LITTLE,
BROWN

LB

LARGE
PRINT

STRANGE
THE
DREAMER

LAINI TAYLOR

LITTLE, BROWN AND COMPANY

LARGE PRINT EDITION

Little, Brown and Company
Hachette Book Group
1290 Avenue of the Americas, New York, NY 10104
Visit us at lb-teens.com

First Edition: March 2017

Little, Brown and Company is a division of Hachette Book Group, Inc. The Little, Brown name and logo are trademarks of Hachette Book Group, Inc.

The publisher is not responsible for websites (or their content) that are not owned by the publisher.

ISBNs: 978-0-316-34168-4 (hardcover), 978-0-316-43120-0 (int'l), 978-0-316-46427-7 (large print), 978-0-316-34164-6 (ebook)

Printed in the United States of America

LSC-C

10 9 8 7 6 5 4 3 2 1

For Alexandra, unique in the world

PROLOGUE

On the second Sabbat of Twelfthmoon, in the city of Weep, a girl fell from the sky.

Her skin was blue, her blood was red.

She broke over an iron gate, crimping it on impact, and there she hung, impossibly arched, graceful as a temple dancer swooning on a lover's arm. One slick finial anchored her in place. Its point, protruding from her sternum, glittered like a brooch. She fluttered briefly as her ghost shook loose, and torch ginger buds rained out of her long hair.

Later, they would say these had been hummingbird hearts and not blossoms at all.

They would say she hadn't *shed* blood but *wept* it. That she was lewd, tonguing her teeth at them, upside down and dying, that she vomited a serpent that turned to smoke when it hit the ground. They would say a flock of moths came, frantic, and tried to lift her away.

That was true. Only that.

They hadn't a prayer, though. The moths were no bigger than the startled mouths of children, and even dozens together could only pluck at the strands of her darkening hair until their wings sagged, sodden with her blood. They were purled away with the blossoms as a grit-choked gust came blasting down the street. The earth heaved underfoot. The sky spun on its axis. A queer brilliance lanced through billowing smoke, and the people of Weep had to squint against it. Blowing grit and hot light and the stink of saltpeter. There had been an explosion. They might have died, all and easily, but only this girl had, shaken from some pocket of the sky.

Her feet were bare, her mouth stained damson. Her pockets were all full of plums. She was young and lovely and surprised and dead.

She was also blue.

Blue as opals, pale blue. Blue as cornflowers, or dragonfly wings, or a spring—not summer—sky.

Someone screamed. The scream drew others. The others screamed, too, not because a girl was dead, but because the girl was blue, and this meant something in the city of Weep. Even after the sky stopped reeling, and the earth settled, and the last fume spluttered from the blast site and dispersed, the screams went on, feeding themselves from voice to voice, a virus of the air.

The blue girl's ghost gathered itself and perched, bereft, upon the spearpoint-tip of the projecting finial, just an inch above her own still chest. Gasping in shock, she tilted back her invisible head and gazed, mournfully, up.

The screams went on and on.

And across the city, atop a monolithic wedge of seamless, mirror-smooth metal, a statue stirred, as though awakened by the tumult, and slowly lifted its great horned head.

Part I

* * *

shrestha (SHRES·thuh) *noun*

When a dream comes true—but not for the dreamer.

Archaic; from Shres, the bastard god of fortune, who was believed to punish supplicants for inadequate offerings by granting their hearts' desire to another.

🌿 1 🌿

MYSTERIES OF WEEP

Names may be lost or forgotten. No one knew that better than Lazlo Strange. He'd had another name first, but it had died like a song with no one left to sing it. Maybe it had been an old family name, burnished by generations of use. Maybe it had been given to him by someone who loved him. He liked to think so, but he had no idea. All he had were *Lazlo* and *Strange*—*Strange* because that was the surname given to all foundlings in the Kingdom of Zosma, and *Lazlo* after a monk's tongueless uncle.

"He had it cut out on a prison galley," Brother Argos told him when he was old enough to understand. "He was an eerie silent man, and you were an eerie silent babe, so it came to me: *Lazlo*. I had to name so many babies that year I went with whatever popped into my head." He added, as an afterthought, "Didn't think you'd live anyway."

That was the year Zosma sank to its knees and bled great gouts of men into a war about nothing. The war, of course, did not content itself with soldiers. Fields were burned; villages, pillaged. Bands of displaced peasants roamed the razed countryside, fighting the crows for gleanings. So many died that the tumbrils used to cart thieves to the gallows were repurposed to carry orphans to the monasteries and convents. They arrived like shipments of lambs, to hear the monks tell it, and with no more knowledge of their provenance than lambs, either. Some were old enough to know their names at least, but Lazlo was just a baby, and an ill one, no less.

"Gray as rain, you were," Brother Argos said. "Thought sure you'd die, but you ate and you slept and your color came normal in time. Never cried, never once, and that was unnatural, but we liked you for it fine. None of us became monks to be nursemaids."

To which the child Lazlo replied, with fire in his soul, "And none of us became children to be orphans."

But an orphan he was, and a Strange, and though he was prone to fantasy, he never had any delusions about that. Even as a little boy, he understood that there would be no revelations. No one was coming for him, and he would never know his own true name.

Which is perhaps why the mystery of Weep captured him so completely.

There were two mysteries, actually: one old, one new. The old one opened his mind, but it was the new one that climbed inside, turned several circles, and settled in with a grunt—like a satisfied dragon in a cozy new lair. And there it would remain—the mystery, in his mind—exhaling enigma for years to come.

It had to do with a name, and the discovery that, in addition to being lost or forgotten, they could also be stolen.

He was five years old when it happened, a charity boy at Zemonan Abbey, and he'd snuck away to the old orchard that was the haunt of nightwings and lacewings to play by himself. It was early winter. The trees were black and bare. His feet breached a crust of frost with every step, and the cloud of his breath accompanied him like a chummy ghost.

The Angelus rang, its bronze voice pouring through the sheepfold and over the orchard walls in slow, rich waves. It was a call to prayer. If he didn't go in, he would be missed, and if he was missed, he would be whipped.

He didn't go in.

Lazlo was always finding ways to slip off on his own, and his legs were always striped from the hazel switch that hung from a hook with his name on it. It was worth it. To get away from the monks and the

9

rules and the chores and the life that pinched like tight shoes.

To *play*.

"Turn back now if you know what's good for you," he warned imaginary enemies. He held a "sword" in each hand: black apple branches with the stout ends bound in twine to make hilts. He was a small, underfed waif with cuts on his head where the monks nicked it, shaving it against lice, but he held himself with exquisite dignity, and there could be no doubt that in his own mind, in that moment, he was a warrior. And not just any warrior, but a Tizerkane, fiercest that ever was. "No outsider," he told his foes, "has ever set eyes on the forbidden city. And as long as I draw breath, none ever will."

"We're in luck, then," the foes replied, and they were more real to him in the twilight than the monks whose chanting drifted downhill from the abbey. "Because you won't be drawing breath for much longer."

Lazlo's gray eyes narrowed to slits. "You think you can defeat *me*?"

The black trees danced. His breath-ghost scudded away on a gust, only to be replaced by another. His shadow splayed out huge before him, and his mind gleamed with ancient wars and winged beings, a mountain of melted demon bones and the city on the far side of it—a city that had vanished in the mists of time.

This was the old mystery.

It had come to him from a senile monk, Brother Cyrus. He was an invalid, and it fell to the charity boys to bring him his meals. He wasn't kind. No grandfather figure, no mentor. He had a terrible grip, and was known to hold the boys by the wrist for hours, forcing them to repeat nonsense catechisms and confess to all manner of wickedness they could scarce understand, let alone have committed. They all had a terror of him and his gnarled raptor hands, and the bigger boys, sooner than protect the smaller, sent them to his lair in their stead. Lazlo was as scared as the rest, yet he volunteered to bring *all* the meals.

Why?

Because Brother Cyrus told stories.

Stories were not smiled upon at the abbey. At best, they distracted from spiritual contemplation. At worst, they honored false gods and festered into sin. But Brother Cyrus had gone beyond such strictures. His mind had slipped its moorings. He never seemed to understand where he was, and his confusion infuriated him. His face grew clenched and red. Spittle flew when he ranted. But he had his moments of calm: when he slipped through some cellar door in his memory, back to his boyhood and the stories his grandmother used to tell him. He couldn't remember the other monks' names, or even the prayers that had been his vocation for decades, but the stories poured from him, and Lazlo listened. He listened the way a cactus drinks rain.

In the south and east of the continent of Namaa—far, far from northerly Zosma—there was a vast desert called the Elmuthaleth, the crossing of which was an art perfected by few and fiercely guarded against all others. Somewhere across its emptiness lay a city that had never been seen. It was a rumor, a fable, but it was a rumor and fable from which marvels emerged, carried by camels across the desert to fire the imaginations of folk the world over.

The city had a name.

The men who drove the camels, who brought the marvels, they told the name and they told stories, and the name and the stories made their way, with the marvels, to distant lands, where they conjured visions of glittering domes and tame white stags, women so beautiful they melted the mind, and men whose scimitars blinded with their shine.

For centuries this was so. Wings of palaces were devoted to the marvels, and shelves of libraries to the stories. Traders grew rich. Adventurers grew bold, and went to find the city for themselves. None returned. It was forbidden to *faranji*—outsiders—who, if they survived the Elmuthaleth crossing, were executed as spies. Not that that stopped them from trying. Forbid a man something and he craves it like his soul's salvation, all the more so when that something is the source of incomparable riches.

Many tried.

None ever returned.

The desert horizon birthed sun after sun, and it seemed as if nothing would ever change. But then, two hundred years ago, the caravans stopped coming. In the western outposts of the Elmuthaleth—Alkonost and others—they watched for the heat-distorted silhouettes of camel trains to emerge from the emptiness as they always had, but they did not.

And they did not.

And they did not.

There were no more camels, no more men, no more marvels, and no more stories. *Ever.* That was the last that was ever heard from the forbidden city, the unseen city, the *lost* city, and this was the mystery that had opened Lazlo's mind like a door.

What had happened? Did the city still exist? He wanted to know everything. He learned to coax Brother Cyrus into that place of reverie, and he collected the stories like treasure. Lazlo owned nothing, not one single thing, but from the first, the stories felt like his own hoard of gold.

The domes of the city, Brother Cyrus said, were all connected by silk ribbons, and children balanced upon them like tightrope walkers, dashing from palace to palace in capes of colored feathers. No doors were ever closed to them, and even the birdcages were open for the birds to come and go as they pleased, and wondrous fruits grew everywhere, ripe for the plucking, and cakes were left out on window ledges, free for the taking.

Lazlo had never even *seen* cake, let alone tasted it, and he'd been whipped for eating windfall apples that were more worm than fruit. These visions of freedom and plenty bewitched him. Certainly, they distracted from spiritual contemplation, but in the same way that the sight of a shooting star distracts from the ache of an empty belly. They marked his first consideration that there might be other ways of living than the one he knew. Better, sweeter ways.

The streets of the city, Brother Cyrus said, were tiled with lapis lazuli and kept scrupulously clean so as not to soil the long, long hair the ladies wore loose and trailing behind them like bolts of blackest silk. Elegant white stags roamed the streets like citizens, and reptiles big as men drifted in the river. The first were spectrals, and the substance of their antlers—spectralys, or lys—was more precious than gold. The second were svytagors, whose pink blood was an elixir of immortality. There were ravids, too—great cats with fangs like scythes— and birds that mimicked human voices, and scorpions whose sting imparted superhuman strength.

And there were the Tizerkane warriors.

They wielded blades called *hreshtek*, sharp enough to slice a man off his shadow, and kept scorpions in brass cages hooked to their belts. Before battle, they would thrust a finger through a small opening to be stung, and under the influence of the venom, they were unstoppable.

"You think you can defeat *me*?" Lazlo defied his orchard foes.

"There are a hundred of us," they replied, "and only one of you. What do *you* think?"

"I think you should believe every story you've ever heard about the Tizerkane, and turn around and go home!"

Their laughter sounded like the creaking of branches, and Lazlo had no choice but to fight. He poked his finger into the little lopsided cage of twigs and twine that dangled from his rope belt. There was no scorpion in it, only a beetle stunned by the cold, but he gritted his teeth against an imagined sting and felt venom bloom power in his blood. And then he lifted his blades, arms raised in a V, and *roared*.

He roared the city's name. Like thunder, like an avalanche, like the war cry of the seraphim who had come on wings of fire and cleansed the world of demons. His foes stumbled. They gaped. The venom sang in him, and he was something more than human. He was a whirlwind. He was a *god*. They tried to fight, but they were no match for him. His swords flashed lightning as, two by two, he disarmed them all.

In the thick of play, his daydreams were so vivid that a glimpse of reality would have shocked him. If he could have stood apart and seen the little boy crashing through the frost-stiff bracken, waving branches around, he would scarcely have recognized himself, so deeply did he inhabit the warrior in his mind's eye, who had just disarmed a hundred enemies and sent them staggering home. In triumph, he tipped back his head, and let out a cry of...

...a cry of...

"*Weep!*"

He froze, confused. The word had broken from his mouth like a curse, leaving an aftertaste of tears. He had reached for the city's name, as he had just a moment ago, but...it was gone. He tried again, and again found *Weep* instead. It was like putting out his hand for a flower and coming back with a slug or sodden handkerchief. His mind recoiled from it. He couldn't stop trying, though, and each time was worse than the one before. He groped for what he knew had been there, and all he fished up was the awful word *Weep*, slick with wrongness, damp as bad dreams, and tinged with its residue of salt. His mouth curled with its bitterness. A feeling of vertigo swept over him, and the mad certainty that it had been *taken*.

It had been taken *from his mind*.

He felt sick, robbed. Diminished. He raced back up the slope, scrabbling over low stone walls, and pelted through the sheepfold, past the garden and through the cloister, still gripping his apple branch swords. He saw no one, but was seen. There was a rule against running, and anyway, he ought to have been at vespers. He ran straight to Brother Cyrus's cell and shook him awake. "The name," he said, gasping for breath. "The name is missing. The city from the stories, tell me its name!"

He knew deep down that he hadn't forgotten it, that this was something else, something dark and strange, but there was still the chance that maybe, maybe Brother Cyrus would remember, and all would be well.

But Brother Cyrus said, "What do you mean, you fool boy? It's *Weep*—" And Lazlo had just time to see the old man's face buckle with confusion before a hand closed on his collar and yanked him out the door.

"Wait," he implored. "Please." To no avail. He was dragged all the way to the abbot's office, and when they whipped him this time, it wasn't with his hazel switch, which hung in a row with all the other boys' switches, but one of his apple boughs. He was no Tizerkane now. Never mind a hundred enemies; he was disarmed by a single monk and beaten with his own sword. Some hero. He limped for weeks, and was forbidden from seeing Brother Cyrus, who'd grown so agitated by his visit that he'd had to be sedated.

There were no more stories after that, and no more escapes—at least, not into the orchard, or anywhere outside his own mind. The monks kept a sharp eye on him, determined to keep him free of sin—and of joy, which, if not explicitly a sin, at least clears a path to it. He was kept busy. If he wasn't working, he was praying. If he wasn't praying, he was working, always under "adequate supervision" to prevent his vanishing like a wild creature into the trees. At night he slept, exhausted as a gravedigger, too tired even to dream. It did seem as though the fire in him was smothered, the thunder and the avalanche, the war cry and the whirl-wind, all stamped out.

As for the name of the vanished city, it had van-ished, too. Lazlo would always remember the feel of it in his mind, though. It had felt like calligraphy, if calligraphy were written in honey, and that was as close to it as he—or anyone—could come. It wasn't just him and Brother Cyrus. Wherever the name had been found—printed on the spines of books that held its stories, in the old, yellowed ledgers of merchants who'd bought its goods, and woven into the memories of anyone who'd ever heard it—it was simply erased, and *Weep* was left in its place.

This was the new mystery.

This, he never doubted, was magic.

2

THE DREAM CHOOSES THE DREAMER

Lazlo grew up.

No one would ever call him lucky, but it could have been worse. Among the monasteries that took in foundlings, one was a flagellant order. Another raised hogs. But Zemonan Abbey was famous for its scriptorium. The boys were early trained to copy—though not to read; he had to teach himself that part—and those with any skill were drafted into scribing. Skill he had, and he might have stayed there his whole life, bent over a desk, his neck growing forward instead of upright, had not the brothers taken ill one day from bad fish. This *was* luck, or perhaps fate. Some manuscripts were expected at the Great Library of Zosma, and Lazlo was charged to deliver them.

He never came back.

The Great Library was no mere place to keep

books. It was a walled city for poets and astronomers and every shade of thinker in between. It encompassed not only the vast archives, but the university, too, together with laboratories and glasshouses, medical theaters and music rooms, and even a celestial observatory. All this occupied what had been the royal palace before the current queen's grandfather built a finer one straddling the Eder and gifted this one to the Scholars' Guild. It ranged across the top of Zosimos Ridge, which knifed up from Zosma City like a shark's fin, and was visible from miles away.

Lazlo was in a state of awe from the moment he passed through the gates. His mouth actually fell open when he saw the Pavilion of Thought. That was the grandiose name for the ballroom that now housed the library's philosophy texts. Shelves rose forty feet under an astonishing painted ceiling, and the spines of books glowed in jewel-toned leather, their gold leaf shining in the glavelight like animal eyes. The glaves themselves were perfect polished spheres, hanging by the hundreds and emitting a purer white light than he'd ever seen from the rough, ruddy stones that lit the abbey. Men in gray robes rode upon wheeled ladders, seeming to float through the air, scrolls flapping behind them like wings as they rolled from shelf to shelf.

It was impossible that he should leave this place. He was like a traveler in an enchanted wood. Every step deeper bewitched him further, and deeper he did go, from room to room as though guided by instinct, down secret stairs to a sublevel where dust lay thick on books undisturbed for years. He disturbed them. It seemed to him that he *awoke* them, and they awoke him.

He was thirteen, and he hadn't played Tizerkane for years. He hadn't played anything, or strayed out of step. At the abbey, he was one more gray-clad figure going where he was told, working, praying, chanting, praying, working, praying, sleeping. Few of the brothers even remembered his wildness now. It seemed all gone out of him.

In fact, it had just gone deep. The stories were still there, every word that Brother Cyrus had ever told him. He cherished them like a little stash of gold in a corner of his mind.

That day, the stash grew bigger. Much bigger. The books under the dust, they were *stories*. Folktales, fairy tales, myths, and legends. They spanned the whole world. They went back centuries, and longer, and whole shelves of them—entire, beautiful shelves—were stories of Weep. He lifted one down with more reverence than he'd ever felt for the sacred texts at the abbey, blew off the dust, and began to read.

He was found days later by a senior librarian, but only because the man was looking for him, a letter from the abbot in the pocket of his robes. Elsewise, Lazlo might have lived down there like a boy in a cave for who knows how long. He might have grown feral: the wild boy of the Great Library, versed in three dead languages and all the tales ever written in them, but ragged as a beggar in the alleys of the Grin.

Instead, he was taken on as an apprentice.

"The library knows its own mind," old Master Hyrrokkin told him, leading him back up the secret stairs. "When it steals a boy, we let it keep him."

Lazlo couldn't have belonged at the library more truly if he were a book himself. In the days that followed—and then the months and years, as he grew into a man—he was rarely to be seen without one open in front of his face. He read while he walked. He read while he ate. The other librarians suspected he somehow read while he slept, or perhaps didn't sleep at all. On the occasions that he did look up from the page, he would seem as though he were awakening from a dream. "Strange the dreamer," they called him. "That dreamer, Strange." And it didn't help that he sometimes walked into walls while reading, or that his favorite books hailed from that dusty sublevel where no one else cared to go. He drifted about with his head full of myths, always at least half lost in some otherland of story. Demons and wingsmiths, seraphim and spirits, he loved it all. He believed in magic, like a child, and in ghosts, like a peasant. His nose was broken by a falling volume of fairy tales his first day on the job, and that, they said, told you everything you needed to know about strange Lazlo Strange: head in the clouds, world of his own, fairy tales and fancy.

That was what they meant when they called him a dreamer, and they weren't wrong, but they missed the main point. Lazlo was a dreamer in more profound a way than they knew. That is to say, he *had* a dream—a guiding and abiding one, so much a part of him it was like a second soul inside his skin. The landscape of his mind was all given over to it. It was a deep and ravishing landscape, and a daring and magnificent dream. *Too* daring, *too* magnificent for the likes of him. He knew that, but the dream chooses the dreamer, not the other way around.

"What's that you're reading, Strange?" asked Master Hyrrokkin, hobbling up behind him at the Enquiries desk. "Love letter, I hope."

The old librarian expressed this wish more often than was seemly, undaunted that the answer was always no. Lazlo was on the verge of making his usual response, but paused, considering. "In a way," he said, and held out the paper, which was brittle and yellowed with age.

A gleam lit Master Hyrrokkin's faded brown eyes, but when he adjusted his spectacles and looked at the page, the gleam winked out. "This appears to be a receipt," he observed.

"Ah, but a receipt for what?"

Skeptical, Master Hyrrokkin squinted to read, then gave a crack of a laugh that turned every head in the huge, hushed room. They were in the Pavilion of Thought. Scholars in scarlet robes were hunched at long tables, and they all looked up from their scrolls and tomes, eyes grim with disapproval. Master Hyrrokkin bobbed a nod of apology and handed Lazlo back the paper, which was an old bill for a very large shipment of aphrodisiacs to a long-dead king. "Seems he wasn't called the Amorous King for his poetry, eh? But what are you doing? Tell me this isn't what it looks like. For god's sake, boy. Tell me you aren't archiving receipts on your free day."

Lazlo was a boy no longer, no trace remaining—outwardly—of the small bald foundling with cuts on his head. He was tall now, and he'd let his hair grow long once he was free of the monks and their dull razors. It was dark and heavy and he tied it back with bookbinder's twine and spared it very little thought. His brows were dark and heavy, too, his features strong and broad. "Rough-hewn," some might have said, or even "thuggish" on account of his broken nose, which made a sharp angle in profile, and from the front skewed distinctly to the left. He had a raw, rugged look—and sound, too: his voice low and mas-culine and not at all smooth, as though it had been left out in the weather. In all this, his dreamer's eyes were incongruous: gray and wide and guileless. Just now they weren't quite meeting Master Hyrrokkin's gaze. "Of course not," he said unconvincingly. "What kind of maniac would archive receipts on his free day?"

"Then what *are* you doing?"

He shrugged. "A steward found an old box of bills in a cellar. I'm just having a look."

"Well, it's a shocking waste of youth. How old are you now? Eighteen?"

"Twenty," Lazlo reminded him, though in truth he couldn't be certain, having chosen a birthday at random when he was a boy. "And you wasted your youth the same way."

"And I'm a cautionary tale! Look at me." Lazlo did. He saw a soft, stooped creature of a man whose dandelion-fluff hair, beard, and brows encroached upon his face to such a degree that only his sharp little nose and round spectacles showed. He looked, Lazlo thought, like an owlet fallen out of its nest. "Do you want to end your days a half-blind troglodyte hobbling through the bowels of the library?" the old man demanded. "Get out of doors, Strange. Breathe air, see things. A man should have squint lines from looking at the horizon, not just from reading in dim light."

"What's a horizon?" Lazlo asked, straight-faced. "Is it like the end of an aisle of books?"

"No," said Master Hyrrokkin. "Not in any way."

Lazlo smiled and went back to the receipts. Well, that word made them sound dull, even in his head. They were old cargo manifests, which sounded marginally more thrilling, from a time when the palace had been the royal residence and goods had come from every corner of the world. He wasn't archiving them. He was skimming them for the telltale flourishes of a particular rare alphabet. He was looking, as he always was on some level, for hints of the Unseen City— which was how he chose to think of it, since *Weep* still brought the taste of tears. "I'll go in a moment," he assured Master Hyrrokkin. It might not have seemed like it, but he took the old man's words to heart. He had, in fact, no wish to end his days at the library— half blind or otherwise—and every hope of earning his squint lines by looking at the horizon.

The horizon he wished to look at, however, was very far away.

And also, incidentally, forbidden.

Master Hyrrokkin gestured to a window. "You're at least aware, I hope, that it's summer out there?" When Lazlo didn't respond, he added, "Large orange orb in the sky, low necklines on the fairer sex. Any of this ring a bell?" Still nothing. *"Strange?"*

"What?" Lazlo looked up. He hadn't heard a word. He'd found what he was looking for—a sheaf of bills from the Unseen City—and it had stolen his attention away.

The old librarian gave a theatrical sigh. "Do as you will," he said, half doom and half resignation. "Just take care. The books may be immortal, but *we* are not. You go down to the stacks one morning, and by the time you come up, you've a beard down to your belly and have never once composed a poem to a girl you met ice-skating on the Eder."

"Is that how one meets girls?" asked Lazlo, only half in jest. "Well, the river won't freeze for months. I have time to rally my courage."

"Bah! Girls are not a hibernal phenomenon. Go *now*. Pick some flowers and find one to give them to. It's as simple as that. Look for kind eyes and wide hips, do you hear me? *Hips*, boy. You haven't lived until you've laid your head on a nice, soft—"

Mercifully, he was interrupted by the approach of a scholar.

Lazlo could as easily will his skin to turn color as he could approach and speak to a girl, let alone lay his head on a nice, soft anything. Between the abbey and the library, he had hardly known a female person, much less a *young* female person, and even if he'd had the faintest idea what to say to one, he didn't imagine that many would welcome the overtures of a penniless junior librarian with a crooked nose and the ignominious name of Strange.

The scholar left, and Master Hyrrokkin resumed his lecture. "Life won't just happen to you, boy," he said. "*You* have to happen to *it*. Remember: The spirit grows sluggish when you neglect the passions."

"My spirit is fine."

"Then you're going sadly wrong. You're young. Your spirit shouldn't be 'fine.' It should be *effervescent*."

The "spirit" in question wasn't the soul. Nothing so abstract. It was spirit of the body—the clear fluid pumped by the second heart through its own network of vessels, subtler and more mysterious than the primary vascular system. Its function wasn't properly understood by science. You could live even if your second heart stopped and the spirit hardened in your veins. But it did have some connection to vitality, or "passion," as Master Hyrrokkin said, and those without it were emotionless, lethargic. Spiritless.

"Worry about your own spirit," Lazlo told him. "It's not too late for you. I'm sure plenty of widows would be delighted to be wooed by such a romantic troglodyte."

"Don't be impertinent."

"Don't be imperious."

Master Hyrrokkin sighed. "I miss the days when you lived in fear of me. However short-lived they were."

Lazlo laughed. "You had the monks to thank for those. They taught me to fear my elders. You taught me not to, and for that, I'll always be grateful." He said it warmly, and then—he couldn't help himself—his eyes flickered toward the papers in his hand.

The old man saw and let out a huff of exasperation. "Fine, fine. Enjoy your receipts. I'm not giving up on you, though. What's the point of being old if you can't beleaguer the young with your vast stores of wisdom?"

28

"And what's the point of being young if you can't ignore all advice?"

Master Hyrrokkin grumbled and turned his attention to the stack of folios that had just been returned to the desk. Lazlo turned his to his small discovery. Silence reigned in the Pavilion of Thought, broken only by the wheels of ladders and the *shush* of pages turning.

And, after a moment, by a low, slow whistle from Lazlo, whose discovery, it transpired, wasn't so small after all.

Master Hyrrokkin perked up. "More love potions?"

"No," said Lazlo. "Look."

The old man performed his usual adjustment of spectacles and peered at the paper. "Ah," he said with the air of the long-suffering. "Mysteries of Weep. I might have known."

Weep. The name struck Lazlo as an unpleasant twinge behind his eyes. The condescension struck him, too, but it didn't surprise him. Generally, he kept his fascination to himself. No one understood it, much less shared it. There had been, once upon a time, a great deal of curiosity surrounding the vanished city and its fate, but after two centuries, it had become little more than a fable. And as for the uncanny business of the name, in the world at large it hadn't caused much stir. Only Lazlo had *felt* it happen. Others had learned of it later, through a slow trickle of rumors, and to them it just felt like something they'd forgotten.

Some did whisper of a conspiracy or a trick, but most decided, firmly closing a door in their minds, that it had always been Weep, and any claims to the contrary were nonsense and fairy dust. There just wasn't any other explanation that made sense.

Certainly not magic.

Lazlo knew that Master Hyrrokkin wasn't interested, but he was too excited to mind. "Just read it," he said, and held the paper under the old man's nose.

Master Hyrrokkin did, and failed to be impressed. "Well, what of it?"

What of it? Among the goods listed—spice and silk and the like—was an entry for svytagor blood candy. Up until now, Lazlo had only ever seen it referred to in tales. It was considered folklore—that the river monsters even existed, let alone that their pink blood was harvested as an elixir of immortality. But here it was, bought and paid for by the royal house of Zosma. There might as well have been an entry for dragon scales. "Blood candy," he said, pointing. "Don't you see? It was *real*."

Master Hyrrokkin snorted. "*This* makes it real? If it was *real*, whoever ate it would still be alive to tell you so."

"Not so," argued Lazlo. "In the stories, you were only immortal so long as you *kept* eating it, and that wouldn't have been possible once the shipments stopped." He pointed out the date on the bill. "This is two hundred years old. It might even have come from the last caravan."

The last caravan ever to emerge from the Elmuthaleth. Lazlo imagined an empty desert, a setting sun. As always, anything touching on the mysteries had a quickening effect on him, like a drumbeat pulling at his pulse—at *both* his pulses, blood and spirit, the rhythms of his two hearts interwoven like the syncopation of two hands beating at different drums.

When he first came to the library, he'd thought surely he would find answers here. There were the books of stories in the dusty sublevel, of course, but there was so much more than that. The very history of the world, it had seemed to him, was all bound into covers or rolled into scrolls and archived on the shelves of this wondrous place. In his naïveté, he'd thought even the secrets must be hidden away here, for those with the will and patience to look for them. He had both, and for seven years now he'd been looking. He'd searched old journals and bundled correspondences, spies' reports, maps and treaties, trade ledgers and the minutes of royal secretaries, and anything else he could dig up. And the more he learned, the more the little stash of treasure had grown, until it spilled from its corner to quite fill his mind.

It had also spilled onto paper.

As a boy at the abbey, stories had been Lazlo's only wealth. He was richer now. Now he had books.

His books were *his* books, you understand: *his* words, penned in his own hand and bound with his own neat stitches. No gold leaf on leather, like the books in the Pavilion of Thought. These were humble. In the beginning, he'd fished paper from the bins, half-used sheets that thriftless scholars had tossed away, and he'd made do with the snipped ends of binder's twine from the book infirmary where they made repairs. Ink was hard to come by, but here, too, scholars unwittingly helped. They threw away bottles that still had a good quarter inch at the bottom. He'd had to water it down, so his earliest volumes were filled with pale ghost words, but after a few years, he'd begun to draw a pittance of a salary that enabled him to at least buy ink.

He had *a lot* of books, all lined up on the window ledge in his little room. They contained seven years of research and every hint and tidbit that was to be found about Weep and its pair of mysteries.

They did *not* contain answers to them.

Somewhere along the way, Lazlo had accepted that the answers weren't here, not in all these tomes on all these great, vast shelves. And how could they be? Had he imagined that the library had omniscient fairies on staff to record everything that happened in the world, no matter how secret, or how far away? No. If the answers were anywhere, they were in the south and east of the continent of Namaa, on the far side of the Elmuthaleth, whence no one had ever returned.

Did the Unseen City still stand? Did its people yet live? What happened two hundred years ago? What happened fifteen years ago?

What power could erase a name from the minds of the world?

Lazlo wanted to go and find out. That was his dream, daring and magnificent: *to go there*, half across the world, and solve the mysteries for himself.

It was impossible, of course.

But when did that ever stop any dreamer from dreaming?

3

THE COMPLETE WORKS OF LAZLO STRANGE

Master Hyrrokkin was immune to Lazlo's wonder. "They're *stories*, boy. Stuff and fantasy. There was no elixir of immortality. If anything, it was just sugared blood."

"But look at the price," Lazlo insisted. "Would they have paid *that* for sugared blood?"

"What do we know of what kings will pay? That's proof of nothing but a rich man's gullibility."

Lazlo's excitement began to wane. "You're right," he admitted. The receipt proved that something called blood candy had been purchased, but nothing more than that. He wasn't ready to give up, though. "It suggests, at least, that svytagors were real." He paused. "Maybe."

"What if they were?" said Master Hyrrokkin. "We'll never know." He put a hand on Lazlo's shoulder. "You're not a child anymore. Isn't it time to let all this go?" He had no visible mouth, his smile discernible only as a ripple where his dandelion-fluff mustache overlapped his beard. "You've plenty of work for little enough pay. Why add more for none? No one's going to thank you for it. Our job is to find books. Leave it to the scholars to find answers."

He meant well. Lazlo knew that. The old man was a creature of the library through and through. Its caste system was, to him, the just rule of a perfect world. Within these walls, scholars were the aristocracy, and everyone else their servants—especially the librarians, whose directive was to support them in their important work. Scholars were graduates of the universities. Librarians were not. They might have the minds for it, but none had the gold. Their apprenticeship was their education, and, depending on the librarian, it might surpass a scholar's own. But a butler might surpass his master in gentility and remain, nevertheless, the butler. So it was for librarians. They weren't forbidden to study, so long as it didn't interfere with their duties, but it was understood that it was for their personal enlightenment alone, and made no contribution to the world's body of knowledge.

"Why let scholars have all the fun?" Lazlo asked. "Besides, no one studies Weep."

"That's because it's a dead subject," Master Hyrokkin said. "Scholars occupy their minds with important matters." He placed gentle emphasis on *important*.

And just then, as if to illustrate his point, the doors swung open and a scholar strode in.

The Pavilion of Thought had been a ballroom; its doors were twice the height of normal doors, and more than twice the width. Most scholars who came and went found it adequate to open one of them, then quietly close it behind himself, but not this man. He laid a hand to each massive door and thrust, and by the time they hit the walls and shuddered he was well through them, boot heels ringing on the marble floor, his long, sure stride unhindered by the swish of robes. He disdained full regalia, except on ceremonial occasions, and dressed instead in impeccable coats and breeches, with tall black riding boots and a dueling blade at his side. His only nod to scholar's scarlet was his cravat, which was always of that color. He was no ordinary scholar, this man, but the apotheosis of scholars: the most famous personage in Zosma, save the queen and the hierarch, and the most popular, bar none. He was young and glorious and golden. He was Thyon Nero the alchemist, second son of the Duke of Vaal, and godson to the queen.

Heads lifted at the jarring of the doors, but unlike the irritation mirrored on all faces when Master Hyrrokkin had laughed, this time they registered surprise before shifting into adulation or envy.

Master Hyrrokkin's reaction was pure adulation.

He lit up like a glave at the sight of the alchemist. Once upon a time, Lazlo would have done the same. Not anymore, though no one was looking at him to notice the way he froze like a prey creature and seemed to shrink at the approach of "the golden god-son," whose purposeful stride carried him straight to the Enquiries desk.

This visit was out of the ordinary. Thyon Nero had assistants to perform such tasks for him. "My lord," said Master Hyrrokkin, straightening as much as his old back would allow. "It's so good of you to visit us. But you needn't trouble yourself to come in person. We know you've more important things to attend to than running errands." The librarian shot Lazlo a sideward glance. Here, in case Lazlo might miss his meaning, was the best possible example of a scholar occupying his mind with "important matters."

And with what important matters did Thyon Nero occupy his mind?

With no less than the animating principle of the universe: "azoth," the secret essence alchemists had sought for centuries. He had distilled it at the age of sixteen, enabling him to work miracles, among them the highest aspiration of the ancient art: the transmutation of lead into gold.

"That's good of you, Hyrrokkin," said this paragon, who had the face of a god, in addition to the mind of one. "But I thought I'd better come myself"—he held up a rolled request form—"so that there could be no question whether this was a mistake."

"A mistake? There was no need, my lord," Master Hyrrokkin assured him. "There could be no quibbling with a request of yours, no matter who delivered it. We're here to serve, not to question."

"I'm glad to hear that," said Nero, with the smile that had been known to render parlors full of ladies mute and dazed. And then he looked at Lazlo.

It was so unexpected, it was like sudden immersion in ice water. Lazlo hadn't moved since the doors burst open. This was what he did when Thyon Nero was near: He seized up and felt as invisible as the alchemist pretended he was. He was accustomed to cutting silence, and a cool gaze that slid past him as though he didn't exist, so the look came as a shock, and his words, when he spoke, an even greater one. "And you, Strange? Are you here to serve, or to question?" He was cordial, but his blue eyes held a brightness that filled Lazlo with dread.

"To serve, my lord," he answered, his voice as brittle as the papers in his hands.

"Good." Nero held his gaze, and Lazlo had to battle the urge to look away. They stared at each other, the alchemist and the librarian. They held a secret between them, and it burned like alchemical fire. Even old Master Hyrrokkin felt it, and glanced uneasily between the two young men. Nero looked like a prince from some saga told by firelight, all luster and gleam. Lazlo's skin hadn't been gray since he was a baby, but his librarian's robes were, and his eyes, too, as though that color were his fate. He was quiet, and had a shadow's talent for passing unremarked, while Thyon drew all eyes like a flare. Everything about him was as crisp and elegant as freshly pressed silk. He was shaved by a manservant with a blade sharpened daily, and his tailor's bill could have fed a village.

By contrast, Lazlo was all rough edges: burlap to Nero's silk. His robe had not been new even when it came to him a year ago. Its hem was frayed from dragging up and down the rough stone steps of the stacks, and it was large, so the shape of him was quite lost within it. They were the same height, but Nero stood as though posing for a sculptor, while Lazlo's shoulders were curved in a posture of wariness. *What did Nero want?*

Nero turned back to the old man. He held his head high, as though conscious of the perfection of his jawline, and when speaking to someone shorter than himself, lowered only his eyes, not his head. He handed over the request form.

Master Hyrrokkin unrolled the paper, adjusted his spectacles, and read it. And...readjusted his spectacles, and read it again. He looked up at Nero. And then he looked at Lazlo, and Lazlo knew. He knew what the request was for. A numbness spread through him. He felt as though his blood and spirit had both ceased to circulate, and the breath in his lungs, too.

"Have them delivered to my palace," Nero said.

Master Hyrrokkin opened his mouth, confounded, but no sound came out. He glanced at Lazlo again, and the glavelight shone on his spectacles so that Lazlo couldn't see his eyes.

"Do you need me to write out the address?" Nero asked. His affability was all sham. Everyone knew the riverfront palace of pale-pink marble gifted him by the queen, and he knew they knew. The address was hardly the issue.

"My lord, of course not," said Master Hyrrokkin. "It's just, ah…"

"Is there a problem?" asked Nero, his pleasant tone belied by the sharpness of his eyes.

Yes, Lazlo thought. *Yes, there is a problem*, but Master Hyrrokkin quailed under the look. "No, my lord. I'm sure… I'm sure it's an honor," and the words were a knife in Lazlo's back.

"Excellent," said Nero. "That's that, then. I'll expect delivery this evening." And he left as he had come, boot heels ringing on the marble floor and all eyes following.

Lazlo turned to Master Hyrrokkin. His hearts hadn't stopped beating after all. They were fast and irregular, like a pair of trapped moths. "Tell me it isn't," he said.

Still confounded, the old librarian just held out the request form. Lazlo took it. He read it. His hands shook. It was what he thought:

In Nero's bold, sweeping script was written: *The Complete Works of Lazlo Strange.*

Master Hyrrokkin asked, in utter mystification, "What in the world could *Thyon Nero* want with *your books*?"

4

THE BASTARD GOD OF FORTUNE

The alchemist and the librarian, they couldn't have been more different—as though Shres, the bastard god of fortune, had stood them side by side and divided his basket of gifts between them: *every gift* to Thyon Nero, one by one, until the very last, which he dropped in the dirt at Lazlo's feet.

"Make what you can of that," he might have said, if there were such a god, and he was feeling spiteful.

To Thyon Nero: birth, wealth, privilege, looks, charm, brilliance.

And to Lazlo Strange, to pick up and dust off, the one thing left over: honor.

It might have been better for him if Nero got that one, too.

Like Lazlo, Thyon Nero was born during the war, but war, like fortune, doesn't touch all folk with the same hand. He grew up in his father's castle, far from the sight and smell of suffering, much less the experience of it. On the same day that a gray and nameless infant was plunked on a cart bound for Zemonan Abbey, a golden one was christened Thyon—after the warrior-saint who drove the barbarians out of Zosma—in a lavish ceremony attended by half the court. He was a clever, beautiful child, and though his elder brother would inherit the title and lands, he claimed all else—love, attention, laughter, praise—and he claimed it loudly. If Lazlo was a silent baby, harshly raised by resentful monks, Thyon was a small, charming tyrant who demanded everything and was given even more.

Lazlo slept in a barracks of boys, went to bed hungry, and woke up cold.

Thyon's boyhood bed was shaped like a war brig, complete with real sails and riggings, and even miniature cannons, so heavy it took the strength of two maids to rock him to sleep. His hair was of such an astonishing color—as the sun in frescoes, where you might stare at it without burning out your eyes—that it was allowed to grow long, though this was not the fashion for boys. It was only cut on his ninth birthday, to be woven into an elaborate neckpiece for his godmother, the queen. She wore it, and—to the dismay of goldsmiths—spawned a fashion for human-hair jewelry, though none of the imitations could compare with the original in brilliance.

Thyon's nickname, "the golden godson," was with him from his christening, and perhaps it ordained his path. Names have power, and he was, from infancy, associated with gold. It was fitting, then, that when he entered the university, he made his place in the college of alchemy.

What was alchemy? It was metallurgy wrapped in mysticism. The pursuit of the spiritual by way of the material. The great and noble effort to master the elements in order to achieve purity, perfection, and divinity.

Oh, and gold.

Let's not forget gold. Kings wanted it. Alchemists promised it—had *been* promising it for centuries, and if they achieved purity and perfection in anything, it was the purity and perfection of their failure to produce it.

Thyon, thirteen years old and sharp as the point of a viper's fang, had looked around him at the cryptic rituals and philosophies and seen it all as obfuscation cooked up to excuse that failure. *Look how complicated this is*, alchemists said, even as they made it so. Everything was outlandish. Initiates were required to swear an oath upon an emerald said to have been pried from the brow of a fallen angel, and when presented with this artifact, Thyon laughed. He refused to swear on it, and flat refused to study the esoteric texts, which he called "the consolation of would-be wizards cursed to live in a world without magic."

"You, young man, have the soul of a blacksmith," the master of alchemy told him in a cold rage.

"Better than the soul of a charlatan," Thyon shot back. "I would sooner swear an oath on an anvil and do honest work than dupe the world with make-believe."

And so it was that the golden godson swore his oath on a blacksmith's anvil instead of the angel's emerald. Anyone else would have been expelled, but he had the queen's favor, and so the old guard had no choice but to stand aside and let him do his own work in his own way. He cared only for the material side of things: the nature of elements, the essence and mutability of matter. He was ambitious, meticulous, and intuitive. Fire, water, and air yielded up secrets to him. Minerals revealed their hidden properties. And at fifteen, to the deep dismay of the "would-be wizards," he performed the first transmutation in western history—not gold, alas, but lead into bismuth—and did so, as he said, without recourse to "spirits or spells." It was a triumph, for which he was rewarded by his godmother with a laboratory of his own. It took over the grand old church at the Great Library, and no expense was spared. The queen dubbed it "the Chrysopoesium"— from *chrysopoeia*, the transmutation of base metal into gold—and she wore her necklace of his hair when she came to present it to him. They walked arm in arm in matching gold: his on his head, hers on her neck, and soldiers marched behind them, clad in gold surcoats commissioned for the occasion.

Lazlo stood in the crowd that day, awed by the spectacle and by the brilliant golden boy who had always seemed to him like a character from a story—a young hero blessed by fortune, rising to take his place in the world. That was what everyone saw—like an audience at the theater, blithely unaware that backstage the actors were playing out a darker drama.

As Lazlo was to discover.

It was about a year after that—he was sixteen—and he was taking the bypass through the tombwalk one evening when he heard a voice as hard and sharp as ax-fall. He couldn't make out the words at first and paused, searching for their source.

The tombwalk was a relic of the old palace cemetery, cut off from the rest of the grounds by the construction of the astronomers' tower. Most of the scholars didn't even know it was there, but the librarians did, because they used it as a shortcut between the stacks and the reading rooms in the base of the tower. That was what Lazlo was doing, his arms full of manuscripts, when he heard the voice. There was a rhythm to it, and an accompanying punctuation of slaps or blows. *Thwop. Thwop.*

There was another sound, barely audible. He

thought it was an animal, and when he peered around the corner of a mausoleum, he saw an arm rising and falling with the steady, vicious *thwop*. It wielded a riding crop, and the image was unmistakable, but he still thought it was an animal that was being beaten, because it was low and cringing and its bitten-off whimpers were no human sound.

A burning anger filled him, quick as the strike of a match. He drew in breath to shout.

And held it.

There was a little light, and in the instant it took his voice to gather up a single word, Lazlo perceived the scene in full.

A bowed back. A crouching boy. Glavelight on golden hair. And the Duke of Vaal beating his son like an animal.

"*Stop!*" Lazlo had almost said. He held in the word like a mouthful of fire.

"Witless—" *Thwop.* "Imbecilic—" *Thwop.* "Lackadaisical—" *Thwop.* "Pathetic."

It went on, merciless, and Lazlo flinched with every *thwop*, his anger smothered by a great confusion. Once he had time to think, it would flare up again, hotter than before. But in the face of such a sight, his overwhelming feeling was shock. He himself was no stranger to punishment. He still had faint scars crisscrossing his legs from all his lashings. He'd sometimes been locked in the crypt overnight with only the skulls

47

of dead monks for company, and he couldn't even count the number of times he'd been called stupid or worthless or worse. But that was *him*. He belonged to no one and had nothing. He had never imagined that *Thyon Nero* could be subject to such treatment, and such words. He had stumbled upon a private scene that belied everything he thought he knew about the golden godson and his charmed life, and it broke something in him to see the other boy brought low.

They weren't friends. That would have been impossible. Nero was an aristocrat, and Lazlo so very much wasn't. But Lazlo had many times fulfilled Thyon's research requests, and once, in the early days, when he'd discovered a rare metallurgical treatise he thought might be of interest, Nero had even said, "Thank you."

It might sound like nothing—or worse, it might appall that he only said it once in all those years. But Lazlo knew that boys like him were trained to speak only in commands, and when Thyon had looked up from the treatise and spoken those simple words, with gravity and sincerity—"Thank you"—he had glowed with pride.

Now his *Stop!* sat burning on his tongue; he wanted to shout it, but didn't. He stood rooted, pressed against the cool side of the mossy mausoleum, afraid even to move. The riding crop fell still. Thyon cradled his head in his arms, face hidden. He made no more sound, but Lazlo could see his shoulders shaking.

"Get up," snarled the duke.

Thyon straightened, and Lazlo saw him clearly. His face was slack and red, and his golden hair stuck to his brow in tear-damp strands. He looked a good deal younger than sixteen.

"Do you know what she spent on your laboratory?" demanded the duke. "Glassblowers all the way from Amaya. A furnace built from your own plans. A smokestack that's the highest point in the entire city. And what have you to show for it all? Notes? Measurements?"

"Alchemy *is* notes and measurements," protested Thyon. His voice was thick with tears, but not yet stripped of defiance. "You have to know the properties of metals before you can hope to alter them."

The duke shook his head with utter contempt. "Master Luzinay was right. You do have the soul of a blacksmith. Alchemy is *gold*, do you understand me? Gold is your life now. Unless you fail to produce it, in which case you'll be lucky to have a life. Do you understand me?"

Thyon drew back, stunned by the threat. "Father, please. It's only been a year—"

"*Only* a year?" The duke's laugh was a dead thing. "Do you know what can happen in a year? Houses fall. *Kingdoms* fall. While you sit in your laboratory *learning the properties of metal*?"

This gave Thyon pause, and Lazlo, too. *Kingdoms fall?* "But...you can't expect me to do in a year what no one has ever done before."

"No one had ever transmuted metal, either, and you did it at fifteen."

"Only to bismuth," the boy said bitterly.

"I am well aware of the inadequacy of your achievement," spat the duke. "All I've heard from you since you started university is how much smarter you are than everyone else. So *be smarter*, damn you. I told her you could do it. I *assured* her."

"I'm trying, Father."

"Try harder!" This, the duke bellowed. His eyes were very wide, the whites showing in a full ring around his irises. There was desperation in him, and Lazlo, in the shadows, was chilled by it. When the queen had named the Chrysopoesium, he had thought it a fine name for an alchemical laboratory. He'd taken it in the spirit of hope: that the greatest ambition of the art might one day be realized there. But it seemed there was no "one day" about it. She wanted gold and she wanted it now.

Thyon swallowed hard and stared at his father. A wave of fear seemed to roil between them. Slowly, and all but whispering, the boy asked, "What if it can't be done?"

Lazlo expected the duke to lash out again, but he only gritted his teeth. "Let me put it to you plainly. The treasury is empty. The soldiers cannot be paid. They are deserting, and our enemies have noticed. If this goes on, they *will* invade. Do you begin to see?"

There was more. Disastrous intrigues and debts called in, but what it added up to was very simple: *Make gold, or Zosma will fall.*

Lazlo watched Thyon go pale as the whole weight of the kingdom settled on him, and he felt it as though it were on his own shoulders.

And it was.

Not because it was put there by a cruel father and a greedy queen, but because he took it. Right there in the tombwalk, as though it were a real, physical burden, he put himself beneath it to help Thyon bear the weight—even if Thyon didn't know it.

Why did he? He might have turned aside and gone about his evening and his life, giddy with relief that such burdens weren't his to bear. Most would have. Moreover, most would have hastened hence to whisper of it and spread the rumor before night finished falling. But Lazlo wasn't most people. He stood in the shadows, furious with thought. He was thinking of war, and the people the last one stole from him before he could know them, and all the children the next one would orphan, and all the names that would die like songs.

Through it all, he was highly sensible of his own uselessness. How could *he* help the golden godson? He wasn't an alchemist, or a hero. He was a librarian, and a dreamer. He was a reader, and the unsung expert on a long-lost city no one cared a thing about. What could *he* possibly...?

It came to him.

He wasn't an alchemist. He was an expert on a long-lost city no one cared a thing about. And it happened that that city, according to its legends, had been practicing alchemy back when Zosma was still a barbarian-plagued wilderness. In fact, the archetypal images of the art and its practitioners came from the old stories brought across the Elmuthaleth: tales of powerful men and women who had tapped the secrets of nature and the cosmos.

Lazlo thought about it. He thought about it as Thyon and the duke left the tombwalk in tense silence, and as he returned his armload of manuscripts to the library, and he kept thinking about it as the library closed for the night and he missed dinner to return to his room and his books.

While resident scholars lived in the grand guest chambers of the palace's upper stories, librarians were housed in the service quarters, one floor above the housekeeping staff, in the rooms once occupied by ladies' maids and valets. Lazlo entered a long, low-ceilinged passage with many identical doors, each with a glave hanging on a hook. He took his down and brought it into his room with him.

Glaves were quarried stones, naturally and perpetually luminous, and they emitted no heat, only radiance, the color and strength of which varied as greatly as the quality of gemstones. This one was poor: an irregular hunk of reddish rock emitting a muddy glow. Small as the room was, it left the corners in shadow. There was a narrow bed on one side and a desk and stool on the other. Two wall pegs held every item of clothing Lazlo owned, and there was no shelf but the window ledge. His books were lined up there. He hung up the glave and started pulling them off and flicking through them. Soon he was sitting on the floor, leaning against the wall, marking pages and jotting down notes. Footsteps passed in the corridor as the other librarians turned in for the night, but Lazlo had no awareness of them, or of the descending silence, or the rise and fall of the moon. Sometime in the night he left his room and made his way down to the dusty sublevel that hadn't been dusty for years.

It was his sanctuary—a realm of stories, not just from the Unseen City, but the world. Weep might have been his dream, but he loved all stories, and knew every single one that resided here, even if he'd had to translate them from a dozen languages with the help of dictionaries and grammars. Here, captured between covers, was the history of the human imagination, and nothing had ever been more beautiful, or fearsome, or bizarre. Here were spells and curses and myths and legends, and Strange the dreamer had for so long fed his mind on them that if one could wander into it, they would discover a fantasia. He didn't think like other people. He didn't dismiss magic out of hand, and he didn't believe that fairy tales were just for children. He *knew* magic was real, because he'd felt it when the name of the Unseen City was stolen from his mind. And as for fairy tales, he understood that they were reflections of the people who had spun them, and were flecked with little truths—intrusions of reality into fantasy, like...toast crumbs on a wizard's beard.

He hoped this might be one such crumb.

At the heart of alchemy was the belief in azoth, the secret essence inherent in all matter. Alchemists believed that if they could distill it, it would enable them to master the underlying structures of the physical world. To transmute lead into gold, derive a universal solvent, and even an elixir of immortality.

It had long been accepted that this would be accomplished by means of some elaborate process involving the elemental trinity: salt, mercury, and sulfur. An absurd number of books and treatises had been written on the subject, considering the utter absence of empirical evidence. They were full of diagrams of dragons swallowing suns and men suckling at the breasts of goddesses, and Lazlo thought them as wild as any fairy tales, although they were shelved more respectably, in the alchemy room of the library, which, tellingly, had once been the palace treasury.

Meanwhile, banished belowstairs where no alchemist would ever look for it, in a book of tales from the Unseen City whimsically titled *Miracles for Breakfast*, there was mention of another theory: that the alchemist was *himself* the secret ingredient—that only the conjunction of human soul with elemental soul could give birth to azoth.

And there it was, a crumb on a wizard's beard.

Perhaps.

5

MIRACLES FOR BREAKFAST

He ought to have waited, at least for a few days. Really, he ought never to have gone at all. He understood that later. Lazlo understood a lot of things later.

Too late.

The sun was rising by the time he emerged from the stacks clutching the book, and he might have been tired from staying up all night, but energy thrummed through him. Excitement. Nerves. He felt as though he were part of something, and forgot that only he knew it. He didn't return to his room, but made his way out of the main palace and across the grounds to the old church that was now the Chrysopoesium.

All the city was spread out below. A radiance lit the Eder where it met the horizon. As the sun climbed, its gleam raced upriver like a lit fuse, seeming to carry daylight with it. The cathedral bells rang out, and all the other church bells followed—light and sweet, like children answering a parent's call.

Lazlo thought Thyon might not have slept, either, not with the terrible burden laid on him. He approached the doors. They were huge, cast-bronze church doors, and weren't exactly built for knocking. He knocked anyway, but he could hardly hear the rap of his own knuckles. He might have given up then, retreated, and given himself time to think better of what he was about to do. If the initial thrill of discovery had been allowed to wear off, surely he would have seen his folly, even naïve as he was. But, instead, he checked around the side of the church, found a door with a bell, and rang it.

And so things fell out as they did.

Thyon answered the door. He looked blank. Lifeless. "Well?" he asked.

"I'm sorry to disturb you," Lazlo said, or something to that effect. This part was a blur to him after. His pulse was pounding in his ears. It wasn't like him to put himself forward. If his upbringing at the abbey had specialized in anything, it was instilling a profound sense of unworthiness. But he was riding the momentum of his outrage on Thyon's behalf, and the flush of solidarity from one beaten boy for another, and above all, the thrill of discovery. Maybe he blurted "I found something for you," and held up the book.

Whatever his words, Thyon stood back so that he might enter. The space was high and hushed, like any church, but the air stank of sulfur, like a pit of hell. Wan shafts of dawn light diffused through stained glass, throwing color onto shelves of gleaming glass and copper. The nave was occupied by a long worktable cluttered with equipment. The whole of the apse had been taken over by a monumental furnace, and a brick chimney cut right up through the center of the frescoed dome, obliterating the heads of angels.

"Well, what is it?" Thyon asked. He was moving stiffly, and Lazlo didn't doubt that his back was covered with welts and bruises. "I suppose you've found me another treatise," he said. "They're all worthless, you know."

"It's not exactly a treatise." Lazlo set the book down on the pocked surface of the worktable, noticing only now the engraving on the cover. It showed a spoon brimming with stars and mythical beasts. *Miracles for Breakfast.* It looked like a children's book, and he had his first pang of misgiving. He hurried to open it, to hide the cover and title. "It *is* to do with gold, though," he said, and launched into an explanation. To his dismay, it sounded as out of place in this somber laboratory as the book looked out of place, and he found himself rushing to keep ahead of his growing mortification, which only made it sound wilder and more foolish the faster he went.

"You know the lost city of Weep," he said. He made himself use the impostor name and immediately tasted tears. "And its alchemists who were said to have made gold in ancient times."

"Legends," said Thyon, dismissive.

"Maybe," said Lazlo. "But isn't it possible the stories are true? That they made gold?"

He registered the look of incredulity on Thyon's face, but misinterpreted it. Thinking it was his premise that the alchemist found unbelievable, he hurried along.

"Look here," he said, and pointed to the passage in the book, about the alchemist himself being the secret ingredient of azoth. "It says the conjunction of human soul and elemental soul, which sounds, I don't know, *unhelpful*, because how do you join your *soul* with metal? But I think it's a mistranslation. I've come across it before. In Unseen...I mean, in the language of Weep, the word for 'soul' and 'spirit' is the same. It's *amarin* for both. So I think this is a mistake." He tapped his finger on the word *soul* and paused. Here it was, his big idea. "I think it means that the key to azoth is *spirit*. Spirit of the body." He held out his wrists, pale side up, exposing the traceries of veins so that Thyon would be sure to take his meaning. And, with that, he found he'd run out of words. A conclusion was needed, something to shine a light on his idea and make it gleam, but he had none, so it just hung there in the air, sounding, frankly, ridiculous.

Thyon stared at him several beats too long. "What is

the meaning of this?" he asked at last, and his voice was ice and danger. "A dare? Did you lose a bet? Is it a *joke*?"

"What?" Startled, Lazlo shook his head. His face went hot and his hands went cold. "No," he said, seeing Thyon's incredulity now for what it was. It wasn't Lazlo's *premise* he was reacting to. It was his *presence*. In an instant, Lazlo's perception shifted and he understood what he'd just done. He—Strange the dreamer, junior librarian—had marched into the Chrysopoesium, brandishing a book of fairy tales, and presumed to share his insights on the deepest mystery of alchemy. As though *he* might solve the problem that had eluded centuries of alchemists—including Nero himself.

His own audacity, now that he saw it, took his breath away. How could he have thought this was a good idea?

"Tell me the truth," commanded Thyon. "Who was it? Master Luzinay? He sent you here to mock me, didn't he?"

Lazlo shook his head to deny the accusation, but he could tell that Thyon wasn't even seeing him. He was too lost in his own fury and misery. If he was seeing anything, it was the mocking faces of the other alchemists, or the cool calculations of the queen herself, ordering up miracles like breakfast. Or maybe—probably—he was seeing the scorn on his father's face last night, and feeling it in the rawness of his flesh and the ache of his every movement. There was, in him, such a simmer of emotions, like chemicals thrown together in an alembic: fear like a sulfur fog, bitterness as sharp as salt, and damned fickle mercury for failure and desperation.

"I would never mock you," Lazlo insisted.

Thyon grabbed up the book, flipping it closed to study the title and cover. "*Miracles for Breakfast*," he intoned, leafing through it. There were pictures of mermaids, witches. "*This* isn't mockery?"

"I swear it isn't. I may be wrong, my lord. I . . . I probably am." Lazlo saw how it looked, and he wanted to tell what he knew to be true, how folklore was sprinkled with truths, but even that sounded absurd to him now—crumbs on wizards' beards and all that nonsense. "I'm sorry. It was presumptuous to come here and I beg your pardon, but I swear to you I meant no disrespect. I only wanted to help you."

Thyon snapped the book shut. "To help *me*. *You*, help *me*." He actually laughed. It was a cold, hard sound, like ice shattering. It went on too long, and with every new bite of laughter, Lazlo felt himself grow smaller. "Enlighten me, Strange," said Thyon. "In what version of the world could *you* possibly help *me*?"

In what version of the world? Was there more than one? Was there a version where Lazlo grew up with a name and a family, and Thyon was put on the cart for the abbey? Lazlo couldn't see it. For all his grand imagination, he couldn't conjure an image of a monk shaving that golden head. "Of course you're right," he stammered. "I only thought...you shouldn't have to bear it all alone."

It was...the wrong thing to say.

"Bear *what* all alone?" asked Thyon, query sharp in his eyes.

Lazlo saw his mistake. He froze, much as he had in the tombwalk, hiding uselessly in the shadows. There was no hiding here, though, and because there was no guile in him, everything he felt showed on his face. Shock. Outrage.

Pity.

And finally Thyon understood what had brought this junior librarian to his door in the earliest hours of dawn. If Lazlo had waited—weeks or even days— Thyon might not have made the connection so instantly. But his back was on fire with pain, and Lazlo's glance strayed there as though he knew it. *Poor Thyon, whose father beat him.* In an instant he knew that Lazlo had seen him at his weakest, and the simmer of emotions were joined by one more.

It was *shame*. And it ignited all the others.

"I'm sorry," Lazlo said, hardly knowing what he was sorry for—that Thyon had been beaten, or that he had chanced to see it.

"Don't you *dare* pity me, you *nothing*," Thyon

snarled with such venom in his voice that Lazlo flinched back as if stung.

What followed was a terrible, sickening blur of spite and outrage. A red and twisted face. Bared teeth and clenched fists and glass shattering. It all got twisted up in nightmares in the days that followed, and embellished by Lazlo's horror and regret. He stumbled out the door, and maybe a hand gave him a shove, and maybe it didn't. Maybe he just tripped and sprawled down the short flight of steps, biting into his tongue so his mouth filled with blood. And he was swallowing blood, trying to look normal as he made his way, limping, back to the main palace.

He'd reached the steps before he realized he'd left the book behind. No more miracles for breakfast. No breakfast at all, not today with his bitten tongue swelling in his mouth. And he hadn't eaten dinner the night before, or slept, but he was so far from hungry or tired, and he had some time to collect himself before his shift began, so he did. He bathed his face in cool water, and winced and rinsed his mouth out, spitting red into the basin. His tongue was grisly, the throb and sting seeming to fill his head. He didn't speak a word all day and no one even noticed. He feared Thyon would have him fired, and he was braced for it, but it didn't happen. Nothing happened. No one found out what he'd done that morning. No one missed the book, either, except for him, and he missed it very much.

Three weeks later, he heard the news. The queen was coming to the Great Library. It was the first time she'd visited since the dedication of the Chrysopoesium, which, it would appear, had been a wise investment.

Thyon Nero had made gold.

6

PAPER, INK, AND YEARS

Coincidence?

For hundreds of years, alchemists had been trying to distill azoth. Three weeks after Lazlo's visit to the Chrysopoesium, Thyon Nero did it. Lazlo had his suspicions, but they were only suspicions—until, that is, he opened the door to his room and found Thyon in it.

Lazlo's pulse stammered. His books were spilled onto the floor, their pages creased beneath them like the broken wings of birds. Thyon held one in his hands. It was Lazlo's finest, its binding nearly worthy of the Pavilion of Thought. He'd even illuminated the spine with flakes of leftover gold leaf it took him three years to save. *The Unseen City*, it read, in the calligraphy he'd learned at the abbey.

It hit the floor with a slap, and Lazlo felt it in his

hearts. He wanted to stoop and pick it up, but he just stood there on his own threshold and stared at the intruder, so composed, so elegant, and as out of place in the dingy little room as a sunbeam in a cellar.

"Does anyone know that you came to the Chrysopoesium?" Thyon asked.

Slowly, Lazlo shook his head.

"And the book. Does anybody else know about it?"

And there it was. There was no coincidence. Lazlo had been right. Spirit was the key to azoth. It was almost funny—not just that the truth had been found in a fairy tale, but that the great secret ingredient should prove so common a thing as a bodily fluid. Every alchemist who had ever lived and died in search of it had had the answer all the time, running through his very veins.

If the truth were to be known, anyone with a pot and a fire would try to make gold, drawing spirit from their veins, or stealing it from others. It wouldn't be so precious then, and nor would the golden godson be so special. With that, he understood what was at stake. Thyon meant to keep the secret of azoth at all costs.

And Lazlo was a cost.

He considered lying, but could think of no lie that might protect him. Hesitant, he shook his head again, and he thought he had never been so aware of anything as he was aware of Thyon's hand on the hilt of his sword.

Time slowed. He watched Thyon's knuckles whiten, saw the span of visible steel lengthen as the sword was drawn up and out of its sheath. It had a curve to it, like a rib. It had a mirror brightness in the glavelight, and caught gold in it, and gray. Lazlo's eyes locked with Thyon's. He saw calculation there, as Thyon weighed the trouble of killing him with the risk of letting him live.

And he knew how that calculus would come out. With him alive, there would always be someone who knew the secret, while killing him would be no trouble at all. Thyon might leave his engraved ancestral sword skewered through Lazlo's corpse, and it would be returned to him cleaned. The whole thing would simply be tidied away. Someone like Nero might do as he liked to someone like Lazlo.

But . . . he didn't.

He sheathed the blade. "You will never speak of it," he said. "You will never write of it. No one will ever know. Do you understand me?"

"Yes," said Lazlo, hoarse.

"Swear to it," Thyon ordered, but then he cast his eyes over the books on the floor and abruptly changed his mind. "On second thought, don't swear." His lips curved in a subtle jeer. "Promise me three times."

Lazlo was startled. A triple promise? It was a child's vow from fairy tales, where breaking it was a curse, and it was more powerful to Lazlo than any vow on god or monarch would have been. "I promise," he said, shaking with the chill of his own near death. "I promise," he said again, and his face was hot and burning. "I promise."

The words, repeated, had the rhythm of an incantation, and they were the last that passed between the two young men for more than four years. Until the day the golden godson came in person to the Enquiries desk to requisition Lazlo's books.

The Complete Works of Lazlo Strange.

Gripping the request form, Lazlo's hands shook. The books were his, and they were *all* that was his. He'd made them, and he loved them in the way one loves things that come of one's own hands, but even that wasn't the extent of it. They weren't just a collection of notes. They were where he kept his impossible dream—every discovery he'd made about the Unseen City, every piece he'd puzzled into place. And it wasn't for the simple accumulation of knowledge, but with the goal of one day...circumventing impossibility. Of somehow going there, where no outsider had ever been. Of crossing the desert, seeing those glittering domes with his own eyes, and finding out, at last, *what happened to the Unseen City.*

His books were a seven-year-long record of his hopes. Even touching them gave him courage. And now they were to fall into Thyon Nero's hands?

"What in the world," Master Hyrrokkin had asked, "could *Thyon Nero* want with *your books*?"

"I don't know," said Lazlo, at a loss. "Nothing. Only to take them away from me."

The old man clucked his tongue. "Surely such pettiness is beneath him."

"You think so? Well, then perhaps he intends to read them cover to cover."

Lazlo's tone was flat, and Master Hyrrokkin took his point. That scenario was indeed the more ridiculous. "But *why*?" Hyrrokkin persisted. "Why should he want to take them away from you?"

And Lazlo couldn't tell him that. What he himself was wondering was: Why *now*, four years later? He had done nothing to break his promise, or to draw Nero's ire in any way. "Because he can?" he asked, bleak.

He fought the requisition. Of course he did. He went straight to the master of archives to plead his case. The books were his own, he said, and not property of the library. It had always been made clear that the expertise of librarians was unworthy of the term *scholarship*. As such, how could they now be claimed? It was contradictory and unjust.

"*Unjust?* You ought to be proud, young man," Villiers, the master, told him. "Thyon Nero has taken an interest in your work. It's a great day for you."

A great day indeed. For seven years, Lazlo had been "Strange the dreamer," and his books had been "scribblings" and "foolishness." Now, just like that, they were his "work," validated and stolen in one fell swoop.

"Please," he begged, urgent and hushed. "Please don't give him my books."

And...they didn't.

They made *him* do it.

"You're disgracing yourself," Villiers snapped. "And I won't have you disgrace the library, too. He's the golden godson, not some thief in the stacks. He'll return them when he's done with them. Now be off with you."

And so he had no choice. He loaded them into a crate and onto a handcart and trundled them out of the library, through the front gates, and down the long road that spiraled around Zosimos Ridge. He paused and looked out. The Eder sparkled in the sun, the rich brown of a pretty girl's eyes. The New Palace arched across it, as fantastical as a painted backdrop in a fairy play. Birds wheeled over the fishing docks, and a long golden pennant flew from the cupola of Nero's pale-pink palace. Lazlo made his slow way there. Rang the bell with deep reluctance. Remembered ringing another bell four years earlier, with *Miracles for Breakfast* clutched in his hands. He'd never seen it again. Would these books be any different?

A butler answered. He bid Lazlo leave the crate, but Lazlo refused. "I must see Lord Nero," he said, and when Thyon at last presented himself, Lazlo asked him simply, "*Why?*"

"Why?" The alchemist was in his shirtsleeves, without his scarlet cravat. His blade was in its place, though, and his hand rested casually on its hilt. "I've always wanted to ask *you* that, you know."

"*Me?*"

"Yes. Why, Strange? Why did you give it to me?" *It?* The secret, and all that followed. "When you might have kept it, and been someone yourself."

The truth was—and nothing would have persuaded Nero to believe it—that it had never occurred to Lazlo to seek his own advantage. In the tombwalk that day, it had been very clear to him: Here was a story of greedy queens and wicked fathers and war on the horizon, and . . . it wasn't *his* story. It was Thyon's. To take it for himself . . . it would have been stealing. It was as simple as that. "I *am* someone," he said. He gestured to the crate. "*That's* who I am." And then, with quiet intensity, "Don't take them. *Please.*"

There was a moment, very brief, when the guarded dispassion fell away from Thyon's face, and Lazlo saw something human in him. Regretful, even. Then it was gone. "Remember your promise," he warned, and shut the door in Lazlo's face.

Lazlo returned to his room late that evening, having

lingered at dinner to avoid it. Reaching his door, he took his glave down off its hook, hesitated, then hung it back up. With a deep breath, he entered. He hoped that darkness might soften the loss, but there was just enough moonlight to bathe his window ledge in a soft glow. Its emptiness was stark. The room felt hollow and dead, like a body with its hearts cut out. Breathing wasn't easy. He dropped onto the edge of his bed. "They're only books," he told himself. Just paper and ink.

Paper, ink, and years.

Paper, ink, years, and his dream.

He shook his head. His dream was in his mind and in his soul. Thyon might steal his books, but he couldn't steal that.

That was what he told himself that first long night bereft of his books, and he had trouble falling asleep for wondering where they were and what Nero had done to them. He might have burned them, or put them into a moldering cellar. He might even now be pulling them apart page by page, folding them into birds, and launching them off his high widow's walk, one by one.

When he finally did sleep, Lazlo dreamed his books were buried beneath the earth, and that the blades of grass that grew up from them whispered "Weep, Weep" when the winds blew, and all who heard it felt tears prick their eyes.

Never once did he consider that Thyon might be

reading them. That, in a room as opulent as Lazlo's was plain, with his feet up on a tufted stool and a glave on either side, he was reading long into the night while servants brought him tea, and supper, and tea again. Lazlo certainly never imagined him taking notes, with a swan quill and octopus ink from an inkwell of inlaid lys that had actually come from Weep some five hundred years ago. His handsome face was devoid of mockery or malice, and was instead intent, alive, and *fascinated*.

Which was so much worse.

Because if Lazlo thought a dream could not be stolen, he underestimated Thyon Nero.

7

IMPOSSIBLE DREAM

Without his books, Lazlo felt as though a vital link to his dream had been cut. The Unseen City had never seemed more distant, or more out of reach. It was as though a fog had lifted, forcing him to confront an uncomfortable truth.

His books were not his dream. Moreover, he had tucked his dream into their pages like a bookmark and been content to leave it there for too long. The fact was: Nothing he might ever do or read or find inside the Great Library of Zosma was going to bring him one step closer to Weep. Only a journey would do that.

Easier said than done, of course. It was so very far. He might conceivably find a way of reaching Alkonost, the crossroads of the continent and western outpost of the Elmuthaleth. He had no qualifications to recommend him, but there was at least a chance he could hire onto a merchant convoy and work his way there. After that, though, he would be on his own. No guide would take faranji across the desert. They wouldn't even sell them camels so that they might make the attempt on their own—which would be suicide in any case.

And even supposing he somehow managed to cross the desert, there would still be the Cusp to confront: the mountain of white glass said in legend to be the funeral pyre of demons. There was only one way over it, and that was through the gates of Fort Misrach, where faranji were executed as spies.

If the city was dead, then he might get through to explore its ruins. The thought was unutterably sad. He didn't want to find ruins, but a city full of life and color, like the one from the stories. But if the city was alive, then he could expect to be drawn and quartered and fed in pieces to the carrion birds.

It wasn't hard to see why he'd tucked his dream into his books for safekeeping. But now it was all he had left, and he had to take a good, hard look at it. It wasn't encouraging. Whatever way he turned it, all he saw was: impossible. If the dream chose the dreamer, then his had chosen poorly. It needed someone far more daring than he. It needed the thunder and the avalanche, the war cry and the whirlwind. It needed *fire*.

It was a low point, the weeks after Thyon Nero took away his books. The days dragged. The walls closed in. He dreamed of deserts and great empty cities and imagined he could feel the minutes and hours of his life running through him, as though he were nothing but an hourglass of flesh and bone. He found himself staring out windows, wistful, yearning for that distant, unattainable horizon.

Which is how he happened to see the bird.

He was up one of the ladders in the Pavilion of Thought, pulling books for an impatient philosopher who paced below. "I haven't got all day," the man called up.

I have, thought Lazlo, pushing off to send his ladder rolling along its tracks. He was at the top tier of the very tall shelves, along the northern wall beyond which the shark-fin ridge fell away in a sheer cliff all the way to the city. There were narrow windows slotted between each section of bookcase, and he caught glimpses of the summer sky as he rolled past them. Bookcase, window, bookcase, window. And there it was: a bird, hovering on an updraft, as birds liked to do on this side of the ridge, hanging in place like tethered kites. But he'd never seen a bird like this one. He halted the ladder to watch it, and something went very still at the core of him. It was pure white, a hook-beaked raptor, and it was immense, larger even than the hunting eagles he'd seen with the nomads who passed through the marketplace. Its wings were like the sails of a small ship, each feather as broad as a cutlass. But it wasn't just its color or size that struck him. There was something about

76

it. Some trick of the light? Its edges…they weren't defined, but seemed to melt against the blue of the sky like sugar dissolving into tea.

Like a ghost diffusing through the veil of the world.

"What are you doing up there?" called the philosopher. Lazlo ignored him. He leaned forward to peer through the glare on the glass. The bird pirouetted on one vast wing and tipped into a slow, graceful spiral. He watched it plummet and soar out to cast its shadow over the roadway below, and over the roof of a carriage.

The royal carriage. Lazlo's forehead clashed against the window in his surprise. There was a procession coming up the long, winding road: not just the carriage but files of mounted soldiers both ahead and behind, the sun glittering on their armor. He squinted. One troop of soldiers didn't look like the others, but they were too distant for a clear view. Their armor didn't glitter. Their mounts moved with a strange gait. The road curved around to the ridge's south face, and soon the whole procession had passed out of view. The huge white eagle glided after them and then…

Perhaps Lazlo looked away. Perhaps he blinked. He didn't think so, but just like that the bird wasn't there anymore. It was and then it wasn't, and even if he *had* blinked, it couldn't have left his sight so quickly. There was no cover nearby, nothing to hide it. The drumbeat of Lazlo's blood and spirit surged. The bird had vanished.

"You there!" The philosopher was getting angry.

Lazlo looked down at him. "Is the queen meant to visit today?" he called.

"What? No."

"Because the royal carriage is coming."

The scholars sitting nearest heard and looked up. Word spread in murmurs. Royal visits were rare, and generally announced well in advance. Soon the scholars were standing up from their tables and leaving their materials behind to go outside and gather in the entrance court. Lazlo descended the ladder and walked out with them, not even hearing the call of his name from the librarian behind the Enquiries desk. "Strange, where are you going? *Strange.*"

The bird had vanished. It was magic. Lazlo knew it, as he'd known before. Whatever had happened to the city's true name, magic was responsible. Lazlo had never doubted it, but he'd feared that he'd never see further proof of it. He had a trio of fears that sat in his gut like swallowed teeth, and when he was too quiet with his own thoughts, they'd grind together to gnaw at him from within. This was the first: that he would never see further proof of magic.

The second: that he would never find out what had happened in Weep.

The third: that he would always be as alone as he was now.

All his life, time had been passing in the only way

he knew time to pass: unrushed and unrushable, as sands running through an hourglass grain by grain. And if the hourglass had been real, then in the bottom and neck—the past and the present—the sands of Lazlo's life would be as gray as his robes, as gray as his eyes, but the top—the future—would hold a brilliant storm of color: azure and cinnamon, blinding white and yellow gold and the shell pink of svytagor blood. So he hoped, so he dreamed: that, in the course of time, grain by grain, the gray would give way to the dream and the sands of his life would run bright.

Now the bird. The presence of magic. And something beyond the reach of understanding. An affinity, a resonance. It felt like...it felt like the turn of a page, and a story just beginning. There was the faintest glimmer of familiarity in it, as though he knew the story, but had forgotten it. And at that moment, for no reason he could put into words, the hourglass *shattered*. No more, the cool gray sift of days, the diligent waiting for the future to trickle forth. Lazlo's dream was spilled out into the air, the color and storm of it no longer a future to be reached, but a cyclone here and now. He didn't know *what*, but as surely as one feels the sting of shards when an hourglass tips off a shelf and smashes, he knew that something was happening.

Right now.

8

TIZERKANE

Soldiers and carriage clattered through the gates. The royal entourage was always a gorgeous spectacle, but that wasn't what stopped Lazlo's feet as abruptly as though his soul had flown on ahead of his body and left it stranded. It hadn't, surely, though maybe it leaned forward, like a craned neck. A craned *soul*.

Such absolute, unjaded wonder he had never experienced in his life.

Warriors. That was the only word for the men who rode behind the queen. They were not of Zosma. Even at war, soldiers of the crown hardly merited that term, which belonged to ancient battles and blood-curdling cries. It belonged to men like this, in tusked helms and bronze chest plates, with axes strapped across their backs. They *towered.* Their mounts were unnaturally tall. Their mounts were unnatural. They weren't horses. They were creatures never seen before, lithe and grand and complicated. Their long necks folded back like egrets'; their legs were sleek and many-jointed, their faces deerlike, with great dark eyes and ears like sheaves of snowy feathers. And then there were their antlers: huge and branching, with a sheen like the play of prisms of warm gold. Lys.

The antlers were spectralys because the creatures were spectrals. Among all those gathered and gathering, only Lazlo recognized the white stags of the Unseen City, and only he knew the warriors for who they were.

"*Tizerkane*," he whispered.

Tizerkane. Alive. The implications were profound. If they were alive, then the city was, too. Not a hint or rumor in two hundred years, and now Tizerkane warriors were riding through the gates of the Great Library. In the sheer, shimmering improbability of the moment, it seemed to Lazlo that his dream had tired of waiting and had simply...come to find him.

There were a score of the warriors. The tusks on their helms were the fangs of ravids, and the cages at their belts held scorpions, and they were not all men. A closer look revealed that their bronze chest plates were sculpted in realistic relief, and while half had square pectorals and small nipples, the other half were full-breasted, the metal etched around the navel with the *elilith* tattoo given to all women of the Unseen City

when they reached their fertility. But this went unno-
ticed in the first thrilling moment of their arrival.

All attention was arrested by the man who rode
vanguard.

Unlike the others, he was unhelmed and
unarmored—more human for being unhidden, but
no less striking for it. He was neither young nor old,
his wild black hair just beginning to gray at his brow.
His face was square and brown and leathered by much
sun, his eyes jet chips set in smiling squints. There
was a stunning vitality to him, as though he breathed
all the world's air and only left enough for others by
sheer benevolence. He was powerful, chest fully twice
as deep as a normal man's, shoulders twice as broad.
Great golden bands caught his sleeves in the dip
between biceps and deltoids, and his neck was dark
with obscure tattoos. Instead of a chest plate, he wore a
vest of tawny fur, and a broad and battered sword belt
from which hung two long blades. *Hreshtek*, thought
Lazlo, and his hands closed around the phantom hilts
of apple bough swords. He felt the texture of them,
their precise weight and balance as he'd twirled them
over his head. The memories flooded him. It had been
fifteen years, but it might have been fifteen *minutes*
since his hundred routed foes fled through the frost.

Long ago, when he was still wild. When he was
powerful.

He scanned the sky but saw no sign of the ghostly

bird. The courtyard was dead silent, save for the hooves of the horses. The spectrals made no sound, moving with dancers' grace. A footman opened the carriage door and, when the queen appeared in it, Master Ellemire, head of the Scholars' Guild and director of the Great Library, took her hand and helped her down. He was a big, swaggering man with a thunderous voice, but he blanched before the new arrivals, at a loss for words. And then, from the direction of the Chrysopoesium, came the ring of boot heels. The long, sure stride.

A wave of heads turned toward the sound. Lazlo didn't have to look. Everything clicked into place. The requisition of his books made sudden sense, and he understood that Thyon would not have burned them or flown the pages off the widow's walk like birds. He would have known of this extraordinary visit in advance. He would have read them. He would have prepared. Of course.

He came into view, walking briskly. He paused to kiss the hand of his godmother, and offered a brief bow to Master Ellemire before turning to the Tizerkane as though *he* were the library's representative and not the older man. *"Azer meret*, Eril-Fane," he said, his voice smooth and strong. *"Onora enet, en shamir."*

Well met, Eril-Fane. Your presence is our honor. Lazlo heard it as though from a distance. It was the traditional greeting of guests in Unseen. Learned, word for word, from his books.

It had taken him years to develop a working dictionary of Unseen, and more to unlock the probable pronunciation of its alphabet. *Years.* And Thyon stood there and spoke that phrase as though it were just lying around, knowable, as common as any pebble picked up off the ground, rather than the rare and precious gem it was.

The warrior—Eril-Fane, Thyon had called him— was amazed to find himself greeted in his own language, and immediately responded in kind. *And your welcome is our blessing*, was what he said. Lazlo understood. It was the first Unseen he had ever heard from a native speaker, and it sounded just as he'd always imagined it would: like calligraphy, if calligraphy were written in honey.

If Lazlo had understood his words, though, Thyon did not. He covered well, spouting a pleasantry before shifting into Common Tongue to say, "This is a day such as dreams are made of. I never thought to set eyes on a Tizerkane warrior."

"I see it's true what they say of the Great Library of Zosma," Eril-Fane replied, shifting to Common Tongue as well. His accent on its smooth syllables was like a patina on bronze. "That the wind is in your employ, and blows all the world's knowledge to your door."

Thyon laughed, quite at ease. "If only it were so simple. No, it's a good deal more work than that, but if it is knowable, I daresay it is known here, and if it is half as fascinating as your history, then it is also savored."

Eril-Fane dismounted and another warrior followed suit: a tall, straight woman who stood like a shadow to him. The rest remained mounted, and their faces weren't impassive like the ranks of Zosma soldiers. They were as vivid, each one, as their general's—sharp with interest, and alive. It made a marked difference. The Zosma guards were like mounted statues, eyes blank and fixed on nothing. They might have been minted, not born. But the Tizerkane looked back at the scholars looking at them, and the faces framed by ravid fangs, though fierce, were also fascinated. Avid, even hopeful, and above all, *human*. It was jarring. It was wonderful.

"This is not the first stop on our sojourn," Eril-Fane said, his voice like rough music. "But it is the first in which we have been greeted with familiar words. I came seeking scholars, but had not anticipated that we might ourselves be a subject of scholarly interest."

"How could you doubt it, sir?" said Thyon, all sincerity. "Your city has been my fascination since I was five years old, playing Tizerkane in the orchard, and felt its name...plucked from my mind."

Sometimes a moment is so remarkable that it carves out a space in time and spins there, while the world rushes on around it. This was one such. Lazlo stood stunned, a white noise roaring in his ears. Without his

85

books, his room felt like a body with its hearts cut out. Now his *body* felt like a body with its hearts cut out.

There was more. The queen and Master Ellemire joined in. Lazlo heard it all: the concern and abiding interest they took in the far, fabled city and its mysteries, and with what excitement they had met the news of this visit. They were convincing. No one listening would suspect they hadn't given Weep a moment's thought until a few weeks ago. No doubt the assembled scholars were wondering how they could have been ignorant of such deep and long-standing interest on the part of their guild master and monarch—who, it was to be noted by the keen-eyed among them, wore a priceless new tiara of lys atop her stiff, graying curls.

"So, sir," said Master Ellemire, perhaps trying to wrest authority from Thyon. "What news of Weep?"

A misstep. The warrior was stoic but couldn't entirely hide his wince, as though the name caused him physical pain.

"I've never liked to call it that," cut in Thyon—softly, like a confession. "It's bitter on my tongue. I think of it as the Unseen City instead."

It was another knife in Lazlo's hearts, and earned Thyon a considering look from Eril-Fane. "We don't use that name, either," he said.

"Then what do you call it?" inquired the queen, querulous.

"We call it *home*, Your Majesty."

"And you're a long way from it," observed Thyon, getting to the point.

"You must be wondering why."

"I confess I am, and so much else besides. I welcome you to our great city of learning and hope that we may be of service."

"As do I," said the warrior. "More than you could know."

They went inside, and Lazlo could only watch them go. There was a sensation in his hearts, though, as a stirring of embers. There *was* fire in him. It wasn't smothered, only banked, but it would burn like the wings of the seraphim before this was over.

9

A Rare Opportunity

Word spread quickly: The visitor wished to address the scholars.

"What can he want?" they wondered, streaming into the Royal Theater. Attendance was voluntary, and unanimous. If the sight of the warriors wasn't enough to stoke their curiosity, there was rumor of a "rare opportunity." They gossiped, taking their seats.

"They say he brought a coffer of gemstones the size of a dowry chest."

"And did you see the tiara? It's *lys*—"

"Did you see the *creatures*? One rack of antlers could ransom a kingdom."

"Just try getting close to one."

"The warriors!"

"Some are *women*."

"Of all the mad indecencies!"

But mostly they wondered at the man himself. "They say he's a hero of some kind," Lazlo overheard. "The liberator of Weep."

"Liberator? From who?"

"Who or *what*?" was the cryptic reply. "I don't know, but he's called the *Godslayer*."

Everything else in Lazlo's mind took a step back to clear space for this new intelligence. *The Godslayer.* He marveled. What had the warrior *slain* that went by the name of *god*? For fifteen years, the mysteries of Weep had never been far from his thoughts. For seven years, he had scoured the library for clues of what had happened there. And now here were Tizerkane, and the answers he sought were under this very roof, and new questions, too. *What were they doing here?* In spite of Nero's treachery, a dazzlement was growing in him. *A rare opportunity.* Could it be what he hoped? What if it was? In all his dreaming—and indeed, all his despairing—he had never foreseen *this*: that his impossible dream might simply... ride through the gates.

He didn't take a seat in the sea of scarlet robes, but stood in the back of the theater, in the shadows. Scholars had been summoned, not librarians, and he didn't want to risk being told to leave.

Eril-Fane took the stage. A hush fell fast. Many of the scholars were seeing him for the first time, and you could almost feel their carefully cultivated skepticism fail.

If there were gods in need of slaying, here was the man for the job.

Lazlo's pulse thrilled through him as the Godslayer began. "It has been two centuries since my city lost the world," the warrior said, "and was lost to it. Someday that story will be told, but not today. Today it is enough to say that we have passed through a long, dark time and come out of it alive and strong. Our difficulties are now behind us. All but one." He paused. A somberness darkened his voice and regard—the mysteries of Weep, writ on its own hero's face. "The...shadow of our dark time still haunts us. It poses no danger. That much I can say. There is nothing to fear. I assure you." Here he paused, and Lazlo leaned forward, hardly breathing. *Why* did he assure them? What did their fear matter? *Could he mean...?*

"You may know," he went on, "that my city was ever forbidden to faranji. 'Outsiders,' as we would call you." He smiled a little and added, "Fondly, of course," and a low laugh rippled through the audience.

"You may also have heard that faranji who insisted on trying their luck were executed, one and all."

The laughter ceased.

"I am grateful to your good queen for giving us a gentler reception here."

Laughter again, if hesitant. It was his manner—the warmth of him, like steam rising from tea. One looked at him and thought, *Here is a great man, and also a good one*, though few men are ever both.

"No one born this side of the Elmuthaleth has ever seen what lies beyond it. But that is about to change." A rushing filled Lazlo's ears, but he didn't miss a word. "I have come to extend an invitation: to visit my city as my personal guest. This last remaining…problem, we have been unable to solve on our own. Our library and university were crushed two hundred years ago. Literally *crushed*, you understand, and our wisdom-keepers with them. So we find ourselves lacking the knowledge and expertise we need. Mathematics, engineering, metallurgy." A vague gesture of his fingers indicated he spoke in broad terms. "We've come far from home to assemble a delegation of men and women—" And as he said this, his eyes sketched the crowd, as though to confirm what he had already noted: that there were no women among the scholars of Zosma. A furrow creased his brow, but he went on. "—who might supply what we lack, and help us to put the last specter of the past where it belongs."

He looked out at them, letting his eyes settle on individual faces. And Lazlo, who was accustomed to the near invisibility his insignificance bestowed on him, was jolted to feel the weight of that gaze on him-self. A second or two it rested there: a blaze of connection, the feeling of being seen and set apart.

91

"And if this chance, in itself," Eril-Fane continued, "does not tempt you to disrupt your life and work—for a year at least, more likely two—rest assured you will be well compensated. Further, for the one who *solves* the problem"—his voice was rich with promise—"the reward will be great."

With that, most every scholar in Zosma was ready to pack a trunk and strike out for the Elmuthaleth. But that wasn't to be the way of it. It was not an open invitation, the Godslayer went on to say. He would select the delegates himself based on their qualifications.

Their qualifications.

The words flattened Lazlo like a sudden shift in gravity. He didn't need to be told that "dreamer" was not a qualification. It wasn't enough to want it more than anyone else. The Godslayer hadn't come halfway around the world to grant a junior librarian's dream. He'd come seeking knowledge and expertise, and Lazlo couldn't imagine that meant a faranji "expert" on his own city. Mathematics, engineering, metallurgy, he'd said. He'd come for practical knowledge.

He'd come for men like Thyon Nero.

10

No Story Yet Told

The Godslayer was two days interviewing scholars at the Great Library of Zosma, and in the end, he invited only *three* to join his delegation. They were: a mathematician, a natural philosopher, and, to no one's surprise, the alchemist, Thyon Nero. Lazlo wasn't even granted an interview. It wasn't Eril-Fane who denied him, but Master Ellemire, who was overseeing the process.

"Well, what is it?" he asked, impatient, when Lazlo reached the front of the queue. "Do you have a message for someone?"

"What? No," said Lazlo. "I'd...I'd like an interview. Please."

"*You*, an interview? I hardly think he's recruiting librarians, boy."

There were other scholars around, and they added

their own mockery. "Don't you know, Ellemire? Strange isn't just a librarian. He's practically a scholar himself. Of *fairy tales*."

"I'm sorry to say," the master told Lazlo, eyes heavy-lidded with disdain, "that Eril-Fane made no mention of fairies."

"Maybe they've an elf problem in Weep," said another. "Do you know anything about elf trapping, Strange?"

"Or dragons. Perhaps it's dragons."

This went on for some time. "I'd just like the chance to speak with him," Lazlo pleaded, but to no avail. Master Ellemire wouldn't "waste their guest's time" by sending in someone so "manifestly unqualified," and Lazlo couldn't find it in himself to argue on his own behalf. He *was* unqualified. The fact was, if he *did* get in to see the Godslayer, he didn't even know what he would say. What *could* he say to recommend himself? *I know a lot of stories?*

It was the first time he ever felt, for himself, a measure of the contempt others felt for him.

Who had ever expended so much passion on a dream, only to stand helpless as it was granted to others? Others, moreover, who had expended no passion on it at all. His impossible dream had, against all probability, crossed deserts and mountains to come to Zosma and extend an unprecedented invitation.

But not to him.

"I owe you a thank-you, Strange," said Thyon Nero later, after everything was decided and the Tizerkane were preparing to depart.

Lazlo could only look at him, blank. A thank-you for what? For helping him when he was desperate and alone? For handing him the secret to his fame and fortune? For rescuing the royal treasury and enabling Zosma to pay its army and avoid war?

No. None of that. "Your books were quite informative," he said. "Of course, I imagine real scholars will take an interest in Weep now, and amateur records won't be needed. Still, it's not bad work. You should be proud."

Proud. Lazlo remembered that solitary thank-you from back when they were boys, and couldn't believe that it had ever been meaningful. "What are you doing here?" he asked. "Shouldn't you be over there with the chosen?"

The Tizerkane were mounted, spectrals gleaming white and lys, the warriors in their bronze, faces fierce and alive. Eril-Fane was bidding the queen farewell, and the mathematician and natural philosopher were with them, too. The chosen scholars weren't leaving with the Tizerkane today. They were to meet them in four months' time at the caravansary in Alkonost, where the full delegation would assemble to strike out together across the Elmuthaleth. It would take them time to wrap up their work and prepare themselves for a long journey. None of them were adventurers, at least not yet. In the meantime, the Tizerkane would continue their travels, searching out more delegates in the kingdoms of Syriza, Thanagost, and Maialen. Still, Lazlo didn't know what Thyon was doing mingling among the unchosen. Besides gloating.

"Oh, I'm going," he said. "I just wanted you to know that your books were helpful. Eril-Fane was most impressed with my knowledge of his city. Do you know, he said I was the first outsider he's met who knew anything about it. Isn't that a fine thing?"

Fine wasn't the word that came to Lazlo's mind.

"Anyway," continued Thyon, "I didn't want you to worry that you'd done all that work for nothing."

And Lazlo wasn't a creature of anger or envy, but he felt the scorch of both—as though his veins were fuses and they were burning through him, leaving paths of ash in their wake. "Why do you even want to go?" he asked, bitter. "It's nothing to you."

Thyon shrugged. Everything about him was smooth—his pressed clothes and perfect shave, his cavalier voice and blithe expression. "Stories will be told about me, Strange. You should appreciate that. There ought to be adventure in them, don't you think? It's a dull legend that takes place in a laboratory."

A legend? The tale of the golden godson, who distilled azoth and saved kingdoms. It was all about *him*, and not Weep at all. He smacked Lazlo on the back. "I'd better go and say good-bye. And don't worry, Strange. You'll get your books back."

It was no comfort. For years, Lazlo's books had represented his dream. Now they would represent the end of it.

"Don't be so glum," said Thyon. "Someday I'll come home, and when I do, I promise"—he put a hand to his hearts—"I'll tell you all about the mysteries of Weep."

Numbly, Lazlo watched him walk away. It wasn't fair. He knew it was a childish thought. Who knew better than he that life wasn't fair? He'd learned that lesson before he could walk, before he could speak. But how could he accept *this*? How could he go on from this, knowing that his chance had come and gone, and he hadn't even been allowed to try? He imagined marching forth right now, right here, in front of everyone, and appealing directly to Eril-Fane. The thought made his face burn and his voice wither, and he might as well have been turned to stone.

Master Hyrrokkin found him there and laid a consoling hand on his arm. "I know it's hard, Strange, but it will pass. Some men are born for great things, and others to *help* great men do great things. There's no shame in it."

Lazlo could have laughed. What would Master Hyrrokkin say if he knew the help that Lazlo had already given the great golden godson? What would everyone say, those scholars who'd mocked him, if they knew a fairy tale had held the key to azoth? When Lazlo had gone to Thyon with his "miracle for breakfast," it had been so clearly Thyon's story that he hadn't even considered keeping it for himself. But... this was *his* story.

He was Strange the dreamer, and this was his dream.

"I *do* want to help a great man do great things," he told the librarian. "I want to help Eril-Fane. I want to help the Unseen City."

"My boy," said Master Hyrrokkin with deep and gentle sadness, "how could *you* help?"

And Lazlo didn't know how, but he knew one thing. He couldn't help if he stayed here. He watched Eril-Fane bid Thyon farewell. The scene dazzled. Royalty and warriors and spectacular beasts. Eril-Fane stepped a foot up into his stirrup and mounted. Thyon stood beside him, a perfect part of a perfect picture. Some people were born to inhabit such scenes. That was what Master Hyrrokkin believed, and what Lazlo had always been taught. And others were born to... what? To stand in the crowd and do nothing, try nothing, say nothing, and accept every serving of bitter *nothing* as their due?

No. Just... *no.*

"Wait! Please."

The words came from *him*. Here, in front of everyone. His heartbeats were deafening. His head felt wrapped in thunder. The scholars craned their necks to see who among them had spoken, and were startled—even astonished—to see the soft-spoken, dreamy-eyed junior librarian cutting his way through the crowd. He was astonished himself, and stepped forth with a sense of unreality. Eril-Fane had heard him and was looking back, inquiring. Lazlo had lost track of his feet and legs. He might have been floating for all he could tell, but he supposed it more likely he was walking and just couldn't feel it. This boldness, such as it was, went against everything in him, but this was it, his last chance: act now, or lose his dream forever. He forced himself forward.

"My name is Lazlo Strange," he called out, and the full complement of Tizerkane warriors turned their heads as one to look at him. Their vivid faces showed their surprise—not because Lazlo had called out, but because he had called out in Unseen, and unlike Thyon, he didn't treat it like a common thing, but the rare and precious gem it was. The words, in the reverent tones of his rough voice, sounded like a magic spell. "Might I beg a moment of your time?" he asked, still in their tongue, and he must not have looked crazed—though it had to be a near thing; he *felt* crazed—because Eril-Fane eased his spectral around to face him, and, with a nod, signaled him to approach.

"Who is that?" Lazlo heard the queen ask, her voice waspish. "What is he saying?"

Thyon stepped forward, his eyes darting between Lazlo and Eril-Fane. "Sir," he said quickly, his veneer of smoothness slipping. "You needn't trouble yourself. He's only a librarian."

Eril-Fane's brow creased. "Only?" he asked.

If Thyon had indeed read *The Complete Works of Lazlo Strange*, then he must know that in Weep of old, the keepers of books had been the keepers of wisdom, and not servants as they were in Zosma. Realizing that his slight had missed its mark, he hurried to say, "I only mean that he lacks the sort of expertise you're looking for."

"I see," said Eril-Fane, turning his attention back to Lazlo. And then, in his own tongue, with what seemed to Lazlo's untrained ear to be slow and careful enunciation, he inquired, "And what can I do for you, young man?"

Lazlo's grasp of the spoken language was tenuous, but he managed to answer, in uncertain grammar, "I want to come with you. Please, let me be of service."

Eril-Fane's surprise showed. "And why did you not come to me before?"

"I . . . wasn't permitted, sir," Lazlo said.

"I see," said Eril-Fane once more, and Lazlo thought he detected displeasure in his tone. "Tell me, how did you learn our language?"

Haltingly, Lazlo did. "I . . . I built a key with old trade documents. It was a place to start. Then there were letters, books." What could he say? How could he convey the *hours*—hundreds of hours—spent bent over ledgers, his eyes swimming in the dim light of a dull glave while his mind traced the arabesques and coils of an alphabet that looked like music sounded? How could he explain that it had fit his mind as nothing else ever had, like numbers to a mathematician, or air to a flute? He couldn't. He only said, "It's taken me seven years."

Eril-Fane took all this in, casting a mild sideward glance at Thyon Nero, who was stiff with alarm, and if he was comparing the alchemist's superficial knowledge with Lazlo's deeper understanding, he didn't call it out.

"And *why* have you learned it?" he asked Lazlo, who stumbled through a reply. He wasn't sure exactly what he said, but he *tried* to say: "Because your city is my fascination. I can still taste its true name, and I know magic is real, because I felt it that day, and all I've ever wanted is to go and find it."

"Find magic? Or my city?"

"Your city," said Lazlo. "Both. Though magic..." He groped for words, and ended up shifting in frustration back to Common Tongue. "I fear that magic must be dark," he said, "to have done such a thing as *erase a name*. That has been my only experience of it. Well," he added, "until the white bird."

"What?" The Godslayer grew suddenly serious. "What white bird?"

"The…the ghost eagle," said Lazlo. "Is it not yours? It arrived with you, so I thought it must be."

"She's here?" Eril-Fane asked, intent. He searched the sky, the line of the rooftops. "When did you see her? Where?"

Her? Lazlo pointed beyond the palace. "When you were first coming up the road," he said. "It—*she*—seemed to be following. She vanished right before my eyes."

"*Please*, Strange," Thyon cut in, pained. "What are you on about? Vanishing birds?" He laughed, as one would at a child with a silly notion, but it rang terribly false. "Now I really must insist you leave our guest in peace. Step back now, and you might yet keep your position."

Lazlo faced him. The alchemist's hand rested—casually—on the hilt of his sword, but there was nothing casual in the malice that burned in his gaze. It wasn't only malice, but fear, and Lazlo understood two things: He would *not* keep his position, not after such insolence as this. And he could not be permitted to leave, either, not with the secret he carried. In putting himself forward, he had risked everything. It was all suddenly very clear. A weird, bright courage sang in him as he turned back to Eril-Fane.

"Sir," he said. "It's true that I am unqualified in engineering and the sciences. But I can be of use to you. No one would work harder, I promise you. I could

102

be your secretary, handle contracts for the delegates, write letters, keep accounts. Anything. Or I'll take care of the spectrals. Carry water. Whatever you need. I...I..." He wasn't fully in possession of himself. His words were spilling out. His mind was racing. *Who am I?* he asked himself. *What do I have to offer?* And before he could bite it back, he heard himself say, "I can tell stories. I know a lot of stories," before faltering into a painful silence.

I know a lot of stories.

Had he really just said that? Thyon Nero laughed. Eril-Fane didn't. He exchanged a look with his second-in-command, the tall, straight woman by his side. Lazlo couldn't read it. He saw that she was beautiful, in a very different way than the women of Zosma were beautiful. She was unpainted and unsmiling. There were lines around her eyes from laughter, and around her mouth from grief. She didn't speak, but something passed between the two. These seconds were the longest of Lazlo's life, and the heaviest with fate. If they left him behind, would he even last the day? What would Nero do to him, and when?

Then Eril-Fane cleared his throat. "It's been a very long time since we heard new stories," he said. "And I could indeed use a secretary. Gather your things. You'll come with us now."

Lazlo's throat trapped his breath. His knees felt turned to water. What had been holding him up all this time? Whatever it was, it let go, and it was all he could do not to stumble. Everyone was watching. Everyone was listening. The shocked hush was threaded with murmurs.

"I have nothing to gather," he breathed. It was true, but even if he'd had a palace full of possessions, he couldn't have gone to fetch them now, for fear of returning to find the Tizerkane gone, and his chance, and his dream—and his *life*—with them.

"Well then, up with you," said Eril-Fane, and a spectral was led forward.

A spectral. For him. "This is Lixxa," said the warrior, putting the reins into Lazlo's hand as though he might know what to do with them. He'd never even ridden a horse, let alone a creature like this. He stood there looking at the reins, and the stirrup, and the faces of the Tizerkane regarding him with curiosity. He was used to hiding behind books or in the shadows. It was midsummer, midmorning, in the full light of day. There were no books to hide behind, and no shadows—only Lazlo Strange in his worn gray robes, with his nose that had been broken by fairy tales, looking like the hero of no story ever told.

Or. No story *yet* told.

He mounted. He was clumsy, and he wasn't dressed for riding, but he got a leg across, and that seemed to be the main thing. His robes hiked up to his knees. His legs were pale, and his soft-soled slippers were worn nearly through. Lixxa knew her business, and followed when the others filed out through the gate. All eyes were on Lazlo, and all were wide—except for Thyon's, which were narrow with fury. "You can keep the books," Lazlo told him, and left him standing there. He took one last look at the gathered crowd—scarlet robes and the occasional gray—and spotted Master Hyrrokkin, looking stunned and proud. Lazlo nodded to the old man—the only person besides Thyon who knew what this meant to him, and the only person in the world who might be happy for him—and he nearly wept.

I'm going to Weep, he thought, and could have laughed at the pun, but he kept his composure, and when the Tizerkane warriors rode out of the Great Library and out of Zosma, Strange the dreamer went with them.

11

TWELFTHMOON

That was Sixthmoon, summer in the north.

It was Twelfthmoon now, and winter in Zosma, the Eder frozen over, and young men perchance composing poems to girls they'd met ice-skating.

Lazlo Strange was not among them. He was riding a spectral at the head of a long, undulating line of camels. Behind them lay all the emptiness of the known world: flat sky above, flat earth below, and between the two nothing at all for hundreds of miles save the name *Elmuthaleth* for parched lips to curse.

The months of travel had altered him. His library pallor had burned and then browned. His muscles had hardened, his hands grown callused. He felt himself toughened, like meat hung to cure, and though he hadn't seen his reflection for weeks, he had no doubt that Master Hyrrokkin would be satisfied.

"A man should have squint lines from looking at the horizon," the old librarian had said, "not just from reading in dim light."

Well, here was the horizon Lazlo had dreamed of since he was five years old. Ahead, at last, lay the desert's hard and final edge: the Cusp. Jagged and glittering, it was a long, low-slung formation of blinding white rock, and a perfect natural battlement for that which lay beyond: Not yet visible and never before seen by faranji eyes, lay the city that had lost its name, and, within it, whatever problem the Godslayer sought help to solve.

It was the first week of Twelfthmoon, on the far side of the Elmuthaleth, and Strange the dreamer—library stowaway and scholar of fairy tales—had never been thirstier, or more full of wonder.

PART II

* * *

thakrar (THAH·krahr) *noun*

The precise point on the spectrum of awe at which wonder turns to dread, or dread to wonder.

Archaic; from the ecstatic priestesses of Thakra, worshippers of the seraphim, whose ritual dance expressed the dualism of beauty and terror.

12

Kissing Ghosts

"You *can* kiss a ghost."

"I suppose you'd know."

"I do know. It's just like kissing a person."

"Now, that's something you *wouldn't* know."

Sarai lingered in the half-light of the gallery, listening to the rhythms of Sparrow and Ruby arguing. It never grew very heated between them, but neither did it ever quite abate. She knew that as soon as she stepped out into the garden they would draw her into it, and she wasn't awake enough for that. It was late afternoon; she'd only just risen, and it took her some time to shake off the effects of lull, the draught she drank to help her sleep.

Well, she didn't need help *sleeping*. Her nights were long and filled with dark work; she was exhausted by dawn, and drifted off as soon as she let her eyes shut.

But she didn't let them shut until she'd had her lull, because lull kept her from *dreaming*.

Sarai didn't dream. She didn't dare.

"I've kissed people," said Ruby. "I've kissed *you*."

"Pecks on the cheek don't count," replied Sparrow.

Sarai could see the pair of them, shimmering in the late-day sun. Sparrow had just turned sixteen, and Ruby would in a few more months. Like Sarai, they wore silk slips that would have been considered undergarments if there were anyone around to see them. Anyone *alive*, that is. They were picking plums, their two sets of bare arms reaching in among the whip-like boughs, their two dark heads turned away from her, one tidy, the other wild as wind. The wild one was Ruby. She refused to wear her hair in braids and then acted as though she were dying when they tried to brush out the tangles.

Sarai gathered, from the tenor of the debate, that she had been kissing the ghosts. She sighed. It wasn't a surprise, exactly. Of the five of them, Ruby was the most ardent, and the most prone to boredom. "It's easy for *you*," she'd told Sarai just the other evening. "You get to see people every night. You get to *live*. The rest of us are just stuck in here with the ghosts."

Sarai hadn't argued. It would seem that way to the others, of course. She did see the people of Weep every night, but it made nothing easier. On the contrary.

Every night she bore witness to what she could never have. It wasn't living. It was torture.

"Good, you're awake," said Feral, coming into the gallery. It was a long, vaulted arcade that overlooked the garden from the dexter arm of the citadel, and was where dinner would soon be laid out for the five of them. Here, the slick blue mesarthium of which the entire citadel was constructed was softened almost to an afterthought by Sparrow's orchids. Hundreds of them, dozens of varieties, spiking, trailing, billowing, they dressed the colonnade in a forest of blooms. Vines wrapped the pillars, and epiphytes clung to the ceiling like anemones, or roosting butterflies. It was sumptuous, illusory. You could almost forget where you were. You could almost imagine yourself free, and walking in the world.

Almost.

As for Feral, he was Sarai's ally and fellow acting parent to the other three. He was seventeen years old, like her, and had, this year, fallen almost all the way over the line into adulthood. He was tall, still lean from his fast growth, and had begun to shave—or, as Sparrow put it, to "abuse his poor face with knives." It was true he hadn't yet mastered the art, but he was getting better. Sarai saw no new wounds on him, only the healing pucker of an old one on the sharp edge of his jaw.

She thought he looked tired. "Bad day?" she asked. The girls weren't always easy to manage, and since Sarai was nocturnal by necessity, it mostly fell to Feral to see that they did their chores and obeyed The Rule.

"Not bad," said Feral. "Just long."

It was odd for Sarai to think of days being long. She slept through them all, from sunrise nearly till sunset, and it always felt as though she were opening her eyes only a moment after closing them. It was the lull. It ate her days in one gray gulp.

"How about you?" he asked, his brown eyes soft with concern. "Bad night?"

All of Sarai's nights were bad. Bad seemed to her the very nature of night. "Just long," she echoed with a rueful smile, laying one hand to her slender neck and rolling her head from side to side. She knew he couldn't understand. He did his part to keep the five of them alive, and she did hers. There was no point complaining.

"Where's Minya?" she asked, noting the absence of the fifth member of their peculiar family.

Feral shrugged. "I haven't seen her since breakfast. Maybe she's with Great Ellen."

Great Ellen had run the citadel nursery before the Carnage. Now she ran everything. Well, everything that was still running, which wasn't much.

"Ghost-kisser," they heard from the garden. Sparrow's

soft voice curled with laughter, and was cut off by an "Ow!" as Ruby pelted her with a plum.

"Who was it?" Sarai asked Feral. "Who did she aim her lips at?"

Feral made a sound that was the verbal equivalent of a shrug. "Kem, I think."

"Really? Kem?" Sarai wrinkled her nose. Kem had been with them since the beginning. He'd been a footman before the Carnage, and still wore the livery he'd died in, which to Sarai's mind suggested a distinct lack of imagination.

"Why?" Feral asked Sarai, waggling his eyebrows. "Who would *you* kiss?"

In a tone both arch and light, Sarai replied, "I kiss dozens of people every night." And she touched a spot just above the outer curve of one cinnamon eyebrow. "Right here. Men and women, babies and grandparents. I kiss them and they shudder." Her voice was like ice, and so were her hearts. "I kiss them and they grieve."

"That's not kissing," said Feral. He had been teasing, merry, and now he wasn't.

He was right, of course. It was not kissing, what Sarai did to people in the deep of night. "Maybe not," she said, still arch, still light, "but it's as close as I'll ever come to it." She pushed down her shoulders and lifted her chin. *End of discussion*, her posture said.

Feral looked like he might press the issue, but all

of a sudden Ruby's voice grew louder. "Well, let's just see about it, shall we?" she said, followed shortly by a singsong call of, "Feral, where are you?"

Feral froze like prey in a raptor's shadow. "Oh no," he said.

Ruby appeared in an arch of the arcade, looking like one more orchid in the forest, her slim form a stem upholding a bloom of riotous hair. Feral tried to melt out of sight, but it was too late. She'd spotted him. "There you are. Oh, hello, Sarai, hope you slept well. Feral, I need you for a second."

Sparrow was right behind her. "You do *not* need him," she said. "Leave him alone!"

And the chain of events that followed was a perfect illustration of the minor chaos that passed for life in the citadel.

Ruby seized Feral by his collar and yanked his face down to hers. He struggled. She held on, mashing her lips against his and doing something to his mouth that looked and sounded less like kissing than *devouring*.

The temperature dropped. The air over their heads churned and darkened, a cloud coalescing out of nowhere, gray and dense and gravid with rain. Within a second the gallery was full of the wild tang of ozone and a fullness of moisture that made them feel they were inside a storm even before the first drops burst forth, fat and full and very cold, like the bottom dropping out of a bucket. Sarai felt the frigid spatter, but

Ruby was the target, and the girl was soaked in an instant.

Her gasp freed Feral's lips from suction. He wrenched himself away and staggered back, glaring and wiping his mouth, which was undevoured but glistening with spit. Ruby tried to skitter clear of the cloud, but it pursued her.

"Feral, call it off!" she cried, but he didn't, so she charged straight toward him, cloud and all. He dodged and ducked behind Sarai, into whom Ruby caromed in a plash of sodden, icy silk.

It was Sarai's turn to gasp. The rain was *arctic*. "Feral!" she managed to croak. The cloud vanished as it had come, and Sarai pushed away from Ruby, shocked and streaming. Beneath her feet the floor had become a wide, shallow lake. The orchids glistened, rivulets of rain streaming from their fleshy petals. Her own slip was wet-dark and clinging to her body, and she was now thoroughly awake. "Thank you so much," she said to Feral, who was still wiping the saliva off his face.

"You're welcome," he replied, surly.

When they were little, they'd thought he *made* the clouds, and why wouldn't they? There was no one to explain it to them, or Sarai's gift to her, or the girls' gifts to them. The gods had died and left them to their own devices.

Feral wished, and clouds appeared. Even before

he'd known to wish for them, they'd come, tied to his moods and terribly inconvenient, to hear Great Ellen tell it. How many times had the nursery flooded because when this little boy was angry or excited, clouds filled the air around him? Now he could control it, more or less, and called them on purpose. Sometimes they were rain clouds, heavy and dark, and sometimes airy tufts of white that cast delicate shade and twisted into shapes like hunting ravids or castles in the air. There was snow from time to time, always a treat, and hail, less of a treat, and sometimes sultry, muggy vapors that smelled of growth and decay. Occasionally, perilously, there was lightning. Sarai and Feral were ten or eleven when a paper kite appeared with some fog, and they realized he didn't *make* the clouds. He ripped them out of faraway skies. He *stole* them.

Cloud Thief, they called him now, and this was his part to play in keeping them alive. The river was out of their reach and rain was seasonal. Their only source of water for much of the year was Feral's clouds.

Ruby's riot of hair had gone otter-pelt sleek, still sluicing off the remnants of rain. Her white slip was plastered to her body and quite transparent, her small nipples and the divot of her navel plainly visible. She made no move to cover herself. Feral averted his eyes.

Ruby turned to Sparrow and conceded, with evident surprise, "You know, you're right. It's *not* like kissing ghosts. It's warmer. And...wetter." She laughed and shook her head, fountaining spumes of rain from the ends of her hair. "A lot wetter."

Sparrow didn't share her laughter. Stricken, the girl spun on one bare heel and darted back out to the garden.

Ruby turned to Sarai. "What's wrong with *her*?" she asked, perfectly oblivious to what had been clear to Sarai for months now: that Sparrow's affection for Feral had changed from the sisterly feelings they all had for him into something...well, to use Ruby's words...*warmer*. Sarai wasn't going to explain it to Ruby—or to Feral, who was equally oblivious. It was just one of the ways life was getting more complicated as they grew up.

She slapped at her wet slip and sighed. At least hers was dark gray, and so hadn't gone see-through like Ruby's, but she would still have to change. "It's almost dinnertime," she said to Ruby. "I suggest you get dry."

Ruby looked down at herself, then back up at Sarai. "All right," she said, and Sarai saw the telltale spark in her eye.

"Not like that—" she said, but it was too late.

Ruby burst into flames. Sarai had to lurch back from the blast of heat as Ruby was engulfed in a crackling, deep-orange column of fire. It kindled in an instant, like lamp oil kissed by a spark, but died more slowly, the flames receding until her form was visible within them, her flesh absorbing each lick of fire one by one. Her eyes were the last reservoir of flame, burning as red as her name so that she looked, for a second, like a temple icon to an evil goddess, and then she was just herself again—herself and *only* herself, nary a shred or ashen tatter remaining of her dress.

They called her Bonfire, for obvious reasons. While a baby Feral might have caused inconvenience, a baby Ruby had had a more dangerous effect, compounded by the volatility of her nature. It was a good thing, then, that their nursemaids had been dead already. Ghosts were not combustible, and neither was mesarthium, so there had been no risk of her setting the citadel alight.

"All dry," said the girl, and so she was. Her hair, unburned, was wild once more, still crackling with the fire's kinesis, and Sarai knew that if she touched it, it would feel like a bed of coals, and so would her bare skin. She shook her head, glad Sparrow had missed this display.

Feral was still standing with his back turned. "Tell me when it's safe to look," he said, bored.

Sarai told Ruby, "That was a waste of a dress."

Ruby shrugged. "What does it matter? We won't live long enough to run out of dresses."

Her voice was so casual, so matter-of-fact, that her words swept past all of Sarai's defenses and pierced her. It was more of a shock than the rain.

Won't live long enough . . .

"Ruby!" said Sarai.

Feral, equally shocked, turned back around, naked girl or not. "Is that really what you think?" he asked her.

"What, you don't?" Ruby looked genuinely amazed, standing there fire-dried and beautiful, naked, at ease with herself, and blue. Blue as opals, pale blue. Blue as cornflowers, or dragonfly wings, or a spring—not summer—sky. Just like the rest of them.

Blue as five murders waiting to happen.

"You think we're going to grow old here?" she asked, looking back and forth between them, gesturing to the walls around them. "You must be joking. Is that really a future you can picture?"

Sarai blinked. It wasn't a question she allowed herself to ask. They did their best. They obeyed The Rule. Sometimes she almost believed it would be enough. "A lot of things could happen," she said, and heard how half her voice was carved away by uncertainty, and how utterly weak she sounded.

"Like what?" Ruby asked. "Besides dying, I mean."

And Sarai couldn't think of a single thing.

13

PURGATORY SOUP

Sarai stepped out of her clammy, wet slip and let it fall to the floor of her dressing room. Puddled gray silk on the blue metal floor. Blue toes, blue legs, blue self reflected in the blue mirror, which wasn't glass but only more mesarthium, polished to a high gloss. The only thing that wasn't blue was her hair—which was the red-brown of cinnamon—and the whites of her eyes. The whites of her teeth, too, if she were smiling, but she very much wasn't.

"We won't live long enough to run out of dresses," Ruby had said.

Sarai regarded the row of slips hanging from the slim mesarthium dowel. There were so many, and all so fine. And yes, they were underclothes, but she and Ruby and Sparrow preferred them to the alternative: the gowns.

The only clothes they had or would ever have—like the only life they had or would ever have—was what the citadel provided, and the citadel provided the garments of dead goddesses.

The dressing room was as large as a lounge. There were dozens of gowns, all of them too grand to wear, and too terrible. Satins and foils and stiff brocades, encrusted with jewels and trimmed in furs with the heads still on, glassy eyes, bared fangs and all. One had a skirt like a cage carved of whalebone, another a long train made of hundreds of doves' wings all stitched together. There was a bodice of pure molded gold, made to look like a beetle's carapace, and a fan collar fashioned from the spines of poisonous fish, with tiny teeth sewn in patterns like seed pearls. There were headdresses and veils, corsets with daggers concealed in the stays, elaborate capes, and teetering tall shoes carved of ebony and coral. Everything was gaudy and heavy and cruel. To Sarai, they were clothes a monster might wear if it were trying to pass as human.

Which was near enough to the truth. The monster had been Isagol, goddess of despair.

Her mother, dead now these fifteen years.

Sarai had a thousand memories of Isagol, but none of them were her own. She'd been too young—only two years old when it happened. *It.* The Carnage. Knifeshine and spreading blood. The end of one world and start of another. Her memories of her mother

123

were all secondhand, borrowed from the humans she visited in the night. In some the goddess was alive, in others dead. She'd been murdered in an iridescent green gown jeweled with jade and beetle wings, and she'd looked enough like Sarai that the visions of her body were like seeing a prophecy of her own death. Except for the black bar Isagol had painted across her eyes, temple to temple, like a slim mask.

Sarai eyed the shelf of her mother's paints and perfumes. The pot of lampblack was right there, untouched in all this time. Sarai didn't use it. She had no desire to look more like the goddess of despair than she already did.

She focused on the slips. She had to get dressed. White silk or scarlet, or black trimmed in burgundy. Gold or chartreuse, or pink as the dawn sky. She kept hearing the echo of Ruby's words—*won't live long enough*—and seeing in the row of slips two possible endings:

In one, she was murdered and they went unworn. Humans burned or shredded them, and they burned and shredded her, too. In the other, she lived and spent years working her way through them all. Ghosts laundered them and hung them back up, again and again over years, and she wore them out one by one and eventually grew old in them.

It seemed so far-fetched—the idea of growing old—that she had to admit to herself, finally, that she had no more real hope of the future than Ruby did.

It was a brutal revelation.

She chose black to suit her mood, and returned to the gallery for dinner. Ruby had come back from her own dressing room clad in a slip so sheer she might as well have stayed naked. She was making tiny flames dance off her fingertips, while Feral leaned over his big book of symbols, ignoring her.

"Minya and Sparrow?" Sarai asked them.

"Sparrow's still in the garden, pouting about something," said Ruby, her self-absorption apparently admitting no hint as to what that something might be. "Minya hasn't turned up."

Sarai wondered at that. Minya was usually waiting to pester her as soon she came out of her room. "Tell me something nasty," she would say, bright-eyed, eager to hear about her night. "Did you make anyone cry? Did you make anyone *scream*?" For years, Sarai had been happy to tell her all about it.

Not anymore.

"I'll fetch Sparrow," she said.

The garden was a broad terrace that stretched the breadth of the citadel, abutting the high, indomitable body of the structure on one side, and falling away to a sheer drop on the other, edged only by a hip-high balustrade. It had been formal once, but now was wild. Shrubs that had been tidy topiaries had grown into great shaggy trees, and bowers of blooming vines had overspilled their neat beds to riot up the walls and columns and drape over the railing. Nature flourished, but not on its own. It couldn't, not in this unnatural place. It was Sparrow who made it flourish.

Sarai found her gathering anadne blossoms. Anadne was the sacred flower of Letha, goddess of oblivion. Distilled, it made lull, the draught Sarai drank to keep from dreaming.

"Thank you for doing that," Sarai said.

Sparrow looked up and smiled at her. "Oh, I don't mind. Great Ellen said it was time for a new batch." She dropped a handful of flowers into her bowl and dusted off her palm. "I just wish you didn't need it, Sarai. I wish you were free to dream."

So did Sarai, but she wasn't free, and wishing wouldn't make her so. "I might not have my own dreams," she said, as though it scarcely mattered, "but I have everyone else's."

"It's not the same. That's like reading a thousand diaries instead of writing your own."

"A thousand?" said Sarai. "More like a hundred thousand," which was close to the population of Weep.

"So many," said Sparrow, marveling. "How do you keep them straight?"

Sarai shrugged. "I don't know that I do, but you can learn a lot in four thousand nights."

"*Four thousand.* Have we been alive so long?"

"Longer than that, silly."

"Where do the days go?" There was such sweetness

126

in Sparrow's wisp of a smile. She was as sweet as the scent of the garden and as gentle, and Sarai couldn't help thinking how perfectly her gift suited her. Orchid Witch, they called her. She felt the pulse of life in things and nursed it forth to make them grow. She was, Sarai thought, like springtime distilled into a person.

Ruby's gift, too, was an extension of her nature: Bonfire, blazing like a beacon, burning like a wildfire out of control. And Minya and Feral, did their gifts suit them? Sarai didn't like the thought, because if it was so and their abilities spoke some essential truth about their souls, what did that say about *her*?

"I was just thinking," said Sparrow, "how our waking life is like the citadel. Enclosed, I mean. Indoors, no sky. But dreaming is like the garden. You can step out of prison and feel the sky around you. In a dream you can be anywhere. You can be *free*. You deserve to have that, too, Sarai."

"If the citadel is our prison," Sarai replied, "it's our sanctuary, too." She plucked a white blossom from its stem and dropped it into Sparrow's bowl. "It's the same with lull." Sleep might be a gray wasteland to her, but she knew what was lurking beyond the safe circle of lull, and she was glad of the gray. "Besides," she said, "my dreams wouldn't be like a garden." She tried not to envy that Sparrow's were—or that her gift was such a simple and beautiful one, while her own was neither.

"Maybe one day they can be," said Sparrow.

"Maybe," said Sarai, and hope had never felt like such a lie. "Let's go have dinner," she said, and together they went inside.

"Good evening, brood," Less Ellen greeted them, carrying a tureen from the kitchen. Like Great Ellen, Less Ellen had been with them from the beginning. She had worked in the citadel nursery, too, and with two Ellens, a distinction had been needed. The one being greater in both status and size, so it was that Skathis himself, the god of beasts and high lord of the Mesarthim, had dubbed them the greater and lesser Ellens.

Ruby breathed a woeful sigh as her dinner was put before her. "Kimril soup. Again." She scooped up a spoonful and let it dribble back into her bowl. It was beige, with the consistency of stagnant water. "You know what this is? It's *purgatory soup*." Turning to Sparrow, she asked, "Couldn't you grow something *new* for us to eat?"

"Certainly I could," Sparrow replied, a tartness in her tone that had not been there when she was speaking with Sarai, "if my gift were conjuring seeds from thin air." She took a dainty sip from her spoon. "Which it isn't."

Sparrow might make things grow, but she had to have something to start with. For the most part, the citadel gardens had been ornamental—full of exotic flowers, with little in the way of edibles. It was their good luck that some long-ago gardener had made a small kitchen garden of herbs, fresh greens, and a few vegetables, and their *very* good luck that their some-time visitor, the great white bird they called Wraith for its habit of vanishing into thin air, had seen fit to drop some kimril tubers into the garden once, else they'd have starved long ago. Kimril was easy to grow, nourishing though nearly flavorless, and was now the staple of their boring diet. Sarai wondered if the bird knew that it had made the difference between life and death for five blue abominations, or if it had simply been a fluke. It had never brought them anything else, so she supposed it must be the latter.

Sparrow grew their food. Feral kept the rain barrels filled. Ruby did her part, too. There was no fuel to burn, so *she* burned. She made the fires that cooked their meals and heated their baths, and Minya, well, she was responsible for the ghosts, who did most of the work. Sarai was the only one who had no part in the mundane tasks of their days.

Purgatory soup, she thought, stirring hers with her spoon. The simplest possible fare, served on the finest porcelain, and set on an elaborate charger of chased silver. Her goblet was chased silver, too, in a design of twined myrantine branches. Once upon a time, the gods had drunk wine from it. Now there was only rainwater.

Once upon a time, there had *been* gods. Now there were only children going about in their dead parents' undergarments.

"I can't do it anymore," said Ruby, dropping her spoon into her soup. It splattered the table and the front of her new slip. "I can't put one more bite of this insipid mush into my mouth."

"Must you be so dramatic?" Feral asked, bypassing his spoon in favor of tipping back his bowl and drinking from it. "It's not as though it's terrible. At least we still have some salt in the pantry. Imagine when that runs out."

"I didn't say it was terrible," said Ruby. "If it was terrible, it wouldn't be *purgatory* soup, would it? It would be *hell* soup. Which would have to be more interesting."

"Mm-hm," agreed Sparrow. "In the same way that being eternally tortured by demons is more 'interesting' than *not* being eternally tortured by demons."

They had an ongoing debate on the merits of "interesting." Ruby contended that it was always worth it, even if it came with danger and ended in doom. "Purgatory's more than just not being tortured," she argued now. "It's not being *anything, ever.* You might not be tortured, but you'll also never be *touched.*"

"Touched?" Sparrow's eyebrows went up. "How did we get to touching?"

"Don't you want to be touched?" Ruby's eyes

glimmered red, and the corners of her lips curled up, feline. There was such longing in her words, such hunger. "Don't you wish you had someone to sneak off and *do things with?*"

Sparrow flushed at this, a roseate warmth creeping into the blue of her cheeks and giving them a violet cast. She darted a glance at Feral, who didn't notice. He was looking at Ruby.

"Don't get any ideas," he told her, flat. "You've debauched me enough for one day."

Ruby rolled her eyes. "Please. That's an experiment I won't be repeating. You're a terrible kisser."

"*Me?*" he demanded. "That was all you! I didn't even *do* anything—"

"That's why it was terrible! You're *supposed* to do something! It's not facial paralysis. It's *kissing*—"

"More like *drowning*. I never knew one person could produce so much saliva—"

"My darlings, my vipers," came the soothing voice of Great Ellen, floating into the room. Her voice floated, and she floated after it. She didn't touch the floor. She didn't bother with the illusion of walking. Great Ellen, more than any other ghost, had shed all pretense of mortality.

Ghosts were not bound by the same laws as the living. If they appeared exactly as they had in life, it was because they chose to, either out of believing themselves perfect as is, or from fear of losing their last

131

touchstone to reality in the form of their own familiar face, or—as in the case of Kem the footman—because it just didn't occur to them to change. That was relatively rare, though. Most of them, given time, made at least small adjustments to their phantom forms. Less Ellen, for example, had, while alive, been in possession of but a single eye (the other having been extracted by a goddess in a foul mood). But in death she restored it, and made both eyes larger and thicker-lashed in the bargain.

But it was *Great* Ellen who was the true master of the postmortal state. Her imagination was an instrument of wonder, and she fashioned, of the stuff of her ghostliness, an ever-shifting expression of her marvelous self.

This evening she wore a bird's nest for a crown, and an elegant green bird was perched in it, singing. It was only an illusion, but a perfect illusion. Her face was more or less her own: a matron's face, cheeks high, red, and round—"happiness cheeks," Sarai called them—but in place of her wool-white hair were leaves, streaming behind her as though caught in a breeze. She set a basket of biscuits on the table. Kimril-flour biscuits, as bland as the soup. "No more of your sniping and snarling," she said. "What's this about kissing?"

"Oh, nothing," said Feral. "Ruby tried to drown me in saliva, that's all. Come to think of it, has anyone seen Kem lately? He's not dead in a puddle of drool somewhere, is he?"

"Well, he's definitely dead," remarked Sarai. "I couldn't say about the drool."

"He's probably hiding," said Sparrow. "Or maybe pleading with Minya to release him from his torment."

Ruby was unfazed. "Say what you like. He loved it. I bet he's writing a poem about it."

Sarai let out a muffled snort at the idea of Kem writing a poem. Great Ellen sighed. "Those lips will lead you into trouble, my pretty flame."

"I *hope* so."

"Where is Minya, anyway?" asked Great Ellen, regarding the girl's empty chair.

"I thought she might be with you," said Sarai.

Great Ellen shook her head. "I haven't seen her all day."

"I checked her rooms," said Ruby. "She wasn't there, either."

They all looked at one another. It wasn't as though one could go missing in the citadel—not unless you took a leap off the terrace, anyway, which Sarai thought Minya the least likely of the five of them to do. "Where could she be?" mused Sparrow.

"I haven't seen much of her lately," said Feral. "I wonder where she's been spending her time."

"Are you missing me?" asked a voice from behind

them. It was a child's voice, bell-bright and as sweet as icing sugar.

Sarai turned, and there was Minya in the doorway. A six-year-old child to all appearances, she was grubby and round-faced and stick-limbed. Her eyes were big and glossy as only a child's or spectral's can be, minus the innocence of either.

"Where have you been?" Great Ellen asked her.

"Just making friends," said the little girl. "Am I late for dinner? What is it? Not soup again."

"That's what *I* said," chimed Ruby.

Minya came forward, and it became clear what she meant by "making friends."

She was leading a ghost behind her like a pet. He was newly dead, his face blank with shock, and Sarai felt a tightness in her throat. Not another one.

He moved in Minya's wake, stiffly, as though fighting a compulsion. He might strain all he liked. He was hers now, and no amount of struggle would restore his free will. This was Minya's gift. She fished spirits from the air and bound them to her service. Thus was the citadel staffed with the dead: a dozen servants to see to the needs of five children who were no longer children.

She didn't have a moniker, the way Feral was Cloud Thief and Ruby was Bonfire and Sparrow was Orchid Witch. Sarai had a name, too, but Minya was just

Minya, or "mistress" to the ghosts she bound in iron gossamers of will.

It was an extraordinary power. After death, souls were invisible, incorporeal, and ephemeral, lasting a few days at the most between death and evanescence, during which time they could only cling to their bodies or drift helplessly upward toward their final unmaking—unless, that is, Minya caught and kept them. They were made solid by her binding—substance and matter, if not flesh and blood. They had hands to work with, mouths to kiss with. They could speak, dance, love, hate, cook, teach, tickle, and even rock babies to sleep at night, but only if Minya let them. They were hers to control.

This one was a man. He still wore the semblance of his worldly body. Sarai knew him. Of course she did. She knew the people of Weep better than anyone, including their leaders, including their priestesses. *They* were her dark work. They were her nights. Sooner or later they would all die and find themselves at Minya's mercy, but while they lived, it was Sarai's mercy that mattered.

"Tell us your name," Minya commanded the ghost.

He gritted his teeth, choking to keep his name to himself. He held out for four or five seconds and looked exhausted but determined. He didn't understand that Minya was toying with him. She was leaving him just enough will to believe he stood a chance against her. It was cruel. Like opening a birdcage to let the bird fly out, whilst all the while it's tethered by the leg, and freedom is only an illusion. Minya marshaled a dozen ghosts at all times, even in her sleep. Her power over them was entire. If she wanted him to say his name, he would say his name. If she wanted him to sing it, he would sing it. Just now, it amused her to let him believe he could resist her.

Sarai said nothing. She couldn't help him. She shouldn't want to. He would kill her if he could, and the others, too. If he were alive, he would rip them apart with his bare hands.

And she couldn't really blame him for it.

Finally, Minya tore his name from his lips. "Ari-Eil!" he gasped.

"You're young," said Ruby, who was fixed on him with uncommon interest. "How did you die? Did someone kill you?" she asked, in much the same tone as if she were inquiring after his health.

He stared at them in raw horror, his eyes skipping from Ruby to Feral to Sparrow to Sarai, trying to process the sight of their blue flesh.

Blue. As blue as tyranny and thrall and monsters in the streets. His eyes caught on Sarai for a long tremulous moment and she knew what he was seeing: Isagol the Terrible, resurrected from the dead. But Sarai's face was too young, and must seem naked without the black band painted across her eyes. She wasn't Isagol. She saw it dawn on him: *what* she was, if not who. What they all were.

"*Godspawn*," he whispered, and Sarai felt his revulsion as powerfully as though it, too, were given substance by Minya's binding. The air felt slippery with it. Rank. He shook his head and squeezed his eyes shut, as though he could deny their existence. It served as an affirmation, if nothing else. Every new ghost who recoiled from them in shock proved that they had not yet broken The Rule.

The Rule, the one and only. Self-imposed, it contained, in its simplicity, countless forbiddens. If they lived a thousand years, they'd still be discovering new things they mustn't do.

No evidence of life.

That was it: the four-word mantra that governed their existence. They must betray *no evidence of life.* At all costs, the citadel must appear abandoned. They must remain hidden, and give the humans no hint that they were here, or that, unthinkably, five abominations had survived the Carnage and eked out an existence here *for fifteen years.*

In this ghost's reaction, they saw that all was well. They were still a secret: the fruits of slaughter, slipped through bloody fingers. "You're dead," he said, almost pleading for it to be true. "We killed you."

"About that . . ." said Ruby.

Minya gave the ghost's invisible leash a tug that

felled him to his knees. "We're not dead," she said. "But *you* are."

He must have known already, but the plain words were a sucker punch. He looked around, taking it all in: this place that he only knew from his worst nightmares. "Is this hell?" he asked, hoarse.

Ruby laughed. "I *wish*," she said. "Welcome to purgatory. Care for some soup?"

14

Beautiful and Full of Monsters

Lazlo clutched his spear and moved slowly over the desert sand, Ruza on his left, Tzara on his right. The two Tizerkane held spears as well, and though Ruza had been teaching him to throw, Lazlo still felt like an impostor. "I won't be any help if it comes to it," he'd said before they set out on their hunt.

The creature they sought was something out of stories. He'd never imagined they were real, much less that he would ever track one.

"Don't underestimate yourself, faranji," Ruza had replied, his voice full of assurance. "I can always push you into its mouth and run. So you see, you'll have saved my life, and I'll never forget it."

"Nice," Lazlo had said. "That's exactly the sort of heroism that inspired me to play Tizerkane as a little boy."

"It won't come to anything," Tzara had cut in, giving Ruza a shove. "We're just going to poke it. You can't appreciate a threave until you've seen one. That's all."

Just poke it. Poke a monster. And then?

"Behold the horror," Eril-Fane had said, approving the excursion. The caravan had adjusted its course to give the thing a wide berth, but Ruza had been keen for Lazlo to see the Elmuthaleth's ugliest species. Threaves were ambush predators. They burrowed under the sand and lay in wait, for years even, for prey to happen along, and they were only a threat if you had the poor fortune of walking over one. But thanks to the caravan's threave hawks, they knew exactly where the thing was.

Low in the sky, one of the birds flew circles to mark the place where the threave lay buried. The caravans had always employed falconers with special birds that could scent the stench of the creatures and avoid them—and occasionally to hunt them, as they were doing now, though with no intent to kill. They were only twenty yards from it, and the back of Lazlo's neck prickled. He'd never stalked anything before.

"It knows we're coming," Ruza said. "It can feel the vibrations of our footsteps. It must be getting excited. Its mouth will be filling with digestive juices, all bubbly and hot. It would be like falling into a bath if it ate you. A really awful bath." He was the youngest of the Tizerkane, only eighteen, and had been the first to make Lazlo welcome. Not that any of them had made him *un*welcome. It was just that Ruza had an eager nature—eager to tease, more than anything else— and had taken it upon himself to teach Lazlo basic skills, such as riding, spear-throwing, cursing. He was a good language teacher all around, mainly because he talked so much, but he was unreliable—as Lazlo had discovered early on when he'd asked Azareen, Eril-Fane's second-in-command, what turned out to mean not "Can I help you with that?" but "Would you like to sniff my armpits?"

She had declined.

That was early on. His Unseen had improved enough now to know when Ruza was trying to trick him.

Which was most of the time.

"Hush," said Tzara. "Watch the sand."

Lazlo did. The hawk drew a circle with its shadow, but he saw no hint within of buried beasts. There was nothing to distinguish the sand there from the sand anywhere.

Tzara stopped short. "Would you like to do the honors?" she asked him. She was another of the younger warriors. Her face was smooth and bronze, with a high-bridged, regal nose and a scar bisecting her right eyebrow. She wore her head shaved—all but an inch-thick strip down the center of her scalp, which she left long and wove into a single braid.

"Honors?" asked Lazlo.

She handed him a pebble. "Just throw it in."

Lazlo held his spear in one hand and the pebble in the other. He stared at the stretch of sand and the shadow of the bird going round and round, took a deep breath, and…tossed the pebble. It arced through the air. And…he did expect *something* to happen. He even expected it to be monstrous, but perhaps there was no preparing for one's first monster. The instant the pebble struck the surface of the sand, the desert floor *erupted*.

Sand flew. It stung his face and got in his eyes so that the thing that sprang up in front of him was at first sight just a big, bristling blur. He leapt backward, spear heavy in his hand, and managed to trip over his own feet and land with a thud sitting down. Ruza and Tzara didn't fall back, though, or even heft their spears, and so he took his cue from their calm, wiped the sand from his eyes, and stared.

It was like an immense spider, he thought, his mind groping for comparisons that might make sense of the thing. But it didn't make sense. It might resemble a great, bloated abdomen bristling with legs, but the proportions were wrong. The legs were too short, and couldn't possibly lift the creature's bulk. They weren't legs at all, Lazlo realized. They were *chelicerae*.

Mouthparts.

They were moving wildly—a dozen black-bristled appendages roughly the size of his own arms and with pincers for grasping prey and dragging it toward . . . its mouth.

Lazlo couldn't tell how much of the threave lay buried still beneath the sand, but from what he could see, it was made up almost entirely of mouth. It didn't even have eyes, just a great, pulsating sphincter, gaping, tooth-spiked, hot, and red. The chelicerae writhed, questing for prey, and the sphincter-maw spasmed, teeth clicking open and shut, searching for something to bite into. Finding nothing, it hissed out a blast of hot air flecked with something foul—the digestive juices Ruza had mentioned?

Like "a really awful bath" indeed. Lazlo had to wonder how many adventurers, crossing the desert without the benefit of threave hawks, had ended their quest in jaws like these. "Nature's booby trap," Ruza called it, and they left it there, unharmed, to await the next wave of faranji adventurers foolish enough to attempt the crossing.

They rejoined the caravan, which had stopped to make camp. "Well?" asked Eril-Fane. "What do you say about threaves?"

"I need to amend my 'Ways I Hope Not to Die' list," said Lazlo.

Eril-Fane laughed. "Indeed. We might have come west sooner, you know, but no one had trained a threave hawk in two hundred years. We decided to wait until that had been mastered."

"Wise decision," said Lazlo. Two hundred years. The first mystery of Weep, the one that had opened his mind like a door. "My city lost the world, and was lost to it," Eril-Fane had said back in Zosma. Lazlo had been daily in his company ever since, and was no closer to knowing what any of it meant.

Soon, though.

Tomorrow.

"I'm going to put up the fog nets," he said.

"You needn't," Eril-Fane replied. He was currying his spectral, Syrangelis. "We have enough water for tomorrow."

The nets were designed to leach condensation out of the cool night air, and were an important supplementary source of water in the Elmuthaleth. It was the last night of their crossing, though, and the water in the skins would last until they reached their destination. Lazlo shrugged. "There's nothing like freshly harvested fog," he said, and went off to do it anyway. The water in the skins was two months stale, and besides, he'd gotten used to the labor—which involved an ironwood mallet and pounding stakes deep into the sand. It loosened him up after a long day in the saddle, and though he would have been embarrassed to admit it, he liked the change it had made to his body. When he stripped off his white chaulnot to bathe—what passed for "bathing" in the desert, that is, scrubbing his skin with a mixture of sand

and pulverized negau root—there was a hardness and sculpt that hadn't been there before.

Even his hands hardly seemed his own these days. Before, he'd had a single callus from holding his pen. Now his palms were tough all over and the backs of his hands were as brown as his face. His gray eyes seemed shades lighter by contrast to his darkened skin, and the months of traveling into the sun hadn't only earned him squint lines. They had reshaped his eyes, cutting them narrower against the light, and altered the line of his brow, drawing it forward and knitting it between his black eyebrows in a single furrow. Those small changes wrought an undue transformation, replacing his dreamy vagueness with a hunting intensity.

Such was the power of a half year of horizons.

Lazlo had reason to know that he bore little resemblance now to the junior librarian who'd ridden out of Zosma six months ago with the Tizerkane. In fact, when the delegates had all assembled in Alkonost to cross the desert together, Thyon Nero had failed to recognize him.

It had been four months by then since they had seen each other last, and, to Lazlo's surprise, the golden godson had several times passed him right by in the caravansary before registering, with a visible start, who he was.

With his long dark hair and hooded white

chaulnot, riding a spectral with panache and speaking Unseen as though his smoky voice were made for it, Lazlo could almost pass for one of the Tizerkane. It was hard to believe he was the same hapless dreamer who used to walk into walls while reading.

Horizons instead of books. Riding instead of reading. It was a different life out here, but make no mistake: Lazlo was every bit the dreamer he had always been, if not more. He might have left his books behind, but he carried all his stories with him, out of the glave-lit nooks of the library and into landscapes far more fit for them.

Like this one.

He straightened the fog net and peered over it at the Cusp. He'd thought at first that it was a mirage. In the midst of the Elmuthaleth, sky had met ground in an unbroken circle, flat and featureless, as far as the eye could see. To travel across it, day after day, for weeks, to make and break camp each dusk and dawn with a sameness that merged the days to a blur, it defied the mind to believe that it could end. When the first shimmer had appeared in the distance, he'd thought it must be an illusion, like the lakes they sometimes saw that vanished as they drew near, but this hadn't vanished. Over the past several days it had grown from a pale streak on the horizon to ... well, to the Cusp, whatever the Cusp *was*.

It formed the eastern edge of the Elmuthaleth,

and the other faranji were content to call it a mountain range, but it didn't look like a mountain range. It lacked peaks. The entire formation—a kind of immense mound—was white, from the dun desert floor to the blue of the sky. It looked like milky crystal, or perhaps ice.

Or...it looked like what the myths said it was.

"Almost there. Hard to believe."

It was Calixte's voice. She was one of the other faranji. Coming up beside Lazlo to share the view, she pushed back the hood of her chaulnot to reveal her fine, small head. It had been naked as an egg the first time Lazlo saw her—forcibly shaved, as his own had once been, and just as crudely—but her hair was growing in now. It was a soft brown fluff like fledgling plumage. Her bruises were long gone, but she still had scars where her manacles had rubbed her wrists and ankles raw.

Calixte was not only the first girl Lazlo counted as a friend, but also the first criminal.

"By this time tomorrow..." he said. He didn't need to finish the thought. The anticipation was palpable. By this time tomorrow they would be there. They would climb the single track that led through Fort Misrach to the top of the Cusp, and they would get their first sight of that which lay beyond it.

Weep.

"Last chance for a theory," said Calixte. Her ragged

147

notebook was in her hands. She held it up and flapped it like a butterfly.

"You don't give up, do you?"

"It's been said. Look, there's one page left." She showed him. "I saved it for you."

"You shouldn't have."

"Yes, I should. Don't think I'm letting you reach the Cusp without giving me at least one."

One theory.

When the delegates had met up in Alkonost, they had assumed they would be enlightened as to the reason for their journey. The nature of Weep's "problem," as it were. They'd earned that much, surely, by coming so far. And when Eril-Fane rose to his feet at the head of the table at their first shared meal, they'd waited with hushed expectancy for the information that was their due. The next morning they would set foot to the great and terrible Elmuthaleth. It was only fair that they should know *why*—and preferably while they could still turn back if they chose.

"In your time among us," Eril-Fane had told them then, "you will be called upon to believe things you would not at this moment find it possible to believe. You are rational men and women who believe what you can see and prove. Nothing would be gained by telling you now. On the contrary. You will find that the relentless nothingness of the Elmuthaleth has a way of amplifying the workings of your mind. I would sooner it amplify your curiosity than your skepticism."

In other words: *It's a surprise.*

And so they'd gone on in mystery, but not without resentment and a vast deal of speculation. The crossing had been hard: bleak and monotonous, physically and mentally grueling. The theory purse had been Calixte's idea, and a good one. Lazlo had seen how it gave the others a spark of life, to play a game of sorts, to have something to *win*. It didn't hurt that they liked to hear themselves talk, and it gave them opportunity. It was simple: You made a guess as to what the problem was, and Calixte wrote it down in her book. You could make as many guesses as you wanted, but each one cost ten silver, paid into the purse, which was a shabby affair of old green brocade held closed with a gaudy brooch. Calixte said it had been her grandmother's, but then she also said she came from a family of assassins—or else a family of acrobats, depending on her mood—so it was hard to know what to believe.

Once they reached Weep and all was revealed, whoever had made the closest guess would win the purse—which was up to some five hundred silver now, and bursting at its frayed green seams.

Lazlo had not entered a theory into the book. "There couldn't possibly be an idea left unclaimed," he said.

"Well, there's not a *boring* one left unclaimed, that's for certain. If I hear one more manly variation on the conquest theory I might kill myself. But you can do better. I know you can. You're a storyteller. Dream up something wild and improbable," she pleaded. "Something beautiful and full of monsters."

"Beautiful *and* full of monsters?"

"All the best stories are."

Lazlo didn't disagree with that. He made a final adjustment to the net, and turned back toward camp. "It isn't a story contest, though."

Calixte fell into step beside him. "But it is. It's a *true*-story contest, and I think the truth must be stranger than *that lot* is fit to dream up." She flicked her notebook dismissively toward the center of camp, where the rest of the faranji were gathered waiting for their dinner to be cooked for them. They'd early established themselves in the role of guests—most of them, anyway—and were content to stand idle while the caravan drovers and the Tizerkane—and Lazlo— saw to all the work. They had already covered their lightweight chaulnots with their heavy woolen ones against the coming evening chill—proof that not one joule of energy had been converted to heat by means of respectable labor. With their hoods up and their purposeless milling, Lazlo thought they looked like a pack of ghosts on coffee break.

"Maybe not," he allowed.

"So it's all up to you," said Calixte. "You can't help but come up with a strange idea. Any idea you have is a *Strange* idea. Get it?"

Lazlo laughed in spite of himself. Usually, plays on his name were much less good-humored. "I'm not a member of the delegation," he reminded her. What was he? Storyteller and secretary and doer of odd jobs, neither Tizerkane nor delegate, just someone along for the dream.

"But you *are* a faranji," she countered. And this was true, though he didn't fit with the rest of them. He'd ridden into their cities mounted on a spectral, after all, and most of them assumed he was from Weep—at least, until Thyon Nero disabused them of that notion.

"He's just an orphan peasant from Zosma, you know," he'd said, lest they be tempted to feel anything like respect for him.

"Even if I won," Lazlo said to Calixte, "the others would just say I already had the answer from Eril-Fane."

"I don't care what they'd say," Calixte replied. "It's my game. *I* decide the winner, and *I* believe you."

And Lazlo was surprised by the strength of his gratitude—to be believed, even by a tomb raider from a family of assassins. Or perhaps especially by a tomb raider from a family of assassins. (Or acrobats, depending on her mood.)

Calixte, like he, didn't fit with the rest. But she,

unlike he, *was* a member of the delegation. The most puzzling member, perhaps, and the least anticipated. She was even a surprise to Eril-Fane, who'd gone to Syriza seeking a builder, not an acrobat.

It was their first destination after Zosma, and so Lazlo's first experience as the Godslayer's secretary had been the recruitment of Ebliz Tod, builder of the Cloudspire, tallest structure in the world. And what a structure it was. It looked like an enormous auger shell, or a unicorn's horn upthrust from the earth, and was said to stand at over six hundred feet. It was a simple, elegant spiral, windowless and unadorned. Syriza was known for its spires, and this was the king of them all.

Eril-Fane had been duly impressed, and had agreed to Ebliz Tod's every demand in order to woo him to Weep. A formal contract was prepared by Lazlo, in his official capacity, and signed, and the Unseen party was set to continue its journey when Lazlo mentioned a bit of gossip he'd heard:

That a girl had *climbed* the Cloudspire.

"Without ropes," he'd relayed to Eril-Fane. Only her hands and bare feet, wedged in the single cleft that ran spiral from the base of the tower to its tip.

"And did she reach the top?" Eril-Fane had wanted to know, squinting up at the tower to gauge the feasibility of such a feat.

"They say so. Apparently they've put her in jail for it."

"*Jail?* For climbing a tower?"

"For raiding a tomb," Lazlo corrected.

Never mind that the man for whom it had been built was still living, the Cloudspire was a royal tomb, and all manner of luxuries had already been laid in for the king's postmortal comfort. Besides the oculus at the top (for the "respiration of souls"), there was only one way in. It was never left unguarded, but when a treasurer entered the tomb with his arms full of *itzal* (jars containing the souls of animals, the practice of slave itzal and wife itzal having been—happily— abolished), he found a girl sitting cross-legged on the jeweled sarcophagus, *juggling emeralds*.

She confirmed that she had scaled the spire and entered through the oculus, but claimed she hadn't come to steal. She was only practicing her juggling, she said. Wouldn't anyone do the same? When Eril-Fane went to the jail—and found a bruised, bald waif in rusty manacles, half starved and defending herself with a nail—he asked her why she'd done it, and she replied with pride, "Because I could."

And Lazlo supposed that must also be the reason he had brought her along with them: because she could climb a six-hundred-foot tower with only her small hands and bare feet. He didn't know why this skill might be of value. It was a piece of the puzzle.

—Ebliz Tod: a man who could build a tower.
—Calixte Dagaz: a girl who could climb one.

153

—Thyon Nero: the alchemist who had distilled azoth.

—Jonwit Belabra: mathematician.

—Phathmus Mouzaive: natural philosopher; liked to declare that his field was no less than "the physical laws of the universe," but whose focus, in reality, was somewhat narrower: magnetic fields.

—Kae Ilfurth: engineer

—The Fellerings: metallurgists; twin brothers.

—Fortune Kether: an artist—renowned publicly for his frescoes and privately for the catapults and siege engines he designed for skirmishing kings.

—Drave: just Drave, a so-called explosionist, whose job was setting blast charges in mines, and whose credits included blowing the sides off of mountains.

—Soulzeren and Ozwin Eoh, a married couple: she a mechanist, he a farmer-botanist, who together had invented a craft they called a silk sleigh. A craft that could *fly*.

These were the Godslayer's delegates. Being told nothing more of the problem in Weep than that it was "the shadow of a dark time," the only real clue they had to go on in their theorizing was...themselves. The answer, they reasoned, must be found in some configuration of their areas of expertise. Working backward, what sort of problem might such skills solve?

As Calixte had bemoaned, most of the theories were martial ones, involving conquest, weapons, and defense. Lazlo could see why—siege engines, explosives, and metal did suggest such a direction—but he didn't think it would be anything like that. Eril-Fane had said the problem posed no danger to them, and he could ill imagine that the Tizerkane general would leave his city for so long if it were under threat. But something, he had said, still haunted them. He had used that word. *Haunt.* Lazlo alone had considered that he might mean it literally. Suppose there were ghosts. *Godslayer.* The ghosts of dead gods? He wouldn't be putting *that* into Calixte's book. For one thing, these were hardly the people you would summon to address such a dilemma, and, for another, how they would laugh at him if he did.

Was *that* why he hadn't given a theory, because he was afraid of being laughed at? No. He thought it was because he wanted Calixte to be right: for the truth to be stranger than anything they could imagine. He didn't want to guess the answer, not even for five hundred silver. He wanted to climb to the top of the Cusp tomorrow and open his eyes and *see.*

"The moment you see the city," Eril-Fane had promised them, "you will understand what this is about."

The moment you see the city.

The moment.

Whatever the problem was, it would be clear at a glance. That was another piece of the puzzle, but Lazlo didn't want to ponder it. "I don't want to guess," he told Calixte. "I want to be surprised."

"So be surprised!" she said, exasperated. "You don't have to guess *right*, you only have to guess *interesting*."

They were back in camp now. The low-slung woolen tents had gone up, and the Tizerkane had penned the spectrals in a larger pavilion of the same boiled wool. The camels, with their shaggy coats, passed their nights under the cold of the stars. The drovers had unloaded them, stacking their bales into a windbreak, though thus far the evening was still. The plume of smoke from the fire rose straight up, like the charmed ropes in the marketplace in Alkonost that had hung suspended in thin air whilst small boys clambered up and down them.

The faranji were still waiting for their dinner. There were carrion birds in the sky, circling and cawing ugly cries that Lazlo imagined translated as *Die so we can eat you.*

Eril-Fane released a message falcon and it rose through the ranks of them, screaming a raptor's warning before striking out for the Cusp. Lazlo watched it go, and this, more than anything, drove home to him the nearness of their destination.

The unbelievable imminence of his impossible dream.

"All right," he told Calixte. "You win."

She put back her head and ululated, and everyone in camp turned to look.

"Hush, banshee," he said, laughing. "I'll give you *one* theory, as wild and improbable as I can make it."

"*And* beautiful and full of monsters," she reminded him.

"And beautiful and full of monsters," he agreed, and he knew then what he would tell her.

It was the oldest story in the world.

❧ 15 ❧

THE OLDEST STORY IN THE WORLD

The seraphim were the world's earliest myth. Lazlo had read every book of lore in the Great Library, and every scroll, and every song and saga that had made its way from voice to voice over centuries of oral tradition to finally be captured on paper, and this was the oldest. It went back several millennia—perhaps as many as seven—and was found in nearly every culture—including the Unseen City, where the beings had been worshipped. They might be called enkyel or anjelin or angels, s'rith or serifain or seraphim, but the core story remained constant, and it was this:

They were beings of surpassing beauty with wings of smokeless fire—six of them, three male, three female—and long, long ago, before time had a name, they came down from the skies.

They came to look and see what manner of world it

was, and they found rich soil and sweet seas and plants that dreamed they were birds and drifted up to the clouds on leaves like wings. They also found the ijji, a huge and hideous race that kept humans as slaves, pets, or food, depending on the version of the tale. The seraphim took pity on the humans, and for them they slew the ijji, every one, and they piled the dead at the edge of the great dust sea and burned them on a pyre the size of a moon.

And that, the story went, is how man claimed ascendency over the world that was Zeru, while the demons were stricken from it by the angels. Once upon a long-lost time, people had believed it, and had believed, too, that the seraphim would return one day and sit in judgment over them. There had been temples and priestesses and fire rites and sacrifice, but that was a long time ago. No one believed in the old myths anymore.

"Get out your pencil," Lazlo told Calixte, emerging from his tent. He had taken the time, first, to groom his spectral, Lixxa, and then himself. His last sand bath. He wouldn't miss it. "Are you ready for this? It's going to be good. Extremely improbable."

"Let's have it, then."

"All right." He cleared his throat. Calixte waggled her pencil, impatient. "The problem," he said, as though it were perfectly reasonable, "is that the seraphim have returned."

She looked delighted. She bent her head and started scribbling.

From the direction of the faranji, Lazlo heard a laugh. "Seraphim," someone scoffed. "Absurd."

He ignored them. "Of course you know the seraphim," he told Calixte. "They came down from the skies, but do you know where they came *to*? They came *here*." He gestured around him. "The great dust sea, it's called in the tales. What else but the Elmuthaleth? And the funeral pyre the size of a moon?" He pointed to the single feature in the great flat land.

"The Cusp?" Calixte asked.

"Look at it. It's not crystal, it's not marble, and it's definitely not ice."

The sun had melted to a stripe of copper and the sky was deepening blue. The Cusp looked more otherworldly even than by daylight, aglow as though lit from within. "Then what is it?" Calixte asked.

"The fused bones of slaughtered demons," said Lazlo, just as Brother Cyrus had once told him. "Thousands of them. The holy fire burned away their flesh, and whatever their bones were made of, it melted into glass. You can still see their skulls, all full of teeth, and make out their curved spines and long skeletal feet. Carrion birds nest in their great eye sockets. Nothing can survive there but eaters of the dead."

Calixte had stopped writing. Her eyes were wide. "*Really?*" she asked, breathless.

Lazlo broke into a smile. *Extremely improbably*, he was about to remind her, but someone else answered first.

"Of course not really," said the voice, with a drawl of exaggerated patience. It was Ebliz Tod, the builder. He had not appreciated sharing the Godslayer's invitation with the girl who'd "scuttled up the Cloudspire like a bug," and had been heard to voice such complaints as, "it demeans those of us of true accomplishment to count a *thief* in our number." Now he said to her, with utmost condescension, "Dear girl, your credulity is as vast as this desert. One might get lost in it and never again encounter fact or reason."

A couple of the others laughed with him, marveling that anyone could believe such nonsense. Thyon Nero was leaning back against the windbreak, gilded by both sunset and firelight. "Strange believes it, too," he told Drave, the explosionist, who sat by his side, faring poorly by proximity. The golden godson managed to look dashing even in the midst of a desert crossing. The sun had treated his skin to a happy golden hue, and bleached the tips of his hair to a pale gleam. The lean travel rations had only accentuated the exquisite modeling of his features, and his short beard—kept trimmed, unlike everyone else's—lent him maturity and consequence without sacrificing any of his youthful splendor.

Drave, by contrast, was wiry and weather-beaten

beyond his years, which were somewhere near thirty. Hailing from Maialen, where sun was scant, he was very fair, and had suffered in the Elmuthaleth more than anyone, burning and peeling, burning and peeling, his face a patchwork of pink and red with brownish curls of dead skin sloughing away.

The two made an unlikely pair: the alchemist and the explosionist. They had fallen into step back in Alkonost, and taken to riding and eating meals together. In anyone else, it would have looked like friendship, but Lazlo couldn't see it as anything so benign. Thyon Nero hadn't had "friends" in Zosma so much as admirers, and Drave seemed willing to fill that role, even fetching him his breakfast, and shaking the sand out of his boots for him, and all without the reward of gratitude. Lazlo wondered if his own long ago "thank you" was the only one Nero had ever spoken. He didn't pity Drave, though. It was clear to him that the explosionist wasn't after friendship, but the secret of gold.

Good luck with that, he thought, wry.

"He believes in everything, even ghosts," Thyon added, drawing a willing snigger from Drave before turning his eyes on Lazlo. "Don't you, Strange?"

It reminded Lazlo of that awful day at the Enquiries desk when he'd requisitioned Lazlo's books: the sudden cut of his eyes singling Lazlo out. The barbed question, intended to discomfit. And he felt a shade of his old fear, too. This whole journey, Nero had hardly spoken to him except to make little sharp jibes, but Lazlo felt the burn of his gaze sometimes, and wondered if the alchemist still counted him a cost—the only person alive who knew his secret.

As to Thyon's question, his reply was noncommittal. "I admit, I prefer an open mind to a closed one," he said.

"You call it an open mind to believe men flew down from the skies on fiery wings?"

"And women," said Lazlo. "It's a woeful species that's all male."

"More like a nonexistent species," remarked Calixte. "Men lacking both wombs and good sense."

A disturbing thought occurred to Lazlo. He turned to Ruza, shifting into Unseen to ask him, "Are there male and female threaves? Dear god, tell me those things don't mate."

"Baby threaves must come from somewhere," said Ruza.

"But how would they even find each other?" Lazlo wondered. "Let alone...?" He let the rest pass unsaid.

"I don't know, but I bet when they do, they make the most of it." The young warrior waggled his eyebrows.

Lazlo grimaced. Ruza shrugged. "What? For all we know, threave love stories are the most beautiful of all time—"

Calixte snorted. She, too, had troubled herself to learn the language, with Tzara her principle teacher, as Ruza was Lazlo's. The two women were sitting together now, and Calixte whispered something to Tzara that made the warrior bite her lip and flush.

"Pardon me," cut in Thyon, with the pinched look of someone who believes he's being mocked. And since he hadn't bothered to learn Unseen, he could almost be forgiven for thinking so. He restated his question. "You believe men *and women* flew down from the skies on fiery wings?"

Lazlo had never said he believed in the seraphim. Even in his books he'd made no such claim. He had nothing like proof, or even faith. It simply interested him—greatly—how all the cultures of Zeru were underpinned by the same story. At the very least, it spoke to the migration patterns of ancient people. At the very *most*, it spoke to a good deal more. But all that was neither here nor there. He wasn't trying to win the theory purse, after all. He was only satisfying Calixte. "I see no harm in entertaining all ideas," he said. "For example, could you have arrived at azoth if you'd arbitrarily closed your mind to certain chemical compounds?"

Thyon's jaw clenched. When he spoke again a tightness had replaced the mockery in his tone. "Alchemy is a science. There is no comparison."

"Well, I'm no alchemist," Lazlo said, affable. "You

know me, Strange the dreamer, head in the clouds." He paused and added with a grin, "Miracles for breakfast."

Thyon's face went stony at the mention of the book. Was Lazlo threatening him? Absolutely not. He would never break his triple promise, and he heard his own taunts with a sense of unreality. He wasn't a junior librarian at the golden godson's mercy anymore, and whatever awe he had felt for him was gone. Still, it was stupid to goad him. He turned back to Calixte. "Now, where was I?"

She referred to her notebook. "The fused bones of slaughtered demons," she supplied.

"Right. So it was *here* the seraphim came down— or more like *there*, in the city." He gestured toward the Cusp and beyond. "And there they slew the unwholesome ijji, leaving the young and attractive race of man and woman free of foes, and went away again. Millennia passed. Humans thrived. And then one day, as prophesied . . . the seraphim returned."

He waited for Calixte's pencil to catch up. "Okay," she said. "You've got the monsters part, and I suppose I'll grant you beauty. For your lovely face, if not for the seraphim," she added in a tease. Lazlo didn't even blush. If Calixte *did* find his face lovely— which he found distinctly implausible, considering its centerpiece—there was nothing like attraction or desire behind it. No, he had seen the way she looked

165

at Tzara, and the way Tzara looked at her, and that made for a fairly thorough education on the subject of desire. "But what," Calixte asked him, "is *the problem*?"

"I'm getting to it," said Lazlo, though in truth he hadn't quite figured out that part of his wild and improbable theory. He looked around. He saw that it wasn't only the faranji paying attention, but the Unseen as well: the Tizerkane, the camel drovers, and old Oyonnax, the shaman. They couldn't understand Common Tongue, but his voice naturally caught their ear. They were accustomed to listening to him tell stories, though that usually happened after dinner, when the sky was dark and he could only see their faces by the flickering light of the fire. He did a quick translation for their benefit. Eril-Fane was listening with wry amusement, and Azareen, too, who was perhaps more to him than his second-in-command, though Lazlo couldn't work out the nature of their relationship. The closeness between them was palpable but also somehow...painful. They didn't share a tent, as several pairs of warriors did, and though they showed no physical affection, it was clear to anyone with eyes that Azareen loved Eril-Fane. Eril-Fane's feelings were harder to interpret. For all his warmth, there was something guarded about him.

The two shared a history, but what kind?

In any case, this wasn't Lazlo's current puzzle. *The problem*, he thought, casting about. *Seraphim and ijji*.

He caught sight of Mouzaive, the natural philosopher, standing over the cook, Madja, with his plate in his hand and a sour look on his face, and that was where his spark of inspiration came from.

"The Second Coming of the seraphim. It may have begun with awe and reverence, but what do you suppose?" he said, first in Common Tongue and then in Unseen. "It turns out they make *terrible* guests. Extremely impressed with themselves. Never lift a finger. Expect to be waited on hand and foot. They won't even put up their own tents, if you can credit it, or help with the camels. They just . . . lurk about, waiting to be fed."

Calixte wrote, biting her lip to keep from laughing. Some of the Tizerkane did laugh, as did Soulzeren and Ozwin, the married couple with the flying machines. They could laugh because the criticism wasn't aimed at them. Accustomed to farming the Thanagost badlands, they weren't the sort to sit idle, but helped out however they could. The same could not be said of the others, who were stiff with affront. "Is he suggesting we ought to perform *labor*?" asked Belabra, the mathematician, to a stir of astonished murmurs.

"In short," Lazlo concluded, "the purpose of this delegation *is* to persuade the seraphim to be on their

way. Politely, of course. Failing that: forcible eviction."
He gestured to the delegates. "Explosions and catapults and so forth."

Soulzeren started clapping, so he bowed. He caught
sight of Eril-Fane again, and saw that his wry amusement had sharpened to a kind of keen appraisal. Azareen was giving him the same frank look, which Lazlo
met with an apologetic shrug. It was a ridiculous
notion, as well as petty and impolitic, but he hadn't
been able to resist.

Calixte filled the last page of the book, and he dug
out his ten silver, which was more money than he'd
ever held before receiving his first wage from Eril-
Fane. "Farewell, good coin," he bid it, surrendering it,
"for I shall never see thee more."

"Don't be glum, Strange. You might win," said
Calixte without conviction. She examined the coin and
declared that it had "a damned triumphant look about
it," before shoving it into the overstuffed purse. The
seams strained. It appeared as though one more coin
might split it wide open. The last page in the book, the
last space in the purse, and the theory game was ended.

They had only now to wait until tomorrow and see
who won.

The temperature plummeted as the desert fell dark.
Lazlo layered his woolen chaulnot over the linen one
and put up his hood. The campfire burned against
the deep blue night, and the travelers all gathered in

168

its glow. Dinner was served, and Eril-Fane opened a bottle of spirits he'd saved for this night. Their last night of thirst and bland journey food and aching buttocks and saddle chafe and dry bathing and grit in every crease of cloth and flesh. The last night of lying on hard ground, and falling asleep to the murmured incantations of the shaman stirring his powders into the fire.

The last night of wondering.

Lazlo looked to the Cusp, subtle in the starlight. The mysteries of Weep had been music to his blood for as long as he could remember. This time tomorrow, they would be mysteries no longer.

The end of wondering, he thought, but not of *wonder*. That was just beginning. He was certain of it.

16

A HUNDRED SMITHEREENS OF DARKNESS

Sarai was out of sorts. After dinner, Feral ripped a snowstorm from some far-off sky and they had snow for dessert with plum jam stirred in, but she could scarcely enjoy it. Sparrow and Ruby threw snowballs at each other, their laughter a bit too sharp, their aim a bit too true, and Minya slipped away somewhere, promising to release the ghost, Ari-Eil, to his natural evanescence.

Sarai hated it when Minya brought new ghosts into the citadel. Each one was like a mirror that reflected her monstrosity back at her.

Lest you forget you are an abomination, here's an old woman who'll wail at the sight of you. Here's a young man who'll think he's in hell.

It did wonders for her sense of self.

"Why must she do it?" she said aloud. It was only

her and Feral in the gallery now, and he was bent over his book. It wasn't paper, but sheets of thin mesarthium, etched all in symbols. If they were letters, they couldn't have been more different from the fluid and beautiful alphabet of Weep, which Great Ellen had taught them to read and write. That had no angles, only curves. This had no curves, only angles. Sarai thought it looked brutal, somehow. She didn't know how Feral could keep poring over it, when for years he'd had no luck deciphering it. He said he could almost *sense* the meaning, as though it were *right there*, waiting to resolve, like a kaleidoscope in need of turning.

He traced a symbol with his fingertip. "Why must who do what?" he asked.

"Minya. Drag ghosts in here. Bring their hate into our home." Sarai heard herself. How petty she sounded, complaining about the inconvenience to herself. She couldn't say what she was really feeling, though. It was unspeakable that she should pity a human, ghost or living.

"Well," said Feral, distractedly. "At least we have you to bring *our* hate into *their* homes."

Sarai blinked a series of rapid blinks and looked down at her hands. There was no malice in Feral's words, but they stung like a pinch. Maybe she was sensitive in the wake of Ruby's certainty of doom, and the revelation that she herself shared it. And maybe it was her envy that Feral conjured snow and Sparrow grew flowers and Ruby made warmth and fireworks, while she . . . did what she did. "Is that what I do?" she asked, her voice coming out brittle. "It's a wonder you don't call me Hate Bringer."

Feral looked up from his book. "I didn't mean it in a *bad* way," he said.

Sarai laughed without mirth. "Feral, how could hate ever *not* be bad?"

"If it's deserved. If it's vengeance."

Vengeance. Sarai heard the way he said it, and she understood something. *Vengeance* ought to be spoken through gritted teeth, spittle flying, the cords of one's soul so entangled in it that you can't let it go, even if you try. If you feel it—if you really *feel* it—then you speak it like it's a still-beating heart clenched in your fist and there's blood running down your arm, dripping off your elbow, and *you can't let go.* Feral didn't speak it like that at all. It might have been any word. *Dust* or *teacup* or *plum.* There was no heat in it, no still-beating heart, no blood. *Vengeance* was just a word to him.

The realization emboldened her. "What if it isn't?" she asked, hesitant.

"What if what isn't what?"

Sarai wasn't even sure what she meant. If it wasn't vengeance? If it wasn't deserved? Or, still more primary: What if it wasn't even *hate* she felt for humans, not anymore? What if everything had changed, so slowly she hadn't even felt it while it was happening? "It's not vengeance," she said, rubbing her temples. "I spent that years ago." She looked at him, trying to read him. "*You* don't still feel it, do you? Not really? I'm sure Ruby and Sparrow don't."

Feral looked uneasy. Sarai's words were simple enough, but they challenged the basic tenet of their lives: that they had an enemy. That they *were* an enemy. She could tell there was no great hate left in him, but he wouldn't admit it. It would be a kind of blasphemy. "Even if we didn't," he hedged, "Minya's got enough for all of us."

He wasn't wrong about that. Minya's animus burned brighter than Ruby's fire, and for good reason: She was the only one of them who actually remembered the Carnage. It had been fifteen years. Sarai and Feral were seventeen now; Sparrow was sixteen, and Ruby not quite. And Minya? Well. She might look like a six-year-old child, but she wasn't one. In truth, she was the eldest of the five of them, and the one who had saved them fifteen years back when she really *was* six years old, and the rest of them only babies. None of them understood why, or how, but she hadn't aged since that bloody day when the humans had celebrated their victory over the gods by executing the children they'd left behind.

Only the five of them had survived, and only

because of Minya. Sarai knew the Carnage from stolen dreams and memories, but Minya *remembered*. She had burning coals for hearts, and her hate was as hot now as it had ever been.

"I think that's why she does it," said Sarai. "Why she brings the ghosts, I mean. So we have to see how they look at us, and we can't ever forget what we are."

"That's good, though, isn't it?" countered Feral. "If we did forget, we might slip up. Break The Rule. Give ourselves away."

"I suppose," Sarai allowed. It was true that fear kept them careful. But what purpose did hate serve?

She thought it was like the desert threave, a sand beast that could survive for years eating nothing but its own molted skin. Hate could do that, too—live off nothing but itself—but not forever. Like a threave, it was only sustaining itself until some richer meal came along. It was waiting for prey.

What were *they* waiting for?

Sarai could see that Feral wouldn't share her conflict, and how could he? The only humans he ever saw were ghosts, still reeling with the first shock of death to find themselves *here*, in the theater of their nightmares, enslaved to a pitiless little girl as blue as their worst memories. It didn't exactly bring out the best in them. But after four thousand nights among them— in their homes, on their skin—Sarai knew humans in a way the others couldn't, and she'd lost that easy ability to hate. She let the matter drop.

"What Ruby said earlier," she ventured. "Do you feel that way, too?"

"Which part?" he asked. "About the soup being insipid, or hell being interesting?"

Sarai shook her head, smiling. "You know which part I mean."

"Ah yes. How it's all right to burn our clothes when the mood strikes us because we're going to die young?"

"That's the one." Sarai grew hesitant. "Feral, can you imagine us growing old?"

"Of course I can," he said without hesitation. "I'll be a distinguished elderly gentleman with great long whiskers, three doting wives, a dozen children—"

"Three wives?" Sarai cut in. "Who, *us*? You're going to marry all of us, are you?"

"Well, naturally. I wouldn't want anyone to feel left out. Except Minya, and I don't think she'll mind."

"No, I think you're right about that," said Sarai, amused. "She's not exactly wifely."

"Whereas *you*..."

"Oh yes. So wifely. But how will it work? Will you rotate between us on a schedule, or choose as the mood strikes you?"

"A schedule does seem more *fair*," he said, solemn. "I know it won't be easy, you all having to share me,

175

but we must make the best of an imperfect situation." He was fighting to keep his mouth composed in its line of earnest gravity, but he couldn't keep the humor from his eyes.

"An imperfect situation," Sarai repeated. "Is *that* what we have here?" She gestured all around. The gallery. The citadel. Their precarious, doomed existence.

"A *bit* on the imperfect side, yes," said Feral with regret, and they just couldn't maintain their seriousness in the face of such an understatement. Sarai cracked first, tipping into helpless laughter, and Feral followed, and mirth worked its mundane magic, leaching the tension from Sarai's spine and relieving the cold dread that had been pressing on her all evening.

And that's how you go on. You lay laughter over the dark parts. The more dark parts, the more you have to laugh. With defiance, with abandon, with hysteria, any way you can. Sarai suspected that her mother, the goddess of despair, would not have approved.

She would have loved her daughter's gift, though.

The night grew late. The others went to their rooms. Sarai went, too, but not to sleep. Her day was just beginning.

Her rooms had been her mother's, and were second in size and splendor only to Minya's, which were a full palace in their own right, enclosed within the body of the citadel, and had been the domain of her father:

Skathis, god of beasts and high lord of the Mesarthim, most monstrous of them all.

Sarai's were at the extremity of the dexter arm—which was a way of saying *right*, as *sinister* was a way of saying *left*—down the long, curved corridor from the gallery. Her door didn't close. Every door in the citadel—every *thing* in the citadel—was frozen as it had been at the moment of Skathis's death. Doors that had been open remained resolutely open. Doors that had been closed were permanently impassable. Vast sectors of the citadel were, in fact, sealed off, their contents a mystery. When the five of them were younger, they had liked to imagine other children surviving in those closed-off wings, leading parallel lives, and they had played at imagining who they might be, and what gifts they had to make their cloistered existence bearable.

Great Ellen had told them of children she had known in her years in the nursery. A girl who could project illusions with her mind. A boy who could mimic others' faces. Another whose tears could heal any hurt—a beautiful gift, but he was destined to spend his whole life crying.

Most enviable to them back then had been the girl who could bring things out of dreams. If she could dream it, she could carry it out with her. Toys and harps and kittens, cakes and crowns and butterflies. They'd loved imagining all the things they'd get if they had that gift: seed packets for Sparrow to grow a real garden, and books for Feral, who longed to learn more than what the ghosts could teach. For Sarai: a doll she coveted from down in Weep, that she'd seen hugged in a sleeping girl's arms during one of her nocturnal visits. An army for Minya, who had always been grim. For Ruby, a whole jar of honey to eat without sharing.

"You should have that gift instead," she had told Sarai. "It's much nicer than yours."

"Nice enough until you have a nightmare," Sarai had replied, grudging.

"What if she dreamed a ravid," said Minya, grinning, "and when she woke up it bit off her head?"

They understood now that if anyone *had* been locked away in other sectors of the citadel they would have died within days. The five of them were the only living beings here.

Sarai couldn't close her door, but she drew the curtain she'd fixed to cover it. They were supposed to respect one another's curtains, but it was an imperfect system, especially where Minya was concerned. *An imperfect situation*, Sarai recalled, but the fizz of laughter had gone flat.

An antechamber led into the bedroom. Unlike the austere walls of the corridor, this room mimicked the architecture of Weep, with columns supporting an ornamental entablature and soaring, fan-vaulted ceiling. Down in the city, the buildings were stone, intricately carved with scenes from the natural world and the mythic one. Among the loveliest was the Temple of Thakra, at which a dozen master sculptors had labored for forty years, two of them going blind in the process. The frieze alone boasted a thousand sparrows so lifelike that real birds had been known to while away their lives romancing them in vain. Here in these chambers were twice as many songbirds, mingling with seraphim and lilies, spectrals and vines, and though the work was likely accomplished in a mere hour or two, they were even more perfect than the ones on the temple. They were wrought in mesarthium, not stone, and had been neither carved nor cast. That wasn't how mesarthium worked.

The curtained bed occupied a dais in the center of the chamber. Sarai didn't sleep in it. It was too big—like a stage. There was another, more reasonable bed tucked in an alcove behind the dressing room. When she was younger, she'd supposed it had belonged to a maid, but at some point she came to understand that it had been for Isagol's consorts, paramours, whatever you chose to call them. Sarai's own father would have slept in this bed when Isagol didn't want him in hers. Her father. When she'd realized that, it had felt like a violation of her own safe place, to imagine him here, taking solace in this little bit of privacy while he lay awake, plotting the slaughter of the gods.

It was Sarai's bed now, but she wouldn't need it yet for hours. She crossed to the terrace door, barefoot, and stepped out into the moonlight.

Sarai was seventeen years old, a goddess and a girl. Half her blood was human, but it counted for nothing. She was blue. She was godspawn. She was anathema. She was young. She was lovely. She was afraid. She had russet hair and a slender neck, and wore a robe that had belonged to the goddess of despair. It was too long, and trailed behind her, its hem worn to a sheen from dragging over the floor, back and forth, back and forth. Pacing this terrace, Sarai might have walked as far as the moon and back.

Except, of course, that if she could walk to the moon, she wouldn't *come* back.

It was time. She closed her eyes. She closed them tight. Her gift was ugly. She never let anyone see her call it forth. She could teach Ari-Eil a thing or two yet about revulsion, she thought. She took a deep breath. She could feel it burgeoning within her, welling up like tears. She held it in a moment longer. There was always that impulse: to keep it inside, this part of herself. To hide it. But she didn't have that luxury. She had work to do, so she opened her mouth.

And *screamed*.

It was clearly a scream—the rictus tension in her face, head thrust forward, throat stretched taut—but no sound came out. Sarai didn't scream *sound*. She screamed something else. It issued forth: a soft, boiling darkness. It looked like a cloud.

It wasn't a cloud.

Five seconds, ten. She screamed her silent scream. She screamed *an exodus*.

Streaming forth into the night, the darkness fractured into a hundred fluttering bits like windblown scraps of velvet. A hundred smithereens of darkness, they broke apart and re-formed and siphoned themselves into a little typhoon that swept down toward the rooftops of Weep, whirling and wheeling on soft twilight wings.

Sarai screamed *moths*. Moths and her own mind, pulled into a hundred pieces and flung out into the world.

🍃 17 🍃

THE MUSE OF NIGHTMARES

All the godspawn had magical gifts, though some of their abilities deserved the term *gift* more than others. There was no predicting what they would be, and each manifested in its own time, in its own way. Some, like Feral's and Ruby's, made themselves known spontaneously— and vividly—while they were still babies. Storms and fires in the nursery. Snowdrifts and lightning strikes, or bedclothes burned away, leaving nothing but an angry, naked baby steaming in a mesarthium bassinet. Other abilities took longer to discover, and depended on environment and circumstance—like Sparrow's, which needed a garden, or at the very least a seed, in order to show itself. She'd still been crawling when it had. Great Ellen loved to tell the story: how small Sparrow had beelined across the gallery on chubby hands and knees to the orchids that hadn't bloomed since the Carnage.

They'd looked like potted sticks, and Great Ellen hadn't stopped the little girl from grabbing at them. There was little enough to play with in the citadel, and the orchids were past hope. She'd been distracted—probably by Ruby—and when next she looked, it wasn't potted sticks she saw, but Sparrow's small, upturned face transfixed by the sight of a bloom unfurling from the dead wood she clutched in her tiny hands.

Orchid Witch. Cloud Thief. Bonfire. Their gifts had manifested effortlessly, naturally. The same could not be said for Sarai's.

While Feral, Ruby, and Sparrow couldn't remember the time before their magic, she could. She remembered wondering what her gift would turn out to be, and hoping for a good one. The others hoped, too. Well, the girls were very small, but Feral and Minya were highly aware: Sarai's gift was their last unknown. They were trapped in the citadel to scrape up a life for themselves however they could and for as long as they could, and there were gifts that might make that easier. As for Sarai, she didn't just want to make it easier. That wasn't enough. She wanted to save them.

There was one gift, above all, that might have done that. It was Skathis's gift, and though most likely to be inherited by his children, godspawn powers were unpredictable, and there was a chance that it could manifest in others. Sarai knew she didn't have it, though. She'd been tested for it as a baby. They all were. Korako, goddess of secrets, had been the one to see to it, and to administer other tests to determine the more elusive godspawn abilities. Korako was dead now, along with Skathis and Isagol, Letha, Vanth, and Ikirok—the Mesarthim, all murdered by the Godslayer, Eril-Fane.

The gift Sarai had most wished for wasn't Skathis's gift, anyway, but flight. There had been godspawn who could fly, according to Great Ellen, and she had imagined that one day she might just begin to rise, and rise, and rise to freedom. In her fantasies, she carried the others away with her, but they never reached a destination because she couldn't imagine what place there could be in the world for the likes of them. There were good gifts to wish for, and there were bad ones to fear, and the more time passed, the more she worried that hers would be one of those. She was five years old, and nothing had happened. Six, and still nothing.

And then...not nothing. Not *something*, either. Not yet, not quite. Just a feeling, growing inside her, and not a good one.

At first, it had felt a little like holding in cruel words instead of speaking them—how they sit burning on the back of your tongue like a secret poison, ready to spew into the world. She held it in. She didn't tell anyone. It grew stronger, heavier. She resisted it. From the very beginning, it felt *wrong*, and it only got worse. There was restlessness in her, an urgency to *scream*, and all this wrongness, this urgency...it only happened at night. By the light of day she was fine, and that seemed a further clue that it was a dark, bad thing inside her. Welling up, building up, rising, filling her—something *in* her that should not have been there, and every night that passed it was harder to resist its compulsions.

Her throat wanted to scream. Her soul wanted it, too. She fought against it as though there were demons in her trying to claw their way out and ravage the world.

Let them, Minya would have said. *The world deserves ravaging.*

It was Minya who finally dragged it out of her— dragged *them* out, her hundred smithereens of darkness. "I see what you're doing," she'd accused Sarai one night, cornering her in the garden. That was the year they were the same age. Sarai had caught up to her, and would soon grow past her, while Minya stayed forever the same. "You think I can't tell?" the little girl had demanded. "You're hiding your gift. Well, it's not yours to hide. Whatever it is, it belongs to all of us."

Sarai didn't dispute that. They were in this together, and she'd had such hopes that her gift might set them free. But those hopes were all gone. "What if it's bad?" she'd whispered, fearful.

"Bad would be good," Minya had said, fervent. "We *need* bad, Sarai. *For vengeance.*"

She knew how to say the word, gritted teeth and spittle flying, all her hate bound up in it. Her own gift was what it was. She could punish the humans, but only once they were dead, and that did not satisfy. Sarai might have dreamed of flying and escape, but not Minya. She'd hoped Sarai's magic would prove a weapon against their enemy. And the two little girls might have looked like equals that night in the garden—like playmates—but they weren't. Minya was the fearsome elder sister who had saved all their lives, and they would do anything for her, even hate for her. That part was easy, really. Natural. They'd known nothing else. Ghosts, the citadel, and hating the humans who hated them.

So Sarai gave in to the scream that night, and the dark things within her took wing. They came boiling out between her lips, and they weren't demons after all, but *moths*.

The horror of it. *Insects emerging from her body.*

When it was finally over—that first emergence, five or ten seconds that felt like an eternity—she'd fallen to her knees and lost her supper between the roots of a plum tree. Minya had watched it all with wide eyes and sick fascination. The moths were frantic, because Sarai was frantic. They whipped and whirled through a desperate choreography. Sarai's throat burned—from the vomit, not the moths. Later, she would come to understand that they didn't actually boil up her throat. They weren't really *in* her, not like that. They were *of* her—a dimension of her mind or soul that took form only as they emerged. Somewhere in the air of her scream they coalesced. She felt the brush of fursoft wings against her lips, but that was all. She didn't choke on them. She wasn't a living hive with a bellyful of chrysalids that hatched at darkfall. Nothing so terrible. But it was terrible enough that first time, and wild and jarring and *dizzying*. She knelt between plum roots and reeled. Her mind felt peeled open, skinned and scattered. She clung to a knob of root as the world broke into pieces and spun.

She could see through the moths' eyes. All hundred of them at once. That was the dizziness, the reeling and spinning. She could see what they could see, and hear what they could hear, and smell and taste what they could, too, and even feel whatever their wings and feet and feather antennae touched. This was her gift, grotesque and marvelous:

Her consciousness had wings. *She* couldn't fly, but *it* could. It was a kind of escape, but it mocked freedom. She was still a prisoner, a secret monster. But now she was a prisoner and secret monster who could spy on the life that she could never have.

If that had been all, it would still have been useful: to have a window into Weep, at night at least, if not by day—the moths being strictly nocturnal—to see something of the enemy and know what they were

187

doing. But it wasn't all. It was only the beginning of her dark, strange ability.

Tonight, a child no longer, Sarai did as she had done four thousand nights before. She stepped out onto her terrace, and screamed her moths at the sky. They descended on Weep, fanning out over the roof-tile topography as though it had been sectored on a map. They divvied it between them, dove down chimneys, squeezed through cracks in shutters. They were dark, small, and lovely—the exact purple of the lining of night, with the shot-silk shimmer of starlight on dark water. Their antennae were plumes fit to fan a tiny queen, their bodies like willow buds: compact, furred, marvelous.

Up on her terrace, Sarai paced. Restless energy coursed through her. She could never be still when her moths were abroad. Her eyes were open but out of focus. She left just enough of her consciousness seated in her body to do that much: pace the length of her terrace and know if anyone came near her. The rest of her mind was in Weep, in a hundred places at once.

She entered Ari-Eil's house, among others. The window was open. Her moth flew right in. His corpse was laid out on the kitchen table. She didn't touch him, but only looked. He was handsome even now, but his stillness was terrible, the gulf between sleep and death immense. It was strange to see his empty shell when his ghost had so recently been in the citadel. When humans died, their souls clung invisibly to their bodies for as long as they could—a day or two—and then they lost their grip and were claimed by the natural pull of evanescence. The sky took them. They rose up and returned to it, and were subsumed by it.

Unless Minya caught them, of course, and kept them to play with.

Ari-Eil had been unmarried; this was his family home, and his younger sister nodded at his side, asleep at her vigil. Her name was Hayva; she was Sarai's age, and Sarai couldn't help thinking how different the girl's life would be if the gods were still alive.

At the same time that she was there, in Ari-Eil's kitchen, she was entering other houses, watching other faces. Among them were women who hadn't been as lucky as Hayva, but had been young when the gods ruled Weep. It hadn't been Weep then, of course. That name came with the bloodshed, but it suited the two centuries of Mesarthim reign. If there had been anything in abundance in all those years, it had surely been tears.

All these homes, all these people. Scattered toys and battered boots and everything so different than it was in the citadel. There was no mesarthium in these houses, but tile and wood and stone. Handmade quilts and woven rugs and cats curled right beside the humans in their mussed-up beds. Sarai went to them. The humans, not the cats. Her moths found the sleepers in their beds. Their touch was light. The sleepers never woke. Men and women, children and grandparents. The moths perched on their brows, or on the ridges of their cheekbones. There was intimacy in it. Sarai knew the scents of humans, and the rhythms of their breathing. She was a connoisseur of eyelashes—the way they rested, the way they fluttered. And the texture of skin around the eyes, how fragile it was, and earliest to wrinkle, and the dart and flicker of the orb beneath the lid. She could tell at a glance if a sleeper was dreaming or was in that restful state between dreams. No one who ever lived, she thought, knew more of shut eyes than she did.

She saw her share of bare skin, too—brown, not blue—and watched the pulse of unprotected throats and tender, pale wrists. She saw people at their most vulnerable, both alone and together, sleeping or else doing the other things that are done in the dark. There were, it turned out, an untold number of ways that bodies could intertwine. That was an education. It used to be funny and shocking. She would tell the others about it first thing in the mornings, and they would gasp and giggle, but it wasn't funny or shocking anymore. It had crept over her imperceptibly: a kind of stirring, an allure. Sarai understood Ruby's hunger. She didn't spy on such private moments anymore, but even the sight of a strong, bare arm crooked gently round a waist or shoulder could make her ache with the yearning to be held. To be one of a pair of bodies that knew that melting fusion. To reach and find. To be reached for and found. To belong to a mutual certainty.

To wake up holding hands.

Up in the citadel, Sarai's throat constricted. Her hands clenched into fists. Such was not for the likes of her. "I kiss dozens of people every night," she'd told Feral earlier that evening.

"That's not kissing," he'd said, and he was right. Kissing was not what Sarai did to humans in their sleep. In fact, everything up to this point was preamble—the flight from the citadel, the squeezing down chimneys and perching on brows. Sight and feel, smell, taste and touch, they were just the threshold of her gift. Here was the fullness of it:

When a moth made contact with a person, Sarai could step inside their dreams as easily as stepping through a door, and once she was there, she could do as she pleased.

Their minds lay open to her—or at least, the surfaces did, and whatever bubbled up from beneath to paint them in streams of imagery, sensation, and emotion, endlessly combining and recombining in the ceaseless effort at making *sense*, at making *self*. For what was a person but the sum of all the scraps of their memory and experience: a finite set of components with an infinite array of expressions. When a moth perched on a sleeper's brow, Sarai was plunged into their dream. What the dreamer was experiencing, she experienced, and not as some hapless spectator. As soon as she entered—an invisible marauder, unseen and unfelt—the dream was hers to control. In the realm of the real, she might have been just a girl, in hiding and in peril, but in the unconscious mind she was all-powerful: sorceress and storyteller, puppeteer and dark enthraller.

Sarai was the Muse of Nightmares.

Minya had given her the name, and the purpose that went with it. Minya had made her what she was. "We need bad, Sarai," the little girl had said. "For vengeance." And Sarai had become the weapon Minya wanted her to be, and punished humans in the only way she could: through their dreams. Fear was her medium, and nightmares her art. Every night, for years, she had tormented the sleepers of Weep. "Did you make anyone cry?" Minya would ask her in the morning. "Did you make anyone scream?"

The answer was always *yes*.

For a long time, this new, exciting thing had been the focus of their lives. The other four would come to her room at dawn to crowd into her bed with her as soon as her moths returned, and she would tell them everything: what and whom she had seen, what the homes were like in the city, what the people were like. Minya just wanted to know about the nightmares, but the others were more interested in Weep itself. She would tell them about parents who came to comfort their children when nightmares woke them, and they would all go still and quiet, listening with a terrible intensity. There was always, among them, such a stew of envy and longing. They hated the humans, but they also wanted to *be* them. They wanted to punish them, and they wanted to be embraced by them. To be accepted, honored, loved, like someone's child. And since they couldn't have any of it, it all took the form of *spite*. Anyone who has ever been excluded can understand what they felt, and no one has ever been quite so excluded as they.

So they layered cynicism atop their longing, and it was something like laying laughter over the darkness— self-preservation of an uglier stripe. And thus did they harden themselves, by choosing to meet hate with hate.

Sarai settled a moth on Hayva, Ari-Eil's sister, and on other sleepers in other houses. All across the city, she sank into the dreams of Weep. Most were mundane, the mind's rote bookkeeping. Some dreams stood out. One man was dancing with his neighbor's wife. An old woman was hunting a ravid with nothing but a demonglass knife. A pregnant woman imagined her baby born blue, and hoped it were the blue of death sooner than the blue of gods.

Hayva dreamed of her brother.

Two children played in a courtyard. It was a simple snippet of memory. There was a dead tree, and Ari-Eil

193

was holding Hayva on his shoulders so she could hang paper flowers on its branches. Like most of the trees in Weep, it would never bloom again. They were playing that it was still alive.

Sarai stood by, invisible to them. Even if she'd wanted them to see her, they wouldn't. This was the limit of her gift as she knew it from long experience. In the early days she'd tried everything to catch their attention. She'd hollered and hissed and they never heard her, pinched them and they never felt her. In the dreams of others, she was as a ghost, fated to never be seen.

She was used to it now. She watched the two children decorate the dead branches with paper flowers, and wondered if that was the most that Weep could ever hope for. A pretense of life.

Wasn't that what *she* had, too?

What was she doing here, in this home, in this dream? If she were trying to earn Minya's praise, she wouldn't hold back, but would use Hayva's tenderness and grief against her. Sarai had an arsenal of terrors. She *was* an arsenal of terrors. All these years she'd been collecting them, and where could she keep them but within herself? She felt them at the core of her, every image and scene of fright and foreboding, of shame, shock, and misery, of bloodshed and agony. It was why she dared no longer dream: because in her own sleep she was like any dreamer, at the mercy of

194

her unconscious. When she fell asleep, she was no sorceress or dark enthraller, but just a sleeping girl with no control over the terrors within her.

When she was younger, she wouldn't have hesitated to plague Hayva with dread visions of her dead brother. She might have had him die a hundred new ways, each more gruesome than the last. Or else she might have made the little boy in this sweet memory into a ravenous undead thing who would hurl his sister to the ground and sink his teeth into her scalp as she woke screaming.

Once upon a time, Sarai would have imagined Minya's delight, and done her worst.

Not anymore.

Tonight, she imagined Hayva's delight, and did her best. Channeling Sparrow, her sweet Orchid Witch, she willed the dead tree back to life and watched it set forth leaf and bud while the two memory-children danced around it, laughing. In the real room where the girl was slouched in a chair beside her dead brother's body, her lips curved into a soft smile. The moth left her brow, and Sarai left the dream and flew back out into the night.

It's funny, how you can go years seeing only what you choose to see, and picking your outrage like you pick out a slip, leaving all the others hanging on their slim mesarthium dowel. If outrage *were* a slip, then for years Sarai had worn only the one: the Carnage.

How well she knew it from dreams. Over and over she'd seen it play out in the minds of the men who'd done it—Eril-Fane's most of all.

Knifeshine and spreading blood. The Ellens dead on the floor so the men who'd slain them had to step over their bodies. The terror and pleading of little girls and boys old enough to understand what was happening. The wail and lamb bleat of babies too small to know, but infected by the terror of the others. All those screams: subtracted one by one as though *silence* were the goal.

And the goal was achieved.

Nearly thirty voices were subtracted from the world that day, not even counting the six gods or the dozen humans who, like the Ellens, had gotten in the way. If it weren't for Minya, then Sarai and Feral, Ruby and Sparrow would have been four more small bodies in the nursery that day. The humans had done that. They had slaughtered babies. It was no surprise that Sarai had become the Muse of Nightmares, a vengeful goddess to haunt their dreams.

But, as she had told Feral, she'd spent her vengeance years ago.

The wretched thing—and the thing she never dared talk about—was that in order to exploit the humans' fears, she'd had to dwell in them. And you couldn't do that for four thousand nights without coming to understand, in spite of yourself, that the humans were survivors, too. The gods had been monsters, and had deserved to die.

But their children didn't. Not then, and not now.

The citadel was their prison, and it was their sanctuary, but for how much longer could it be either? No matter how well they obeyed The Rule, someday the humans would come. If the horror of Minya's fresh-caught ghosts told them anything, it was that the people of Weep would do again what they had done before, and how could they hope to defend themselves?

Moths and clouds and flowers and fire and ghosts. They weren't powerless, but Sarai had no delusions. They couldn't survive a second Carnage. Their only hope was in *not being found*.

She paced on her terrace, back and forth beneath the moon, while down in the city her moths went from house to house like bees from flower to flower. Her consciousness was a subtle instrument. It could divide evenly among her hundred sentinels, or shift between them in any configuration, honing in where attention was required and receding where it wasn't. Every moment her perception was shifting. She had to react on a wing's edge, trust her instincts, carom through the city dipping in and out of minds, spin a hundred moths through their wild dance, twist dreams and sharpen them, harry gods and beasts down the paths of the unconscious. And always, always, whatever else she did, whatever fears she deployed, to each she attached a sneak postscript, like devastating news at the end of a letter. It was always the same. Every nightmare that shook every sleeper in Weep carried the same subliminal warning.

It was a nameless horror of the citadel and all it contained.

This was the work she set herself: to weave through all the dreams of Weep a dread so potent that none could bear to *look* at the citadel, much less go near it. So far it had been enough.

The night felt very long, but it ended as all nights do, and Sarai called her moths home. She stopped her pacing, and waited. They winged through the last gleams of starlight, re-forming into their siphon of whirling wings, and she opened her mouth and took them back in.

In the beginning, the return had been even worse than the exodus. That first time, she hadn't managed it at all. She just couldn't open her mouth to them, and had had to watch them turn to smoke when the sun rose.

She'd been mute all day, as though her voice had turned to smoke with them.

Come nightfall, though, she'd felt the burgeoning again, as the whole cycle began anew, and she'd learned that if she wished to be able to speak, she'd better open her mouth and let the moths back in.

"Who would ever want to kiss a girl who eats moths?" Ruby had once asked her in a spirit of commiseration. And Sarai had thought then—as she did now—that kissing wasn't a problem likely to arise for her. But she didn't *eat* the moths, in any case. There was nothing to choke down, no creatures to swallow. Just the feather-soft brush of wings against her lips as they melted back into her, leaving an aftertaste of salt and soot. Salt from tears, soot from chimneys, and Sarai was whole again. Whole and weary.

She'd hardly stepped back inside when Less Ellen entered, carrying her morning tray. This held her lull in a small crystal vial, with a dish of plums to cut the bitterness. "Good morning, lovely," said the ghost.

"Good morning, sweet," replied Sarai. And she reached for her lull, and downed her gray oblivion.

18

The Fused Bones of Slaughtered Demons

For all his fanciful storytelling and talk of open minds, what had Lazlo really expected to find as the caravan approached the Cusp? A fissured cliff face of weather-riven marble? Rock that looked enough like bones to spawn a myth, with a boulder here and there in the rough shape of a skull?

That was not what he found.

"They're really bones," he said to Eril-Fane, and tried to read confirmation in the hero's expression, but Eril-Fane only gave a ghost of a smile and maintained the silence that he'd carried with him all day.

"They're really bones," Lazlo said again, faintly, to himself. That, over there. That wasn't a boulder that looked like a skull. It *was* a skull, and there were hundreds of them. No, there had to be thousands in all this vast white mass, of which hundreds were visible just from the track. Teeth in the jaws, sharp as any hreshtek, and, in the great eye sockets, just as he had said: carrion bird nests. They were strange and shaggy affairs, woven out of stolen things—dropped ribbons and hanks of hair, fringe torn off shawls and even shed feathers. The birds themselves swooped and cried, weaving in and out of immense, curved ridges that could only be spines, segmented and spurred, and, unmistakably: giant hands, giant feet. Tapering carpals as long as a man's arm. Knucklebones like fists. They were melted, they were fused. The skulls were warped, like candles left too near the fire, so that none held the same shape. But they held shape enough. These had been living creatures once.

Though not generally given to gloating, he would have liked to see the other faranji's faces just now, Thyon's in particular. But the golden godson was stuck on a camel, farther back in the caravan, and Lazlo had to be content with echoing exclamations from Calixte, who *was* given to gloating.

"Hey, Tod, am I really seeing this?" he heard her call. "Or am I lost in my *vast credulity*?" And, a moment later: "What are *you* doing here, Tod? Don't you know it's rude to wander about in someone else's credulity?" And then: "Is this fact or reason I'm encountering? Wait, no, it's more demon bones."

He suspected she wouldn't soon tire of the joke.

"You're surprised," Eril-Fane remarked to Lazlo. "The way you talked last night, I thought you knew."

"Knew? No, I thought...I don't know what I thought. I thought that even if it were true, it wouldn't be so *obviously* true."

It was strikingly obvious, and somehow too big to fit into his mind—like trying to cram the actual Cusp into his own small skull. It wasn't every day you got proof of myth, but if this wasn't proof, he didn't know what was. "The seraphim?" he asked Eril-Fane. "Were they real, too?"

"Is there proof, do you mean?" Eril-Fane asked. "Nothing like this. But then, they didn't die here, so they couldn't have left bones. The Thakranaxet has always been proof enough for us."

The Thakranaxet was the epic of the seraphim. Lazlo had found a few passages over the years, though the poem in its entirety had never found its way to Zosma. Hearing the reverence of Eril-Fane's tone, he understood that it was a holy text. "You worship them."

"We do."

"I hope I didn't offend you with my theory."

"Not at all," said Eril-Fane. "I enjoyed it."

They continued riding. Dazzled, Lazlo took in the extraordinary formations around him. "That one was a juvenile," he said, pointing to a skull smaller than the rest. "That's a baby demon skull. And this is a mountain of melted demon bones. And I'm riding over it on a spectral." He stroked Lixxa's long white ears and she whickered, and he murmured sweet things to her before continuing. "I am riding over the funeral pyre of the ijji with the Godslayer. Whose secretary I am."

Eril-Fane's ghost of a smile became somewhat less ghostly. "Are you narrating?" he asked, amused.

"I should be," Lazlo said, and began to, in a dramatic voice. "The Cusp, which had looked low on the horizon, was formidable at close range, and it took the caravan several hours to climb the switchback track to Fort Misrach. It was the only way through. It was also the place where, for centuries, faranji had been drawn and quartered and fed to the sirrahs. Lazlo Strange looked to the sky"—here, Lazlo paused to look to the sky—"where the foul birds circled, screeching and crying and all but tying dinner napkins around their foul, sloped throats. And he wondered, with a frisson of concern: Was it possible he'd been brought so far just to serve as food for the carrion-eaters?"

Eril-Fane laughed, and Lazlo counted it a small victory. A kind of grimness had been growing on the Godslayer the nearer they drew to their destination. Lazlo couldn't understand it. Shouldn't he be eager to get home?

"A *frisson of concern*?" repeated Eril-Fane, cocking an eyebrow.

Lazlo gestured to the birds. "They are ominously glad to see us."

"I suppose I might as well tell you. Due to a shortfall in faranji adventurers, the sirrahs were becoming malnourished. It was deemed necessary to lure some travelers here to make up the lack. After all, the birds must eat."

"Damn. If only you'd told me sooner, I'd have put it in Calixte's book. Then I could have used the prize money to bribe the executioners."

"Too late now," said Eril-Fane with regret. "We're here."

And here, indeed, they were. The fortress gates loomed before them. Helmed Tizerkane drew them open, welcoming their leader and comrades home with solemn gladness. Lazlo they regarded with curiosity, and the rest of the strangers as well, once their camels had been brought through the gates into the central plaza of the fortress. It was sliced right into the rock—or rather, into the melted, heat-rendered bones—which rose in high walls on either side, keeping the sky at a distance. Barracks and stables lined the walls, and there were troughs and a fountain—the first unrationed water they had seen for two months. Dead ahead at some twenty meters was another gate. The way through, Lazlo thought, and he almost couldn't process it.

"The moment you see the city," Eril-Fane had said, "you will understand what this is about."

What could it be, that would be clear at a glance?

He dismounted and led Lixxa to a trough, then turned to the fountain and scooped water over his head with both hands. The feel of it, cold and sharp, soaking to his scalp and rushing down his neck, was unimaginably good. The next scoop was for drinking, and the next, and the next. After that: scrubbing his face, digging his fingertips into the itchy growth of unaccustomed beard. Now that they were nearly arrived, he allowed himself a brief daydream of comfort. Not luxury, which was beyond his ken, but simple comfort: a wash, a shave, a meal, a bed. He would buy some clothes with his wages as soon as he had the chance. He'd never done that before and didn't know the first thing about it, but supposed he'd figure it out. What did one wear, when one might wear anything?

Nothing gray, he thought, and remembered the sense of finality he'd felt throwing away his librarian's robes after joining Eril-Fane—and the regret, too. He had loved the library, and had felt, as a boy, as though it had a kind of sentience, and perhaps loved him back. But even if it was just walls and a roof with papers inside, it had bewitched him, and drawn him in, and given him everything he needed to become himself.

Would he ever see it again, or old Master Hyrrokkin? Though it had been only half a year, the Great Library had become memory, as though his mind had sorted his seven years there and archived them into a more distant past. Whatever happened here, Lazlo knew that that part of his life was over. He had crossed continents and drunk starlight from rivers without names. There was no going back from that.

"Strange!" cried Calixte, springing toward him in her dancing way. Her eyes were alight as she grabbed his shoulders with both hands and shook him. "*Bones*, Strange! Isn't it ghoulish?" Her tone made clear that she meant *good*-ghoulish, if there were such a thing. Lazlo didn't think there was. However you looked at it—whatever the ijji had been, and whatever had killed them, angels or not—this mound of bones was an epic mass grave. But there would be time for pondering the implications later. For now, he allowed himself wonder.

Calixte thrust a cupped hand at him. "Here. I knew you'd be too virtuous to do it yourself." Curious, he put out his hand, and she dropped a sharp, curved fragment of glittering white glass onto it. "It's a Cusp cuspid," she said, beaming.

An ijji tooth. "You broke this off?" he marveled. She'd have had to dismount, perhaps even climb.

"Well, no one said *not* to deface the mountain."

Lazlo shook his head, smiling, and thought how, if he hadn't heard the rumor in Syriza, if he hadn't mentioned it to Eril-Fane, Calixte might still be in jail, if she was even still alive. "Thank you," he said, closing his hand around the tooth.

It was the first gift he had ever been given.

There was a small meal waiting for them—simple fare but exquisite for being fresh. Soft, salty bread and white cheese, slices of spiced meat, and quarters of some big, globed fruit that tasted of sugared rain. No one spoke, and there were, for the moment, no divisions among them—rich or poor, outsider or native, scholar or secretary. Never mind that Thyon Nero had grown up on delicacies and Lazlo Strange on crusts, neither had ever enjoyed a meal more.

"Hey, Tod," said Calixte, around a mouthful of bread. "Are we still in my credulity? Because if we are, you owe me for this meal."

Okay, maybe *some* divisions persisted.

The sirrahs continued to circle, squalling their ravenous chorus, and their ranks were disrupted once more, as they had been yesterday, by the passage of a message falcon. Half their size, it dove through the scribble of their ragged, stinking wings, driving them back with its piercing cry. Eril-Fane held up his arm, and the bird spiraled an elegant descent, luffed into the wind, and landed.

The Godslayer retrieved the message and read it, and when he looked up from the page, he sought out Lazlo, first with his eyes, then with his feet.

"News?" asked Lazlo as he approached.

"What, this?" He held up the message. "More like orders."

"Orders?" From whom? A commander? A governor? "I thought *you* gave the orders."

Eril-Fane laughed. "Not to my mother," he said.

Lazlo blinked. Of every improbability packed into that moment, this struck him the most forcefully. He had crossed the Elmuthaleth at the Godslayer's side and now carried, in his pocket, the tooth of a creature from the world's oldest myth. But myth was the ordinary terrain of his mind, whereas it had never occurred to him that the Godslayer might have a mother.

Because he was a hero. Because he seemed cast from bronze, not born like a mortal man. Because Lazlo, lacking one himself, tended to forget about mothers. It occurred to him that he might not ever have met one, or at least never exchanged more than a word or two with one. It hardly seemed possible, but there it was.

"She's looking forward to meeting you," said Eril-Fane.

Lazlo looked at him, blank. "Me," he said. "But how could she know...?" He trailed off, a lump forming in his throat. The Godslayer had a mother waiting for him in Weep. He had sent her word of his imminent arrival, and in his note he had seen fit to mention Lazlo.

"You'll stay with her when you reach the city."

"Oh," said Lazlo, surprised. The faranji were to be hosted at the Merchants' Guildhall; he had assumed he would be, too.

"She insists, I'm afraid. I hope you don't mind. It won't be as grand as the guild. Comfortable, though." And Lazlo hardly knew what was more extraordinary: that Eril-Fane was subject to his mother's insistence, or that he imagined Lazlo might mind.

"No," he said. "Comfortable is good." Those were the words his mind served up to him. *Comfortable is good.* "Wait." Eril-Fane's word choice struck him. "You said when *I* reach the city. Aren't you coming?"

"Not tonight."

"What? Why?"

Eril-Fane looked weary. The vitality that usually radiated from him was all but gone. Averting his eyes as though ashamed, he said, "I don't sleep well in Weep."

It was the only time Lazlo had heard him use that name, and it chilled him.

"So you see," said Eril-Fane, trying to smile, "I'm offering you up to my mother as proxy. I hope you can endure a fuss. She's had no one to look after for some time, so I expect she'll make the most of it."

"It will be the first fuss I have ever endured," said Lazlo, hearing something raw in his voice that could not be put down to a dry throat. "But I imagine I'll do all right."

The Godslayer smiled, eyes warm and crinkling,

and reached out to thump him on the shoulder. And Lazlo, who lacked not only a mother but a father, too, thought that having one might feel something like this.

"Well then," said the great man. "Here we are." He looked across to the far gate and seemed to steel himself. "Are you ready?"

Lazlo nodded.

"Then let's go."

19

THE SHADOW OF OUR DARK TIME

Eril-Fane led the party to the far gate. He didn't go through it, but turned his spectral around to face them. He didn't speak at once. There was a weight to his silence. There was tension and resignation in his face, even a hint of dread.

"Two hundred years ago, there was a storm." He paused. They all hung on the word *storm*. The twin metallurgists exchanged a hopeful glance, because one of their theories had involved a hurricane.

"It wasn't like other storms," Eril-Fane continued. "There was no rain, only wind and lightning, and the lightning was like nothing that had come before. It was directly above the city, furious. It formed *a sphere*... as though some great hands had skimmed the sky and gathered a world's worth of lightning into a ball." He acted this out, his great shoulders bunching as his hands dragged the specter of lightning and shaped it, and held it.

"It stopped." He dropped his hands. "The night fell dark. There was no moon, no stars. The people could see nothing, but they felt a change in the atmosphere, a pressure. And when the sun rose, they saw why. As you will see."

And with that, he turned his mount and led them through the gate. The path was carved deep through the demonglass, and narrow, so that they had to go in single file. It curved and rose, gradually widening. Onward and upward they rode. The sky grew larger, a deep and cloudless blue.

And then, quite suddenly, they came to an edge and it was all before them.

The Elmuthaleth had been high desert plateau, flat and sere. On this side of the Cusp, the world fell away into a deep canyon. It was long and curving, carved by a river—such a river as made the Eder look like a dribble, its catastrophic rush audible even from here. But no amazement could be spared for a river, no matter how epic. There just wasn't enough amazement in the world.

"The shadow of our dark time still haunts us," the Godslayer had said. And Lazlo had fixed on *dark time*, and he had wondered at the word *haunts*, but he had never thought to consider *shadow*.

It was a literal shadow.

There was the city—fabled Weep, unseen no longer—and the day was bright, but it lay dark.

Lazlo felt as though the top of his head were open and the universe had dropped a lit match in. He understood in that moment that he was smaller than he had ever known, and the realm of the unknowable was bigger. So much bigger. Because there could be no question:

That which cast Weep in shadow was not of this world.

"Strange," said Calixte, and she didn't mean the adjective *strange*, which fell immensely short of the sight before them. No, she was addressing Lazlo. She weighed the theory purse on her palm and said, in a bright, stunned whisper, "I think you win."

❧ 20 ❧

DEAD MAN'S NEWS

There were ghosts in the room. Sarai heard them whispering before she opened her eyes, and the golden daylight wavered—light, shadow, light, shadow—as they moved back and forth between the window and her bed. At first she thought it must be Less Ellen, along with perhaps Awyss and Feyzi, the chambermaids, and she felt a flicker of annoyance that they had entered unbidden. It wasn't time yet to wake. She could feel it in the heaviness of her limbs and eyelids: The lull had not yet spent its thick gray spell.

The whispers sharpened. "The hearts, go for the hearts."

"Not the hearts. You might hit a rib. The throat's better."

"Here, let me."

Sarai's eyes flew open. It was not Less Ellen or

Awyss or Feyzi or any of the servants. It was a cluster of old women, and they startled and skittered back from the bedside, clinging together. "It's awake!" one of them cried.

"Do it now!" shrieked another.

And before Sarai could process what was happening, one of the ghosts lunged toward her and raised a knife, her face savage with hate and intent, and Sarai couldn't get out of the way. She just couldn't move fast enough, not through the lull fog. The knife blade flashed and all her borrowed memories of the Carnage came spilling out—knifeshine and babies screaming—and *she* was screaming, and the old women were screaming, but not the one with the knife. She was sobbing with rage, and the knife was still upraised, her arm trembling wildly as it fought to complete the arc it had begun and bring the blade down on Sarai's throat.

"I can't," she keened with pure frustration. Tears streaked her face. She tried with all her will, but her arm would not obey her, and the knife fell from her grip to embed itself tip down in the mattress, just beside Sarai's hip.

Sarai was able to move then, finally. She rolled to her knees and backed away from the ghosts. Her heartbeats churned within her, sending trills of panic coursing through her body, even though she knew she was safe. The ghosts couldn't hurt her. It was the first imperative of Minya's binding: that the dead not harm the living. These ghosts didn't know that, though. The one who had come forth was distraught. Sarai knew her, and hadn't known she'd died. Her name was Yaselith, and her story was that of most of the women of her generation—and all the generations born and raised under Mesarthim rule, when Skathis went riding Rasalas, his great metal beast, and plucked girls and boys from their homes.

What happened up in the citadel, none ever told. Before they were returned, Letha saw to them. Letha: goddess of oblivion, mistress of forgetting. She could blank a mind with a blink of her eye, and did, stealing whole years from the girls and boys of the city, so that when Skathis brought them back they had no recollection of their time with the gods. Their bodies, however, bore traces that could not so easily be erased, for more had been stolen from them than their memories.

Yaselith's eyes now were wet and red, her hair as white and weightless as a puff of smoke. She was shaking violently, her breath coming in little snatches, and when she spoke, her voice was as rough as the strike of a match. "Why?" she demanded. "Why can't I kill you?"

And Sarai, confronted with a would-be murderer in the person of an old dead woman, didn't feel anger. Not at *her*, anyway. Minya was another story. What were new ghosts doing wandering the citadel?

"It's not your fault," she said, almost gently. "But you can't hurt me."

"Then you should hurt yourself," hissed Yaselith, pointing to the knife. "Put Weep out of its misery. Kill yourself, girl. Have mercy on us all. Do it. *Do it*."

And then they were all hissing it, crowding in, pushing back the curtains of Isagol's big bed to encircle Sarai on all sides. "Do it," they urged her. "Have some decency. *Do it*." There was savage glee in their eyes, and she knew them all, and she didn't understand how they could be here because none of them were dead, and her panic surged and swelled as she watched her own hand reach out for the knife. Her first thought was that *she* was dead and Minya was making her do it, because she couldn't stop herself. Her hand closed around the hilt and pulled it free from the bedding. Where the blade had been, up from the small slash in the fabric, blood pulsed in arterial spurts.

And even that mad unreality failed to bring her to her senses. Beds might bleed. She was too steeped in the landscape of nightmare even to question it. Her hand turned itself, positioning the dagger point against her breast, and she searched the jeering faces of the old women of Weep, finding no end to them. Where there had been five or six now there were dozens, their faces thrust up against the gauzy bedcurtains so that their mouths and eye sockets looked like black pits, and even then, the thing that struck her wasn't their faces but the curtains.

What was she doing in her mother's bed?

That was her last thought before she plunged the knife into her own hearts and sat upright with a great raw gasp to find herself in her proper bed. Alone. No ghosts, no knife, no blood. No breath, either. There seemed no end to the gasp. She was choking on it and couldn't exhale. Her hands were claws, every muscle rigid, a scream caught in her skull, scouring out all thought. On and on it all went until she thought she'd die of the simple failure to breathe, and then at last the gasp let her go and she doubled over, coughing out air as her body remembered what to do. She was long minutes curled around herself just breathing, her throat raw, eyes squeezed shut, before she could even face the truth.

She'd had a dream.

She started to tremble uncontrollably. A dream had gotten through. "Oh no," she whispered, and curled up tighter as she grappled with what this meant. "Oh no."

The lull was supposed to keep her from dreaming. Had she forgotten to drink it? No, she could still taste its bitterness on the back of her tongue.

Then how had she dreamed?

She thought back to the time before lull, and the onslaught of nightmares that had prompted Great

Ellen to start brewing it for her. It had felt, then, like being hunted by all the terrors she had collected over the years—her entire arsenal, turned against her. That was what the creeping gray nothing protected her from—or was supposed to.

Eventually she got out of bed. She'd have liked a bath, but that would mean going to the rain room and filling the tub, then calling for Ruby to heat it, and that was more trouble than she could face. So she poured out cold water from her pitcher and washed with that. She brushed and braided her hair, and changed into a fresh slip all before emerging into the main chamber, where her mother's big bed stood untouched, its hangings free of ghost women and their haggard faces. Still, she shuddered and hurried past it, out through her door-curtain and down the corridor, where she met Less Ellen bringing her afternoon tray. This held tea—not true tea, which they'd run out of long ago, but an herbal infusion to help shake off the lull—and biscuits, since Sarai always slept through lunch.

"You're up early," said the ghost, surprised, and Sarai strove to conceal her distress.

"I don't know that I'd call afternoon *early*," she said with a frail smile.

"Well, early for you. Did something wake you?"

"Is that my tea?" Sarai asked, evading the question, and she took her cup from the tray in Less Ellen's hands and filled it from the little teapot. The scent of

219

mint filled the air. "Thank you, Ellen," she said, and carried the cup with her on her way, leaving the ghost, bewildered, behind her.

She bypassed the gallery and headed instead to the kitchen to talk to Great Ellen, whom she asked, in strict confidence, if it were possible to strengthen her lull.

"Strengthen it?" repeated the woman, eyes going wide, then narrow. "What's happened?" she demanded.

"Nothing's happened," Sarai lied. "I just worry that it might become less effective, over time." And she *had* worried about that, but... it hadn't become less effective over time. It had stopped working overnight, and that wasn't something she was prepared to deal with.

"Well, *has* it? Don't fib to me. You know I can tell." Her voice was stern, and as Sarai looked into her eyes, Great Ellen morphed her face into a hawk's, eyes yellow and severe beneath the sharp slant of feathered brow ridges, a deadly hooked beak where her nose should have been.

"Don't," Sarai protested, laughing in spite of herself. "You know I can't withstand the hawk."

"Look into my eyes and just try lying."

It was a game from when they were younger. Great Ellen had never tried forcing or commanding them to behave or obey. That would have gone ill, especially when their gifts were still volatile and not fully under their control. She'd used craftier methods, like this, and gotten better results. It was, in fact, quite difficult to lie to a hawk. "That's not fair," said Sarai, covering her eyes. "Can't you just trust me, and help me?"

"Of course I can, but I ought to know how urgent it is. I've wondered when you'd build up a tolerance." *When*, not *if*. "Is it happening?"

Sarai uncovered her eyes and found Great Ellen restored to human form, the excoriating hawk gaze replaced by a piercing but compassionate human one. In answer, she gave her the tiniest of nods, and was grateful when she didn't probe deeper. "All right, then," Great Ellen said, all competence, no fuss. "An extra half dose in the morning, and I'll tinker with the next batch and see what can be done."

"Thank you," said Sarai.

Her relief must have been audible, because Great Ellen gave her a look that was hawk even without the transformation. She said, with caution, "It won't work forever, you know. No matter what we do."

"Don't worry about me," said Sarai with feigned carelessness, but as she went out to the gallery she added, in an undertone only she could hear, "I don't think we have to worry about forever."

She saw Sparrow first, kneeling among her orchids, her face dreamy and her hands full of vines, which were visibly growing, slowly cascading out between her fingers to twine through those already in place and fill in gaps where mesarthium still showed through.

At the table, Minya and Feral were faced off across the quell board, deep in a game. It was evident from Feral's glower that he was losing, while Minya looked half bored, and stifled a yawn before moving her piece.

Sarai had never been so glad of the predictable monotony of life in the citadel as she was now. She would even welcome kimril soup in all its comforting dullness.

This evening, however, was to be neither comforting nor dull.

"Poor thing," she heard Ruby croon, and, turning to look, saw her standing squarely in front of Ari-Eil. Sarai stopped in her tracks. It was jarring, seeing him again after seeing his corpse. Minya had promised to release him, but he was very much still with them, and if he had come to grips with the basic fact of his new existence—that they were alive and he was not—he had in no way softened in his attitude toward them. His confusion was gone, which only left more room in his expression for hostility. Minya had put him in the corner, the way one might lean a broom or umbrella when not using it, and he was, amazingly, still trying to resist her.

Or not so amazingly, perhaps. As Sarai watched, he managed, with incredible effort, to slide his foot a few inches, which could only mean that Minya was still toying with him, holding him imperfectly to allow him false hope.

Ruby was standing in front of him, demure—for her—in a knee-length black slip. Her hands were clasped behind her back, and one foot curled coyly around the ankle of the other. "I know it must be an awful shock," she was saying to him. "But you'll see we're not really so bad. What happened before, none of that was us. We're not like our parents." She reached out to touch his cheek.

It was a tender gesture. Ruby was thoughtless, but she wasn't toying with the ghost as Minya was. Sarai knew she meant to be consoling. The dead man was, however, in no mood for consolation. "Don't touch me, *godspawn*," he snarled, and snapped at her hand like an animal.

Ruby snatched it back. "*Rude*," she said, and turned to Minya. "You *let* him do that."

"No biting," Minya told the ghost, though of course Ruby was right: He wouldn't have been able to do it unless she'd let him. Knowing her, Sarai thought she probably *made* him do it. She used them like puppets sometimes. Sarai remembered her nightmare, and having no control over her own knife-wielding hand, and shuddered at the thought of being Minya's toy.

"Minya," she said, remonstrating. "You promised you'd let him go."

Minya's eyebrows shot up. "Did I? That doesn't sound like me at all."

Nor did it. Minya was many things—perverse,

223

capricious, and obstinate among them. She was like a wild creature, by turns furtive and barging, ever unwashed, and with the staring lack of empathy that belongs to murderers and small children. Attempts at civilizing her rolled right off her. She was invulnerable to praise, reason, and shame, which meant she couldn't be coaxed or persuaded, and she was cunning, which made her hard to trick. She was ungovernable, flawlessly selfish, resentful, and sly. One thing she was not—*ever*—was obliging.

"Well, you did," Sarai persisted. "So...would you? Please?"

"What, *now*? But I'm right in the middle of a game."

"I'm sure you'll survive the inconvenience."

Feral had been studying the game board, chin sunk in hand, but he looked up now with just his eyeballs, surprised to hear Sarai arguing with Minya. As a rule, that was something they avoided, but Sarai's anger made her careless. She was in no mood for tiptoeing around the little girl's whims right now. After the dream she'd had, the last thing she needed was another baleful ghost glaring at her.

"What's the matter with *you*?" Minya asked. "I suppose you're bleeding."

It took Sarai a moment to understand what she meant, because she thought of the blood spurting up from the wound in the bed, and of the phantom

224

pressure of the knifepoint against her breast. But it was her monthly bleeding that Minya meant, and the suggestion only made her angrier. "No, Minya. Unlike you, the rest of us experience a normal range of emotion, including but not limited to distress when forced to endure the disgust of the dead." And it wasn't Ari-Eil's face in her mind when she said it, but the old women all crowded round her, and she knew that at least part of her anger at Minya was left over from the dream and was irrational—because Minya hadn't *actually* turned old women loose to wander the citadel and attempt to murder her. But part of being irrational is not caring that you're being irrational, and right now she just didn't.

"Is he bothering you so much?" Minya asked. "I can make him face the wall, if it helps."

"It doesn't help," said Sarai. "Just let him go."

The others were watching, breath all but held, eyes overlarge. Minya's eyes were always large, and now they glittered. "Are you sure?" she asked, and it felt like a trap.

But what kind of trap could it possibly be? "Of course I'm sure," said Sarai.

"All right," said Minya in a lilting tone that signified it went against her better judgment. "But it is strange you don't want to hear his news first."

News?

Sarai tried to match Minya's feigned calm. "What news?"

"First you don't want to hear and now you do." She rolled her eyes. "Really, Sarai. Make up your mind."

"I never *didn't* want to hear," Sarai snapped. "You never said there was anything *to* hear."

"Touchy," said Minya. "Are you sure you aren't bleeding?"

What would you know about that? Sarai wanted to demand. *If you ever decide to grow up, then maybe we'll talk about it.* But she wasn't nearly angry enough— or foolish enough—to speak the words *grow up* to Minya. She just gritted her teeth and waited.

Minya turned to Ari-Eil. "Come over here," she said, and he did, though she still asserted only partial control, allowing him to fight against her at every step so that he came lurching and stumbling. It was grotesque to watch, which was, of course, the point. She brought him to the opposite end of the long table from where she sat. "Go on, then," she said. "Tell them what you told me."

"Tell them yourself," he spat.

And it wasn't him she was toying with now by dragging out the suspense of it, but the rest of them. Minya paused to study the quell board, taking her time to move one of her game pieces, and Sarai could tell from Feral's expression that it was a devastating move. Minya collected her captured piece with a look of smug satisfaction. A scream was building in Sarai's mind, and, with it, an awful presentiment that the pall of doom of the past day had been leading to this moment.

What news?

"It's lucky for us you happened to die," Minya said, redirecting herself at the ghost. "Else we might have been taken entirely by surprise."

"It doesn't matter whether you're surprised," snarled the dead man. "He killed you once, he'll do it again."

A jolt went through Sarai. Sparrow gasped. Feral sat bolt upright. "Minya," he said. "What is he talking about?"

"Tell them," commanded Minya. Her voice was still bright, but not like a bell now. Like a knife. She rose to her feet, which were bare and dirty, and stepped from her chair onto the table. She prowled the length of it, until she was standing right in front of him. They were nearly eye-to-eye: he, an imposing grown man; she, a slight and messy child. No more suspense, and no more delusion of freedom. Her will clamped onto him and his words reeled out as though she'd reached down his throat and ripped them from him.

"The Godslayer is coming!" he cried out, gasping. That much Minya made him tell, but the rest he spoke freely. Savagely. *And he's going to tear your world apart.*

Minya looked over her shoulder. Sarai saw Skathis

in her eyes, as though the god of beasts were somehow alive in his small daughter. It was a chilling look:
cold and accusing, full of blame and triumph. "Well,
Sarai?" she asked. "What do you have to say about
that? Your papa's come back home."

❧ 21 ❧

THE PROBLEM IN WEEP

"*What is that?*" Lazlo asked. He felt himself perfectly poised at the midpoint between wonder and dread, and didn't know which to feel. Dread, it had to be, because he'd glimpsed dread on Eril-Fane's face, but how could he not feel wonder at such a sight?

"That," said Eril-Fane, "is the citadel of the Mesarthim."

"Mesarthim?" said Lazlo, at the same moment that Thyon Nero asked, "Citadel?" Their voices clashed, and their glances, too.

"Citadel, palace, prison," said Eril-Fane. His voice was rough, and dropped almost to nothing on the last word.

"That's a *building*?" Ebliz Tod demanded, brash and incredulous. His Cloudspire, it would seem, was *not* the tallest structure in the world.

The height of the thing was but one element of its magnificence, and not even the foremost. It was tall, certainly. Even at a distance of miles, it was clearly *massive*, but how to properly gauge its height, in light of the fact that...it didn't stand upon the ground?

The thing was *floating*. It was fixed in space, absolutely motionless, high above the city with no possible means of suspension—unless, indeed, there were some scaffolding in the heavens. It was composed of dazzling blue metal with an almost mirror shine to it, as smooth as water, and nowhere rectilinear or planar, but all flowing contours, as supple as skin. It didn't look like a thing built or sculpted, but rather poured of molten metal. Lazlo could scarcely decide what was more extraordinary: that it was *floating*, or that it took the form of *an immense being*, because here was where his wild and improbable theory came wildly and improbably true. In a manner of speaking.

The entire impossible structure took the form of a seraph. It was a statue too huge to be conceived: upright, straight, feet toward the city, head in the sky, arms outheld in a pose of supplication. Its wings were spread wide. *Its wings.* The great metal span of them. They were fanned out to such a tremendous breadth that they made a canopy over the city, blocking out the sunlight. Moonlight, starlight, all natural light.

This wasn't what Lazlo had meant by his theory, even in jest, but he was hard-pressed now to say which was wilder or more improbable: the return of mythic beings from beyond the sky, or a thousand-foot-high metal statue of one, hovering in the air. The imagination, he thought, no matter how vivid, was still tethered in some measure to the known, and this was beyond anything he could have imagined. If the Godslayer had told them in advance, it would have sounded absurd even to *him*.

The delegates found their voices and poured forth a deluge of questions.

"How is it floating?"

"What is that metal?"

"Who made it?"

"How did it get there?"

Lazlo asked, "Who are the Mesarthim?" and that was the first question Eril-Fane answered. Sort of.

"The question is: Who *were* the Mesarthim. They're dead now." Lazlo thought he saw a trace of grief in the Godslayer's eyes, and he couldn't make sense of it. The Mesarthim could only be the "gods" whose deaths had earned him his name. But if he had killed them, why should he grieve? "And that," he added, nodding to it, "is dead, too."

"What do you mean, it's dead?" someone asked. "Was it *alive*? That... *thing*?"

"Not exactly," said Eril-Fane. "But it moved as though it were. It breathed." He wasn't looking at anyone. He seemed very far away. He fell silent, facing the immensity of the strangeness before them, and then breathed out. "When the sun rose that day two hundred years ago, it was there. When the people came out of their houses and looked up and saw it, there were many who rejoiced. We have always worshipped the seraphim here. It might sound like a fairy tale to some of you, but our temples are timbered with the bones of demons, and it is no fairy tale to us." He gestured toward the great metal angel. "Our holy book tells of a Second Coming. This isn't what anyone thought it would look like, but many wanted to believe. Our priestesses have always taught that divinity, by virtue of its great power, must encompass both beauty and terror. And here were both." He shook his head. "But in the end, the form of the citadel might only have been a twisted joke. Whatever they were, the Mesarthim weren't seraphim."

The whole party was silent. All the faranji looked as dazed as Lazlo felt. Some brows creased as rational minds grappled with this proof of the impossible— or at least the hitherto inconceivable. Others were smooth on faces gone slack with astonishment. The Tizerkane looked grim, and...this was odd, but Lazlo noticed, first seeing Azareen and the way she kept her eyes pinned on Eril-Fane, that none of them were looking at the citadel. Not Ruza or Tzara or anyone. It seemed to Lazlo they were looking anywhere *but* there, as though they couldn't bear the sight of the thing.

"They didn't have wings. They weren't beings of fire. Like the seraphim, though, there were six of them, three male, three female. No army, no servants. They needed none," said Eril-Fane. "They had magic." He gave a bitter smile. "Magic isn't a fairy tale, either, as we here have cause to know. I wanted you to see this before I tried to explain. I knew your minds would fight it. Even now, with the proof before you, I can see you're struggling."

"Where did they come from?" Calixte asked.

Eril-Fane just shook his head. "We don't know."

"But you say they were gods?" asked Mouzaive, the natural philosopher, who was hard-pressed to believe in the divine.

"What is a god?" was Eril-Fane's reply. "I don't know the answer to that, but I can tell you this: The Mesarthim were powerful, but they were nothing holy."

He sank into silence, and they waited to see if he would break it. There were so many questions they wanted to ask, but even Drave, the explosionist, felt the pathos of the moment and held his tongue. When Eril-Fane did speak, though, it was only to say, "It's getting late. You'll want to reach the city."

"We're going *there*?" some among them demanded,

fear thick in their voices. "Right underneath that thing?"

"It's safe," the Godslayer assured them. "I promise you. It's just a shell now. It's been empty for fifteen years."

"Then what's the problem?" Thyon Nero asked. "Why exactly have you brought us here?"

Lazlo was surprised he hadn't figured it out. He gazed at the dazzling behemoth and the darkness beneath it. "The shadow of our dark time still haunts us." Eril-Fane might have slain the gods and freed his people from thrall, but that thing remained, blocking out the sun, and lording their long torment over them. "To get rid of it," he told the alchemist, as sure as he had ever been of anything. "And give the city back its sky."

22

PATTERN OF LIGHT, SCRIBBLE OF DARKNESS

Lazlo looked up: at the shining citadel of alien blue metal floating in the sky.

Sarai looked down: at the gleam of the Cusp, beyond which the sun was soon to sink, and at the fine thread winding down the valley toward Weep. It was the trail. Squinting, she could just make out a progress of specks against the white.

Lazlo was one of the specks.

Around them both, voices jangled and jarred—speculation, debate, alarm—but they heard them only as noise. Both were absorbed in their own thoughts. Lazlo's mind was afire with marvel, the lit match touching off fuse after fuse. Burning lines raced through his consciousness, connecting far-flung dots and filling in blanks, erasing question marks and adding a dozen more for every one erased. A *dozen*

dozen. There could be no end to the questions, but the sketch outlines of answers were beginning to appear, and they were astonishing.

If his absorption were a pattern of light, though, Sarai's was a scribble of darkness. For fifteen years, she and the others had survived in hiding, trapped in this citadel of murdered gods and scraping a meager existence from it. And maybe they had always known this day would come, but the only life—the only *sanity*—had been in believing it could be held at bay. Now those specks in the distance, almost too small to be seen, were coming inexorably toward them to attempt to dismantle their world, and what tatters remained of Sarai's belief deserted her.

The Godslayer had returned to Weep.

She had always known who her father was. Long before she ever screamed moths and sent her senses down to the city, she knew about the man who had loved and killed her mother, and who would have killed her, too, if she had been in the nursery with the others. Images rose from her arsenal of horrors. His strong hand, drawing a knife across Isagol's throat. Children and babies screaming, the bigger ones thrashing in the arms of their killers. Spuming arterial fountains, leaping sprays of red. "The throat's better," the old woman had said in Sarai's nightmare. She reached up for her own throat and wrapped her hands around it as though she could protect it. Her pulse was frantic, her breathing ragged, and it seemed impossible that people could live at all with such flimsy stuff as skin keeping blood, breath, and spirit safe inside their bodies.

At the garden balustrade in the citadel of the Mesarthim, with ghosts peering over their shoulders, the godspawn watched their death ride down to Weep.

And in the sky overhead—empty, empty, empty and then *not*—a white bird appeared in the blue, like the tip of a knife stabbed through a veil, and wherever it had been, and however it had come, it was here now, and it was watching.

PART III

* * *

mahal (muh·HAHL) *noun*

A risk that will yield either tremendous reward or disastrous consequence.

Archaic; from the mahalath, a transformative fog of myth that turns one either into a god or a monster.

23

UNSEEN NO LONGER

Fabled Weep, unseen no longer.

From the top of the Cusp, where the Godslayer's delegation stood, a trail descended into the canyon of the River Uzumark, with the white of demonglass gradually giving way to the honey-colored stone of cliff faces and natural spires and arches, and to the green of forests so dense that their canopies looked, from above, like carpets of moss one might walk across. And the waterfalls might have been curtains of pale silk hung from the cliff tops, too numerous to count. With its waterfall curtains and carpets of forest, the canyon was like a long and beautiful room, and Weep a toy city—a gilded model—at its center. The shocking surreality of the citadel—the sheer size of the thing played havoc with the mind's sense of scale.

"Does Eril-Fane want me to climb *that*?" Calixte asked, staring up at the great seraph.

"What's the matter? Couldn't do it?" taunted Ebliz Tod.

"Have to reach it first," she quipped. "I suppose that's where *you* come in." She waved her hand at him, queenly. "Be a dear and build me some stairs."

Tod's umbrage rendered him momentarily speechless, during which pause Soulzeren interjected, "Be faster to fly, anyway. We can have the silk sleighs ready in a few days."

"That's just getting to it, though," her husband, Ozwin, pointed out. "That'll be the easy part. Getting rid of it, now, there's another matter."

"What do you reckon?" Soulzeren mused. "Move it? Dismantle it?"

"Blow it up," said Drave, which drew him flat looks from everyone.

"You do see that it's directly above the city," Lazlo pointed out.

"So they get out of the way."

"I imagine they're trying to avoid further destruction."

"Then why invite *me*?" he asked, grinning.

"Why indeed?" Soulzeren murmured in an undertone.

Drave reached out to smack Thyon Nero on the shoulder. "Did you hear that?" he asked, as Thyon had failed to laugh. "Why invite *me* if you don't want destruction, eh? Why bring ten camels' worth of powder if you don't want to blow that thing right back to the heavens?"

Thyon gave him a thin smile and half nod, though it was clear that his mind was elsewise occupied. No doubt he was processing the problem in his own way. He kept his own counsel, while the other delegates were vociferous. For months their intellects had been hamstrung by mystery. Now the sky presented the greatest scientific puzzle they had ever encountered, and they were all considering their place in it, and their chances of solving it.

Mouzaive was talking to Belabra about magnets, but Belabra wasn't listening. He was muttering indecipherable calculations, while the Fellerings—the twin metallurgists—discussed the possible composition of the blue metal.

As for Lazlo, he was awed and humbled. He'd known from the first that he had no qualifications to recommend him for the Godslayer's delegation, but it wasn't until he beheld the problem that he realized that some part of him had still hoped he might be the one to solve it. Ridiculous. A storybook might have held the secret of azoth, and knowledge of stories might have earned him a place in the party, but he hardly thought that tales would give him an edge now.

Well, but he was *here*, and he would help in any

way he could, even if it was only running errands for the delegates. What was it Master Hyrrokkin had said? "Some men are born for great things, and others to help great men do great things." He'd also said there was no shame in it, and Lazlo agreed.

Still, was it too much to hope that the "man born for great things" should *not* turn out to be Thyon Nero? *Anyone but him*, thought Lazlo, laughing a little at his own pettiness.

The caravan descended the trail into the valley, and Lazlo looked about himself, amazed. He was really here, seeing it. A canyon of golden stone, swaths of unbroken forest, a great green river blurred by waterfall mist, flowing as far as the shadow of the citadel. There, just shy of the city, the Uzumark broadened into a delta and was sliced into ribbons by boulders and small islands before simply vanishing. Beyond the city it reappeared and continued its tumultuous journey eastward and away. The river, it seemed, flowed *under* the city.

From a distance, Weep was stunningly like Lazlo's long-held picture of it—or at least, like his long-held picture as seen through a veil of shadow. There were the golden domes, though fewer than he'd pictured, and they didn't gleam. The sunlight didn't strike them. By the time the sun angled low enough to slant its rays under the citadel's outspread wings, it had gone beyond the edge of the Cusp, and only traded one shadow for another.

But it was more than that. There was a forlorn look about it, a sense of lingering despair. There were the city's defensive walls, built in a harmonious oval, but the harmony was broken. In four places, the wall was obliterated. Set down with geometric precision at the cardinal points were four monumental slabs of the same alien metal as the citadel. They were great tapered blocks, each as big in its own right as a castle, but they appeared entirely smooth, windowless and doorless. They looked, from above, like a set of great map weights holding down the city's edges so it wouldn't blow away.

It was difficult to make out from this distance, but there seemed to be something atop each one. A statue, perhaps.

"What are those great blocks?" he asked Ruza, pointing.

"Those are the anchors."

"Anchors?" Lazlo squinted across the distance, gauging the blocks' position relative to the great seraph overhead. It appeared to be centered in the air above them. "Do they act like anchors?" he asked. He thought of ships in harbor, in which case there would be anchor chain. Nothing visible connected the seraph to the blocks. "Are they keeping it from drifting away?"

Ruza's smile was wry. "They never took the time to explain it to us, Strange. They set them down the day they came—never mind what was under them—and there they are still." Ruza jerked his head at the procession behind them. "Think one of these geniuses will be able to move them?"

"Move the anchors? Do you think that's how to move the citadel?"

Ruza shrugged. "Or what? Attach towlines to it and pull? All I know is it won't be leaving the way it came. Not with Skathis dead."

Skathis.

The name was like a serpent's hiss. Lazlo took it in, and the realization dawned that Ruza was talking. Well, he was always talking. The fine point was: The secrecy that had bound them all until now was apparently broken. Lazlo could ask questions. He turned to his friend.

"Don't look at me like that," said Ruza.

"Like what?"

"Like I'm a beautiful book you're about to open and plunder with your greedy mad eyes."

Lazlo laughed. "Greedy mad eyes? Plunder? Are you afraid of me, Ruza?"

Ruza looked suddenly steely. "Do you know, Strange, that to ask a Tizerkane if he fears you is to challenge him to single combat?"

"Well then," said Lazlo, who knew better than to believe anything Ruza said. "I'm glad I only said it to *you* and not one of the fearsome warriors like Azareen or Tzara."

"Unkind," said Ruza, wounded. His face crumpled. He pretended to weep. "I *am* fearsome," he insisted. "I *am*."

"There, there," Lazlo consoled. "You're a very fierce warrior. Don't cry. You're terrifying."

"Really?" asked Ruza in a pitiful little hopeful voice. "You're not just saying that?"

"You two idiots," said Azareen, and Lazlo felt a curious twinge of pride, to be called an idiot by her, with what might have been the tiniest edge of fondness. He exchanged a chastened glance with Ruza as Azareen passed them on the trail and took the lead.

A short time ago, Lazlo had seen her arguing with Eril-Fane, and had heard just enough to understand that she'd wanted to stay with him at Fort Misrach. "Why must you face everything alone?" she had demanded before turning away and leaving him there. And when Lazlo last looked back to wave, the caravan starting down the trail and the Godslayer staying behind, he had seemed not only diminished, but haunted.

If it was safe in the city, as he promised, then why did he look like that, and why did he not come with them?

What happened here? Lazlo wondered. He didn't

ask any more questions. In silence, they rode the rest of the way down to Weep.

✳ ✳ ✳

Eril-Fane stood on the ridge and watched the caravan make its way to the city. It took them an hour to reach it, weaving in and out of view among stands of trees, and by the time they left the forest for good, they were too distant for him to make out who was who. He could tell spectral from camel, and that was all. It was getting dark, which didn't help.

Azareen would be leading. She would be straight-backed, face forward, and no one behind her would suspect the look on her face. The loneliness. The raw, bewildered *mourning*.

He did that to her. Over and over.

If she would only give up on him, he could stop destroying her. He could never be what she hoped for—what he had once been. Before he was a hero. Before he was even a man.

Before he was the lover of the goddess of despair.

Eril-Fane shuddered. Even after all these years, the thought of Isagol the Terrible stirred such a storm in him—of rancor and longing, desire and disgust, violence and even affection—all of it seething and bleeding and writhing, like a pit of rats eating one another alive. That was what his feelings were now, what Isagol had made of them. Nothing good or pure could survive in him. All was corruption and gore, suffocating in his self-loathing. How *weak* he was, how pitiful. He might have killed the goddess in the end, but he wasn't free of her, and he never would be.

If only Azareen would let him go. Every day that she waited for him to become who he had been, he bore the burden of her loneliness in addition to his own.

His mother's, too. At least he could send her Lazlo to take care of, and that would help. But he couldn't very well send someone home with Azareen to take his place as . . . as her husband.

Only she could make that choice, and she wouldn't.

Eril-Fane had told Lazlo he didn't sleep well in Weep. Well, that rather downplayed the matter. It turned his blood cold to even think of closing his eyes in the city. Even from up here, where distance made a toy of it—a pretty glimmer of far-off glaves and old gold—he felt its atmosphere like tentacles waiting to drag him back in, and he couldn't stop shaking. Better that no one should see him like this. If the Godslayer couldn't keep his countenance, how could anyone else?

Feeling like the world's greatest coward, he turned away from his city, and his guests, and his wife, whom he could not love because *he could not love*, and he rode the short track back to Fort Misrach.

Tomorrow, he told himself. Tomorrow he would

face Weep, and his duty, and the nightmares that stalked him. Somehow, he would find the courage to finish what he had started fifteen years ago, and free his people from this last vestige of their long torment.

Even if he could never free himself.

24

OBSCENITY. CALAMITY. GODSPAWN.

"I told you we'd die before we ran out of dresses," said Ruby, and all of her saucy bravado was gone. She might have been blithe about dying when it was abstraction, but she wasn't now.

"No one's dying," said Feral. "Nothing's changed."

They all looked at him. "Nothing except the God-slayer's back," Ruby pointed out.

"With clever men and women from the outside world," Sparrow added.

"Intent on destroying us," Minya concluded.

"Not destroying *us*," argued Feral. "They don't know we're here."

"And what do you think they'll do when they find us?" asked Minya. "Express polite surprise and apologize for barging into our home?"

"It won't come to that," he said. "How would they

get anywhere near us? It's not as though they can *fly*. We're safe up here."

He was dismissive, but Sarai could tell that he was worried, too. It was the outsiders. What did the five of them know of the rest of the world and the capabilities of its people? Nothing at all.

They were on the garden terrace, which was at the top of the great seraph's breast, stretching from shoulder to shoulder, and overlooked the city all the way to the Cusp. Helplessly, they watched the procession of specks move down the slope and disappear inside the city. Sarai was between plum trees, her hands trembling, resting on the balustrade. Over the edge was nothing but empty air—a straight drop far, far down to the rooftops. She was uneasy, standing so close. She made the descent every night through her moths' senses, but that was different. The moths had wings. She did not. She took a careful step back and wrapped her hand around a strong branch.

Ruby was reckless, though, leaning too far out. "Where do you suppose they are now?" she asked. She picked a plum and threw it out as hard as she could. Sparrow gasped. They watched the fruit arc out into air.

"Ruby! What are you doing?" Sparrow demanded.

"Maybe I'll hit one of them."

"The Rule—"

"*The Rule*," Ruby repeated, rolling her eyes. "You think they don't fall off the trees by themselves? Oh look, a plum!" She mimicked picking something up, examining it, then tilting back her head to gaze up. "Must be someone living up there! Let's go kill them!"

"I hardly think a plum would survive the fall," Feral pointed out.

Ruby gave him the flattest look that had, perhaps, ever been given in all of time. Then, unexpectedly, she began to laugh. She clutched her middle and doubled over. "I hardly think a plum would survive the fall," she repeated, laughing harder. "And how about *me?*" she asked. She flung a leg over the balustrade, and Sarai's stomach dropped. "Do you think *I'd* survive the fall? Now, *that* would be breaking The Rule."

Sparrow gasped. "Enough," said Sarai, jerking Ruby back. "Don't be stupid." She could feel panic pulsing beneath the skin of the moment, and made an effort to smother it. "Feral's right. It's too soon to worry."

"It's never too soon to worry," said Minya, who, unlike the rest of them, didn't seem worried in the least. On the contrary, she seemed *excited.* "Worry spurs preparation."

"What kind of preparation?" Sparrow asked, a quaver slipping into her voice. She looked around at her garden, and at the graceful arches of the gallery, through which the dining table could be seen, and the ghost, Ari-Eil, still standing rigid where Minya had left him. A breeze stirred the drapery of vines that were the only thing standing between outside and in.

"We can't hide," she said. "If we could just shut the doors—"

"Doors" in the citadel were nothing like the hand-carved timber ones Sarai knew from the city. They didn't swing open and shut. They didn't latch or lock. They weren't objects at all, but only apertures in the smooth mesarthium. The *open* ones were apertures, anyway. Closed, they weren't doors at all, but only smooth expanses of wall, because back when the citadel was "alive," the metal had simply *melted* open and shut, re-forming seamlessly.

"If we could shut the doors," Minya reminded her slowly, "that would mean we could control mesarthium. And if we could control mesarthium, we could do a lot more than *shut the doors*." There was an acid edge to her voice. Minya, being Skathis's daughter, had always had a festering bitterness at the core of her, that she hadn't inherited his power—the one power that could have set them free. It was the rarest of gifts, and Korako had monitored the babies closely for any sign of it. In all of Great Ellen's years in the nursery it had manifested only once, and Korako had taken the baby away on the spot.

Mesarthium was no ordinary metal. It was perfectly adamant: impenetrable, unassailable. It could not be cut or pierced; no one had ever succeeded in making so much as a scratch in it. Nor did it melt. The hottest forge fire and the strongest blacksmith

254

could make not the slightest dent in it. Even Ruby's fire had no effect on it. At Skathis's will, however, it had rippled, shifted, reshaping itself into new configurations with the fluidity of mercury. Hard and cool to the touch, it had, nevertheless, been molten to his mind, and the creatures who gave him his title—"god of beasts" instead of merely "god of metal"—had been, for all intents and purposes, living things.

They were four mesarthium monsters, one to each of the huge metal blocks positioned at the perimeter of the city. Rasalas had been his favorite, and though the citizens of Weep had understood that the beast was only metal animated by Skathis's mind, the understanding was buried under their terror. Their fear of him was its own entity, and Sarai understood why. Thousands upon thousands of times she'd seen him in their dreams, and it was hard even for her not to believe he had been alive. The citadel in the sky had seemed alive, too. Back then, anyone looking up at it was likely to find it looking back with its immense, inscrutable eyes.

Such had been Skathis's gift. If they'd had it, then the doors would be an afterthought. They could bring the whole citadel back to life and move it anywhere they wanted—though Sarai didn't imagine there was anywhere in the world that would want *them*.

"Well, we can't, can we?" said Sparrow. "And we can't *fight* "

"*You* can't," agreed Minya with scorn, as though

Sparrow's gift, which had kept them fed for years, had no worth because it had no dimension for violence. "And you," she said to Feral with equal scorn. "If we wanted to frighten them with thunder, then you might be useful." She had goaded him for years to learn to summon and aim lightning, with dismal results. It was beyond his control, and though this was due to the natural parameters of his gift and no personal failing, it didn't spare him Minya's judgment. Her eyes flicked to Sarai next, and here her gaze went beyond scorn to something more combative. Spite, frustration, venom. Sarai knew it all. She'd endured its sting ever since she stopped blindly doing everything Minya told her to do.

"And then there's Bonfire," Minya said, moving on to Ruby without scorn so much as cool consideration.

"What about me?" asked Ruby, wary.

Minya's gaze focused in on her. "Well, I suppose you might do more with your gift than heat bathwater and burn up your clothes."

Ruby paled to a bloodless cerulean. "You mean... burn *people*?"

Minya let out a little laugh. "You're the only one of the five of us who's actually a weapon and you've never even considered—"

Ruby cut her off. "I'm not a weapon."

Minya's mirth vanished. She said coolly, "When it comes to the defense of the citadel and our five lives... yes, you are."

Sometimes you can glimpse a person's soul in just a flicker of expression, and Sarai glimpsed Ruby's then: the longing that was the core of her. Yesterday she'd had the thought that Ruby's gift expressed her nature, and it did, but not the way Minya wanted it to. Ruby was heat and volatility, she was *passion*, but not violence. She wanted to kiss, not kill. It sounded silly but it wasn't. She was fifteen years old and furiously alive, and in a glimmer of a moment, Sarai saw her hopes both exposed and destroyed, and felt in them the echo of her own. To be someone else.

To not be... *this*.

"Come on," said Feral. "If it comes to fighting, what chance do you think we have? The Godslayer slew the Mesarthim, and they were far more powerful than we are."

"He had the advantage of surprise," said Minya, all but baring her teeth. "He had the advantage of treachery. Now *we* have it."

A little sob escaped from Sparrow. Whatever calm they'd been pretending, it was slipping away. No, Minya was tearing it away deliberately. *What's wrong with you?* Sarai wanted to demand, but she knew she would get no satisfaction. Instead, she said, with all the authority she could muster, "We don't know anything yet. Feral's right. It's too soon to worry. I'll find out what I can tonight, and tomorrow we'll know if we need to have this conversation or not. For now, it's dinnertime."

"I'm not hungry," said Ruby.

Neither was Sarai, but she thought if they could act normal, they might feel normal. A little bit, anyway. Though it was hard to feel normal with a ghost glaring at you from the head of the table. "Minya..." she said. It pained her to be gracious, but she forced herself. "Would you please send Ari-Eil away so that we can eat in peace?" She didn't ask her to release him. She understood that Minya meant to keep him around, if only to torment Sarai.

"Certainly I will, since you ask so nicely," said Minya, matching her gracious tone with just an edge of mockery. She gave no visible signal, but in the dining room, the ghost unfroze and pivoted toward the interior door. Minya was done toying with him, apparently, because he didn't shuffle his steps or fight against her now, but virtually glided from their sight.

"Thank you," said Sarai, and they went inside.

Dinner was not kimril soup, though Sarai doubted Ruby would have voiced any objection to it tonight. She was uncharacteristically silent, and Sarai could imagine the tenor of her thoughts. Her own were grim enough, and she wasn't faced with the notion of burning people alive. What Feral said was true. They could never win a battle. Once they were discovered, there simply was no scenario in which life went on.

She didn't linger in the gallery after dinner, but asked Ruby to heat a bath for her.

Their suites all had bathrooms with deep mesarthium pools in them, but water no longer came from the pipes, so they used a copper tub in the rain room instead. The "rain room" was the chamber off the kitchens they'd designated for Feral's cloud summoning. They'd fitted it with barrels, and a channel in the floor caught runoff and funneled it out to the gardens. Kem, the ghost footman, said it had been the butchering room before, and the channel was for blood and the big hooks on the ceiling were for hanging meat. No trace of blood remained, though, just as none remained in the nursery or the corridors. One of Minya's first commands to the ghosts in the aftermath of the Carnage had been to clean up all the blood.

Sarai scooped water into the tub with a bucket, and Ruby put her hands on the side and ignited them. Just her hands, like she was holding fireballs. The copper conducted the heat beautifully, and soon the water was steaming and Ruby left. Sarai submerged herself and soaked, and washed her hair with the soap Great Ellen made them from the herbs in the garden, and all the while she had the peculiar sense that she was preparing herself—as though her body would be going out from the citadel and not merely her senses. She was even nervous, as if she were about to meet new people. *Meet* them, ha. She was about to *spy on* new people and violate their minds. What did it matter if her hair was clean? They wouldn't see her, or have any awareness of her presence. They never did. In Weep it was she who was the ghost, and an unbound one, invisible, incorporeal, insubstantial as a murmur.

Back in her dressing room, she put on a slip. Staring at herself in the mirror, she found that she'd lost the ability to see herself through her own eyes. She saw only what humans would see. Not a girl or a woman or someone in between. They wouldn't see her loneliness or fear or courage, let alone her humanity. They would see only obscenity. Calamity.

Godspawn.

Something took hold of her. A surge of defiance. Her eyes swept the dressing room. Past the slips to the terrible gowns, the headdresses and fans and pots of her mother's face paint and all the macabre accoutrements of the goddess of despair. And when she emerged, Less Ellen, who had brought her tea, did a double take and nearly dropped her tray. "Oh, Sarai, you gave me a fright."

"It's just me," said Sarai, though she didn't feel quite herself. She'd never desired to be anything like her mother before, but tonight she craved a little goddess ferocity, so she'd painted Isagol's black band across her eyes from temple to temple and mussed her cinnamon-red hair as wild as she could make it.

She turned to the terrace—which was the outstretched right hand of the huge metal seraph—and went out to meet the night and the newcomers.

25

THE NIGHT AND THE NEWCOMERS

Sarai screamed her moths at Weep, and down and down they whirled. On a normal night they would split up and divide the city a hundred ways between them, but not tonight. She needed all her focus on the newcomers. Tonight, the citizens of Weep would not weep because of her.

The ghost Ari-Eil had told them—or been compelled by Minya to tell them—that the faranji were to be housed at the Merchants' Guildhall, where a wing had been outfitted as a hostelry just for them. Sarai had never gone there before. It wasn't a residence, so she'd never looked there for sleepers, and it took her a few minutes to locate the right wing. The place was palatial, with a large central structure topped with a golden dome, and walls of the native honey stone. All was carved in the traditional style. Weep wasn't a city that feared ornamentation. Centuries of carvers had embellished every stone surface with patterns and creatures and seraphim.

Graceful open pavilions were connected by covered walkways to outbuildings capped in smaller domes. There were fountains, and once upon a time there had been gardens full of fruit and flowers, but those had all withered in the accursed shade.

The whole city had been a garden once. Not anymore. Orchid Witch, Sarai thought in passing, could do a sight of good down here.

If not for the fact that she would be murdered on sight.

The moths tested the terrace doors first, but found most of them closed, and far too well made for any cracks that might admit them, so they flew down the chimneys instead. Inside, the rooms were sumptuous, as befitted the first foreign delegation ever welcomed beyond the Cusp. For centuries, the city had been famed the world over for its craftsmanship, and these chambers might have served as a showplace: the finest of carpets laid over floors of mosaic gold and lys, with embroidered bedcovers, frescoed walls, carved ceiling timbers, and marvelous objects on shelves and walls, every one a masterpiece.

But Sarai wasn't here for the art. Among eleven occupied rooms, she counted thirteen sleepers, one of whom was not a faranji but a Tizerkane warrior,

Tzara, wrapped in the slender arms of a slight young woman with very short, soft hair. That made a dozen outsiders all told, most of whom were musty old men. There was only one other woman: less young, less slender, sleeping beside a stocky man. These were the only couples, and the only women; all the rest were men, and slept alone. More than half snored. Slightly less than half stank. It was easy to tell who had availed themselves of the baths drawn for them, because their tubs were coated in the brown scum of weeks of unwash. Those with clean tubs simply had not yet transferred the scum from their persons, and Sarai was loath to perch her moths on them. Up in the sky, her nose wrinkled as though she were experiencing the concentrated male stench firsthand.

With all her moths divided among so few rooms, she was able to study each person from multiple vantage points and take in every detail of them. Two of the men looked so alike that she grew confused for a moment, thinking that two sets of moths were relaying her the same information. They weren't; she realized the men were twins. One man was especially ill-favored. He had a sour, thin-lipped look even in sleep, and another resembled a reptile in molt, the skin of his face sloughing away in curls of dead skin. His knuckles were gnarled with burn scars, too, like melted candle wax, and he smelled like a dead animal. The young women were much pleasanter—smooth-skinned and sweet-smelling. Around Tzara's navel, Sarai saw the eli-lith tattoo given to all girls of Weep when they become women. Tzara's was a serpent swallowing its tail, which symbolized the cycle of destruction and rebirth and had become popular since the defeat of the gods. The older couple wore matching gold bands on their rough and callused ring fingers, and the man's nails, like Sparrow's, bore dark crescents from working with soil. The soil was in the room, too: The elegant table was covered with dozens of little canvas sacks filled with seedlings, and Sarai wondered how *plants* figured into the Godslayer's plans to conquer the citadel.

On one sleeper in particular, though, she found an undue portion of her attention fix, without her even meaning it to. It was an instinctive process, her focus flowing among her sentinels according to need. But this wasn't need. This stranger didn't seem more important than the others. He was simply more beautiful.

He was *golden*.

His hair was such a color as she'd never seen. Her own red-brown was unusual enough in Weep where everyone had black hair, but his was the color of sunlight, long enough in the front and with just enough wave to make a curl you wanted to reach out and coax around your finger. Aside from the girl entwined with Tzara, he was the only one of the faranji who was young, though not so young as Sarai was herself. He was princely and broad-shouldered, and had nodded off propped up on cushions with a book open on his bare chest. Through the moths' vision, Sarai saw that the cover was a picture of a spoonful of stars and creatures, but her attention was drawn to his face, which was every bit as fine an artwork as the room's collection of marvels. There was such an elegance in the lines of it, such a perfect sculpt to every angle and curve that he was almost unreal. A museum piece.

She reminded herself that she wasn't here to be enraptured by this stranger's beauty, but to discover who he was, and what nature of threat he posed, and the same with the rest whose humbler looks presented less distraction. She looked at them all and they were just sleeping humans, so vulnerable with their slack mouths and their long pale toes poking out from under the covers. With few exceptions, they were very nearly ridiculous. It seemed impossible that they might be the death of her.

Enough. She wouldn't learn anything about the Godslayer's guests by looking at them. It was time to look *in* them.

In eleven rooms, where thirteen humans slept— ten men and three women, one of whom was not an outsider and thus not a subject—moths that were perched on the walls and bedposts bestirred themselves and took to the air, fluttering the little distance to land on flesh. None of the humans felt the feather-light feet of winged creatures alighting on their brows

265

and cheekbones, much less the smooth intrusion of the Muse of Nightmares into their minds.

Invisible, incorporeal, insubstantial as a murmur, Sarai slipped into their dreams, and what she discovered there, in the hours that followed, proved that the strangers were far from ridiculous.

And would indeed be the death of her.

* * *

Azareen lived in a set of rooms above a bakery in Windfall—the district so named for the plums that fell on it from the trees of the gods. She walked up the back steps, from the courtyard where the bakery and adjacent tavern kept their waste bins. It stank, and there was that other smell, distinct to Windfall: ferment. Always, the plums were raining down, as though the trees were enchanted and would never die.

Azareen hated plums.

She put the key in the lock, pushed open the door, and went in. Two years' worth of dust lay over everything. The blankets would be musty, the cupboards empty. Her mother or sisters would have kept the rooms fresh for her, but having them here would open the door to conversations she didn't wish to have, such as why she still lived here, alone, when she might stay with any of them, or even marry, and have a family, before it was too late.

"I'm already married," she would tell them, and what could they say to that? It was true in its way, even if her husband had released her from the promise she'd made eighteen years ago, when she was only a girl. *Sixteen years old*, and Eril-Fane had been all of seventeen. How beautiful he'd been. They'd been too young to marry, but it hadn't stopped them. In the shadow of the Mesarthim, all time had seemed borrowed, and they just couldn't wait.

Oh, the memories. They would surface from the wreckage, fast and sharp enough to impale her: of wanting him so much she didn't know how she'd survive a night without him. And then, at last, not having to.

Their wedding night. How young and smooth they'd been, and eager and tireless and *burning*. Five nights. That was what they'd had: five nights, eighteen years ago. That was her marriage. And then... what came after.

Azareen dropped her pack on the floor and looked around. Small, stifling, and quiet, it made quite a change from the Elmuthaleth. She had a sitting room, a bedroom, and a small kitchen with a water closet. She'd stopped by her sister's house to see her family after settling the faranji in at the guildhall, and she'd had some dinner there. She needed a bath, but that could wait until the morning. She went straight to her bed. Where, eighteen years ago, she had spent five eager, tireless, burning nights with her beautiful young husband before the gods stole him away.

The quiet closed in. Azareen imagined she could *feel* the shadow, the weight and press of the citadel overhead. It was the weight and press of everything that had happened in it—and everything that had never happened because of it.

She didn't change her clothes, but just took off her boots and reached into her pack, into the little pocket she'd sewn into it to hold her most cherished possession.

It was a ring of tarnished silver. She put it on, as she did always and only at night, tucked her hands under her cheek, and waited for sleep to take her.

✳ ✳ ✳

A mile or so away, down a street paved in lapis lazuli just like in a mean old monk's childhood tales, in a house much less grand than the Merchants' Guildhall and far cozier than Azareen's rooms, Lazlo was just getting to bed. The sun would rise in an hour. He hadn't meant to stay up all night, but how could he help it?

He was *here*.

"There's only one way to celebrate the end of such a journey," his hostess had told him when she greeted him at the Merchants' Guildhall and whisked him away home with her. "And that is with food, a bath, and a bed, in the order of your preference."

Suheyla was her name. Her hair was a cap of white, cropped short as a man's, and her face was a perfect example of how someone can be beautiful without being beautiful. She shone with good nature and the same vitality that Eril-Fane radiated, but without the shadow that had grown over him as they drew nearer to Weep. There was gravity in her, but nothing grim or bleak. Her eyes were the same deep-set smiles as her son's, with more extensive deltas of creases at the corners. She was short and vigorous, colorfully dressed in an embroidered tunic adorned with tassels and gathered in by a wide, patterned belt. Discs of hammered gold at her temples were connected by spans of fine chain across her brow. "You are most welcome here, young man," she'd said with such heartfelt sincerity that Lazlo almost felt as if he'd come home.

Home—about which he knew as little as he did about mothers. Before today, he had never set foot in a home. As to having a preference, that was new, too. You take what you're given and you're grateful for it. Once that message is well and truly ingrained in you, it feels like vainglory to imagine one's own likes and dislikes could matter to other people. "Whatever order makes the most sense," he had replied, almost like a question.

"Sense be damned! You can eat in the bath if that's what you wish. You've earned it."

And Lazlo had never had a bath he'd had any desire

to linger in, bathing in the monastery having been characterized by shivering in buckets of well water, and at the library by quick, lukewarm pull showers. Still, feeling deeply that his filth was an unforgivable imposition, he'd chosen to bathe first, and thus had he discovered, at the age of twenty, the incomparable pleasure of submergence in hot water.

Who knew?

He had *not* elected to eat in the bath, however—or even to linger beyond the not inconsiderable time it took to get clean—being far too eager to continue talking with Suheyla. She had, on the walk from the guild-hall, joined his admittedly short list of favorite people, along with Eril-Fane, Calixte, Ruza, and old Master Hyrrokkin. When he saw the quantity of food she'd laid out for him, though, his ingrained abnegation rose to the surface. There were small roast birds and pastries glistening with honey, cubes of meat in fragrant sauce, and curled crustaceans impaled on sticks. There was a salad of grains and another of greens, and a platter of fruit and a half-dozen small bowls of pastes and another half-dozen of salts, and the bread was a disc too big for the table, hanging instead from a hook that existed for this purpose, so that you might just reach up and tear some off. And there were sweets and peppers and tea and wine and . . . and it was all too much for him.

"I'm so sorry to put you to such trouble," he'd said, earning himself a sharp look.

"Guests aren't trouble," Suheyla had replied. "They're a blessing. Having no one to cook for, now, that's a sadness. But a young man gaunt from the Elmuthaleth and in need of fattening? That's a pleasure."

And what could he do but say thank you and eat his fill?

Oh glory, he'd never had a better meal. And he'd never felt so full, or lingered at a table so long, or talked so much or been so comfortable with someone he'd only just met. And so his introduction to the world of homes and mothers was powerfully good, and though he had felt, on his first walk through the city of his dreams, that he would never be tired again, he was in fact very, very tired, which Suheyla couldn't help but notice. "Come along," she said. "I've kept you up too late."

Earlier, he had left his travel bag near the door. "Let me," he said as she bent to pick it up.

"Nonsense," she replied, and in a flash of a glimpse he perceived that she had no right hand, only a smooth, tapering wrist, though it didn't hinder her in the slightest as she hooked the strap of his bag with it and slung it over her shoulder. He wondered that he hadn't noticed it earlier.

She showed him to one of the green painted doors

that opened off the courtyard. "This was my son's room," she said, gesturing for him to enter.

"Oh. But won't he be wanting it?"

"I don't think so," she said with a tinge of sadness in her voice. "Tell me, how does he sleep...out there?" She made a vague gesture to the west, indicating, Lazlo supposed, the whole rest of the world.

"I don't know," he answered, surprised. "Well enough." How inadequate an offering to a worried mother. *Well enough.* And how would Lazlo know? It had never crossed his mind that Eril-Fane might have vulnerabilities. He realized that all this time he'd been looking to the Godslayer as a hero, not a man, but that heroes, whatever else they are, are also men—and women—and prey to human troubles just like anybody else.

"That's good," said Suheyla. "Perhaps it's gotten better, with his being away from here."

"It?" asked Lazlo, remembering the way Eril-Fane had averted his eyes and said he didn't sleep well in Weep.

"Oh, nightmares." Suheyla waved away the subject and laid her hand to Lazlo's cheek. "It's very good to have you here, young man. Do sleep well."

* * *

Moths effused from the chimneys of the Merchants' Guildhall.

It was the hour before dawn. Some in the city were waking. The bakers were already at work, and carts rolled quietly toward the market square, bringing their daily burdens of produce from the valley farms. Sarai hadn't meant to stay so long in the outsiders' dreams, but she'd found in them such an alien world, so full of visions she had no context for, that she had barely felt time passing.

The ocean: a vastness unspeakable. Leviathans as big as palaces, harnessed to pontoons to keep them from submerging to their freedom. Glave mines like buried sunlight. Towers like tusks. Men with leashed wolves patrolling dazzling blue fields. Such images spoke of a world beyond her ken, and, scattered throughout them—strange among strange and as difficult to separate from the wild vagaries of dreams as snowflakes from a basket of lace—were the answers she had been seeking.

Who were these strangers and what nature of threat did they pose?

As to the first, they were men and women driven by ideas and powered by intelligence and rare skills. Some had families, some did not. Some were kind, some were not. She couldn't possibly *know them* in one night of trespass. She'd formed impressions; that was all. But as to the second question...

Sarai was reeling with visions of explosions and contraptions and impossibly tall towers—and girls *climbing* impossibly tall towers—and magnets and saws and bridges and flasks of miraculous chemicals and . . . and . . . and *flying machines*.

"It's not as though they can *fly*," Feral had said, but it would seem that he was wrong. When Sarai first glimpsed the craft in the dreams of the older of the two faranji women, she had dismissed it as fantasy. Dreams are full of flying. It hadn't worried her. But when she saw the same craft in the husband's mind, she had to take notice. The thing was sleek and simple in design and far too specific to occur by coincidence in two people's dreams, no matter that they lay side by side, touching. Dreams didn't transfer from one sleeper to another. And there was something else that made Sarai believe. She lived in the sky. She knew the world from above in a way that humans didn't, and most dreams of flying just didn't get it right—the reflection of the setting sun on the tops of clouds, the tidal ebb and flow of winds, the look of the world from on high. But this couple with their rough hands, they knew what it was like. No question about it: They'd been there.

So how long before their flying machines were in the air, delivering invaders to the garden terrace and to the flat of the seraph's palm, right where Sarai now stood?

"Tomorrow we'll know if we need to have this conversation or not," she had told the others last evening, when Minya was rattling them all with her talk of fighting. Well, they *would* have to have it, and quickly, little good it would do. Sarai felt sick.

Up in the citadel, she turned in her relentless pacing. Her eyes were open, her surroundings a blur. No one was nearby, but she knew the others must be waiting. If they'd slept at all they'd have risen early to meet her as soon as her moths returned, and hear what she had to tell. Were they just on the other side of her curtain, even now? She hoped they would stay there until she was ready for them.

She considered calling her moths back. Already the eastern horizon was paling and they would fall dead at the first appearance of the sun. But there was something she still had to do. She'd been putting it off all night.

She had to pay a call on the Godslayer.

26

BROKEN PEOPLE

Sarai had come many times to this window. More than to any other in Weep. It was her father's window, and rarely had she let a night pass without a visit to him.

A visit to *torment* him—and herself, too, as she tried to imagine being the sort of child that a father could love instead of kill.

The window was open. There was no obstacle to entering, but she hesitated and perched the moths on the window ledge to peer inside. There wasn't much to the narrow room: a clothes cupboard, some shelves, and a bed of tidy, tightly packed feather mattresses covered with hand-embroidered quilts. There was just enough light through the window to give depth to the darkness, so she saw, in shades of black, the contour of a form. A shoulder, tapering downward. He was sleeping on his side, his back to the window.

Up in her own body, Sarai's hearts stammered. She was nervous, flustered even, as though it were some sort of reunion. A one-sided reunion, anyway. It had been two years since he went away, and it had been such a relief when he did—to be free of Minya's constant harassment. Every day—*every day*—the little girl had demanded to know what he'd dreamed about, and what Sarai had unleashed on her father. Whatever the answer, she was never content. She had wanted Sarai to visit on him such a cataclysm of nightmares as would shatter his mind and leave him spinning through darkness forever. She had wanted Sarai to drive him mad.

The Godslayer had always been a threat to them— the greatest threat. He was Weep's beating heart, the liberator of his people, and their greatest hero. No one was more beloved, or possessed of more authority, and so no one was more dangerous. After the uprising and the liberation, the humans had been kept very busy. They'd had two centuries of tyranny to overcome, after all. They'd had to create a government from nothing, along with laws and a system of justice. They'd had to restore defenses, civil life, industry, and at least the hope of trade. An army, temples, guilds, schools—they'd had to rebuild it all. It had been the work of years, and through it all, the citadel had loomed over their heads, out of their reach. The people of Weep had had no choice but to work at what they could change and tolerate what they could not—which meant never feeling the sun on their faces, or teaching the constellations to their children, or picking fruit from their own garden trees. There had been talk of moving the city out from under the shadow, starting anew someplace else. A site had even been chosen downriver, but there was far too deep a history here to simply give up. This land had been won for them by angels. Shadowed or not, it was sacred.

They had lacked the resources, then, to take on the citadel, but they were never going to tolerate it forever. Eventually, their resolve was going to focus upward. The Godslayer would not give up.

"If *you're* not the end of *him*," Minya would say, "*he'll* be the end of *us*."

And Sarai had been Minya's willing weapon. With the Carnage red and bloody in her hearts, she had tried her best and done her worst. So many nights, she'd covered Eril-Fane in moths and unleashed every terror in her arsenal. Waves of horrors, ranks of monsters. His whole body would go rigid as a board. She'd heard teeth cracking with the clench of his jaw. Never had eyes been squeezed so tightly shut. It had seemed as though they must rupture. But she couldn't break him; she couldn't even make him cry. Eril-Fane had his own arsenal of horrors; he hardly needed hers. Fear was the least of it. Sarai hadn't understood before that fear could be the lesser torment. It was *shame* that tore him apart. It was despair. There was no darkness she could send him to rival what he'd endured already. He had lived three years with Isagol the Terrible. He had survived too much to be driven mad by dreams.

It was strange. Every night Sarai split her mind a hundred ways, her moths carrying pieces of her consciousness through the city, and when they came back to her, she was whole again. It was easy. But something began to happen, the more she tormented her father—a different kind of division within her, and one not so easily reconciled at night's end.

To Minya, there would only ever be the Carnage. But, in fact, there was so much more. There was *before*. Stolen girls, lost years, broken people. And always, there were the savage, merciless gods.

Isagol, reaching into your soul and playing your emotions like a harp.

Letha, dredging your mind, taking out memories and swallowing them whole.

Skathis at the door, come for your daughter.

Skathis at the door, bringing her back home.

The function of hate, as Sarai saw it, was to stamp out compassion—to close a door in one's own self and forget it was ever there. If you had hate, then you could see suffering—and cause it—and feel nothing except perhaps a sordid vindication.

But at some point...here in this room, Sarai thought...she had lost that capacity. Hate had failed

279

her, and it was like losing a shield in battle. Once it was gone, all the suffering had risen up to overwhelm her. It was too much.

It was then that her nightmares turned against her, and she started needing lull.

With a deep breath, Sarai disengaged a moth from the ledge and spurred it forward, a single smithereen of darkness dispatched into the dim. In that one sentinel she focused her attention, and so she was as good as *there*, hovering just inches above the Godslayer's shoulder.

Except...

She could hardly have said which sense first vibrated with a small shock of difference, but she understood at once:

This was not the Godslayer.

The bulk didn't match. Nor did the scent of him. Whoever this was, he was slighter than Eril-Fane, and sank less deeply into the down. As she adjusted to the scant ambient light, she was able to make out dark hair spilled across the pillow, but little more than that.

Who was this, asleep in the Godslayer's bed? Where was Eril-Fane? Curiosity overtook her, and she did something she would never have considered in ordinary times. That is to say: in times of less certain doom.

There was a glave on the bedside table, with a black knit cover drawn down over it. Sarai directed a score of moths to it to grasp the weave with their tiny feet and shift it back just enough to uncover a slice of light. If anyone were ever to witness the moths behaving in such a coordinated way, they would have to grow suspicious that these were no natural creatures. But such a fear seemed quaint to Sarai now, compared to her other concerns. With that small task accomplished, she studied the face that was illuminated by the sliver of glave.

She beheld a young man with a crooked nose. His brows were black and heavy, his eyes deep-set. His cheeks were high and flat, and cut to his jaw with the abruptness of an ax chop. No finesse, no elegance. And the nose. It had clearly met with violence, and lent an aspect of violence to the whole. His hair was thick and dark, and where it gleamed in the glavelight the glints were warm reds, not cool blues. He was shirtless, and though mostly covered by the quilt, the arm that rested over it was corded with lean muscle. He was clean, and must just have shaved for the first time in weeks, as his jaw and chin were paler than the rest of his face and all but smooth—in that way that a man's face is never truly smooth, even right after an encounter with a perfectly sharpened razor. This Sarai knew from years of perching on sleeping faces, and not from Feral who, though he had begun to shave, could go days between with no one the wiser. Not this man. He wasn't, like Feral, *almost* all the way over the line into adulthood, but *all the way* over it: a man in no uncertain terms.

He wasn't handsome. He was certainly no museum piece. There was something of the brute about him with that broken nose, but Sarai found herself lingering longer in the appraisal of him than she had over any of the others, save the golden one. Because they were both young men, and she wasn't so immaculate as to be free of the longings that Ruby expressed so openly, nor so detached that the physical presence of young men had no effect on her. She just kept it to herself, as she kept so many things to herself.

Looking at his lashes resting closed, she wondered what color his eyes were, and experienced a pang of alienation, that it should be her lot to see and never be seen, to pass in secret through the minds of others and leave no trace of herself but fear.

She took quick stock of the sky. Better hurry. She wouldn't have time to glean much of an impression from this one, but even a hint of who he was might prove useful. A stranger in Eril-Fane's house. What did it mean?

She drifted a moth onto his brow.

And promptly fell into another world.

27

ANOTHER WORLD

Every mind is its own world. Most occupy a vast middle ground of ordinary, while others are more distinct: pleasant, even beautiful, or sometimes slippery and unaccountably wrong-feeling. Sarai couldn't even remember what her own had been like, back before she had made of it the zoo of terrors it was now—her own mind a place she was afraid to be caught out in after dark, so to speak, and had to shelter herself from by means of a drink that dulled her with its seeping gray nothing. The Godslayer's dreams were a realm of horrors, too, uniquely his own, while Suheyla's were as soft as a shawl that wraps a child against the cold. Sarai had trespassed in thousands of minds—tens of thousands—and she had sifted her invisible fingers through dreams beyond counting.

But she had never known anything like this.

She blinked and looked around.

Here was a street paved in lapis lazuli, the carved facades of buildings rising up on either side. And there were domes of gold, and the luster of the Cusp in the distance. All night long Sarai had sojourned in dreamscapes wholly alien to her. This wasn't, and yet was. She spun slowly, taking in the curious twinning of familiarity and the strange that was stranger in its way than the wholly alien had been. Clearly this was Weep, but it was not the Weep she knew. The lapis was bluer, the gold brighter, the carvings unfamiliar. The domes—of which there were hundreds instead of merely dozens—weren't quite the right shape. Nor were they of smooth gold leaf as in reality, but were patterned instead in fish-scale tiles of darker gold and brighter, so the sun didn't merely glint on them. It played. It danced.

The sun.

The sun on Weep.

There was no citadel, and no anchors. No mesarthium anywhere, and not a trace of lingering gloom or hint of bitterness. She was experiencing a version of Weep that existed only in this dreamer's mind. She couldn't know that it was born of tales told years ago by a monk slipping into senility, or that it had been fed ever since by every source Lazlo could get his hands on. That he knew everything that it was possible for an outsider to know about Weep, and *this* was the vision he'd built out of pieces. Sarai had entered into an idea of the city, and it was the most wonderful thing that she had ever seen. It danced over her senses the way the dream sun danced over the domes. Every color was deeper, richer than the real, and *there were so many of them.* If the weaver of the world itself had kept the snipped ends of every thread she'd ever used, her basket might look something like this. There were awnings over market stalls, and rows of spice shaped into cones. Rose and russet, scarlet and sienna. Old men blew colored smoke through long painted flutes, etching the air with soundless music. Saffron and vermilion, amaranth and coral. From each dome rose a needlelike spire, all of them snapping with swallowtail flags and interconnected by ribbons across which children ran laughing, clad in cloaks of colored feathers. Mulberry and citrine, celadon and chocolate. Their shadows kept pace with them down below in a way that could never happen in the true Weep, enshrouded as it was in one great shadow. The imaginary citizenry wore garments of simple loveliness, the women's hair long and trailing behind them, or else held aloft by attendant songbirds that were their own sparks of color. Dandelion and chestnut, tangerine and goldenrod.

Over the walls, vines grew, as they must have done in bygone days, before the shade. Fruits burgeoned, fat and glistening. Sunset and thistle, verdigris and violet. The air was redolent with their honey perfume and with another scent, one that transported Sarai back to childhood.

When she was small, before the pantries of the citadel kitchens were emptied of irreplaceable provisions like sugar and white flour, Great Ellen used to make them a birthday cake each year: one to share, to stretch the sugar and white flour across as many years as possible. Sarai had been eight for the last one. The five of them had savored it, made a game of eating it with excruciating slowness, knowing it was the last cake they would ever taste.

And here in this strange and lovely Weep were cakes set out on window ledges, their icing glittering with crystal sugar and flower petals, and passersby stopped to help themselves to a slice of this one or that one, and folks inside handed cups out through the windows, so that they might have something to wash it down with.

Sarai drank it all in in a daze. This was the second time tonight she had been surprised by the stark dissonance between a face and a mind. The first had been the golden faranji. However fine his face, not so his dreams. They were as cramped and airless as coffins. He could barely breathe or move in them, and neither could she. And now this.

That this rugged countenance with its air of violence should give her entrance into such a realm of wonder.

She saw spectrals parading unattended, side by side like couples out for a stroll, and other such creatures as she recognized and didn't. A ravid, its arm-long fangs festooned in beads and tassels, rose up on its hind legs to lick a cake with its long, rasping tongue. She saw a genteel centaur bearing a princess sidesaddle, and such was the atmosphere of magic that they weren't out of place here. He turned his head and the pair shared a lingering kiss that brought warmth to Sarai's cheeks. And there were small men with the feet of chickens, walking backward so their tracks would point the wrong way, and tiny old ladies racing about on saddled cats, and goat-horned boys ringing bells, and the flit and flutter of gossamer wings, and more and lovelier things everywhere she looked. She had been inside the dream for less than a minute—two mere spans of the great seraph's hand, paced forth and back—when she realized that she had a smile on her face.

A smile.

Smiles were rare enough, given the nature of her work, but on such a night as this, with such discoveries, it was unthinkable. She pushed it flat with her hand, ashamed, and paced on. So this faranji was good at dreams? So what. None of this was useful to her. Who was this dreamer? What was he doing here? Hardening herself to wonder, she looked around again and saw, up ahead, the figure of a man with long dark hair.

It was him.

This was normal. People manifest in their own dreams more often than they don't. He was walking away from her, and she willed herself nearer—no sooner wishing it than she was right behind him. This dream might be special, but it was still a dream and, as such, hers to control. She could, if she wished, vanquish all this color. She might turn it all to blood, smash the domes, send the feather-cloaked children tumbling to their deaths. She might drive that tame ravid with its tassels and beads to maul the lovely women with their long black hair. She could turn all this into nightmare. Such was her gift. Her vile, vile gift.

She did none of that. It wasn't why she'd come, for one thing, but even if it was, it was unthinkable that she should mangle this dream. It wasn't just the colors and the fairy-tale creatures, the magic. It wasn't even the cakes. There was such a feeling here of...of sweetness, and safety, and Sarai wished...

She wished it were real, and she could live in it. If ravids could walk here side by side with men and women and even share their cakes, then maybe godspawn could, too.

Real. Foolish, foolish thought. This was a stranger's mind. *Real* was the other four waiting for her in an agony of wondering. *Real* was the truth she had to tell them, and *real* was the dawn glow creeping up the horizon. It was time to go. Sarai gathered up her moths. Those perched on the knitted glave cover released it and it eased back down, swallowing the slice of light and returning the dreamer to darkness. They fluttered to the window and waited there, but the one on his brow remained. Sarai was poised, ready to withdraw it, but she hesitated. She was so many places at once. She was on the flat of the seraph's palm, barefoot, and she was hovering in the window of the Godslayer's bedroom, and she was perched, light as a petal, on the dreamer's brow.

And she was inside his dream, standing right behind him. She had an unaccountable urge to see his face, here in this place of his creation, with his eyes open.

He reached out to pluck a fruit from one of the vines.

Sarai's hand twitched at her side, wanting one, too. Wanting *five*, one for each of them. She thought of the godspawn girl who could bring things out of dreams, and wished she could return with her arms full of fruit. A cake balanced on her head. And riding the tame ravid that now had icing on its whiskers. As though, with gifts and whimsy, she might soften the blow of her news.

Some children were climbing a trellis, and they paused to toss some more fruit down to the dreamer. He caught the yellow orbs and called back, "Thank you."

The timbre of his voice sent a thrill through Sarai. It was deep, low, and raw—a voice like woodsmoke, serrated blades, and boots breaking through snow. But for all its roughness, there was the most endearing hint of shyness in it, too. "I believed it when I was a little boy," he told an old man standing nearby. "About the fruit free for the taking. But later I thought it had to be a fantasy dreamed up for hungry children."

Belatedly, it struck Sarai that he was speaking the language of Weep. All night long, in all those other strangers' dreams, she'd heard scarcely a word she could understand, but this one was speaking it without even an accent. She drifted to one side, coming around finally to get a look at him.

She went right up close, studying him—in profile— in the same shameless way that one might study a statue—or, indeed, in which a ghost might study the living. Earlier in the night, she had done the same with the golden faranji, standing right beside him while he did furious work in a laboratory of spurting flames and shattered glass. Everything had been jagged there, hot and full of peril, and it didn't matter how beautiful he was. She'd been eager to get away.

There was no peril here, or desire for escape. On the contrary, she was drawn in closer. A decade of invisibility had done away with any hesitancy she might once have felt about such flagrant staring. She saw that his eyes were gray, and that his smile wore the same hint of shyness as his voice. And yes, there was the broken line of his nose. And yes, the cut of his cheeks to his jaw was harsh. But, to her surprise, his face, awake and animate, conveyed none of the brutality that had been her first impression. On the contrary.

It was as sweet as the air in his dream.

He turned his head her way, and Sarai was so accustomed to her own acute nonbeing that it didn't even startle her. She only took it as an opportunity to see him better. She had seen so many closed eyes, and eyelids trembling with dreams, and lashes fluttering on cheeks, that she was transfixed by his open ones. They were so near. She could see, in this indulgence of sunlight, the patterns of his irises. They weren't solid gray, but filaments of a hundred different grays and blues and pearls, and they looked like reflections of light wavering on water, with the softest sunburst of amber haloing his pupils.

And…every bit as avidly as she was looking at him, he was looking at…No, not at her. He could only be looking through her. He had an air of one bewitched. There was a light in his eyes of absolute wonder. *Witchlight*, she thought, and she suffered a deep pang of envy for whoever or whatever it was behind her that enthralled him so completely. For just a moment, she let herself pretend that it was her.

That he was looking at *her* in that rapt way.

It was only pretend. An instant of self-indulgence— like a phantom that interposes itself between lovers to feel what it is to be alive. All of this happened in a flutter of seconds, three at the very most. She stood quiet inside the remarkable dream and pretended the dreamer was captivated by her. She tracked the movement of his pupils. They seemed to trace the lines of her face and the band of black she'd painted across it. They dropped, only to rise again at once from the sight of her slip-clad form and her immodest blue skin. He blushed, and sometime in those three seconds it had ceased being pretend. Sarai blushed, too. She fell back a step and the dreamer's eyes followed her.

His eyes followed her.

There was no one behind her. There was no one else at all. The whole dream shrank to a sphere around the pair of them, and there could be no question that the witchlight was for her, or that it was her he meant when he whispered, with vivid and tender enthrallment, "*Who are you?*"

Reality came slamming down. She was seen. *She was seen.* Up in the citadel Sarai jerked back. She snapped the tether of consciousness and cut the moth loose, losing the dream in an instant. All the focus she'd poured into the single sentinel was shunted back into her physical body, and she stumbled and fell, gasping, to her knees.

It was impossible. In dreams, she was a phantom. He couldn't have seen her.

Yet there was no question in her mind that he had.

* * *

Down in Weep, Lazlo woke with a start and sat up in bed just in time to witness ninety-nine smithereens of

292

darkness spook from his window ledge and burst into the air, where, with one frantic eddy, they were sucked up and out of sight.

He blinked. All was quiet and still. Dark, too. He might have doubted that he'd seen anything at all if, at that moment, the one-hundredth moth hadn't tumbled off his brow to fall dead into his lap. Gently he scooped it into his palm. It was a delicate thing, its wings furred in plush the color of twilight.

Half tangled in the remnants of his dream, Lazlo was still seeing the wide blue eyes of the beautiful blue girl, and he was frustrated to have wakened and lost her so abruptly. If he could get back to the dream, he wondered, might he find her again? He laid the dead moth on the bedside table and fell back to sleep.

And he did find the dream, but not the girl. She was gone. In those next moments the sun rose. It seeped a pallid light into the citadel's gloom and turned the moth to smoke on the table.

When Lazlo woke again, a couple of hours later, he'd forgotten them both.

28

No Way to Live

Sarai fell to her knees. All she was seeing was the pure and potent focus of the dreamer's eyes—*on her*—as Feral, Ruby, and Sparrow rushed out to her from the doorway where they'd been watching and waiting.

"Sarai! Are you all right?"

"What is it? What's wrong?"

"Sarai!"

Minya came behind them, but she didn't rush to Sarai's side. She held herself back, watching with keen interest as they took her elbows and helped her up.

Sarai saw their distress and mastered her own, pushing the dreamer from her mind—for now. *He had seen her. What could it mean?* The others were peppering her with questions—questions she couldn't answer because her moths hadn't yet come back to her. They were in the sky now, racing the rising sun. If they didn't make it back in time, she would be voiceless until dark fell and a new hundred were born in her. She didn't know why it worked that way, but it did. She clutched her throat so the others would understand, and she tried to wave them inside so they wouldn't see what happened next. She hated for anyone to see her moths come or go.

But they only drew back, apprehension on their faces, and all she could do when the moths came frothing up over the edge of the terrace was turn away to hide her face as she opened her mouth wide to let them back in.

Ninety-nine.

In her shock, she'd severed the connection and left the moth on the dreamer's brow. Her hearts gave a lurch. She reached out with her mind, fumbling for the cut tether, as though she might revive the moth and draw it back home, but it was lost to her. First she'd been seen by a human, and then she'd left a moth behind like a calling card. Was she coming undone?

How had he seen her?

She was pacing again, out of habit. The others came beside her, demanding to know what had happened. Minya still stood back, watching. Sarai reached the end of the palm, turned, and stopped. There were no railings on this terrace to prevent one from stepping off the edge. There was, instead, the subtle curve of the cupped hand—the metal flesh sloping gently upward to form a kind of great shallow bowl so that you couldn't simply walk off the edge. Even at her most distracted, Sarai's feet kept track of the slope, and knew to stay in the palm's flat center.

Now the panic of the others brought her back to herself.

"Tell us, Sarai," said Feral, holding his voice steady to show that he could take it. Ruby was on one side of him, Sparrow on the other. Sarai drank in the sight of their faces. She'd taken so little time over the past years simply to *be* with them. They lived by day and she by night, and they shared one meal in between. It was no way to live. But... it was living, and it was all they had.

In a fragile whisper, she said, "They have flying machines," and watched, desolate, as the understanding changed their three faces, bullying out the last defiant shred of hope, leaving nothing but despair.

She felt like her mother's daughter then.

Sparrow's hands flew to her mouth. "So that's it, then," said Ruby. They didn't even question it. Somehow, in the night, they'd passed through panic to defeat.

Not Minya. "Look at you all," she said, scathing. "I swear, you look ready to fall to your knees and expose your throats to them."

Sarai turned to her. Minya's excitement had brightened. It appalled her. "How can you be *happy* about this?"

"It had to happen sooner or later," was her answer. "Better to get it over with."

"Over with? What, *our lives?*"

Minya scoffed. "Only if you'd sooner die than defend yourselves. I can't stop you if you're that set on dying, but it's not what *I'll* be doing."

A silence gathered. It occurred to Sarai, and perhaps to the other three at the same time, that yesterday, when Minya had scorned their varying levels of uselessness in a fight, she had made no mention of what her own part might be. Now, in the face of their despair, she radiated eagerness. *Zeal.* It was so utterly wrong that Sarai couldn't even take it in. "What's wrong with you?" she demanded. *"Why are you so pleased?"*

"I thought you'd never ask," Minya said, with a grin that showed all her little teeth. "Come with me. I want to show you something."

* * *

The Godslayer's family home was a modest example of the traditional Weep *yeldez*, or courtyard house. From the outside, it presented a stone facade carved in a pattern of lizards and pomegranates. The door was stout, and painted green; it gave access to a passage straight through to a courtyard. This was open, and was the home's central and primary room, used for cooking, dining, gathering. Weep's mild climate meant that most living happened out of doors. It also meant that, once upon a time, the sky had been their ceiling, and now the citadel was. Only the bedrooms, water closet, and winter parlor were fully enclosed. They surrounded the courtyard in a U and opened onto it through four green doors. The kitchen was recessed into a covered alcove, and a pergola around the dining area would once have been covered with climbing vines for shade. There would have been trees, and an herb garden. Those were gone now. A scrub of pallid shrubs survived, and there were some pots of delicate forest flowers that could grow without much sun, but they were no match for the lush picture in Lazlo's mind.

When he stepped out of his room in the morning, he found Suheyla pulling a fish trap out of the well. This was less strange than it might seem, as it wasn't really a well, but a shaft cut down to the river that flowed beneath the city.

The Uzumark wasn't a single, massive subterranean channel, but an intricate network of waterways that carved their way through the valley bedrock. When the city was built, the brilliant early engineers had adapted these to a system of natural plumbing. Some streams were for freshwater, some for waste disposal. Others, larger, were glave-lit subterranean canals plied by long, narrow boats. From east to west, there was no faster way to traverse the long oval of the city than by underground boat. There was even rumor of a great buried lake, deeper than everything, in which a prehistoric svytagor was trapped by its immense size and lived like a goldfish in a bowl, feeding on eels that bred in the cool springwater. They called it the *kalisma*, which meant "eel god," as it would, to the eels, certainly seem that way.

"Good morning," said Lazlo, coming into the courtyard.

"Ah, you're up," returned Suheyla, merry. She opened the trap and the small fish flickered green and gold as she spilled them into a bucket. "Slept well, I hope?"

"Too well," he said. "And too *late*. I hate to be a layabout. I'm sorry."

"Nonsense. If ever there's a time for sleeping in, I'd say it's the morning after crossing the Elmuthaleth. And my son hasn't turned up yet, so you haven't missed anything."

Lazlo caught sight of the breakfast that was set out on the low stone table. It was almost equal to the dinner spread from the night before, which made sense, since it was Suheyla's first opportunity to feed Eril-Fane in over two years. "Can I help you?" he asked.

"Put the cover back on the well?"

He did as she asked, then followed her to the open fire, where he watched as she cleaned the fish with a few deft flicks of a knife, dunked them in oil, dredged them in spices, and laid them on the grill. He could hardly imagine her being more dexterous if she'd had two hands instead of just the one.

She saw him looking. More to the point, she saw him look away when caught looking. She held up the smooth, tapered stump of her wrist and said, "I don't mind. Have an ogle."

He blushed, abashed. "I'm sorry."

"I'm going to impose a fine on apologies," she said. "I didn't like to mention it last night, but today is your new beginning. Ten silver every time you say you're sorry."

Lazlo laughed, and had to bite his tongue before apologizing for apologizing. "It was trained into me," he said. "I'm helpless."

"I accept the challenge of retraining you. Henceforth you are only allowed to apologize if you tread on someone's foot while dancing."

"Only then? I don't even dance."

"*What?* Well, we'll work on that, too."

She flipped the fish on the grill. The smoke was fragrant with spice.

"I've spent all my life in the company of old men," Lazlo told her. "If you're hoping to make me fit for society, you'll have your hands full—"

The words were out before he could consider them. His face flamed, and it was only her holding up a warning finger that prevented him from apologizing. "Don't say it," she said. Her affect was stern but her eyes danced. "You mustn't worry about offending me, young man. I'm quite impervious. As for this..." She held up her wrist. "I almost think they did me a favor. Ten seems an excessive number of fingers to keep track of. And so many nails to pare!"

Her grin infected Lazlo, and he grinned, too. "I never thought of that. You know, there's a goddess with six arms in Maialen myth. Think of her."

"Poor dear. But then she probably has priestesses to groom her."

"That's true."

Suheyla forked the cooked fish into a dish, which she handed to him, gesturing toward the table. He carried it over and found a spot for it. Her words were stuck in his head, though: "I almost think they did me a favor." Who was *they*? "Forgive me, but—"

"Ten silver."

"What?"

"You apologized again. I warned you."

"I didn't," Lazlo argued, laughing. "'Forgive me' is a command. *I command that you forgive me.* It's not an apology at all."

"Fine," allowed Suheyla. "But next time, no qualifiers. Just ask."

"All right," said Lazlo. "But...never mind. It's none of my business."

"Just *ask.*"

"You said they did you a favor. I was just wondering who you meant."

"Ah. Well, that would be the gods."

For all the floating citadel overhead, Lazlo had as yet no clear context for what life had been under the gods. "They . . . cut off your hand?"

"I assume so," she said. "Of course I don't remember. They may have made me do it myself. All I know is I had two hands before they took me, and one after."

All of this was spoken like ordinary morning conversation. "Took you," Lazlo repeated. "Up there?"

Suheyla's brow furrowed, as though she were perplexed by his ignorance. "Hasn't he told you anything?"

He gathered that she meant Eril-Fane. "Until we stood on the Cusp yesterday, we didn't even know why we'd come."

She chuffed with surprise. "Well, aren't you the trusting things, to come all this way for a mystery."

"Nothing could have kept me from coming," Lazlo confessed. "I've been obsessed with the mystery of Weep all my life."

"Really? I had no idea the world even remembered us."

Lazlo's mouth skewed to one side. "The world doesn't really. Just me."

"Well, that shows character," said Suheyla. "And what do you think, now that you're here?" All the while she'd been chopping fruit, and she made a broad gesture with her knife. "Are you satisfied with the resolution of your mystery?"

"Resolution?" he repeated with a helpless laugh, and looked up at the citadel. "I have a hundred times more questions than I did yesterday."

Suheyla followed his glance, but no sooner did she lift her eyes than she lowered them again and shuddered. Like the Tizerkane on the Cusp, she couldn't bear the sight of it. "That's to be expected," she said, "if my son hasn't prepared you." She laid down her knife and swept the chopped fruit into a bowl, which she passed to Lazlo. "He never could talk about it." He'd started to turn away to carry the bowl to the table when she added, quietly, "They took him longer than anyone, you know."

He turned back to her. No, he really did *not* know. He wasn't sure how to form his thoughts into a question, and before he could, Suheyla, busying herself wiping up the cutting board, went on in the same quiet way.

"Mostly they took girls," she said. "Raising a daughter in Weep—and, well, *being* a daughter in Weep—was...very hard in those years. Every time the ground shook, you knew it was Skathis, coming to your door." *Skathis.* Ruza had said that name. "But sometimes they took our sons, too." She scooped tea into a strainer.

"They took *children*?"

"One's child is always one's child, of course, but technically—or, physically, at least—he waited until they were...of age."

Of age.

Those words. Lazlo swallowed a rising sensation of nausea. Those words were like . . . they were like seeing a bloody knife. You didn't need to have witnessed the stabbing to understand what it meant.

"I worried for Azareen more than for Eril-Fane. For her, it was only a matter of time. They knew it, of course. That's why they married so young. She . . . she said she wanted to be his before she was theirs. And she was. For five days. But it wasn't her they took. It was him. Well. They got her later."

This was . . . it was unspeakable, all of it. Azareen. Eril-Fane. The routine nature of atrocity. But . . . "They're *married*?" was what Lazlo asked.

"Oh." Suheyla looked rueful. "You didn't know. Well, no secret's safe with me, is it?"

"But why should it be a secret?"

"It's not that it's a secret," she said carefully. "It's more that it's . . . not a marriage anymore. Not after . . ." She tipped her head up toward the citadel without looking at it.

Lazlo didn't ask any more questions. Everything he'd wondered about Eril-Fane and Azareen had taken on a much darker cast than he could ever have imagined, and so had the mysteries of Weep.

"We were taken up to 'serve,'" Suheyla went on, her pronoun shift reminding him that she had herself been one of these taken girls. "That's what Skathis called

304

it. He would come to the door, or the window." Her hand trembled, and she clasped it tight over her stump. "They hadn't brought any servants with them, so there *was* that. Serving at table, or in the kitchens. And there were chambermaids, gardeners, laundresses."

In this litany, it was somehow very clear that these jobs, they were the exceptions, and that "service" had mostly been of another kind.

"Of course, we didn't know any of this until later. When they brought us back—and they didn't always, but usually, and usually within a year—we wouldn't remember a thing. Gone for a year, a year gone from us." She dropped her stump, and her hand fluttered briefly to her belly. "It was as though no time had passed. Letha would eat our memories, you see." She looked up at Lazlo then. "She was the goddess of oblivion."

It made sense now—horrible sense—why Suheyla didn't know what had become of her own hand.

"And...Eril-Fane?" he asked, steeling himself.

Suheyla looked back down at the teapot she was filling with steaming water from the kettle. "Oblivion was a mercy, it turns out. He remembers everything. Because he slew them, and there was no one left to take his memories away."

Lazlo understood what she was telling him, what she was saying without saying it, but it didn't seem possible. Not Eril-Fane, who was power incarnate. He was a liberator, not a slave.

"Three years," said Suheyla. "That's how long she had him. Isagol. Goddess of despair." Her eyes lost focus. She seemed to slip into some great hollow place within her, and her voice sank to a whisper. "But then, if they'd never taken him, we would all of us still be slaves."

For that brief moment, Lazlo felt a tremor of the quaking grief within her: that she had not been able to keep her child safe. That was a simple and profound grief, but under it was a deeper, stranger one: that in some way she had to be *glad* of it, because if she *had* kept him safe, he couldn't have saved his people. It mixed up gladness, grief, and guilt into an intolerable brew.

"I'm so sorry," said Lazlo, from the depths of both his hearts.

Suheyla snapped out of whatever faraway, hollow place she was lost in. Her eyes sharpened back to smiling squints. "Ha," she said. "Ten silver please." And she held out her palm until he put the coin in it.

29

THE OTHER BABIES

Minya led Sarai and the others back inside, through Sarai's chambers, and back up the corridor. All of their rooms were on the dexter side of the citadel. Sarai's suite was at the extremity of the seraph's right arm, and the others' were along that same passage, except for Minya's. What had been Skathis's palace occupied the entire right shoulder. They passed it, and the entrance to the gallery, too, and Sarai and Feral exchanged a glance.

The doors that led up or down, into the head or body of the citadel, were all closed, just as they had been when Skathis died. It wasn't even possible to discern where they had been.

The sinister arm—as it was called—was passable, though they rarely went there. It held the nursery, and none of them could bear the sight of the empty cribs, even if the blood was long since washed away. There were a lot of small cell-like rooms beyond with nothing but beds in them. Sarai knew what those were. She'd seen them in dreams, but only the dreams of the girls who'd occupied them last—like Azareen— whose memories had outlived Letha. Sarai could think of no reason that Minya would take them there.

"Where are we going?" Feral asked.

Minya didn't reply, but they had their answer in the next moment when she didn't turn toward the sinister arm, but toward another place they never went— if for different reasons.

"The heart," said Ruby.

"But..." said Sparrow, then cut herself off with a look of realization.

Sarai could guess both what she'd almost said and what had stopped her, because they had occurred to her at the same moment as Sparrow. *But we can't fit anymore.* That was the thought. *But Minya can.* That was the realization. And Sarai knew then where Minya had been spending her time when the rest of them lost track of her. If they'd really wanted to know, they might have figured it out easily enough, but the truth was they'd just been glad she was elsewhere, so they'd never bothered to look for her.

They rounded a corner and came to the door.

It couldn't properly be called a door anymore. It was less than a foot wide: a tall, straight gap in the metal where, near as they could guess, a door hadn't quite finished closing when Skathis died. By its height, which was some twenty feet, it was clear that it had been no ordinary door, though there was no way to gauge what its width might have been when open.

Minya barely fit through it. She had to ease one shoulder in, then her face. It seemed for a moment that her ears would hang her up, but she pressed on and they were forced flat, and she had to work her head side to side to get it through, then exhale fully to narrow her chest enough for the rest of her body to pass. It was a near thing. Any bigger and she couldn't have made it.

"Minya, you know we can't get in," Sparrow called after her as she disappeared into the corridor on the other side.

"Wait there," she called back, and was gone.

They all looked at one another. "What could she want to show us here?" Sarai asked.

"Could she have found something in the heart?" Feral wondered.

"If there was anything to find we'd have found it years ago."

Once, they'd all been small enough to get in. "How long has it been?" Feral asked, running his hand over the sleek edge of the opening.

"Longer for you than for us," said Sparrow.

"That big head of yours," added Ruby, giving him a little shove.

Feral had outgrown it first, then Sarai, and the girls a year or so later. Minya obviously never had. When they were all small, it had been their favorite place to play, partly because the narrow opening made it feel forbidden, and partly because it was so strange.

It was an enormous, echoing chamber, perfectly spherical, all smooth, curved metal, with a narrow walkway wrapping around its circumference. In diameter it was perhaps one hundred feet, and, suspended in its dead center was a smaller sphere of perhaps twenty feet diameter. That, too, was perfectly smooth, and, like the entirety of the citadel, it floated, held in place not by ropes or chains but some unfathomable force. The chamber occupied the place where hearts would go in a true body, so that was what they called it, but that was just their own term. They had no idea what its name or purpose had been. Even Great Ellen didn't know. It was just a big metal ball floating in a bigger metal room.

Oh, and there were monsters perched on the walls. Two of them.

Sarai knew the beasts of the anchors, Rasalas and the others. She had seen them with her moths' eyes, inert as they were now, but she had also seen them as they were before, through the dreams of the people of Weep. She had, in her arsenal, a seemingly infinite number of visions of Skathis mounted on Rasalas, carrying off young women and men no older than she was now. It had been her go-to terror, Weep's worst collective memory, and she shuddered now to think how blithely she had inflicted it, not understanding, as a child, what it had meant. And the beasts of the anchors were big, make no mistake. But the monsters perched like statues on the walls of the citadel's heart were bigger.

They were wasplike, thorax and abdomen joined in narrow waists, wings like blades, and stingers longer than a child's arm. Sarai and the others had climbed on them when they were children, and "ridden" them and pretended they were real, but if, in the reign of the gods, they had been anything more than statues, Sarai had no visions to attest to it. These monsters, she was fairly sure, had never left the citadel. By their size, it was hard to imagine them even leaving this room.

"Here she comes," said Ruby, who'd been peering through the opening at the dark corridor beyond. She stepped out of the way, but the figure that emerged was not Minya. It didn't have to pause and carefully fit any flesh-on-skeleton mass through the gap, but flowed out with the ease of a ghost, which was what it was.

It was Ari-Eil. He glided past them without turning his head, and was followed immediately by another ghost. Sarai blinked. This one was familiar, but she couldn't immediately place him, and then he was past and she had no time to search her memory because another was coming after him.

And another.

And another.

...*So many?*

Ghosts poured out of the citadel's heart, one after the next, passing the four of them without acknowledgment to continue right on by, up the long doorless corridor that led toward the gallery and the garden terrace and their bedchambers. Sarai found herself flattened against the wall, trying to make sense of the flow of faces, and they were all familiar but not as familiar as they would be if she had seen them recently.

Which she had not.

She picked out a face, then another. They were men, women, and children, though most were old. Names began to come to her. Thann, priestess of Thakra. Mazli, dead in childbirth with twins who died, too. Guldan, the tattoo master. The old woman had been famous in the city for inking the most beautiful elilith. All the girls had wanted her to do theirs. Sarai couldn't remember exactly when she had passed away, but it was certainly before her own first bleeding, because her reaction to discovering the old woman's death had been so foolish. It had been *disappointment*—that Guldan wouldn't be able to do *her* elilith, when her time came. As though such a thing could ever have come to pass. What had she been, twelve? Thirteen? Behind her closed eyelids, she had imagined the skin of her tummy brown instead of blue, decorated with the old woman's exquisite flourishes. And oh, the hot flush of shame that chased that picture. To have forgotten, even for an instant, what she was.

As though a human would ever touch her for any reason other than to kill her.

At least four years had passed since then. *Four years.* So how could Guldan be here now? It was the same with the others. And there were *so many of them.* They all stared straight ahead, expressionless, but Sarai caught the desperate plea in more than a few eyes as they flowed past her. They moved with ghostly ease, but also with a severe, martial intent. They moved like soldiers.

Understanding came slowly and then all at once. Sarai's hands flew to her mouth. Both hands, as though to hold in a wail. All this time. How was it possible? Tears sprang to her eyes. So many. So terribly many.

All, she thought. Every man, woman, and child who had died in Weep since...since when?...and passed near enough the citadel in their evanescent journey for Minya to catch. It had been ten years since Sparrow and Ruby outgrew the entrance to the heart. Was that when she had begun this...*collection*?

"Oh, Minya," Sarai breathed from the depths of her horror.

Her mind sought some other explanation but there was none. There was only this: For years, unbeknownst to the rest of them, Minya had been catching ghosts and...keeping them. *Storing* them. The heart of the citadel, that great spherical chamber where only Minya could still go, had served, all this time, as a...a vault. A closet. A lockbox.

For an army of the dead.

* * *

Finally, Minya emerged, easing herself slowly through the gap to stand defiant before Sarai and Feral, Sparrow and Ruby, all of whom were stunned into speechlessness. The procession of ghosts vanished around the corner.

"Oh, Minya," said Sarai. "What have you done?"

"What do you mean, *what have I done*? Don't you see? We're safe. Let the Godslayer come, and all his new friends, too. I'll teach *them* the meaning of 'carnage.'"

Sarai felt the blood leave her face. Did she think they didn't know it already? "You of all people should have had enough carnage in your life."

Minya eternal, Minya unchanging. Evenly, she met Sarai's gaze. "You're wrong," she said. "I'll have had enough *when I've paid it all back*."

A tremor went through Sarai. Could this be a nightmare? A waking one, maybe. Her mind had finally broken and all the terrors were pouring out.

But no. This was real. Minya was going to force a decade's worth of the city's dead to fight and kill their own kith and kin. It hit her with a wave of nausea that she had been wrong, all these years, to hide her empathy for humans and all that they'd endured. She'd been ashamed at first, and afraid that it was weakness on her part, to be unable to hate them as she should. She would imagine words coming out of her mouth, like *They're not monsters, you know*, and she would imagine, too, what Minya's response would be: *Tell that to the other babies.*

The other babies.

That was all she ever had to say. Nothing could trump the Carnage. Arguing for any redeeming quality in the people who had committed it was a kind of rank treason. But now Sarai thought she might have tried. In her cowardice, she had let the others go on with this simplicity of conviction: They had an enemy. They *were* an enemy. The world was carnage. You either suffered it or inflicted it. If she had told them what she saw in the warped memories of Weep, and what she felt and heard—the heartbreaking sobbing of fathers who couldn't protect their daughters, the horror of girls returned with blank memories and violated bodies—maybe they would have seen that the humans were survivors, too.

"There has to be some other way," she said now.

"What if there was?" challenged Minya, cool. "What if there was another way, but you were too pathetic to do it?"

315

Sarai bristled at the insult, and shrank from it, too. Too pathetic to do *what*? She didn't want to know, but she had to ask. "What are you talking about?"

Minya considered her, then shook her head. "No, I'm sure of it. You are too pathetic. You'd let us die first."

"*What*, Minya?" Sarai demanded.

"Well, you're the only one of us who can reach the city," said the little girl. She really was a pretty child, but it was hard to see it—not so much because she was unkempt, but because of the queer, cold *lack* in her eyes. Had she always been like that? Sarai remembered laughing with her, long ago, when they had all properly been children, and she didn't think she had been. When had she changed and become...*this*? "You couldn't manage to drive the Godslayer mad," she was saying.

"He's too strong," Sarai protested. Even now she couldn't bring herself to suggest—even to herself, really—that perhaps he didn't deserve madness.

"Oh, he's strong," agreed Minya, "but I daresay even the great Godslayer couldn't manage to breathe if a hundred moths flew down his throat."

If a hundred moths flew down his...

Sarai could only stare at her. Minya laughed at her blank shock. Did she understand what she was saying? Of course she did. She just didn't care. The moths weren't...they weren't scraps of rag. They weren't

316

even trained insects. They were *Sarai*. They were her own consciousness spun out from her on long, invisible strings. What they experienced, she experienced, be it the heat of a sleeper's brow or the red wet clog of a choking man's throat. "And in the morning," Minya went on, "when he's found dead in his bed, the moths will have turned to smoke, and no one will even know what killed him."

She was triumphant—a child pleased with a clever plan. "You could only kill one person a night, I suppose. Maybe two. I wonder how many moths it would take to suffocate someone." She shrugged. "Anyway, once a few faranji die without explanation, I think the others will lose heart." She smiled, cocked her head. "Well, was I right? Are you too pathetic? Or can you endure a few minutes of disgust to save us all?"

Sarai opened her mouth and closed it. A few minutes of disgust? How trivial she made it sound. "It's not about disgust," she said. "God forbid a strong stomach should be all that stands between killing and not. There's *decency*, Minya. *Mercy*."

"Decency," spat the girl. "*Mercy*."

The way she said it. The word had no place in the citadel of the Mesarthim. Her eyes darkened as though her pupils had engulfed her irises, and Sarai felt it coming, the response that brooked no comeback: *Tell that to the other babies.*

But that wasn't what she said. "You make me sick,

Sarai. You're so soft." And then she spoke words that she never had, not in all these fifteen years. In a low and deadly hiss, she said, "*I should have saved a different baby.*" And then she spun on her heel and stalked out behind her terrible, heartbreaking army.

Sarai felt slapped. Ruby, Sparrow, and Feral surrounded her. "I'm glad she saved you," said Sparrow, stroking her arms and hair.

"Me too," echoed Ruby.

But Sarai was imagining a nursery full of godspawn—kindred little girls and boys with blue skin and magic yet unguessed—and humans in their midst with kitchen knives. Somehow, Minya had hidden the four of them away. Sarai had always felt the narrow stroke of luck—like an ax blow passing close enough to shave the tips from the down of her cheek—that Minya had saved *her*. That *she* had survived instead of one of the others.

And once upon a time, survival had seemed like an end unto itself. But now...it began to feel like an expedient with no object.

Survive *for what*?

🌿 30 🌿

STOLEN NAME, STOLEN SKY

Lazlo didn't stay at Suheyla's house for breakfast. He thought that mother and son might like some time alone after two years' separation. He waited to greet Eril-Fane—and tried hard to keep his new knowledge quiet in his eyes when he did. It was hard; his horror seemed to shout inside of him. Everything about the hero looked different now that he knew even this small sliver of what he had endured.

He saddled Lixxa and rode through Weep, getting quite agreeably lost. "You look well rested," he told Calixte, who was eating in the dining room of the guildhall when he finally found it.

"You don't," she returned. "Did you forget to sleep?"

"How dare you," he said mildly, taking a seat at her

table. "Are you suggesting that I look less than perfectly fresh?"

"I would never be so uncivil as to suggest imperfect freshness." She took a large bite of pastry. "However," she said with her mouth full, "you're cultivating patches of blue under your eyes. So unless you got yourself punched very symmetrically, my guess is not enough sleep. Besides, with the state of ecstatic dazzlement you were in yesterday, I didn't expect you'd be able to sit still, let alone sleep."

"First of all: Who would want to punch me? Second of all: *ecstatic dazzlement*. Nicely put."

"First of all: Thank you. Second of all: Thyon Nero would love to punch you."

"Oh, *him*," said Lazlo. It might have been meant as a joke, but the golden godson's animosity was palpable. The others felt it, even if they had no clue as to what was behind it. "I think he's the only one, though."

Calixte sighed. "So naïve, Strange. If they didn't before, they *all* want to punch you over the theory purse. Drave especially. You should hear him rant. He put way too much into it, the fool. I think he thought it was a lottery, and if he made more guesses he'd be likelier to win. Whereas you make one—a *ridiculous* one— and win. I'm amazed he hasn't punched you already."

"Thakra save me from the theory purse," said Lazlo, blithely invoking the local deity, Thakra. She had been commander of the six seraphim, according

320

to legend—and holy book—and her temple stood just across a broad boulevard from the guildhall.

"Save you from five hundred silver?" queried Calixte. "I think I could help you out there."

"Thanks, I think I'll manage," said Lazlo, who in truth had no idea where to begin with so much money. "More like save me from bitter explosionists and grudging alchemists."

"I will. Don't worry. It's my fault, and I take full responsibility for you."

Lazlo laughed. Calixte was as slim as a hreshtek, but far less dangerous-looking than one. Still, he didn't mistake her for harmless, whereas he knew *he* was, Ruza's spear-throwing lessons notwithstanding. "Thank you. If I'm attacked, I'll scream hysterically and you can come save me."

"I'll send Tzara," said Calixte. "She's magnificent when she fights." She added, with a secret smile, "Though she's even more magnificent doing other things."

Calixte had not been wrong in calling Lazlo naïve, but even as remote as such things as lovers were to him, he understood the smile, and the warm tone of her voice. Heat rose to his cheeks—much to her delight. "Strange, you're *blushing*."

"Of course I am," he admitted. "I'm a perfect innocent. I'd blush at the sight of a woman's collarbones."

As he said that, an almost-memory tickled his mind. A woman's collarbones, and the wonderful space between them. But where would he have seen...? And then Calixte yanked her blouse askew to reveal *hers*—her collarbones, that is—and he laughed and lost the memory.

"Nice job denuding your face, by the way," she said, waggling her fingers under her chin to indicate his shave. "I'd forgotten what it looked like under there."

He grimaced. "Oh. Well, I'm sorry to have to remind you, but it itched."

"What are you talking about, sorry? You have an excellent face," she said, examining him. "It isn't *pretty,* but there are other ways for a face to be excellent."

He touched the sharp angle of his nose. "I do have a face," was about as far as he was willing to go.

"Lazlo," called Eril-Fane from across the room. "Gather everyone, will you?"

Lazlo nodded and rose. "Consider yourself gathered," he informed Calixte, before going in search of the rest of the team.

"Scream if you need saving," she called after him.

"Always."

* * *

The time had come to discuss Weep's "problem" in earnest. Lazlo knew some of it already from Ruza and Suheyla, but the others were hearing it for the first time.

"Our hope in bringing you here," Eril-Fane said,

addressing them in a beautiful salon of the guildhall, "is that you will find a way to free us of the thing in our sky." He looked from one face to the next, and Lazlo was reminded of that day in the theater back at the Great Library, when the Godslayer's gaze had fallen on him, and his dream had taken on this new clarity: not merely to *see* the Unseen City, but to *help*.

"Once, we were a city of learning," said Eril-Fane. "Our ancestors would never have had to seek outsiders for help." He said this with a tinge of shame. "But that's in the past. The Mesarthim, they were... remarkable. God or other, they might have nurtured our awe into reverence and won themselves true worship. But nurture was not their way. They didn't come to offer themselves as a choice, or to win our hearts. They came to rule, totally and brutally, and the first thing they did was break us.

"Before they even showed themselves, they released the anchors. You'll have seen them. They didn't *drop* them. The impact would have knocked down every structure in the city and collapsed the underground waterways, damming the Uzumark that flows under our feet, and flooding the whole valley. They wanted to rule us, not destroy us, and to enslave us, not massacre us, so they set the anchors down deliberately, and crushed only what was beneath them, which happened to include the university and library, the Tizerkane garrison, and the royal palace."

Eril-Fane had mentioned the library before. Lazlo wondered about it, and what precious texts had been lost in it. Might there even have been histories from the time of the ijji and the seraphim?

"It was all terribly tidy. Army, wisdom-keepers, and royal family, obliterated in minutes. Any who escaped were found in the days after. The Mesarthim, they knew all. No secret could be kept from them. And that was all there was to it. They didn't need soldiers, when they had their magic to..." He paused, his jaw clenching. "To control us. And so our learning was lost, along with our leadership, and so much else. A chain of knowledge handed down over centuries, and a library to shame even your great Zosma." Here he smiled faintly at Lazlo. "Gone in a moment. Ended. In the years that followed, pursuit of knowledge was punished. All science and inquiry were dead. Which brings us to you," he told the delegates. "I hope I've chosen well."

Now, finally, their varied areas of expertise made sense. Mouzaive, the natural philosopher: for the mystery of the citadel's suspension. How was it floating? Soulzeren and Ozwin for reaching it in their silk sleighs. The engineers for designing any structures that might be needed. Belabra for calculations. The Fellering twins and Thyon for the metal itself.

Mesarthium. Eril-Fane explained its properties to them—its imperviousness to everything, all heat, all tools. Everything, that is, except for Skathis, who had manipulated it with his mind.

"Skathis controlled mesarthium," he told them, "and so he controlled...everything."

Magical metal telepathically smithed by a god and impervious to all else. Lazlo watched the delegates' reactions, and he could understand their incredulity, certainly, but there *was* a rather large inducement here to believe the unbelievable. He'd have thought that knee-jerk skepticism would have been knuckled under by the sight of the enormous floating seraph in the sky.

"It can certainly be cut," asserted one of the Fellerings. "With the right instruments and know-how."

"Or melted, with sufficient heat," added the other, with a confidence that shaded into arrogance. "The temperatures that we can reach with our furnaces will easily double what your blacksmiths can achieve."

Thyon, for his part, volunteered nothing, and there was more arrogance in his silence than in the Fellerings' bluster. His invitation to the delegation was clearer now, too. Azoth wasn't only a medium for making gold, after all. It also yielded alkahest, the universal solvent—an agent that could eat through any substance in the world: glass, stone, metal, even diamond. Would mesarthium yield to it as well?

If so, then he might well be Weep's second liberator. What a fine accolade for his legend, Lazlo thought with a twinge of bitterness: Thyon Nero, deliverer from shadow.

"Why don't we go over," suggested Eril-Fane, faced with the incredulity of his guests. "I'll introduce you to mesarthium. It's as good a starting point as any."

* * *

The north anchor was closest, near enough to walk—and the trip took them across the strip of light called the Avenue, though it wasn't an avenue. It was the one place where sunlight fell on the city, down through the gap where the seraph's wings came together in front and didn't quite meet.

It was broad as a boulevard, and it almost seemed, crossing it, as though one went from dusk to day and back again in a matter of paces. It ran half the length of the city and had become its most coveted real estate, never mind that much of it fell in humbler neighbor-hoods. There was light, and that was everything. In this single sun-drunk stripe, Weep was as lush as Lazlo had always imagined it to be, and the rest of the city looked more dead for the contrast.

The wings hadn't always been outspread as they were now, Eril-Fane told Lazlo. "It was Skathis's dying act—to steal the sky, as though he hadn't stolen enough already." He looked up at the citadel, but not for long.

And it wasn't only the sky that had been stolen that day, Lazlo learned, finding out, finally, the answer to the question that had haunted him since he was a little boy.

What power can annihilate a name?

"It was Letha," Eril-Fane told him. Lazlo knew the name already: goddess of oblivion, mistress of forgetting. "She ate it," Eril-Fane said. "Swallowed it as she died, and it died with her."

"Couldn't you rename it?" Lazlo asked him.

"You think we haven't tried? The curse is more powerful than that. Every name we give it suffers the same fate as the first. Only Weep remains."

Stolen name, stolen sky. Stolen children, stolen years. What had the Mesarthim been, Lazlo thought, but thieves on an epic scale.

The anchor dominated the landscape, a great mass hulking behind the silhouettes of the overlapping domes. It made everything else seem small, like a half-scale play village built for children. And up on top was one of the statues Lazlo couldn't clearly make out, besides the fact of it being bestial—horned and winged. He saw Eril-Fane look at it, too, and shudder again and skew his gaze away.

They approached the forbidding wall of blue metal, and their reflections stepped forward to meet them. There was something about it, up close—the sheer volume of metal, the sheen of it, the color, some indefinable strangeness—that cast a hush over the lot of them as they reached out with varying degrees of caution to touch it.

The Fellerings had brought a case of instruments, and they set to work at once. Thyon went far from the others to examine it in his own way, with Drave tagging along, offering to carry his satchel.

"It's slick," said Calixte, running her hands over its surface. "It feels wet, but it isn't."

"You'll never climb up this," said Ebliz Tod, touching it, too.

"Care to place a wager?" she countered, the gleam of challenge in her eyes.

"A hundred silver."

Calixte scoffed. "*Silver.* How boring."

"You know how we settle disputes in Thanagost?" asked Soulzeren. "Poison roulette. Pour a row of shot glasses and mix serpaise venom into one of them. You find out you lost when you die gasping."

"You're mad," said Calixte admiringly. She considered Tod. "I think Eril-Fane might want him alive, though."

"*Might?*" Tod bristled. "You're the expendable one."

"Aren't you nasty," she said. "I'll tell you what. If I win, you have to build me a tower."

He laughed out loud. "I build towers for kings, not little girls."

"You build towers for the *corpses* of kings," she

328

replied. "And if you're so sure I can't do it, where's the risk? I'm not asking for a Cloudspire. It can be a small one. I won't need a tomb anyway. Much as I deserve eternal veneration, I intend never to die."

"Good luck with that," said Tod. "And if I win?"

"Mm," she pondered, tapping her chin. "What do you say to an emerald?"

He studied her flatly. "You didn't get away with any emeralds."

"Oh, you're probably right." She grinned. "What would *I* know about it?"

"Show me, then."

"If I lose, I will. But if I win, you'll just have to wonder if I really have it or not."

Tod considered for a moment, his face sour and calculating. "With no rope," he stipulated.

"With no rope," she agreed.

He touched the metal again, gauging its slickness. It must have reinforced his certainty that it was unclimbable, because he accepted Calixte's terms. A tower against an emerald. Fair wager.

Lazlo walked down to where the wall was clear, and skimmed his own hand along the surface. As Calixte had said, it was slick, not merely smooth. It was hard and cool as one would expect of metal in the shade, and his skin slipped right over it without any kind of friction. He rubbed his fingertips together and continued the length of the anchor. Mesarthium,

Mesarthim. Magical metal, magical gods. Where had they come from?

The same place as the seraphim? "They came down from the skies," went the myth—or the *history*, if indeed it was all true. And where from before that? What was behind the sky?

Had they come out of the great star-scattered black entirety that was the universe?

The "mysteries of Weep" weren't mysteries *of Weep*, Lazlo thought. They were much bigger than this place. Bigger than the world.

Reaching the corner of the anchor, he peered around it and saw a narrow alley that dissolved into rubble. He ventured down it, still trailing his hand over the mesarthium. Glancing at his fingertips, he saw that they were grimed a pale gray. He wiped them on his shirt, but it didn't come off.

Opposite the metal wall was a row of ruined houses, still standing as they had before the anchor but with whole sides carved away, like dolls' houses, open on one side. They were decrepit dolls' houses, though. He could see right into old parlors and kitchens, and imagined the people who had lived in them the day their world changed.

Lazlo wondered what lay beneath this anchor. The library? The palace or garrison? The crushed bones of kings or warriors or wisdom keepers? Was it possible that any texts had survived intact?

His eye caught on a patch of color ahead. It was on a forlorn stone wall facing the mesarthium one, and the alley was too narrow for Lazlo to get an angle on it from a distance. Only as he approached could he decipher that it was a painting, and only once he was before it, what it depicted.

He looked at it. He looked. Shock generally hits like a blow, sudden and unexpected. But in this case it crept over him slowly, as he made sense of the image and remembered what he had, until right now, forgotten.

It could only be a rendering of the Mesarthim. There were six of them: three females on one side, three males on the other. All were dead or dying—skewered or laid open or sundered. And between them, unmistakable, larger-than-life, and with six arms to hold six weapons, was the Godslayer. The rendering was crude. Whoever had made the picture was no trained artist, but there was a rough intensity in it that was very powerful. This was a painting of victory. It was brutal, bloody, and triumphant.

The cause of Lazlo's shock wasn't the violence of it—the spurting blood or the liberal quantities of red paint used to illustrate it. It wasn't the *red* paint that got him, but the *blue*.

In all the talk of the Mesarthim so far, no one had seen fit to mention that—if this mural was accurate—they had been *blue*. Just like their metal.

And just like the girl in Lazlo's dream.

How could he have forgotten her? It was as though she'd slipped behind a curtain in his mind and the moment he saw the mural, the curtain fell and she was there: the girl with skin the color of the sky, who had stood so close, studying him as though *he* were a painting. Even the collarbones were hers—the little tickle at his memory, from when he'd glanced down in the dream and blushed to see more of female anatomy than he ever had in real life. What did it say about him that he had dreamed a girl in her underclothes?

But that was neither here nor there. Here she was, in the mural. Crude as it was, capturing none of her loveliness, it was an unmistakable likeness, from her hair—the rich dark red of wildflower honey—to the stark black band painted across her eyes like a mask. Unlike the girl in his dream, though, this one was wearing a gown.

Also...her throat was gaping open and gushing red.

He took a step back, feeling nauseated, almost as though he were seeing a real body and not the cartoonish depiction of a murdered girl he'd glimpsed in a dream.

"All right down there?"

Lazlo looked around. It was Eril-Fane at the top of the alley. Two arms, not six. Two swords, and not a personal armory of spears and halberds. This picture, crude and gory, added yet another dimension to Lazlo's idea of him. The Godslayer had slain gods. Well, of course. But Lazlo had never really formed an image to go along with the idea before, or if he had, it had been vague, and the victims monstrous. Not wide-eyed and barefoot, like the girl in his dream.

"Is this what they looked like?" he asked.

Eril-Fane came to see. His steps slowed as he made out what the mural depicted. He only nodded, never taking his eyes from it.

"They were blue," said Lazlo.

Again, Eril-Fane nodded.

Lazlo stared at the goddess with the painted black mask, and imagined, interposed over her crudely drawn features, the very fine ones he'd seen last night. "Who is she?"

Eril-Fane was a moment answering, and his voice, when he did, was raw and almost too low to hear. "That is Isagol. Goddess of despair."

So this was her, the monster who had kept him for three years in the citadel. There was so much feeling in the way he said her name, and it was hard to read because it wasn't...pure. It *was* hate, but there was grief and shame mixed up in it, too. Lazlo tried to get a look at his face, but he was already walking away. Lazlo watched him go, and he took one last look at the haunting picture before following him. He stared at the daubs and streaks and runnels of red, and this newest mystery, it wasn't a pathway of light burning lines through his mind. It was more like bloody footprints leading into the dark.

How was it possible, he wondered, that he had dreamed the slain goddess before he had any way of knowing what she looked like?

🌿 31 🌿

DARLINGS AND VIPERS

From the heart of the citadel, Sarai returned to her room. Minya's "soldiers" were everywhere, armed with knives and other kitchen tools. Cleavers, ice picks. They'd even taken the meat hooks from the rain room. Somewhere there was an actual arsenal, but it was closed off behind successions of sealed mesarthium doors, and anyway, Minya thought knives appropriate tools for butchery. They were, after all, what the humans had used in the nursery.

There was no escaping the army, especially not for Sarai, since her room gave onto the sunstruck silver-blue palm of the seraph. The ghosts were thickest there, and it made sense. The terrace was the perfect place for a craft to land, much better than the garden with its trees and vines. When the Godslayer came, he would come *here*, and Sarai would be the first to die.

Should she be grateful, then, to Minya, for this protection? "Don't you see?" Minya had said, revealing her army to them. "We're safe!"

But Sarai had never felt *less* safe. Her room was violated by captive ghosts, and she feared that what awaited her in sleep was worse. Her tray was at the foot of her bed: lull and plums, just like any morning, though usually by this time she'd be deep asleep and lost in Letha's oblivion. Would the lull work today? There was an extra half dose, as Great Ellen had promised. Had it only been a fluke yesterday? Sarai wondered. *Please*, she thought, desperate for the bleak velvet of its nothingness. Terrors stirred within her, and she imagined she could hear a din of helpless screaming in the heads of all the ghosts. She wanted to scream, too. There *was* no feeling of safety, she thought, hugging a pillow to her chest.

Her mind offered up an unlikely exception.

The faranji's dream. She had felt safe there.

The memory kicked up a desperate fizz of ... panic? Thrill? Whatever it was, it contradicted the very feeling of safety that had conjured the thought of him to start with. Yes, the dream had been sweet. But ... *he had seen her.*

The look on his face! The wonder in it, the witchlight. Her hearts raced at the thought, and her palms went clammy. It was no small thing to shed a lifetime of nonbeing and suddenly be *seen*.

Who was he, anyway? Of all the faranji's dreams, only his had given her no hint of why Eril-Fane might have brought him here.

Exhausted, fearful, Sarai drank down her lull and laid herself on her bed. *Please*, she thought, fervent—a kind of prayer to the bitter brew itself. *Please work.*

Please keep the nightmares away.

✳ ✳ ✳

Out in her garden, Sparrow kept her eyes down. As long as she fixed on leaves and blossoms, stems and seeds, she could pretend it was a normal day, and there weren't ghosts standing guard under the arches of the arcade.

She was making a birthday present for Ruby, who would be sixteen in a few months...if they were still alive by then.

Considering Minya's army, Sparrow thought their chances were good, but she didn't want to consider Minya's army. They made her feel safe and wretched at the same time, so she kept her eyes down and hummed, and tried to forget they were there.

Another birthday to celebrate without cake. The options for presents were slim, too. Usually they unmade some hideous gown from their dressing rooms and turned it into something else. A scarf maybe. One year Sparrow had made a doll with real rubies for eyes.

Her room had been Korako's, so she had all her gowns and jewels to make use of, while Ruby had Letha's. The goddesses weren't their mothers, as Isagol was Sarai's. They were both of them daughters of Ikirok, god of revelry, who had also served as executioner in his spare time. So they were half sisters, and the only ones of the five related by blood. Feral was the son of Vanth, god of storms—whose gift he had more or less inherited—and Minya was daughter of Skathis. Sarai was the only one whose Mesarthim blood came from the maternal side. Goddess births, according to Great Ellen, had been rare. A woman, of course, could make but one baby at a time, occasionally two. But a man could make as many as there were women to seed them in.

By far, most of the babies in the nursery had been sired on human girls by the trinity of gods.

Which meant that, somewhere down in Weep, Sparrow had a mother.

When she was little, she'd been slow to understand or believe that her mother wouldn't want her. "I could help her in the garden," she'd told Great Ellen. "I could be a really big help, I know I could."

"I know you could, too, love," Great Ellen had said. "But we need you here, pet. How could we live without you?"

She had tried to be gentle, but Minya had suffered no such compunction. "If they found *you* in their

338

garden, they'd bash your head in with the shovel and throw you out with the garbage. You're *godspawn*, Sparrow. They'll *never* want you."

"But I'm human, too," she'd insisted. "Can they have forgotten that? That we're their children, too?"

"Don't you see? They hate us *more* because we're theirs."

And Sparrow *hadn't* seen, not then, but eventually she learned—from a crude and unbelievable assertion of Minya's, followed by a gentle and eye-opening explanation of Great Ellen's—the... *mechanics of begetting*, and that changed everything. She knew now what the nature of her own begetting must have been, and even though the knowing was a blurry, shadowed thing, she felt the horror of it like the weight of an uninvited body and it made her gorge rise. Of course no mother could want her, not after such a beginning.

She wondered how many of the ghosts in Minya's army had been used that way by the gods. Plenty of them were women, most of them old. How many had borne half-caste babies they neither remembered nor wished to remember?

Sparrow kept her eyes on her hands and worked on her present, humming softly to herself. She tried not to think about whether they'd all still be alive by Ruby's birthday, or what kind of life it would be if they were. She just focused on her hands, and the soothing sensation of growth flowing out from them. She was making a cake out of flowers. Oh, it was nothing they could eat, but it was beautiful, and it reminded her of their early years when there had still been sugar in the citadel and some measure of innocence, too, before she understood her own atrocity.

It even had torch ginger buds for little candles: sixteen of them. She'd give it to Ruby at dinner, she thought. She could light them with her own fire, make a wish, and blow them out.

* * *

Feral was in his room, looking at his book. He turned the metal pages and traced the harsh, angular symbols with his fingertip.

If he had to, he could replicate the whole book from memory—that was how well he knew it. Little good that did, since he couldn't wring any meaning from it. Sometimes, when he stared at it long enough, his eyes sliding out of focus, he thought he could see *into* the metal and sense a pulsing, dormant potential. Like a wind vane waiting for a gust to come along and spin it round. Waiting, and also *wanting* it to come.

The book wanted to be read, Feral thought. But what nature of "gust" could move these symbols? He didn't know. He only knew—or at least strongly suspected—that, if he could read this cryptic alphabet, he could unlock the secrets of the citadel. He could protect the girls, instead of merely...well, keeping them hydrated.

He knew that water was no small matter, and that they'd all have died without his gift, so he didn't tend to waste much regret over not having Skathis's power. That particular bitterness was Minya's, but sometimes he fell prey to wistfulness, too. Of course, if they could control mesarthium, they would be free, and safe, not to mention a force to be reckoned with. But they couldn't, so there was no use wasting time wishing for it.

If he could unlock his book, though, Feral felt certain he could do...something.

"What are you up to in here?" came Ruby's voice from the doorway.

He looked up and scowled when he saw that she'd already poked her head inside. "Respect the curtain," he intoned, and looked back down at his book.

But Ruby did not respect the curtain. She just waltzed in on her expressive, blue, highly arched bare feet. Her toenails were painted red, and she was wearing red, and she was also wearing an expression of intent that would have alarmed him had he looked up—which he didn't. He tensed a little. That was all.

She scowled at the top of his bowed head, as he had scowled at her in the doorway. It was an unpromising beginning. *Stupid book*, she thought. *Stupid boy.*

But he was the *only* boy. He had warmer lips than

the ghosts. Warmer everything, she supposed. More important, Feral wasn't afraid of her, which would have to be more fun than draping herself over a half-paralyzed ghost and telling him what to do every few seconds. *Put your hand here. Now here.*

So boring.

"What do you want, Ruby?" Feral asked.

She was close beside him now. "The thing about experiments," she said, "is that they have to be repeated or else they're worthless."

"What? What experiment?" He turned round to her. His brow was furrowed: half confusion, half irritation.

"Kissing," she said. She'd told him before, "That's an experiment I won't be repeating." Well. In light of their acceleration toward doom, she had reconsidered.

He hadn't. "No," he said, flat, and turned away again.

"It's possible I was wrong," she said, with an air of great magnanimity. "I've decided to give you another chance."

Thick with sarcasm: "Thank you for your generosity, but I'll pass."

Ruby's hand came down on his book. "Hear me out." She pushed it away and perched herself on the edge of his table. Her slip hiked up her thighs, her skin as smooth and frictionless as mesarthium, or nearly.

Much softer, though.

She rested her feet on the edge of his chair. "We're probably going to die," she said matter-of-factly. "And anyway, even if we don't, we're here. We're alive. We have bodies. Mouths." She paused and added teasingly, flicking hers over her teeth, "*Tongues.*"

A blush crept up Feral's neck. "Ruby—" he began in a tone of dismissal.

She cut him off. "There's not a lot to do up here. There's nothing to read." She gestured to his book. "The food's boring. There's no music. We've invented eight thousand games and outgrown them all, some of them literally. Why not grow *into* something?" Her voice was getting husky. "We're not children anymore, and we have lips. Isn't that reason enough?"

A voice in Feral's head assured him that it was *not* reason enough. That he did not wish to partake of any more of Ruby's saliva. That he did not, in fact, wish to spend any more time with her than he did already. There might even have been a voice in there somewhere pointing out that if he were to... *spend more time*... with any of the girls, it wouldn't be her. When he'd joked with Sarai about marrying them all, he'd pretended it wasn't something he gave actual thought to, but he did. How could he not? He was a boy trapped with girls, and they might have been *like* sisters, but they *weren't* sisters, and they were... well, they were pretty. Sarai first, then Sparrow, if he were choosing. Ruby would be last.

But that voice seemed to be coming from some way off, and Sarai and Sparrow weren't here right now, whereas Ruby was very near, and smelled very nice.

And, as she said, they were probably going to die.

The hem of her slip was fascinating. Red silk and blue flesh sang against each other, the colors seeming to vibrate. And the way her knees were slung together, one overlapping the other just a little, and the feel of her foot nudging under his knee. He couldn't help but find her arguments...compelling.

She leaned forward, just a little. All thoughts of Sarai and Sparrow vanished.

He leaned back just the same amount. "You said I was terrible," he reminded her, his own voice as husky as hers.

"And you said I drowned you," she replied, coming a fraction closer.

"There *was* a lot of saliva," he pointed out. Perhaps unwisely.

"And *you* were about as sensuous as a dead fish," she shot back, her expression darkening.

It was touch and go for a moment there. "My darlings, my vipers," Great Ellen had called them. Well, they were darlings *and* vipers, all of them. Or, perhaps Minya was all viper and Sparrow was all darling, but the rest of them were just...they were just flesh and spirit and youth and magic and hunger and yes, *saliva*, all bottled up with nowhere to go. Carnage behind them, carnage ahead, and *ghosts everywhere.*

But here all of a sudden was distraction, escape, novelty, sensation. The shift of Ruby's knees was a kind of blue poetry, and when you're that close to someone, you don't *see* their movements so much as you feel the compression of air between you. The slip of flesh, the glide. Ruby twisted, and with a simple serpentine slink she was in Feral's lap. Her lips found his. She was unsubtle with her tongue. Their hands joined the party, and there seemed dozens of them instead of four, and there were words, too, because Ruby and Feral hadn't yet learned that you can't *really* talk and kiss at the same time.

So it took a moment to sort that out.

"I guess I'll give you another chance," conceded a breathless Feral.

"It's *me* giving *you* another chance," Ruby corrected, a string of the aforementioned saliva glistening between their lips when she drew back to speak.

"How do I know you won't burn me?" Feral asked, even as he slid his hand down over her hip.

"Oh," said Ruby, unconcerned. "That could only happen if I completely lost track of myself." Tongues darted, collided. "You'd have to be *really* good." Teeth clashed. Noses bumped. "I'm not worried."

Feral almost took offense, as well he might, but by

then there were a number of rather agreeable things happening, and so he learned to hold his tongue, or rather, to put it to a more interesting purpose than arguing.

You might think lips and tongues would run out of things to try, but they really don't.

"Put your hand here," breathed Ruby, and he obeyed. "Now here," she commanded, and he did not. To her satisfaction, Feral's hands had a hundred ideas of their own, and none of them were boring.

✳ ✳ ✳

The heart of the citadel was empty of ghosts. For the first time in a decade, Minya had it to herself. She sat on the walkway that wound round the circumference of the big spherical room, her legs dangling over the edge—her very thin, very short legs. They weren't swinging. There was nothing childlike or carefree in the pose. There was a very scarcity of *life* in the pose, except for a subtle rocking back and forth. She was rigid. Her eyes were open, her face blank. Her back was straight, and her dirty hands made fists so tight her knuckles looked ready to split.

Her lips were moving. Barely. There was something she was whispering, over and over. She was back in time fifteen years, seeing this room on a different day.

The day. The day to which she was eternally

skewered, like a moth stuck through the thorax by a long, shining pin.

That day, she had scooped two babies up and held them both with one arm. They hadn't liked that, and neither had her arm, but she'd needed the other to drag the toddlers: their two little hands gripped in her one, slick and slippery with sweat. Two babies in one arm, two toddlers stumbling beside her.

She'd brought them *here*, shoved them through the gap in the nearly closed door and turned to race back for more. But there weren't to be any more. She was halfway to the nursery when the screaming started.

It felt, sometimes, as though she were frozen inside the moment that she'd skidded to a halt at the sound of those screams.

She was the oldest child in the nursery by then. Kiska, who could read minds, had been the last led away by Korako, never to return. Before her it was Werran, whose scream sowed panic in the minds of all who heard it. As for Minya, she knew what her gift was. She'd known for months, but she wasn't letting on. Once they found out, they took you away, so she kept a secret from the goddess of secrets, and stayed in the nursery as long as she could. And so she was still there the day the humans rose up and murdered their masters, and that would have been fine with her— she had no love for the gods—if they'd only stopped there.

She was still in that hallway, hearing those screams and their terrible, bloody dwindle. She would always be there, and her arms would always be too small, just as they had been that day.

In one vital way, though, she was different. She would never again allow weakness or softness, fear or ineptitude to hold her frozen. She hadn't known yet what she was capable of. Her gift had been untested. Of course it had been. If she'd tested it, Korako would have found her out and taken her away. And so she hadn't known the fullness of her power.

She could have saved them all, if only she'd known.

There was so much death in the citadel that day. She could have bound those ghosts—even *the gods' ghosts*. Imagine.

Imagine.

She might have bound the gods themselves into her service, Skathis, too. *If only she'd known what to do.* She could have made an army then, and cut down the Godslayer and all the others before they ever reached the nursery.

Instead, she had saved *four*, and so she would always be stuck in that hallway, hearing those screams cut away one by one.

And doing *nothing*.

Her lips were still moving, whispering the same words over and over. "They were all I could carry. They were all I could carry."

There was no echo, no reverberation. If anything, the room *ate* sound. It swallowed her voice, her words, and her eternal, inadequate apology. But not her memories.

She would never be rid of those.

"They were all I could carry.

"They were all I could carry...."

32

THE SPACE BETWEEN NIGHTMARES

Sarai woke up gagging on the feel of a hundred damp moths cramming themselves down her throat. It was so real, *so real.* She actually believed it was her moths, that she had to choke them down, cloying and clogging and alive. There was the taste of salt and soot—salt from the tears of dreamers, soot from the chimneys of Weep—and even after she caught her breath and knew the nightmare for what it was, she could still taste them.

Thank you, Minya, for this fresh horror.

It wasn't the day's first horror. Not even close. Her prayer to lull had gone unanswered. She'd hardly slept an hour altogether, and what little sleep she'd had was far from restful. She had dreamed her own death a half-dozen different ways, as though her mind were making up a list of choices. A menu, as it were, of ways to die.

Poison.

Drowning.

Falling.

Stabbing.

Mauling.

She was even burned alive by the citizens of Weep. And in between deaths, she was...what? She was a girl in a dark wood who has heard a twig snap. The space between nightmares was like the silence after the snap, when you know that whatever made it is holding itself still and watching you in the dark. There was no more seeping gray nothing. The lull fog had thinned to wisps.

All her terrors were free.

She lay on her back, her bedcovers kicked away, and stared up at the ceiling. Her body was limp, her mind numb. How could her lull have simply stopped working? In the pulse of her blood and spirit was a cadence of panic.

What was she supposed to do now?

Thirst and her bladder both urged her to get up, but the prospect of leaving her alcove was grim. She knew what she would find just around the corner, even inside her own room:

Ghosts with knives.

Just like the old women who'd surrounded her bed, despairing of their inability to murder her.

She did get up, finally. She put on a robe and what she hoped passed for dignity, and emerged. There they were, arrayed between the door to the passage and the door out to the terrace: eight of them inside; she couldn't be sure how many out on the hand itself. She steeled herself for their revulsion and walked across her room.

Minya, it would seem, was holding her army under such tight control that they couldn't form facial expressions like the disgust or fear Sarai knew so well, but their eyes remained their own, and it was amazing how much they could convey with just those. There was disgust and fear, yes, as Sarai passed them by, but mostly what she saw in them was pleading.

Help us.

Free us.

"I can't help you," she wanted to say, but the thickness in her throat was more than just the phantom feel of moths. It was the conflict that tore her in two. These ghosts would kill her in a minute if they were free. She shouldn't want to help them. What was wrong with her?

She averted her eyes and hurried past, feeling as though she were still trapped in a nightmare. *Who*, she wondered, *is going to help* me?

No one was in the gallery except for Minya. Well, Minya and the ranks of ghosts that now filled the arches of the arcade, crushing Sparrow's vines beneath their dead feet. Ari-Eil stood at attendance behind Minya's chair, looking like a handsome manservant, but for the set of his features. His face his mistress left free to reflect his feelings, and he did not disappoint. Sarai almost blanched at the vitriol there.

"Hello," said Minya. There were barbs of spite in her bright, childish voice when she asked, insincerely, "Sleep well?"

"Like a baby," Sarai said breezily—by which of course she meant that she had woken frequently crying, but she didn't feel the need to clarify the point.

"No nightmares?" probed Minya.

Sarai's jaw clenched. She couldn't bear to show weakness, not now. "You know I don't dream," she said, wishing desperately that it were still true.

"Really?" said Minya, with a skeptical lift of her eyebrows, and Sarai wondered, all of a sudden, why she was asking. She'd told no one but Great Ellen about her nightmare yesterday, but in that moment, she was certain that Minya knew.

A jolt shot through her. It was the look in Minya's eyes: cool, assessing, malicious. Just like that, Sarai understood: Minya didn't just know about her nightmares. She was the cause of them.

Her lull. Great Ellen brewed it. Great Ellen was a ghost, and thus subject to Minya's control. Sarai felt sick—not just at the idea that Minya might be sabotaging her lull, but to think that she would manipulate Great Ellen, who was almost like a mother to them. It was too horrible.

She swallowed. Minya was watching her closely, perhaps wondering if Sarai had worked it out. Sarai thought she *wanted* her to guess, so that she would understand her position clearly: If she wanted her gray fog back, she was going to have to earn it.

She was glad, then, when Sparrow came in. She was able to produce a credible smile, and pretend— she hoped—that she was fine, while inside her very spirit hissed with outrage, and with shock that Minya would go so far.

Sparrow kissed her cheek. Her own smile was tremulous and brave. Ruby and Feral came in a moment later. They were bickering about something, which made it easier to pretend that everything was normal.

Dinner was served. A dove had been caught in a trap, and Great Ellen had put it in a stew. Dove stew. It sounded so wrong, like butterfly jam, or spectral steaks. Some creatures were too lovely to devour—not that that opinion was shared around the dining table. Feral and Ruby both ate with a gusto that spared no concern for the loveliness of the meat source, and if Minya had never been a big eater, it certainly had nothing to do with delicacy of feeling. She didn't finish her stew, but she did fish out a tiny bone to pick her small white teeth with.

Only Sparrow shared Sarai's hesitation, though they both ate, because meat was rare and their bodies craved it. It didn't matter if they had no appetite. They lived on bare-bones rations and were always hungry.

As soon as Kem cleared away their bowls, Sparrow got up from the table. "I'll be right back," she said. "Don't anyone leave."

They looked at one another. Ruby raised her eyebrows. Sparrow darted out into the garden and came back a moment later holding . . .

"A cake!" cried Ruby, springing up. "How in the world did you—?"

It was a dream of a cake, and they all stared at it, amazed: three tall, frosted layers, creamy white and patterned with blossoms like falling snow. "Don't get too excited," she cautioned them. "It's not for eating."

They saw that the creamy white "frosting" was orchid petals scattered with anadne blossoms and the whole thing was made of flowers, right up to the torch ginger buds on top that looked, for all the world, like sixteen lit candles.

Ruby screwed up her face. "Then what's it for?"

"For wishing on," Sparrow told them. "It's an early birthday cake." She put it down in front of Ruby. "In case."

They all understood that she meant in case there were no more birthdays. "Well, that's grim," said Ruby.

"Go on, make a wish."

Ruby did. And though the ginger already looked like little flames, she lit them on fire with her fingertips and blew them out properly, all in one go.

"What did you wish for?" Sarai asked her.

"For it to be real cake, of course," said Ruby. "Did it come true?" She dug into it with her fingers, but of course there was no cake, only more flowers, but she pantomimed eating it without sharing.

Night had fallen. Sarai got up to go. "Sarai," called Minya, and she stopped but didn't turn. She knew what was coming. Minya hadn't given up. She never would. Somehow, by sheer force of will, the girl had frozen herself in time—not just her body but everything. Her fury, her vengeance, undiminished in all these years. You could never win against such a will. Her voice rang out its reminder: "A few minutes of disgust to save us all."

Sarai kept walking. *To save us all.* The words seemed to curl up in her belly—not moths now but snakes. She wanted to leave them behind her in the gallery, but as she passed through the gauntlet of ghost soldiers that lined the corridor to her room, their lips parted and they murmured all together, "To save us all, to save us all," and after that, the words they'd only spoken with their eyes: *Help us. Save us.* They spoke them aloud. They pleaded at her passing. "Help us, save us," and it was all Minya, playing to Sarai's weakness.

To her mercy.

And then in her doorway, she had to pass a child. *A child.* Bahar, nine years old, who had fallen in the Uzumark three years ago and still wore the sodden clothes of her drowning. It was beyond the pale, even for Minya, to keep a dead child as a pet. The small ghost stood in Sarai's way and Minya's words issued from her lips. "If you don't kill him, Sarai," she said, mournful, "*I'll* have to."

Sarai pressed her palms to her ears and darted past her. But even in her alcove, back where they couldn't see her, she could hear them still whispering "Save us, help us," until she thought she might go mad.

She screamed her moths and curled up in the corner with her eyes tightly closed, wishing more than ever before that she could go with them. In that moment, if she could have poured her whole soul into them and left her body empty—even if she could never return to it—she might have done it, just to be free of the whispered pleas of the dead men and women—and children—of Weep.

The *living* men and women and children of Weep were safe from her nightmares again tonight. She returned to the faranji in the guildhall, and to the Tizerkane in their barracks, and to Azareen alone in her rooms in Windfall.

She didn't know what she would do if she found Eril-Fane. The snakes that curled up in her belly had moved into her hearts. There was darkness in her, and treachery, that much she knew. But everything was so tangled up that she couldn't tell if it was mercy not to kill him, or only cowardice.

But she didn't find him. The relief was tremendous, but quickly bled into something else: a heightened awareness of the stranger who was in his bed instead. Sarai perched on the pillow beside his sleeping face for a long time, full of fear and longing. Longing for the beauty of his dream. Fear of being seen again—and not with wonder this time, but for the nightmare that she was.

In the end she compromised. She perched on his brow and slipped into his dream. It was Weep again, his own bright Weep that ill-deserved the name, but when she saw him at a distance, she didn't follow. She only found a little place to curl up—just as her body was curled up in her room—to breathe in the sweet air, and watch the children in their feather cloaks, and feel safe, for at least a little while.

33

We Are All Children in the Dark

Lazlo's first days in Weep passed in a rush of activity and wonder. There was the city to discover, of course, and all that was sweet and bitter in it.

It wasn't the perfect place he had imagined as a boy. Of course it wasn't. If it ever had been, it had gone through far too much to stay that way. There were no high wires or children in feather cloaks; as near as he could find out, there never had been. The women didn't wear their hair long enough to trail behind them, and for good reason: The streets were as dirty as the streets of any city. There were no cakes set out on window ledges, either, but Lazlo had never really expected that. There *was* garbage, and vermin, too. Not a lot, but enough to keep a dreamer from idealizing the object of his long fascination. The withered gardens were a blight, and beggars lay as though dead, collecting coins on the hollows of their closed eyes, and there were altogether too many ruins.

And yet there was such color and sound, such *life*: wren men with their caged birds, dream men blowing colored dust, children with their shoe harps making music just by running. There was light and there was darkness: The temples to the seraphim were more exquisite than all the churches in Zosma, Syriza, Maialen put together, and witnessing the worship there—the ecstatic dance of Thakra—was the most mystical experience of Lazlo's life. But there were the butcher priests, too, performing divination of animal entrails, and the Doomsayers on their stilts, crying End Times from behind their skeleton masks.

All this was contained in a cityscape of carved honey stone and gilded domes, the streets radiating out from an ancient amphitheater filled with colorful market stalls.

This afternoon he had eaten lunch there with some of the Tizerkane, including Ruza, who taught him the phrase "You have ruined my tongue for all other tastes." Ruza assured him that it was the highest possible compliment to the chef, but the merriness in everyone's eyes suggested a more…prurient meaning. In the market, Lazlo bought himself a shirt and jacket in the local style, neither of them gray. The jacket was the green of far forests, and needed cuffs to catch the sleeves between biceps and deltoids. These came in every imaginable material. Eril-Fane wore gold. Lazlo chose the more economical and understated leather.

He bought socks, too. He was beginning to understand the appeal of money. He bought *four pair*—a profligate quantity of socks—and not only were they not gray, no two pair were even the same color. One was pink, and another had stripes.

And speaking of pink, he sampled blood candy in a tiny shop under a bridge. It was real, and it was *awful*. After fighting back the urge to gag, he told the confectioner, weakly, "You have ruined my tongue for all other tastes," and saw her eyes flare wide. Her shock was chased by a blush, confirming his suspicions regarding the decency of the compliment.

"Thank you for that," Lazlo told Ruza as they walked away. "Her husband will probably challenge me to a duel."

"Probably," agreed Ruza. "But everyone should fight at least one duel."

"*One* sounds just about right for me."

"Because you'd die," Ruza clarified unnecessarily. "And not be alive to fight another."

"Yes," said Lazlo. "That is what I meant."

Ruza clapped him on the shoulder. "Don't worry. We'll make a warrior of you yet. You know…" He eyed the green brocade purse that had belonged to Calixte's grandmother. "For starters, you might buy a wallet while we're here."

"What, you disapprove of my purse?" asked Lazlo, holding it up to show off its gaudy brooch to best advantage.

"Yes, I rather do."

"But it's so handy," said Lazlo. "Look, I can wear it like this." He demonstrated, dangling it from his wrist by its drawstrings and swinging it in circles, childlike.

Ruza just shook his head and muttered, "Faranji."

But mostly, there was work to be done.

Over those first few days, Lazlo had to see to it that all the Godslayer's delegates were set up with workspace to accommodate their needs, as well as materials and, in some cases, assistants. And since most hadn't bothered to learn any of their host language on the journey, they all needed interpreters. Some of the Tizerkane understood a little, but they had their duties to attend to. Calixte was nearly fluent by now, but she had no intention of spending her time helping "small-minded old men." And so Lazlo found himself very busy.

Some of the delegates were easier than others. Belabra, the mathematician, requested an office with high walls he might write his formulas upon and whitewash over as he saw fit. Kether, artist and designer of catapults and siege engines, needed only a drafting table brought into his room at the guildhall.

Lazlo doubted that the engineers needed much more than that, but Ebliz Tod seemed to view it as a matter of distinction—that the more "important" guests should ask for, and receive, the most. And so he dictated elaborate and specific demands that it was then Lazlo's duty to fulfill, with the help of a number of locals Suheyla organized to assist him. The result was that Tod's Weep workshop surpassed his Syriza office in grandeur, though he did indeed spend most of his time at the drafting table in the corner.

Calixte asked for nothing at all, though Lazlo knew she was procuring, with Tzara's assistance, an array of resins with which to concoct sticking pastes to aid in her climbing. Whether she would be called upon by Eril-Fane to do so was much in question—she herself suspected he'd invited her along more to rescue her from jail than from real need of her—but she was determined to win her bet with Tod in any case. "Any luck?" Lazlo asked her when he saw her coming back from a test at the anchor.

"Luck has nothing to do with it," she replied. "It's all strength and cleverness." She winked, flexing her hands like five-legged spiders. "And glue."

As she dropped her hands, it occurred to Lazlo that they bore no gray discoloration. He had discovered, after his own contact with the anchor, that the faint dirty tinge did not wash off, even with soap and water. It had faded, though, and was gone now. The mesarthium, he thought, must be reactive with skin the way some other metals were, such as copper. Not

Calixte's skin, though. She'd just been touching the anchor and bore no trace of it.

The Fellerings, Mouzaive the magnetist, and Thyon Nero all needed laboratory space in which to unload the equipment they had brought with them from the west. The Fellerings and Mouzaive were content with converted stables next to the guildhall, but Thyon refused them, demanding to scout other sites. Lazlo had to go along as interpreter, and at first he couldn't tell what it was the alchemist was looking for. He turned down some rooms as too big and others as too small, before settling on the attic story of a crematorium—a cavernous space larger than others he'd rejected as too big. It was also windowless, with a single great, heavy door. When he demanded no fewer than three locks for it, Lazlo understood: He'd chosen the place for privacy.

He was intent on keeping the secret of azoth, it would seem, even in this city whence, long ago, the secret had come.

Drave required a warehouse to store his powder and chemicals, and Lazlo saw to it that he had one— outside the city, in case of fiery misadventure. And if the distance resulted in less day-to-day Drave, well, that was just a bonus.

"It's a damned inconvenience," the explosionist groused, though the inconvenience proved quite minimal, due to the fact that after overseeing the unloading of his supplies, he spent no further time there.

"Just tell me what you want blown up and I'm good for it," he said, and then proceeded to spend his time scouting the city for pleasures and making women uncomfortable with his leering.

Ozwin, the farmer-botanist, needed a glasshouse and fields for planting, so he, too, had to go out of the city and out of the citadel's shadow, where his seeds and seedlings would see sunlight.

"Plants that dreamed they were birds," that was his work. Those words were from the myth of the seraphim, describing the world as the beings had found it when they came down from the skies: "And they found rich soil and sweet seas and plants that dreamed they were birds and drifted up to the clouds on leaves like wings." Lazlo had known the passage for years, and had assumed it was fantasy—but he had discovered in Thanagost that it was real.

The plant was called ulola, and it was known for two things. One: Its nondescript shrubs were a favorite resting place for serpaise in the heat of the day, which accounted for its nickname, "snakeshade." And two: Its flowers could fly.

Or *float*, if you wanted to be technical. They were saclike blooms about the size of a baby's head, and as they died, their decay produced a powerful lifting gas, which carried them into the sky and wherever the wind blew them, to release seeds in new soil and begin the cycle again. They were a quirk of the badlands—drifting pink balloons that had a way of making landfall in the midst of wild amphion wolf riots—and would most likely have stayed that way if a botanist from the University of Isquith—Ozwin—hadn't braved the dangers of the frontier in search of samples and fallen in love with the lawless land and, more particularly, with the lawless mechanist—Soulzeren—favored by warlords for her extravagant firearm designs. It was quite the love story, even involving a duel (fought by Soulzeren). Only the unique combination of the two of them could have produced the silk sleigh: a sleek, ultralight craft buoyed by ulola gas.

The crafts themselves, Soulzeren was assembling in one of the pavilions of the guildhall. As to the matter of when they would fly, the subject was broached on the fifth afternoon, at a meeting of city leaders that Lazlo attended with Eril-Fane. It did not go at all as he expected.

"Our guests are at work on the problem of the citadel," Eril-Fane reported to the five *Zeyyadin*, which translated as "first voices." The two women and three men constituted the governing body that had been established after the fall of the gods. "And when they are ready, they will make proposals toward a solution."

"To . . . move it," one woman said. Her name was Maldagha, and her voice was heavy with apprehension.

"But how can they hope to do such a thing?" asked a stooped man with long white hair, his voice quavering.

"If I could answer that," said Eril-Fane, with the slightest of smiles, "I would have done it myself and avoided a long journey. Our guests possess the brightest practical minds in half a world—"

"But what is practicality against the magic of gods?" the old man interrupted.

"It is the best hope we have," said Eril-Fane. "It won't be the work of moments, as it was for Skathis, but what else can we do? We might be looking at years of effort. It may be that the best we can hope for is a tower to reach it and to carve it away piece by piece until it's gone. Our grandchildren's grandchildren may well be carting shavings of mesarthium out of the city as the monstrosity shrinks slowly to nothing. But even so, even if that's the only way and we in this room don't live to see it, there *will* come a day when the last piece is gone and the sky is free."

They were powerful words, though spoken softly, and they seemed to lift the hopes of the others. Tentatively, Maldagha said, "Carve it away, you say. *Can* they cut it? *Have* they?"

"Not yet," Eril-Fane admitted. In fact, the Fellerings' confidence had proven misplaced. Like everyone else, they had failed even to make a scratch. Their arrogance was gone now, replaced with disgruntled determination. "But they've only just begun, and we've an alchemist, too. The most accomplished in the world."

As for said alchemist, if he was having any luck with his alkahest, he was keeping it as much a secret as his key ingredient. His doors in the crematorium attic were locked, and he only opened them to receive meals. He'd even had a cot moved in so he could sleep on-site—which did not, however, mean that he never emerged. Tzara had been on watch, and had seen him in the dead of night, walking in the direction of the north anchor.

To experiment on mesarthium in secret, Lazlo supposed. When Tzara mentioned it to him this morning, he had gone himself to examine the surface, looking for any hint that Thyon had been successful. It was a big surface. It was possible he'd missed something, but he didn't really think so. The whole expanse had been as smooth and unnaturally perfect as the first time he saw it.

There was not, in fact, any encouraging news to report to the Zeyyadin, not yet. The meeting had another purpose.

"Tomorrow," Eril-Fane told them, and his voice seemed to weigh down the air, "we launch one of the silk sleighs."

The effect of his words was immediate and... absolutely counterintuitive. In any city in the world, airships—real, functional airships—would be met with wonderment. This ought to have been thrilling news. But the men and women in the room went pale. Five faces in a row uniformly drained of color and went blank with a kind of stunned dread. The old man began to shake his head. Maldagha pressed her lips together to still their sudden trembling, and, in a gesture that pained Lazlo to interpret, laid a hand to her belly. Suheyla had made a similar movement, and he thought he knew what it meant. They all struggled to maintain composure, but their faces betrayed them. Lazlo hadn't seen anyone look this stricken since the boys at the abbey were dragged to the crypt for punishment.

He had never seen adults look like this.

"It will only be a test flight," Eril-Fane went on. "We need to establish a reliable means of coming and going between the city and the citadel. And…" He hesitated. Swallowed. Looked at no one when he said, "I need to see it."

"You?" demanded one of the men. "Are *you* going up there?"

It seemed an odd question. It had never occurred to Lazlo that he might not.

Solemnly, Eril-Fane regarded the man. "I was hoping you would come, too, Shajan. You who were there at the end." The end. The day the gods were slain? Lazlo's mind flashed to the mural in the alley, and the hero depicted in it, six-armed and triumphant. "It has stood dead all these years, and some of us know better than others the . . . state . . . it was left in."

No one met anyone's eyes then. It was very odd. It put Lazlo in mind of the way they avoided looking at the citadel itself. It occurred to him that the bodies of the gods might still be up there, left where they'd died, but he didn't see why that should cause such a trembling and shrinking.

"I couldn't," gasped Shajan, staring at his own shaking hands. "You can't expect it. You see how I am now."

It struck Lazlo as out of all proportion. A grown man reduced to trembling at the thought of entering an empty building—even *that* empty building—because there might be skeletons there? And the disproportion only grew.

"We could still move," Maldagha blurted, looking as harrowed as Shajan. "You needn't go back up there. We needn't do any of this." There was a note of desperation in her voice. "We can rebuild the city at Enet-Sarra, as we've discussed. The surveys have all been done. We need only to begin."

Eril-Fane shook his head. "If we did," he said, "it would mean that they had won, even in death. They haven't. This is *our* city, that our foremothers and forefathers built on land consecrated by Thakra. We won't forsake it. That is our sky, and we will have it back." They were such words as might have been roared before battle. A little boy playing Tizerkane in an orchard would have loved the feel of them rolling off his tongue. But Eril-Fane didn't roar them. His voice sounded faraway, like the last echo before silence redescends.

"What *was* that?" Lazlo asked him after they left.

"That was fear," Eril-Fane said simply.

"But...fear of what?" Lazlo couldn't comprehend it. "The citadel's empty. What can there be to harm them?"

Eril-Fane let out a slow breath. "Were you afraid of the dark as a child?"

A chill snaked up Lazlo's spine. He thought again of the crypt at the abbey, and the nights locked in with dead monks. "Yes," he said simply.

"Even when you knew, rationally, that there was nothing in it that could harm you."

"Yes."

"Well. We are all children in the dark, here in Weep."

34

SPIRIT OF LIBRARIAN

Another day over, another day of work and wonder, and Lazlo was returning to Suheyla's for the night. As he crossed the Avenue, that solitary stripe of sunlight, he saw the errand boy from the guildhall coming toward him with a tray. It held empty dishes, and he realized the boy must be coming back from the crematorium, which lay just ahead. He'd have brought Thyon's dinner, and traded it for his empty lunch tray. Lazlo greeted him, and wondered in passing how Thyon was getting on. He hadn't seen him in the couple of days since he'd hidden himself away, and hadn't had an update to give Eril-Fane when asked. With just a moment's hesitation, he changed his course and made for the crematorium. Passing the anchor on the way, he skimmed his hand over its whole length, and tried to imagine it rippling and morphing as it apparently had for the dark god Skathis.

When he knocked on Thyon's heavy, thrice-locked door, the alchemist actually answered it, which could only mean he thought the boy was back with more provisions—or else he was expecting someone else, because as soon as he saw Lazlo, he started to shut it again.

"Wait," said Lazlo, putting out his foot. It was lucky he wore boots. In the old days of his librarians' slippers his toes would have been crushed. As it was, he winced. Nero wasn't playing around. "I come on behalf of Eril-Fane," he said, annoyed.

"I've nothing to report," said Thyon. "You can tell him that."

Lazlo's foot was still in the door, holding it open some three inches. It wasn't much, but the glave in the antechamber was bright, and he saw Thyon—at least a three-inch-wide strip of him—quite clearly. His brow furrowed. "Nero, are you unwell?"

"I'm fine," the golden godson deigned to say. "Now, if you would remove your foot."

"I won't," said Lazlo, truly alarmed. "Let me see you. You look like death."

It was a drastic transformation, in just a few days. His skin was sallow. Even the whites of his eyes were jaundiced.

Thyon drew back, out of Lazlo's line of sight. "Remove your foot," he said in a low, casual tone, "or I'll test my current batch of alkahest on it." Even his voice sounded sallow, if that were possible.

Alkahest on the foot was an unpleasant prospect to consider. Lazlo wondered how quickly it would eat through his boot leather. "I don't doubt that you would do it," he said, just as casually as Thyon. "I'm only gambling that you don't have it in your hand. You'll have to go and get it, during which time I'll push open the door and get a look at you. Come on, Nero. You're ill."

"I'm not ill."

"You're not *well*."

"It's none of your concern, Strange."

"I really don't know if it is or not, but you're here for a reason, and you may well be Weep's best hope, so convince me you aren't ill or I'll go straight to Eril-Fane."

There was an irritated sigh, and Thyon stood back from the door. Lazlo nudged it open with his foot, and saw that he had not been mistaken. Thyon looked terrible—though, admittedly, his "terrible" was still a cut above how most people could ever hope to look. Still, he looked aged. It wasn't just his color. The skin around his eyes was slack and shadowed. "Gods, Nero," he said, stepping forward, "what's happened to you?"

"Just working too hard," said the alchemist with a grim smile.

"That's ridiculous. No one looks that haggard from working hard for a couple of days."

As he said it, Lazlo's eyes fell on Thyon's worktable. It was a rough-and-tumble version of his table in the Chrysopoesium, scattered with glassware and copper and piles of books. Smoke drifted in the air, a brimstone scent to singe the nostrils, and right in plain view was a long syringe. It was glass and copper, resting on a wadded white cloth spotted with red. Lazlo looked at it, then turned to Thyon, who returned his stare with stony eyes. What had Lazlo just said, that no one looks that haggard from working hard for a couple of days?

But what if their "work" relied on a steady supply of spirit, and their only source was their own body? Lazlo's breath hissed out between his teeth. "You idiot," he said, and saw Thyon's eyes widen in incredulity. No one called the golden godson an idiot. He was, though, in this case. "How much have you taken?" Lazlo asked.

"I don't know what you're talking about."

Lazlo shook his head. He was beginning to lose patience. "You can lie if you want, but I already know your secret. If you're so damned determined to keep it, Nero, I'm the only person in the world who can help you."

Thyon laughed as though this were a good joke. "And why would *you* help *me*?"

It wasn't at all how he'd said it in the Chrysopoesium when they were younger. "*You*, help *me*?" That

375

had been incredulity that Lazlo dared believe himself worthy of helping him. This was more like incredulity that he should *want* to.

"For the same reason I helped you before," said Lazlo.

"And why was that?" Nero demanded. "Why did you, Strange?"

Lazlo stared at him for a moment. The answer really couldn't be simpler, but he didn't think Thyon was equipped to believe it. "Because you needed it," he said, and his words pulled a silence over them both. Here was the radical notion that you might help someone simply because they needed it.

Even if they hated you for it after, and punished you for it, and stole from you, and lied and mocked you? Even then? Lazlo had hoped that, of all the delegates, Thyon wouldn't prove to be Weep's savior, deliverer from shadow. But far greater than that hope was the hope that Weep would be delivered, by *someone*, even if it was him. "Do you need help now?" he asked quietly. "You can't keep drawing your own spirit. It might not kill you," he said, because spirit wasn't like blood, and somehow people went on living without it, if you could call it living. "But it *will* make you ugly," he told him, "and I think that would be very hard for you."

Thyon's brow creased. He squinted at Lazlo to see if he was mocking him. He was, of course, but in the way he might mock Ruza, or Calixte might mock him. It was Thyon's decision whether to take offense or not, and perhaps he was just too tired. "What are you proposing?" he asked, wary.

Lazlo let out a breath and shifted straight into problem-solving mode. Thyon needed spirit to make azoth. At home, he must have had a system, though Lazlo couldn't imagine what it was. How did one keep up a steady supply of something like spirit without anyone finding out? Whatever it was, here, without coming out and asking for it—and revealing his secret ingredient—he had only his own, and he had drawn too much.

Lazlo argued with him, briefly, over whether it was time to let the secret go. But Thyon wouldn't hear it, and finally Lazlo, with a frustrated sigh, stripped off his jacket and rolled up his sleeve. "Just take some of mine, all right? Until we can think of something else."

Through it all, Thyon regarded him with suspicion, as though he were waiting for some hidden motive to reveal itself. But when Lazlo held out his arm, he could only blink, discomfited. It would have been easier if he could believe there *were* some motive, some sort of revenge in the works, or some other manner of scheming. But Lazlo offered up his veins. His own vital fluid. What motive could there be in that? He winced when Thyon jabbed in his needle, and winced again, because the alchemist missed the spirit vein and hit a blood vessel instead. Thyon wasn't an especially skilled phlebotomist, but he didn't apologize and Lazlo didn't complain, and eventually there was a vial of clear fluid on the table, labeled, with a contemptuous flourish, SPIRIT OF LIBRARIAN.

Thyon did not say thank you. He did say, releasing Lazlo's arm to him, "You might try washing your hands occasionally, Strange."

Lazlo only smiled, as the condescension marked a return to familiar territory. He glanced at the hand in question. It did look dirty. He'd trailed it over the anchor on his way here, he remembered. "That's the mesarthium," he said, and asked, curious, "Have you noticed its being reactive to skin?"

"Hardly. It's not reactive to anything."

"Well, have you noticed skin being reactive *to it*?" Lazlo persisted, rolling his sleeve back down.

Thyon only held up his own palms. They were clean, and that was all his answer. Lazlo shrugged and put on his coat. Thyon's response didn't bode well, in its broader context—about mesarthium not being reactive with anything. In the doorway, Lazlo paused. "Eril-Fane will want to know. Is there any reason to be hopeful? Does the alkahest affect mesarthium *at all*?"

He didn't think the alchemist would answer. His hand was on the door, ready to shove it shut. But he paused for half a second, as though Lazlo had earned this single, grudging syllable, and said, grimly, "No."

❧ 35 ❧

BLURRED INK

Sarai felt . . . thinned out. To be so tired was like evapo-
rating. Water to vapor. Flesh to ghost. Bit by bit, from
the surface inward, you feel yourself begin to disappear, or at least to be translated into another state—
from a tangible one, blood and spirit, to a kind of lost
and drifting mist.

How many days had passed in this way, living from
nightmare to nightmare? It felt like dozens, but was
probably only five or six.

This is my life now, she thought, looking at her
reflection in the polished mesarthium of the dressing
room. She touched the skin around her eyes with her
fingertips. It was almost damson, like the plums on
the trees, and her eyes looked too big—as though, like
Less Ellen, she had reimagined them so.

If I were a ghost, she wondered, regarding herself

like a stranger, *what would I change about myself?* The answer was too obvious to admit, and too pathetic. She traced a line around her navel where her elilith would be if she were a human girl. What was it about the tattoos that so beguiled her? They were beautiful, but it wasn't just that. Maybe it was the ritual: the circle of women coming together to celebrate being alive—and being a woman, which is a magic all its own. Or maybe it was the future the mark portended. Marriage, motherhood, family, continuity.

Being a person. With a life. And every expectation of a future. All things Sarai didn't dare to dream about.

Or…things she *shouldn't* dare to dream about. Like nightmares, dreams were insidious things, and didn't like being locked away.

If she did have an elilith, she wouldn't want a serpent swallowing its tail like Tzara and many of the younger women had who'd come of age after the liberation. She already felt like she had creatures inside her—moths and snakes and terrors—and wouldn't want them *on* her, too. Azareen, fierce and stoic as she was, had one of the prettiest tattoos Sarai had seen— done by Guldan, of course, who was now a conscript in Minya's wretched army. It was a delicate pattern of apple blossoms, which were a symbol of fertility.

Sarai knew that Azareen hated the sight of it, and everything it mocked.

The thing about eliliths. They were inked on girls' bellies, which tended to be flat or only gently curved. And when in the course of time their promise of fertility was fulfilled, their bellies swelled, and their tattoos with them. They never really looked the same after. You could see the blurring of the fine ink lines where skin had stretched and then shrunk back again.

The girls whom Skathis stole, their eliliths were pristine when he took them. Not so when he returned them. But since Letha ate their memories, that was all they knew of their time in the citadel—the vague blur of the ink on their bellies, and all that it implied.

Except, that is, for the girls who were in the citadel on the day that Eril-Fane slew the gods. They'd had it worst. They'd had to come down like that, their bellies still full with godspawn and their minds with memories.

Azareen had been one of them. And though she had once been a bride—and before that a girl squeezing the hands of a circle of women while blossoms were etched round her navel in ink—the only time her belly ever swelled was with godseed, and she remembered every second of it, from the rapes that began it to the searing pains that ended it.

She'd never looked at the baby. She'd squeezed her eyes shut until they took it away. She'd heard its fragile cries, though, and heard them still.

Sarai could hear them, too. She was awake, but the terrors were clinging. She shook her head as though she could shake them away.

The things that had been done. By the gods, by the humans. Nothing could shake them away.

She picked out a clean slip. Pale green, not that she noticed. She just reached out blindly and pulled one down. She put it on, and her robe over it, belted tight, and considered her face in the mirror: her huge haunted eyes and the tale they told of nightmares and sleepless days. One look at her and Minya would smile. "Sleep well?" she'd ask. She always did now, and Sarai always answered, "Like a baby," and pretended everything was fine.

There was no pretending away the bruises under her eyes. Briefly, she considered blacking them with her mother's paint, but the effort seemed too great, and would fool no one.

She stepped out of the dressing room. Eyes fixed forward, she passed the ghosts standing guard. They still whispered Minya's words to her, but she had inured herself to them. Even to Bahar, nine years old and soaked to the skin, who followed her down the hall, whispering "Save us," and left wet footprints that weren't really there.

All right, so she could never be inured to Bahar.

"Sleep well?" Minya asked her as soon as she walked into the gallery.

Sarai gave her a wan smile. "Why wouldn't I?" she asked for a change.

"Oh, I don't know, Sarai. Stubbornness?"

Sarai understood her perfectly—that she had only to ask for her lull to be restored to her and Minya would see it done.

Just as soon as Sarai did her bidding.

They hadn't openly acknowledged the situation—that Minya was sabotaging Sarai's lull—but it was in every look they shared.

A few minutes of disgust to save us all.

If Sarai killed Eril-Fane, Minya would let her sleep again. Well? Would her father lose a blink of sleep to save her?

It didn't matter what he would or wouldn't do. Sarai wasn't going to kill anyone. She *was* stubborn, very, and she wasn't about to surrender her decency or mercy for a sound day's sleep. She wouldn't beg Minya for lull. Whatever happened, she would never again serve Minya's twisted will.

Also, she still couldn't *find* him. So there was that.

Not that Minya believed her, but it was true, and she did look. She knew he was back in Weep, partly because Azareen would never have come back without him, and partly because he flickered through the dreams of all the others like a shimmering thread connecting them. But wherever he was sleeping, wherever he stayed at night, she never could find him.

Sarai laughed. "*Me*, stubborn," she said, raising her eyebrows. "Have you met yourself?"

Minya made no denial. "I suppose the question is: Who's more stubborn?"

It sounded like a challenge. "I guess we'll find out," Sarai replied.

Dinner was served and the others came in—Sparrow and Ruby from the garden; Feral, yawning, from the direction of his room. "Napping?" Sarai asked him. Everything had fallen to pieces lately. He used to at least attempt to oversee the girls during the day, and make sure they didn't fall into chaos or break The Rule. Not that anything really mattered anymore.

He only shrugged. "Anything interesting?" he asked her.

He meant news from the night before. This was their routine now. It reminded her of their younger days, when she still told them all about her visits to the city and they all wanted to know different things: Sparrow, the glimpses of normal life; Ruby, the naughty bits; Minya, the screaming. Feral hadn't really had a focus then, but he did now. He wanted to know everything about the faranji and their workshops—the diagrams on their drafting tables, the chemicals in their flasks, the dreams in their heads. Sarai told him what she could, and they tried to interpret the level of threat they posed. He claimed that his interest was defensive, but she saw a hunger in his eyes—for the books and papers she described, the instruments and bubbling beakers, the walls covered in a scrawl of numbers and symbols she couldn't begin to make sense of.

It was his sweetshop window, the life he was missing, and she did her best to make it vivid for him. She could give him that at least. This evening, though, she bore bleak tidings.

"The flying machines," she said. She'd been keeping an eye on them in a pavilion of the guildhall as they took shape in stages, day by day, until finally becoming the crafts she had seen in the faranji couple's dreams. All her dread had at last caught up to her. "They seem to be ready."

This drew a sharp intake of breath from Ruby and Sparrow. "When will they fly?" Minya asked coolly.

"I don't know. Soon."

"Well, I hope it's soon. I'm getting bored. What's the use of having an army if you don't get to use it?"

Sarai didn't rise to her bait. She'd been thinking of what she was going to say, and how she was going to say it. "It needn't come to that," she said, and turned to Feral. "The woman, she worries about the weather. I've seen it in her dreams. Wind is a problem. She won't fly into clouds. I think the crafts must not be terribly stable." She tried to sound calm, rational—not defensive or combative. She was simply making a reasonable suggestion to avoid bloodshed. "If you summon a storm, we can keep them from even getting close."

Feral took this in, glancing with just his eyes toward Minya, who had her elbows on the table, chin in one hand, the other picking her kimril biscuit to bits. "Oh, Sarai," she said. "What an idea."

"It's a good idea," said Sparrow. "Why fight if we can avoid it?"

"Avoid it?" Minya snapped. "Do you think, if they knew we were here, *they* would be worrying about avoiding a fight?" She turned to Ari-Eil, standing behind her chair. "Well?" she asked him. "What do *you* think?"

Whether she gave him leave to answer, or produced his answer herself, Sarai didn't doubt the truth of it. "They'll slaughter you all," he hissed, and Minya gave Sparrow an *I told you so* look.

"I can't believe we're even having this conversation," she said. "When your enemy is coming, you don't gather *clouds*. You gather *knives*."

Sarai looked to Feral, but he wouldn't meet her eye. There wasn't much more to be said after that. She was loath to return to her tiny alcove, which she couldn't help feeling was stuffed with all the nightmares she'd had in it of late, so she went out into the garden with Sparrow and Ruby. There were ghosts all around, but the vines and billows of flowers made nooks you could almost hide in. In fact, Sparrow, sinking her hand into

386

the soil and concentrating for a moment, grew some spikes of purple liriope tall enough to screen them from sight.

"What will we do?" Sparrow asked in a low voice.

"What *can* we do?" Ruby asked, resigned.

"You could give Minya a nice warm hug," suggested Sparrow with an unaccustomed edge to her voice. "What were her words?" she asked. "You might do more with your gift than heat bathwater and burn up your clothes?"

It took both Ruby and Sarai a moment to understand her. They were dumbfounded. "Sparrow!" Ruby cried. "Are you suggesting that I"—she cut herself off, glanced toward the ghosts, and finished in a whisper—"*burn up Minya?*"

"Of course not," said Sparrow, though that was exactly what she'd meant. "I'm not her, am I? I don't want anyone to die. Besides," she said, proving that she'd actually given the matter some thought, "if Minya died, we'd lose the Ellens, too, and all the other ghosts."

"And have to do all our own chores," said Ruby.

Sparrow thwacked her shoulder. "*That's* what you worry about?"

"No," said Ruby, defensive. "Of course I'd miss them, too. But, you know, who would do the cooking?"

Sparrow shook her head and rubbed her face. "I'm not even certain Minya's wrong," she said. "Maybe it is the only way. But does she have to be so *happy* about it? It's gruesome."

"*She's* gruesome," said Ruby. "But she's gruesome *for* us. Would you ever want to be against her?"

Ruby had been much preoccupied of late, and had not noticed the change in Sarai, let alone guessed its cause. Sparrow was a more empathetic soul. She looked at Sarai, taking in her drawn face and bruised eyes. "No," she said softly. "I would not."

"So we let her have her way in everything?" Sarai asked. "Can't you see where it leads? She'd have us be our parents all over again."

Ruby's brow furrowed. "We could never be them."

"No?" countered Sarai. "And how many humans can we kill before we are? Is there a number? Five? Fifty? Once you start, there's no stopping. Kill one—*harm* one—and there is no hope for any kind of life. *Ever.* You see that, don't you?"

Sarai knew Ruby didn't want to harm anyone, either. But she parted the liriope spikes with her hands, revealing the ghosts that edged the garden. "What choice do we have, Sarai?"

One by one the stars came out. Ruby claimed she was tired, though she didn't look it, and went in early to bed. Sparrow found a feather that could only have been Wraith's, and tucked it behind Sarai's ear.

She did Sarai's hair for her, gently combing it out with her fingers and using her gift to make it lustrous.

Sarai could feel it growing, and even sense it brightening, as though Sparrow were infusing it with light. She added inches; she made it full. She fixed her a crown of braids, leaving most of it tumbling long, and wove in vines and sprays of orchids, sprigs of fern, and the one white feather.

And when Sarai saw herself in the mirror again before sending out her moths, she thought that she looked more like a wild forest spirit than the goddess of despair.

36

Shopping for a Moon

Weep slept. Dreamers dreamed. A grand moon drifted, and the wings of the citadel cut the sky in two: light above, dark below.

On the outheld hand of the colossal seraph, ghosts stood guard with cleavers, and some with meat hooks on chains. The moon shone bright on the edges of their blades, and sharp on the points of their terrible hooks, and luminous on their eyes, which were wide with horror. They were bathed in light, while down below, the city foundered in gloom.

Sarai dispatched her moths to the guildhall, where most of the delegates were sleeping soundly, and to the homes of city leaders, and some of the Tizerkane, too. Tzara's lover was with her, and they were ... not sleeping ... so Sarai whisked her moth immediately away. Over in Windfall, Azareen was alone. Sarai watched her unbraid her hair, put on her ring, and lie down to go to sleep. She didn't stay for her dreams, though. Azareen's dreams were...difficult. Sarai couldn't help feeling that she played a part in stealing the life Azareen should have had—as though *she* existed instead of a beloved child that the couple should have had together. It might not have been her fault, but she couldn't feel innocent of it.

She saw the golden faranji—looking unwell—still awake and working. And she saw the ill-favored one, whose sun-ravaged skin was healing in the citadel's shade—though he was no more appealing for it. He was awake, too, out for a stagger with a bottle in his hand. It was as well. She couldn't abide his mind. All the women he dreamed were bruised, and she hadn't stayed long enough to find out how they got that way. She hadn't made herself visit him since the second night.

Every moth, every wingbeat carried the oppressive burden of the ghost army, and of vengeance, and the weight of another Carnage. With the occupation of her terrace, she stayed inside, turning five times oftener in her pacing than she had out on the hand. She craved the moonlight and the wind. She wanted to feel the infinite depth of space above and around her, not this metal cage. She remembered what Sparrow had said, how dreaming was like the garden: You could step out of prison for a little while and feel the sky around you.

And Sarai had argued that the citadel was prison but sanctuary, too. Only a week ago, it had been, and so had lull, and look at her now.

She was so terribly tired.

Lazlo was tired, too. It had been a long day, and giving away his spirit hadn't helped. He ate with Suheyla—and complimented the food without mention of ruined tongues—and took another bath, and though he soaked this time until the water began to cool, the gray didn't fade from his hands. In his state of fatigue, his thoughts dipped like hummingbirds from this to that, always coming round to the fear—the fear of the citadel and all that had happened in it. How haunted they all were by the past, Eril-Fane no less than the rest.

With that, two faces found their way into Lazlo's mind. One from a painting of a dead goddess, the other from a dream: both blue, with red-brown hair and a band of black paint across their eyes. Blue, black, and cinnamon, he saw, and wondered again how he had happened to dream her before ever seeing a likeness of her.

And why, if he'd somehow glimpsed a stray vision of Isagol the Terrible, had she been so . . . *un*terrible?

He stepped from the bath and dried off, pulled on a pair of laundered linen breeches, and was too tired even to tie the drawstring. Back in his room, he tipped onto the bed, prone atop the quilts, and was asleep halfway through his second breath.

And that was how Sarai found him: lying on his stomach with his head cradled in his arms.

The long, smooth triangle of his back rose and fell with deep, even breathing as her moth fluttered above him, looking for a place to settle. The way he was lying, his brow wasn't an option. There was the rugged edge of his cheekbone, but even as she watched, he nestled his head deeper into his arms, and that landing spot shrank and vanished. There was his back, though.

He'd fallen asleep with the glave uncovered, and the low angle of the light threw small shadows over every ripple of muscle, and deep ones under the wings of his shoulder blades and down the channel of his spine. It was a lunar landscape to the moth. Sarai floated it softly into the dark valley of his shoulder blades and as soon as it touched skin, she slipped into his dream.

She was wary, as always. A string of nights now she'd come here since the first time, and each time she'd slipped in as silently as a thief. A thief of what, though? She wasn't stealing his dreams from him, or even altering them in any way. She was just...enjoying them, as one might enjoy music freely played.

A sonata drifting over a garden wall.

Inevitably, though, listening to beautiful music night after night, one grows curious about the player. Oh, she knew who he was. She was, after all, perched on his brow all this while—until tonight, and this new experience of his back—and there was a strange intimacy in that. She knew his eyelashes by heart, and the male scent of him, sandalwood and clean musk. She'd even grown used to his crooked, ruffian nose. But inside the dreams, she'd kept her distance.

What if he saw her again? What if he *didn't*? Had it been a fluke? She wanted to know, but was afraid. Tonight, though, something had shifted. She was tired of hiding. She would find out if he could see her, and maybe even *why*. She was braced for it, ready for anything. At least she thought she was ready for anything.

But really, nothing could have prepared her to enter the dream and find herself *already there*.

* * *

Again, the streets of the magical city—Weep but not Weep. It was night, and the citadel was in the sky this time, but the moon shone down regardless, as though the dreamer wanted it both ways. And again there was unbelievable color, and gossamer wings and fruit and creatures out of fairy tales. There was the centaur with his lady. She walked by his side tonight, and Sarai felt almost restless until she saw them kiss. They were a fixture here; she'd have liked to talk to them and hear their story.

Sarai had the idea that every single person and

creature she saw here was but the beginning of another fantastical story, and she wanted to follow them all. But mostly, she was curious about the dreamer.

She saw him up ahead, riding on a spectral. And here's where things became completely surreal, because riding by his side, astride a creature with the body of a ravid and the head and wings of Wraith the white eagle was...Sarai.

To be clear, Sarai herself—Sarai *actual*—was at a distance, where she had entered the dream at a street crossing. She saw them.

Saw *herself.*

Saw herself riding a mythical creature in the far-anji's dream.

She stared. Her mouth opened and then closed again. *How?* She looked closer. Willed herself closer to see better, though she was careful to keep out of sight.

The other Sarai, near as she could tell, looked just as she herself had on the night that he had seen her: with wild hair, and Isagol's painted black mask. In other circumstances, at a glance, she would have thought she was seeing her mother, because the likeness between them was striking, and humans did dream of Isagol, whereas of course they never dreamed of her. But that wasn't Isagol. Her mother, for all their similarities, had possessed a majesty she didn't, and a cruelty, too. Isagol didn't smile. This girl did. This blue girl had Sarai's face, and she wasn't wearing some gown of beetle wings and daggers, but the same lace-edged white slip Sarai had worn the first night.

She was part of the dream.

The faranji was dreaming *Sarai*. He was dreaming her, and… it was not a nightmare.

Up in the citadel, her pacing feet faltered. Between the dreamer's bare shoulder blades, the perched moth trembled. An ache rose in Sarai's throat, like a sob without the grief. She looked across the street at herself—as seen, remembered, and conjured by the dreamer—and she didn't see obscenity, or calamity, or godspawn. She saw a proud, smiling girl with beautiful blue skin. Because that was what *he* saw, and this was his mind.

Of course, he also thought she was Isagol.

"Forgive me for asking," he was saying to her, "but why despair? Of all things to be goddess of."

"Don't tell anyone," Isagol answered. "I *was* goddess of the moon." She whispered the rest like a secret. "But then I lost it."

"You lost the moon?" the dreamer asked, and peered up at the sky, where the moon was very much present.

"Not that one," she said. "The other one."

"There was another one?"

"Oh yes. There's always a spare, just in case."

"I didn't know that. But… how do you lose a moon?"

"It wasn't my fault," she said. "It was stolen."

The voice was neither Sarai's nor Isagol's, but just some imagined voice. The strangeness of it all dazed Sarai. There was her face, her body, with an unfamiliar voice coming out, speaking whimsical words that had nothing at all to do with her. It was like looking in a mirror and seeing another life reflected back at her.

"We can go to the moon shop for another," the dreamer offered. "If you like."

"Is there a moon shop? All right."

And so the dreamer and the goddess went shopping for a moon. It was like something out of a story. Well, it was like something out of a dream. Sarai followed them in a state of fascination, and they went into a tiny shop tucked under a bridge, leaving their creatures at the door. She stood outside the mullioned window, stroked the gryphon's sleek feathered head, and suffered a pang of absurd envy. She wished it were *she* riding a gryphon and sorting through jeweler's trays for just the right moon. There were crescents and quarters, gibbous and full, and they weren't charms, they were *moons*—real miniature moons, cratered and luminous, as though lit by the rays of some distant star.

Sarai/Isagol—the imposter, as Sarai was beginning to think of her—couldn't decide between them, and so she took them all. The dreamer paid for them out of a silly sort of green brocade purse, and in the next instant they were gleaming at her wrist like a charm bracelet. The pair left the shop and remounted their creatures, Isagol holding up her bracelet so the moons tinkled like bells.

"Will they let you be a moon goddess again?" the dreamer inquired.

What is this moon goddess nonsense? Sarai wondered with a spark of ire. Isagol had been nothing so benign.

"Oh no," said the goddess. "I'm dead."

"Yes, I know. I'm sorry."

"You shouldn't be. I was terrible."

"You don't seem terrible," said the dreamer, and Sarai had to bite her lip. *Because that's not Isagol,* she wanted to snap. *It's me.* But it wasn't her, either. It might have her face, but it was a phantasm—just a scrap of memory dancing on a string—and everything it said and did came from the dreamer's own mind.

His mind, where the goddess of despair dangled moons from a charm bracelet and "didn't seem terrible."

Sarai could have shown him terrible. She was still the Muse of Nightmares after all, and there were visions of Isagol in her arsenal that would have woken him screaming. But waking him screaming was the last thing she wanted, so she did something else instead.

She dissolved the phantasm like a moth at sunup, and slipped into its place.

❧ 37 ❧

A PERFECTLY DELIGHTFUL
SHADE OF BLUE

Lazlo blinked. One moment Isagol had black paint streaked across her eyes and the next she didn't. One moment her hair was draped around her like a shawl and the next it was gleaming down her back like molten bronze. She was crowned with braids and vines and what he first took for butterflies but quickly saw were orchids, with a single long white feather at a jaunty angle. Instead of the slip, she was wearing a robe of cherry silk embroidered with blossoms of white and saffron.

There was a new fragrance, too, rosemary and nectar, and there were other differences, subtler: a slight shift in her shade of blue, an adjustment to the tilt of her eyes. A sort of...sharpening of the lines of her, as though a diaphanous veil had been lifted. She felt more *real* than she had a moment ago.

Also, she was no longer smiling.

"Who are you?" she asked, and her voice had changed. It was richer, more complex—a chord as opposed to a note. It was darker, too, and with it, the whimsy of the moment ebbed away. There were no more moons on her wrist—and none visible in the sky, either. The world seemed to dim, and Lazlo, looking up, perceived the moonlight now only as a nimbus around the citadel's edges.

"Lazlo Strange," he replied, growing serious. "At your service."

"Lazlo Strange," she repeated, and the syllables were exotic on her tongue. Her gaze was piercing, unblinking. Her eyes were a paler blue than her skin, and it seemed to him that she was trying to fathom him. "But who *are* you?"

It was the smallest and biggest of questions, and Lazlo didn't know what to say. At the most fundamental level, he didn't know who he was. He was a Strange, with all that that entailed—though the significance of his name would be meaningless to her, and anyway, he didn't think she was inquiring into his pedigree. So then, who was he?

At that moment, as *she* had changed, so did their surroundings. Gone was the moon shop, and all of Weep with it. Gone the citadel and its shadow. Lazlo and the goddess, still astride their creatures, were transported right to the center of the Pavilion of Thought.

Forty feet high, the shelves of books. The spines in their jewel tones, the glimmer of leaf. Librarians on ladders like specters in gray, and scholars in scarlet hunched at their tables. It was all as Lazlo had seen it that day seven years ago when the good fortune of bad fish had brought him to a new life.

And so it would seem that this was his answer, or at least his first answer. His outermost layer of self, even after six months away. "I'm a librarian," he said. "Or I was, until recently. At the Great Library of Zosma."

Sarai looked around, taking it all in, and momentarily forgot her hard line of questioning. What would Feral do in such a place? "So many books," she said, awed. "I never knew there were this many books in all the world."

Her awe endeared her to Lazlo. She might be Isagol the Terrible, but one can't be irredeemable who shows reverence for books. "That's how I felt, the first time I saw it."

"What's in them all?" she asked.

"In this room, they're all philosophy."

"*This* room?" She turned to him. "There are more?"

He smiled broadly. "So many more."

"All full of books?"

He nodded, proud, as though he'd made them all himself. "Would you like to see my favorites?"

"All right," she said.

Lazlo urged Lixxa forward, and the goddess kept

pace with him on her gryphon. Side by side, as majestic as a pair of statues but far more fantastical, they rode right through the Pavilion of Thought. The gryphon's wings brushed the shoulders of scholars. Lixxa's antlers nearly toppled a ladder. And Lazlo might have been an accomplished dreamer—in several senses of the word— but right now he was like anyone else. He wasn't conscious that this was a dream. He was simply *in it*. The logic that belonged to the real world had remained behind, like luggage on a dock. This world had a logic all its own, and it was fluid, generous, and deep. The secret stairs to his dusty sublevel were too narrow to accommodate great beasts like these, but they slipped down them easily. And he'd long since cleaned off the books with infinite love and care, but the dust was just as he had found it that very first day: a soft blanket of years, keeping all the best secrets.

"No one but me has read any of these in at least a lifetime," he told her.

She took down a book and blew off the dust. It flurried around her like snowflakes as she flipped pages, but the words were in some strange alphabet and she couldn't read them. "What's in this one?" she asked Lazlo, passing it to him.

"This is one of my favorites," he said. "It's the epic of the mahalath, a magic fog that comes every fifty years and blankets a village for three days and three nights. Every living thing in it is transformed, for either better or worse. The people know when it's coming, and most flee and wait for it to pass. But there are always a few who stay and take the risk."

"And what happens to them?"

"Some turn into monsters," he said. "And some to gods."

"So *that's* where gods come from," she said, wry.

"You would know better than me, my lady."

Not really, Sarai thought, because she had no more idea where the Mesarthim had come from than the humans did. She, of course, *was* conscious that this was a dream. She was too accustomed to dream logic to be surprised by any of the trappings, but not too jaded to find them beautiful. After the initial flurry, snow continued to fall in the alcove. It shone on the floor like spilled sugar, and when she slid from her gryphon's back, it was cold under her bare feet. The thing that did surprise her, that she couldn't get her mind around, even now, was that she was having a conversation with a stranger. However many dreams she had navigated, whatever chimerical fancies she had witnessed, she had never *interacted*. But here she was, talking—chatting, even. Almost like a real person.

"What about this one?" she asked, picking up another book.

He took it and read the spine. "Folktales from Vaire. That's the small kingdom just south of Zosma." He leafed pages and smiled. "You'll like this one. It's about a young man who falls in love with the moon. He tries to steal it. Perhaps he's your culprit."

"And does he succeed?"

"No," said Lazlo. "He has to make peace with the impossible."

Sarai wrinkled her nose. "You mean he has to give up."

"Well, it *is* the moon." In the story, the young man, Sathaz, was so enchanted by the moon's reflection in the still, deep pool near his forest home that he would gaze at it, entranced, but whenever he reached for it, it broke into a thousand pieces and left him drenched, with empty arms. "But then," Lazlo added, "if someone managed to steal it from *you*—" He looked to her bare wrist where no moon charms now hung.

"Maybe it was him," she said, "and the story got it wrong."

"Maybe," allowed Lazlo. "And Sathaz and the moon are living happily together in a cave somewhere."

"And they've had thousands of children together, and that's where glaves come from. The union of man and moon." Sarai heard herself, and wondered what was wrong with her. Just moments ago she'd been annoyed at the moon nonsense that was coming out of her phantasm's mouth, and now *she* was doing it. It was Lazlo, she thought. It was his mind. The rules were different here. The *truth* was different. It was...nicer.

He was grinning broadly, and the sight set off a

fluttering in Sarai's belly. "What about that one?" she asked, turning quickly away to point at a big book on a higher shelf.

"Oh hello," he said, reaching for it. He brought it down: a huge tome bound in pale-green velvet with a filigreed layer of silver scrollwork laid over it. "This," he said, passing it to her, "is the villain that broke my nose."

When he released it into her hands, its weight almost made her drop it in the snow. "*This?*" she asked.

"My first day as apprentice," he said, rueful. "There was blood everywhere. I won't disgust you by pointing out the stain on the spine."

"A *book of fairy tales* broke your nose," she said, helpless not to smile at how wrong her first impression had been. "I supposed you were in a fight."

"More of an ambush, actually," he said. "I was on tiptoe, trying to get it." He touched his nose. "But it got me."

"You're lucky it didn't take your head off," said Sarai, hefting it back to him.

"Very lucky. I got enough grief for a broken nose. I'd never have heard the end of a lost head."

A small laugh escaped Sarai. "I don't think you hear very much, if you lose your head."

Solemnly, he said, "I hope never to know."

Sarai studied his face, much as she had done the

first time she saw him. In addition to thinking him some sort of brute, she had also thought him not handsome. Looking now, though, she thought that handsome was beside the point. He was *striking*, like the profile of a conqueror on a bronze coin. And that was better.

Lazlo, feeling her scrutiny, blushed. His assumption as to her opinion of his looks was far less favorable than her actual thoughts on the subject. *His* opinion of *her* looks was simple. She was purely lovely. She had full cheeks and a sharp little chin and her mouth was damson-lush, lower lip like ripe fruit with a crease in the middle, and soft as apricot down. The corners of her smile, turned up in delight, were as neat as the tips of a crescent moon, and her brows were bright against the blue of her skin, as cinnamon as her hair. He kept forgetting that she was dead and then remembering, and he was sorrier about it every time he did. As to how she could be both dead *and* here, dream logic was untroubled by conundrums.

"Dear god in heaven, Strange," came a voice then, and Lazlo looked up to see old Master Hyrrokkin approaching, pushing a library trolley. "I've been looking all over for you."

It was so good to see him. Lazlo enveloped him in a hug, which evidently constituted a surfeit of affection, because the old man pushed him off, incensed. "What's gotten into you?" he demanded, straightening out his robes. "I suppose in Weep they just go around mauling one another like bear wrestlers."

"Exactly like bear wrestlers," said Lazlo. "Without the bears. Or the wrestling."

But Master Hyrrokkin had caught sight of Lazlo's companion. His eyes widened. "Now, who's this?" he inquired, his voice rising an octave or so.

Lazlo made an introduction. "Master Hyrrokkin, this is Isagol. Isagol, Master Hyrrokkin."

In a stage whisper, the old man asked, *"Whyever is she blue?"*

"She's the goddess of despair," Lazlo answered, as though that explained everything.

"No, she isn't," said Master Hyrrokkin at once. "You've got it wrong, boy. *Look* at her."

Lazlo did look at her, but more to offer an apologetic shrug than to consider Master Hyrrokkin's assertion. He knew who she was. He'd seen the painting, and Eril-Fane had confirmed it.

Of course, she looked less like her now, without the black paint across her eyes.

"Did you do as I suggested, then?" asked Master Hyrrokkin. "Did you give her flowers?"

Lazlo remembered his advice. "Pick flowers and find a girl to give them to." He remembered the rest of his advice, too. "Kind eyes and wide hips." He flushed at the memory. This girl was very slender, and Lazlo hardly expected the goddess of despair to have kind

407

eyes. She did, though, he realized. "Flowers, no," he said, awkward, wanting to head off any further exploration of the topic. He knew the old man's lecherous tendencies, and was anxious to see him on his way before he said or did something untoward. "It's not like that—"

But Isagol surprised him by holding up her wrist, upon which the bracelet had reappeared. "He did give me the moon, though," she said. There weren't multiple charms on it now, but just one: a white-gold crescent, pallid and radiant, looking just as though it had been plucked down from the sky.

"Nicely done, boy," said Master Hyrrokkin, approving. Again, the stage whisper: "She could do with more cushioning, but I daresay she's soft enough in the right places. You don't want to be jabbed with bones when you—"

"*Please*, Master Hyrrokkin," Lazlo said, hastily cutting him off. His face flamed.

The librarian chuckled. "What's the point of being old if you can't mortify the young? Well, I'll leave you two in peace. Good day, young lady. It was a real pleasure." He kissed her hand, then turned aside, nudging Lazlo with his elbow and loud-whispering, "What a perfectly delightful shade of blue," as he took his leave.

Lazlo turned back to the goddess. "My mentor," he explained. "He has bad manners but good hearts."

"I wouldn't know about either," said Sarai, who had

found no fault with the old man's manners, and had to remind herself, in any case, that he had been just another figment of the dreamer's mind. "You've got it wrong, boy," the librarian had said. "Look at her." Did that mean that on some level Lazlo saw through her disguise, and didn't believe she was Isagol? She was pleased by this idea, and chided herself for caring. She turned back to the shelves, ran her finger along a row of spines. "All these books," she said. "They're about magic?" She was wondering if he were some sort of expert. If that was why the Godslayer had brought him along.

"They're myths and folktales mostly," said Lazlo. "Anything dismissed by scholars as too *fun* to be important. They put it down here and forget it. Superstitions, songs, spells. Seraphim, omens, demons, fairies." He pointed to one bookcase. "Those are all about Weep."

"Weep is too fun to be important?" she asked. "I rather think its citizens might disagree with you."

"It's not my assessment, believe me. If I were a scholar, I could have made a case for it, but you see, I'm not important, either."

"No? And why is that?"

Lazlo looked down at his feet, reluctant to explain his own insignificance. "I'm a foundling," he said, looking up again. "I have no family, and no name."

"But you told me your name."

"All right. I have a name that tells the world I have no name. It's like a sign around my neck that reads 'No one.'"

"Is it so important, a name?" Sarai asked.

"I think the citizens of Weep would say it is."

Sarai had no answer for that.

"They'll never get it back, will they?" Lazlo asked. "The city's true name? Do *you* remember it?"

Sarai did not. She doubted she had ever known it. "When Letha took a memory," she said, "she didn't keep it in a drawer like a confiscated toy. She *ate* it and it was gone forever. That was her gift. Eradication."

"And *your* gift?" Lazlo asked.

Sarai froze. The thought of explaining her gift to him brought an immediate flush of shame. *Moths swarm out of my mouth*, she imagined herself saying. *So that I can maraud through human minds, like I'm doing right now in yours.* But of course, he wasn't asking about *her* gift. For a moment she'd forgotten who she was—or wasn't. She wasn't Sarai here, but this absurd tame phantasm of her mother.

"Well, she was no moon goddess," she said. "That's all nonsense."

"*She?*" asked Lazlo, confused.

"*I*," said Sarai, though it stuck in her throat. It struck her with a pang of deep resentment, that this extraordinary, inexplicable thing should happen: A human could *see* her—and he was talking to her without hate, with something more like fascination and even wonder—and she had to hide behind this pretense. If she *were* Isagol, she would show him her gift. Like a malefic kitten with a ball of string, she would tangle his emotions until he lost all distinction between love and hate, joy and sorrow. Sarai didn't want to play that part, not ever. She turned the questions back on him.

"Why don't you have a family?" she asked.

"There was a war. I was a baby. I ended up on a cartload of orphans. That's all I know."

"So you could be anyone," she said. "A prince, even."

"In a tale, maybe." He smiled. "I don't believe there were any princes unaccounted for. But what about you? Do gods have families?"

Sarai thought first of Ruby and Sparrow, Feral and Minya, Great and Less Ellen, and the others: her family, if not by blood. Then she thought of her father, and hardened her hearts. But the dreamer was doing it again, turning the questions around on her. "We're made by mist," she said. "Remember? Every fifty years."

"The mahalath. Of course. So you were one who took the risk."

"Would you?" she asked. "If the mist were coming, would you stay and be transformed, not knowing what the result might be?"

"I would," he said at once.

"That was fast. You would abandon your true nature with so little consideration?"

411

He laughed at that. "You have no idea how much consideration I've given it. I lived seven years inside these books. My body may have been going about its duties in the library, but my mind was here. Do you know what they called me? Strange the dreamer. I was barely aware of my surroundings half the time." He was amazed at himself, going on like this, and to the goddess of despair, no less. But her eyes were bright with curiosity—a mirror of his own curiosity about her, and he felt entirely at ease. Certainly despair was the last thing he thought of when he looked at her. "I walked around wondering what kind of wings I would buy if the wingsmiths came to town, and if I'd prefer to ride dragons or hunt them, and whether I'd stay when the mist came, and more than anything else by far, how in the world I was going to get to the Unseen City."

Sarai cocked her head. "The Unseen City?"

"Weep," he said. "I always hated the name, so I made up my own."

Sarai had been smiling in spite of herself, and wanting to ask which book the wingsmiths were in, and whether the dragons were vicious or not, but at this reminder of Weep, her smile slowly melted back to melancholy, and that wasn't all that melted away. To her regret, the library did, too, and they were in Weep once more. But this time it wasn't his Weep, but hers, and it might have been closer to the true city than his version, but it wasn't accurate, either. It was still beautiful, certainly, but there was a forbidding quality to it, too. All the doors and windows were closed—and the sills, it went without saying, were empty of cake—and it was desolate with dead gardens and the telltale hunched hurry of a populace that feared the sky.

There were so many things she wanted to ask Lazlo, who had been called "dreamer" even before she dubbed him that. *Why can you see me? What would you do if you knew I was real? What wings would you choose if the wingsmiths came to town? Can we go back to the library, please, and stay awhile?* But she couldn't say any of that. "Why *are* you here?" she asked.

He was taken aback by the sudden turn in mood. "It's been my dream since I was a child."

"But why did the Godslayer bring you? What is your part in this? The others are scientists, builders. What does the Godslayer need with a librarian?"

"Oh," said Lazlo. "No. I'm not really one of them. Part of the delegation, I mean. I had to beg for a place in the party. I'm his secretary."

"You're Eril-Fane's *secretary*."

"Yes."

"Then you must know his plans." Sarai's pulse quickened. Another of her moths was fluttering in sight of the pavilion where the silk sleighs rested. "When will he come to the citadel?" she blurted out.

It was the wrong question. She knew it as soon as

413

she said it. Maybe it was the directness, or the sense of urgency, or maybe it was the slip of using *come* instead of *go*, but something shifted in his look, as though he were seeing her with new eyes.

And he was. Dreams have their rhythms, their deeps and shallows, and he was caroming upward into a state of heightened lucidity. The left-behind logic of the real world came slanting down like shafts of sun through the surface of the sea, and he began to grasp that none of this was real. Of course he hadn't actually ridden Lixxa through the Pavilion of Thought. It was all fugitive, evanescent: a dream.

Except for her.

She was neither fugitive nor evanescent. Her presence had a weight, depth, and clarity that nothing else did—not even Lixxa, and there were few things Lazlo knew better these days than the physical reality of Lixxa. After six months of all-day riding, she felt almost like an extension of himself. But the spectral seemed suddenly insubstantial, and no sooner did this thought occur than she melted away. The gryphon, too. There was only himself and the goddess with her piercing gaze and nectar scent and ... gravity.

Not gravity in the sense of solemnity—though that, too—but gravity in the sense of a *pull*. He felt as though *she* were the center of this small, surreal galaxy—indeed, that it was *she* who was dreaming *him*, and not the other way around.

He didn't know what made him do it. It was so unlike him. He reached for her hand and caught it—lightly—and held it. It was small, smooth, and very real.

Up in the citadel, Sarai gasped. She felt the warmth of his skin on hers. A blaze of connection—or *colli-sion*, as though they had long been wandering in the same labyrinth and had finally rounded the corner that would bring them face-to-face. It was a feeling of being lost and alone and then suddenly neither. Sarai knew she ought to pull her hand free, but she didn't. "You have to tell me," she said. She could feel the dream shallowing, like a sleek ship beaching on a shoal. Soon he would wake. "The flying machines. When will they launch?"

Lazlo knew it was a dream, and he knew it wasn't a dream, and the two knowings chased circles in his mind, dizzying him. "What?" he asked. Her hand felt like a heartbeat wrapped within his own.

"The flying machines," she repeated. "*When?*"

"Tomorrow," he answered, hardly thinking.

The word, like a scythe, cut the strings that were holding her upright. Lazlo thought that his hand around hers was all that was keeping her standing. "What is it?" he asked. "Are you all right?"

She pulled away, grabbed back her hand. "Listen to me," she said, and her face grew severe. The black band returned like a slash, and her eyes blazed all the brighter for the contrast. "They must not come," she said, in a voice as unyielding as mesarthium. The vines and orchids disappeared from her hair, and then there was blood running out of it, streaming rivulets down her brow to collect in her eye sockets and fill them up until they were nothing but glassy red pools, and still the blood flowed, down over her lips and into her mouth, smearing as she spoke. "Do you understand?" she demanded. "If they do, *everyone will die.*"

❧ 38 ❧

EVERYONE WILL DIE

Everyone will die.

Lazlo jolted awake and was astonished to find himself alone in the small bedroom. The words echoed in his head, and a vision of the goddess was imprinted in his mind: blood pooling in her eye sockets and dripping down to catch in her lush mouth. It had been so real that at first he almost couldn't credit that it had been a dream. But of course it had been. Just a dream, what else? His mind was overflowing with new imagery since his arrival in Weep. Dreams were his brain's way of processing them all, and now it was struggling to reconcile the girl from the dream with the one in the mural. Vibrant and sorrowful versus...bloody and unmourned.

He had always been a vivid dreamer, but this was something altogether new. He could still feel the shape and weight of her hand in his, the warmth and softness of it. He tried to brush it all aside as he got on with the morning, but the image of her face kept intruding, and the haunting echo of her words: *Everyone will die*.

Especially when Eril-Fane invited him to join the ascension to the citadel.

"Me?" he asked, dumbfounded. They were in the pavilion, standing beside the silk sleighs. Ozwin was readying one of the two; to save on ulola gas, only one would go up today. Once they reached the citadel, they were to restore its defunct pulley system so that their future comings and goings would not be dependent on flight.

It was how goods had been brought up from the city back in the days of the Mesarthim. It had a basket just big enough to carry a person or two—as they'd discovered after the liberation, when the freed had used it to get back down to the ground, one trip at a time. But in the wild hours of shock and celebration that greeted the news of the gods' demise, they must have forgotten to secure the ropes properly. They'd slipped from the pulleys and fallen, rendering the citadel forever—or until now—inaccessible. Today they would reestablish the link.

Soulzeren had said she could carry three passengers in addition to herself. Eril-Fane and Azareen made two, and Lazlo was offered the last place.

"Are you sure?" he asked Eril-Fane. "But...one of the Tizerkane—?"

"As you've no doubt observed," said Eril-Fane, "the citadel is difficult for us." *We are all children in the dark*, Lazlo remembered. "Any of them would come if I asked, but they'll be glad to be spared. You needn't come if you don't wish." A sly glint came into his eyes. "I can always ask Thyon Nero."

"Now, that's uncalled for," said Lazlo. "And anyway, he isn't here."

Eril-Fane looked around. "No, he isn't, is he?" Thyon was, in fact, the only delegate who hadn't come to watch the launch. "Shall I send for him?"

"No," said Lazlo. "Of course I want to come." In truth, though, he was less certain after his macabre dream. *Just a dream*, he told himself, glancing up at the citadel. The angle of the climbing sun snuck a slash of rays under the edges of its wings, shining a jagged shimmer along the sharp tips of the huge metal feathers.

Everyone will die.

"Are you sure it's empty?" he blurted out, trying and failing to sound casual.

"I'm sure," said Eril-Fane with grim finality. He softened a little. "If you're afraid, just know that you're in good company. It's all right if you prefer to stay."

"No, I'm fine," Lazlo insisted.

And so it was that he found himself stepping aboard a silk sleigh a scant hour later. In spite of the chill that didn't quite leave him, he was well able to

419

marvel at this latest unfolding of his life. He, Strange the dreamer, was going to fly. He was going to fly in the world's first functional airship, along with two Tizerkane warriors and a badlander mechanist who used to make firearms for amphion warlords, up to a citadel of alien blue metal floating above the city of his dreams.

In addition to the faranji, citizens were gathered to see them off, Suheyla included, and all were marked by the same trepidation as the Zeyyadin the previous evening. No one looked up. Lazlo found their fear more unsettling than ever, and was glad to be distracted by Calixte.

She came over and whispered, "Bring me a souvenir." She winked. "You owe me."

"I'm not going to loot the citadel for you," he said, prim. And then, "What kind of souvenir?" His mind went at once to the god corpses they expected to find, including Isagol's. He shuddered. How long did it take for a corpse to become a skeleton? Less than fifteen years, surely. But he wouldn't be breaking off any pinkie bones for Calixte. Besides, Eril-Fane said that Lazlo and Soulzeren would wait outside while he and Azareen did a thorough search to make sure it was safe.

"I thought you were certain it was empty," Lazlo pointed out.

"Empty of the living," was his comforting reply.

And then they were boarding. Soulzeren put on

goggles that made her look like a dragonfly. Ozwin gave her a kiss and loosened the mooring lines that kept the big silk pontoons firmly on the ground. They had to cast them all off at once if they wanted to rise straight and not "yaw about like drunken camels," as Ozwin put it. There were safety lines that hooked to harnesses Soulzeren had given them to wear—all but Eril-Fane, whose shoulders were far too big for them.

"Hook it on your belt, then," said Soulzeren with a frown. She peered up, squinting at the underside of the vast metal wings, and the soles of the great angel's feet, and the sky she could see around the edges. "No wind, anyway. Should be fine."

Then they were counting down and casting off.

And just like that... they were flying.

* * *

The five in the citadel gathered on Sarai's terrace, watching, watching, watching the city. If you stared at it long enough, it became an abstract pattern: the circle of the amphitheater dead center in the oval formed by the outer walls, which were broken by the four hulking monoliths of the anchors. The streets were mazy. They tempted you to trace pathways with your eyes, finding routes between this place and that. All the godspawn had done it, save Minya, who alone never yearned to see it closer.

"Maybe they aren't coming," said Feral, hoping. Ever since Sarai told him about the silk sleighs' vulnerability, he'd been thinking about it, wondering what he would do if—*when*—it came down to it. Would he defy Minya, or disappoint Sarai? Which was the safer course? Even now he was uncertain. If only they wouldn't come, he wouldn't have to choose.

Choosing wasn't Feral's strong suit.

"There." Sparrow pointed, her hand trembling. She still held the flowers she'd been weaving into Sarai's hair—torch ginger blossoms, like the ones she'd put on Ruby's cake—"for wishing"—except that these weren't buds. They were open blooms, as gorgeous as fireworks. She'd already done Ruby's hair, and Ruby had done hers. All three of them wore wishes in their hair today.

Now Sarai's hearts lurched. They seemed to slam together. She leaned forward, resting against the slope of the angel's hand to peer over the edge and follow the line of Sparrow's finger down to the rooftops. *No no no*, she said inside her head, but she saw it: a flicker of red, rising from the pavilion of the guildhall.

They were coming. Disengaging from the city, leaving rooftops and spires and domes behind. The shape grew larger, steadily more distinct, and soon Sarai could make out four figures. Her hearts went on slamming.

Her father. Of course he was one of the four. He

was easy to discern at a distance for the size of him. Sarai swallowed hard. She had never seen him with her own eyes. A wave of emotion surged through her, and it wasn't wrath, and it wasn't hate. It was longing. To be someone's child. Her throat felt thick. She bit her lip.

And all too soon they were risen close enough that she could make out the other passengers. She recognized Azareen, and would have expected no less from the woman who had loved Eril-Fane for so long. The pilot was the older faranji woman, and the fourth passenger...

The fourth passenger was Lazlo.

His face was upturned. He was still too distant to make out clearly, but she knew it was him.

Why hadn't he listened to her? Why hadn't he believed her?

Well, he would believe soon enough. Waves of hot and cold flushed through her, chased by despair. Minya's army was waiting just inside the open door in Sarai's room, ready to ambush the humans the moment they landed. They would swarm over them with their knives and cleavers and meat hooks. The humans wouldn't stand a chance. Minya stood there like the small general she was, intent and ready. "All right," she said, fixing Sarai and Feral, Ruby and Sparrow with her cool, bright gaze. "Everyone get out of sight," she ordered, and Sarai watched as the others obeyed.

"Minya—" she began.

"*Now*," snapped Minya.

Sarai didn't know what to do. The humans were coming. Carnage was at hand. Numbly, she followed the others, wishing it were a nightmare from which she could awaken.

* * *

It wasn't like soaring. There was nothing of the bird in this steady ascension. They floated upward, rather, like a very large ulola blossom, with a bit more control than the wind-borne flowers had.

Aside from the pontoons, which were sewn of specially treated red silk and contained ulola gas, there was another bladder, this one under the craft, filled with air by means of a foot-pedal bellows. It wasn't for lift, but propulsion. By means of a number of outflow valves, Soulzeren could control thrust in different directions—forward, backward, side to side. There was a mast and sail, too, that worked just like a sailing ship if the winds were favorable. Lazlo had witnessed test flights in Thanagost, and the sight of the sleighs scudding across the skies under full sail had been magical.

Looking down, he saw people in the streets and on terraces, growing steadily smaller until the sleigh had drifted so far above the city that it spread out like a map. They came even with the lowermost part of the citadel—the feet. Up and up, past the knees, the long, smooth thighs up to the torso, seeming draped in robes of gossamer—all mesarthium and solid but so cunningly shaped you could see the jut of hip bones as though through diaphanous cloth.

Whatever else he had been, Skathis had also been an artist.

In order to cast the greatest shadow, the wings were fanned out in an immense circle, with the scapular feathers touching in the back, the secondaries forming the middle of the ring, and the long, sleek primaries reaching all the way around to come parallel to the seraph's outstretched arms. The silk sleigh rose up through the gap between the arms, coming even with the chest. As he squinted up at the underside of the chin, color caught Lazlo's eyes. *Green.* Swaths of green below the collarbones, stretching from one shoulder to the other.

They were the trees that dropped their plums on the district called Windfall, Lazlo thought. It occurred to him to wonder how, with so little rainfall, they were still alive.

* * *

"Feral," Sarai implored. "Please."

Feral's jaw clenched. He didn't look at her. If she were asking him *not* to do something, he wondered if it would be easier than to do something. He glanced at Minya.

"This doesn't have to happen," Sarai went on. "If you call clouds *right now*, you can still force them back."

"Close your mouth," said Minya, her voice like ice, and Sarai saw that it infuriated her that she couldn't compel the living to obey her as easily as she did the dead.

"Minya," she pleaded, "so long as no one's died, there's hope of finding some other way."

"So long as no one's died?" repeated Minya. She gave a high laugh. "Then I'd say it's fifteen years too late for hope."

Sarai closed her eyes and opened them again. "I mean *now*. So long as no one's died *now*."

"If it's not today, then it's tomorrow, or the next day. When there's an unpleasant job to do, it's best to get it over with. Putting it off won't help."

"It might," said Sarai.

"How?"

"I don't know!"

"Keep your voice down," Minya hissed. "You do understand that a necessary condition for ambush is *surprise*?"

Sarai stared at her face, so hard and uncompromising, and again saw Skathis in the set of her features, even the shape of them. If Minya had gotten Skathis's power, she wondered, would she be any different from

426

him, or would she willingly subjugate a whole population, and justify it all within the rigid parameters of *justice*. How had this small, damaged...child...ruled them for so long? It struck her now as ridiculous. Might there have been another way, from the very start? What if Sarai had never given a single nightmare? What if, from the beginning, she had soothed the fears of Weep instead of stoking them? Might she have defused all this hatred?

No. Even she couldn't believe that. For two hundred years it had been building. What could she have hoped to accomplish in fifteen?

She would never know. She had never been given a choice, and now it was too late. These humans were going to die.

And then?

When the silk sleigh and its passengers failed to return? Would they send the other up after it, so more could die?

And then?

Who knows how much time it would buy them, how many more months or years they would have of this purgatorial existence before a bigger, bolder attack came—more crafts, Tizerkane leaping from ships like pirates boarding a vessel. Or the clever outsiders would come up with some grand plan to scuttle the citadel.

Or suppose the humans simply cut their losses and abandoned Weep, leaving a ghost town for them to lord over. Sarai imagined it empty, all those mazy lanes and mussed-up beds deserted, and she felt, for a staggering moment, as though she were drowning in that emptiness. She imagined her moths drowning in silence, and it felt like the end of the world.

Only one thing was sure, whatever happened: From this moment on, the five of them would be like ghosts pretending they were still alive.

Sarai wanted to say all this, but it tangled up inside of her. She'd held her tongue for too long. It was too late. She caught a flash of red through the open door and knew it was the silk sleigh, though her first thought was of blood.

Everyone will die.

Minya's expression was predatory, eager. Her grubby little hand was poised to give the signal, and—

"No!" Sarai cried, shoving her aside and darting forward. She pushed through the throng of ghosts and they were as solid as living bodies, but with none of the warmth and give. She bumped against a knife held fast in a ghost's grip. Its blade slid over her forearm as she thrust her way past. It was so sharp she felt it only as a line of heat. Blood flowed fast, and when a ghost grabbed for her wrist, the slickness made her hard to hold. She twisted free and darted into the doorway.

The silk sleigh was there, maneuvering to a landing. They were already turned in her direction, and startled when she appeared. The pilot was busy with her levers, but the other three stared at her.

Eril-Fane's and Azareen's hands sprang to the hilts of their hreshteks.

Lazlo, amazed, said, "*You.*"

And Sarai, with a sob, screamed, "Go!"

39

UNCANNY ENEMIES

Trees that should have been dead. Movement where there should have been stillness. A figure in the doorway of a long-abandoned citadel.

Where there ought to have been naught but desertion and old death, there was . . . *her*.

Lazlo's first instinct was to doubt he was awake. The goddess of despair was dead and he was dreaming. But he knew the latter, at least, wasn't true. He felt Eril-Fane's sudden stillness, saw his great hand freeze on his hilt, his hreshtek but half drawn. Azareen's wasn't. It came free with a deadly *shink!*

All this was periphery. Lazlo couldn't turn aside to see. He couldn't tear his eyes away from *her*.

She had red flowers in her hair. Her eyes were wide and desperate. Her voice, it carved a tunnel through the air. It was rough and scouring, like rusty anchor chain reeling through a hawse. She was struggling. Hands caught at her from within. *Whose hands?* She gripped the sides of the doorway, but the mesarthium was smooth; there was no frame, nothing to give her purchase, and there were too many hands, grabbing at her arms and hair and shoulders. She had nothing to hold on to.

Lazlo wanted to leap to her defense. Their eyes met. The look was like the scorch of lightning. Her scouring cry still echoed—*Go!*—and then she was gone, ripped back into the citadel.

As others came pouring out.

Soulzeren had, in the instant of the cry, reversed thrust on the sleigh, sending it scudding gently backward. "Gently" was its only speed, except under sail with a good stiff breeze. Lazlo stood rooted, experiencing the full meaning of *useless* as a wave of enemies hurtled toward them, moving with uncanny fluidity, flying at them as though launched. He had no sword to draw, and nothing to do but stand and watch. Eril-Fane and Azareen stood squarely before him and Soulzeren, guarding them from this impossible onslaught. Too many, too swift. They boiled like bees from a hive. He couldn't understand what he was seeing. They were coming. They were fast.

They were here.

431

Steel on steel. The sound—a *skreek*—cut straight to his hearts. He couldn't stand empty-handed—useless—in such a storm of steel. There were no extra weapons. There was nothing but the padded pole Soulzeren kept for pushing the sleigh clear of obstacles when maneuvering to a landing. He grabbed it and faced the fray.

The attackers had knives, not swords—*kitchen* knives—and their shortened reach brought them well inside the warriors' strike zone. If they were ordinary foes, it might have been possible to defend against them with great broad slashes that gutted two or three at a time. But they weren't ordinary foes. It was plain to see they weren't soldiers at all. They were men and women of all ages, some white-haired, and some not even yet adults.

Eril-Fane and Azareen were deflecting blows, sending kitchen knives skittering over the metal surface of the terrace that was still beneath the sleigh. Azareen gasped at the sight of one old woman, and Lazlo noted the way her sword arm fell limp to her side. "Nana?" she said, stunned, and he watched, unblinking, horrified, as the woman raised a mallet—the studded metal sort for pounding cutlets—and brought it arcing down right at Azareen's head.

There was no conscious thought in it. Lazlo's arms did the thinking. He brought the pole up, and just in time. The mallet smashed into it, and *it* smashed into Azareen. He couldn't prevent it. The force of the blow—immense for an old woman!—was too great. But the pole was padded with batting and canvas, and it stopped Azareen's skull from being staved in. Her sword arm jerked back to life. She knocked the pole away and shook her head to clear it, and Lazlo saw...

He saw her blade cut right through the old woman's arm—*right through*—and...nothing happened. The arm, her substance, it simply...rearranged itself around the weapon and became whole again after it had passed through. There wasn't even blood.

It all came clear. These enemies were not mortal, and they could not be harmed.

The realization struck them all, just at the moment that the sleigh glided finally free of the terrace and back into open sky, widening the distance from the metal hand and the army of the dead it held.

There was a feeling of escape, a moment to gasp for breath.

But it was false. The attackers kept coming. They vaulted off the terrace, mindless of the distance. They leapt into the open sky and...failed to fall.

There was no escape. The attackers crashed onto the sleigh. Ghosts poured from the angel's huge metal hand, wielding knives and meat hooks, and the Tizerkane fought them off blow by blow. Lazlo stood between the warriors and Soulzeren, wielding the pole. An attacker slipped around the side—a man with a mustache—and Lazlo cut him in half with a swing, only to watch the halves of him re-form like something from a nightmare. The trick was the weapons, he thought, remembering the mallet. He struck again with the pole, aiming for the man's hand, and knocked the knife from his grip. It clattered to the floor of the sleigh.

This unnatural army was entirely untrained, but what did that matter? There was no end to them, and they could not die. What is skill in such a fight?

The ghost with the mustache, unarmed now, launched at Soulzeren, and Lazlo thrust himself between them. The ghost grabbed for the pole. Lazlo held on. They grappled. Behind the figure he could see all the rest of them—the swarm of them with their blank faces and staring, harrowed eyes, and he couldn't wrest the pole free. The ghost's strength was unnatural. He wouldn't tire. Lazlo was helpless when the next attacker slipped around the Tizerkane's guard. A young woman with haunted eyes. A meat hook in her hands.

She raised it. Brought it down . . .

. . . on the starboard pontoon, puncturing it. The sleigh lurched. Soulzeren cried out. Gas hissed through the hole, and the sleigh began to spin.

It was at just this moment, when it occurred to

Lazlo that he was going to die—exactly as he had been warned, impossibly, in a dream—that the ghost he was grappling with...lost solidity. Lazlo saw his hands, one moment so hard and real on the wood of the pole, melt right through it. The same thing happened to the young woman. The meat hook fell from her grip, though she never loosed her hold on it. It fell right through her hand and into the sleigh. And then the strangest thing. A look of sweetest, purest relief came over her face, even as she began to fade from sight. Lazlo could see through her. She closed her eyes and smiled and was gone. The man with the mustache was next. An instant and his face lost its blankness, flushed with the delirium of *release*, and then he vanished, too. The ghosts were melting. They had gone beyond some boundary and been set free.

Not all of them were so lucky. Most were sucked backward like kites on strings, reeled back to the metal hand to watch as the sleigh, spinning slowly, scudded farther and farther out of their reach.

No time to wonder. The starboard pontoon was leaking gas. The sleigh was keeling over. "Lazlo," barked Soulzeren, pushing her goggles up onto her forehead. "Shift your weight to port, and hold on."

He did as she commanded, his weight balancing the tilt of the craft as she slapped a patch onto the hissing hole the meat hook had made. The weapon still lay on the floor, dull and deadly, and the knife that had fallen there, too. Azareen and Eril-Fane were gasping for breath, their hreshteks still drawn, shoulders heaving. They checked each other frantically for injuries. Both were bleeding from cuts to their hands and arms, but that was all. Amazingly, no one had sustained a serious injury.

Drawing a deep breath, Azareen turned to Lazlo. "You saved my life, faranji."

Lazlo almost said, "You're welcome," but she hadn't actually thanked him, so he held it back and only nodded. He hoped it was a dignified nod, maybe even a little tough. He doubted it, though. His hands were shaking.

His everything was shaking.

The sleigh had stopped its spinning, but was still listing. They'd lost just enough gas for a slow descent. Soulzeren raised the sail and sheeted it, bringing the bow around and aiming for the meadows outside the city walls.

That was good. It would give them time to catch their breath before the others could reach them. The thought of the others, and all the questions they would ask, jolted Lazlo out of his survival euphoria and back into reality. Questions. Questions required answers. What were the answers? He looked to Eril-Fane. "What just happened?" he asked.

The Godslayer stood a good while with his hands on the rail, leaning heavily, looking away. Lazlo couldn't see his face, but he could read his shoulders. Something very heavy was pressing there. Very heavy indeed. He thought of the girl on the terrace, the girl from the dream, and asked, "Was that Isagol?"

"No," said Eril-Fane, sharp. "Isagol is dead."

Then...who? Lazlo might have asked more, but Azareen caught his eye and warned him off with a look. She was badly shaken.

They were silent for the rest of the descent. The landing was soft as a whisper, the craft skimming over the tall grass until Soulzeren dropped the sail and they came at last to a halt. Lazlo helped her secure it, and they climbed back onto the surface of the world. They were out from under the citadel here. The sun was bright, and the crisp line of shadow, downhill, made a visible border.

Against that harsh line where darkness began, Lazlo caught a glimpse of the white bird, wheeling and tilting. It was always there, he thought. Always watching.

"They'll get here soon, I reckon," said Soulzeren. She pulled off her goggles and wiped her brow with her arm. "Ozwin won't tarry."

The Godslayer nodded. He was silent another moment, collecting himself, before he picked up the dropped knife and meat hook from the floor of the silk sleigh and hurled them away. He drew a hard breath and spoke. "I won't order you to lie," he said slowly.

"But I'm asking you to. I'm asking that we keep this to ourselves. Until I can think what to do about it."

It? The ghosts? The girl? This utter upending of what the citizens of Weep thought they knew about the citadel they already feared with such cold, debilitating dread? What manner of dread would this new truth inspire? Lazlo shuddered to think of it.

"We can't...we can't simply do nothing," said Azareen.

"I know," said Eril-Fane, ravaged. "But if we tell, there will be panic. And if we try to attack..." He swallowed. "Azareen, did you *see*?"

"Of course I did," she whispered. Her words were so raw. She hugged her arms around herself. Lazlo thought they should have been Eril-Fane's arms. Even he could see that. But Eril-Fane was trapped in his own shock and grief, and kept his great arms to himself.

"Who were they?" Soulzeren asked. "*What* were they?"

Slowly, like a dancer dropping into a curtsy that keeps going all the way to the ground, Azareen sank down onto the grass. "All our dead," she said. "Turned against us." Her eyes were hard and bright.

Lazlo turned to Eril-Fane. "Did you know?" he asked him. "When we were taking off, I asked if you were certain it was empty, and you said 'Empty of the living.'"

Eril-Fane closed his eyes. He rubbed them. "I didn't

438

mean…ghosts," he said, stumbling on the word. "I meant bodies." He seemed almost to be hiding his face in his hands, and Lazlo knew there were still secrets.

"But the girl," he said, tentative. "She was neither."

Eril-Fane dropped his hands from his eyes. "No." With anguish and a stark glimmer of…something— redemption?—he whispered, *She's alive.*

Part IV

* * *

sathaz (SAH·thahz) *noun*

The desire to possess that which can never be yours.

Archaic; from the Tale of Sathaz, who fell in love with the moon.

🌿 40 🌿

MERCY

What had Sarai just done?

After it was over and they had watched, all five of them, over the edge of the terrace as the silk sleigh escaped down to a far green meadow, Minya turned to her, unspeaking—*unable* to speak—and her silence was worse than screaming could have been. The little girl shook with ill-contained fury, and when the silence stretched on, Sarai forced herself to really look at Minya. What she saw wasn't just fury. It was a wilderness of disbelief and betrayal.

"That man killed us, Sarai," she hissed when she finally found her voice. "You might forget that, but I never can."

"We aren't dead." At that moment, Sarai truly wasn't sure that Minya knew that. Maybe all she knew was ghosts, and could make no distinction. "Minya," she said, pleading, "we're still alive."

"Because *I* saved us from *him*!" She was shrill. Her chest heaved. She was so thin inside her ragged garment. "So that *you* could save *him* from *me*? Is that how you thank me?"

"No!" Sarai burst out. "I thanked you by doing everything you ever told me to do! I thanked you by being your wrath for you, every night *for years*, no matter what it did to me. But it was never enough. It will never *be* enough!"

Minya looked incredulous. "Are you mad you had to keep us safe? I'm so sorry if it was hard for you. Perhaps we should have waited on you, and never made you use your nasty gift."

"That's not what I'm saying. You twist everything." Sarai was shaking. "There might have been another way. You made the choice. *You* chose nightmares. I was too young to know better. You used me like one of your ghosts." She was choking on her own words, astonished at herself for speaking so. She saw Feral, stricken dumb, his mouth actually agape.

"So in turn you betrayed me. You betrayed us all. I might have chosen for you once, Sarai, but today the choice was all yours." Her chest rose and fell with animal breathing. Her shoulders were frail as bird bones. *"And you. Chose. Them!"* She shrieked the last part. Her face went red. Tears burst from her eyes. Sarai

444

had never seen her cry before. Not ever. Even her tears were fierce and angry. No gentle, tragic trails like the ones that painted Ruby's and Sparrow's cheeks. Minya's tears *raged*, practically leaping from her eyes in full, fat drops, like rain.

Everyone was frozen. Sparrow, Ruby, Feral. They were stunned. They looked from Sarai to Minya, Minya to Sarai, and seemed to be holding their breath. And when Minya wheeled on them, pointed at the door, and commanded, "You three. Get out!" they hesitated, torn, but not for long. It was Minya they feared, her icy tantrums, her scalding disappointment, and her they were used to obeying. If Sarai had, in that moment, presented them with a choice, if she had stood proud and defended her actions, she might have won them to her. She didn't, though. Her uncertainty was written all over her: in her too-wide eyes and trembling lip and the way she held her bloody arm limp against her middle.

Ruby clung to Feral and turned away when he did. Sparrow was last to go. She cast a frightened glance back from the doorway and mouthed the words *I'm sorry*. Sarai watched her leave. Minya stood there a moment longer, looking at Sarai as though she were a stranger. When she spoke again, her voice had lost its shrillness, its fury. It was flat, and old. She said, "Whatever happens now, Sarai, it will be your fault."

And she spun on her heel and stalked through the door, leaving Sarai alone with the ghosts.

All the anger was sucked away in her wake, and it left a void. What else was there, when you took away the anger, the hate? The ghosts stood frozen—those who remained, the ones Minya had yanked back from the brink of freedom while others crossed out of her reach and escaped her—and they couldn't turn their heads to look at Sarai, but their eyes strained toward her, and she thought that she saw grace there, and gratitude.

For her mercy.

Mercy.

Was it mercy or betrayal? Salvation or doom? Maybe it was all of those things flashing like a flipped coin, end over end—mercy betrayal salvation doom. And how would it come down? How would it all end? Heads, and the humans live. Tails, the godspawn die. The outcome had been rigged from the day they were born.

A coldness seeped into Sarai's hearts. Minya's army appalled her, but what would have happened today if it hadn't been here? If Eril-Fane had come, expecting to find skeletons, and found *them* instead?

She was left with the desolate certainty that her father would have done again what he did fifteen years ago. His face was fixed in her mind: haunted to start with, just to be returning to this place of his torment. Then startled. Then stricken by the sight of *her*. She'd witnessed the precise moment when he understood.

It was so very fast: the first blanch of shock, when he thought she was Isagol, and the second, when he realized she wasn't.

When he grasped who she was.

Horror. That was what she had seen on his face, and nothing short of it. She had believed she had hardened herself to any further pain he could cause her, but she'd been wrong. This was the first time in her life that she had seen him with her own eyes—not filtered through moths' senses or conjured in his own unconscious or Suheyla's or Azareen's, but *him*, the man whose blood was half her own, her father—and his horror at the sight of her had opened a new blossom of shame in her.

Obscenity, calamity. Godspawn.

And on the dreamer's face? Shock, alarm? Sarai could hardly say. It had all happened in a blink, and all the while the ghosts were wrenching her out of the doorway, dragging her back inside. Her arm. It hurt. She looked down. Blood was crusted dark from her forearm to her fingers, and still oozing bright from the long line of the cut.

There were bruises blooming, too, where the ghosts had gripped her. The pulsing pain made it feel like their hands were still on her. She wanted Great Ellen—her gentle touch to clean and wrap her wound, and her compassion. With resolve, she made to leave, but ghosts blocked her way. For a moment, she didn't grasp what was happening. She'd grown accustomed to their presence, always steeling herself when she had to pass through a cluster of them, but they had never interfered with her before. Now, no sooner did she make for the door than they glided together, preventing her passing. She faltered to a stop. Their faces were impassive as ever. She knew better than to speak to them as though they were under their own control, but the words came out anyway. "What, am I not allowed to leave?"

Of course they didn't answer. They had their orders and would obey them, and Sarai would not be going anywhere.

All day long, nobody came. Ostracized, isolated, and wearier than she had ever been, she rinsed her arm with the last water from her pitcher, and bandaged it with a slip she tore into strips. She kept to her sleeping alcove, as though she were hiding from the ghost guards. Hot waves of panic crashed through her each time she remembered, afresh, the chaos of the morning and the choice that she had made.

Whatever happens now, it will be your fault.

She hadn't meant to choose. In her hearts, she had never and could never make *that* choice—humans over her own kind. That wasn't what she'd done. She wasn't a traitor. But she wasn't a murderer, either. Pacing, she felt as though her life had chased her down a dead-end corridor and trapped her there to taunt her.

Trapped trapped trapped.

Perhaps she had always been a prisoner, but not like this. The walls closed in around her. She wanted to know what was happening down in Weep, and what nature of uproar had greeted the news of her existence. Eril-Fane must have told them by now. They would be gathering weapons, talking strategy. Would they come back up in greater numbers? Could they? How many silk sleighs did they have? She'd only seen two, but they looked easy to build. She supposed it was just a matter of time until they could field an invasion force.

Did Minya think her army could hold them off forever? Sarai pictured a life in which they went on as before but under siege now, alert to attacks at all hours of the day or night, repelling warriors, pushing corpses off her terrace to plunge all the way down to the city below like so many windfall plums. Feral would call rain showers to rinse away the blood, and they would all sit down to dinner while Minya bound the day's new batch of dead into her service.

Sarai shuddered. She felt so helpless. The day was bright, and it went on and on. Her craving for lull was powerful, but there was no more gray waiting for her now, no matter how much lull she drank. She was so tired she felt... threadbare, like the soles of old slippers, but she didn't dare close her eyes. Her terror of what awaited her just over the threshold of consciousness was more powerful still. She wasn't *well*. Ghosts without, horrors within, and nowhere to turn. Her shining blue walls hemmed her in. She wept, waiting for nightfall, and finally it came. Never before had her silent scream been such a release. She screamed everything, and felt as though her very being broke apart in the soft scatter of wings.

Translated into moths, Sarai surged out the windows and siphoned herself away. The sky was huge and there was freedom in it. The stars called to her like signal beacons burning on a vast black sea as she flung herself a hundredfold into the dizzy air. Escape, escape. She flew away from nightmares and privation and the turned backs of her kindred. She flew away from the dead-end corridor where her life had trapped and taunted her. She flew away from *herself.* A wild desire gripped her to fly as far as she could from Weep—a hundred moths, a hundred directions—to fly and fly till sunrise came and turned her to smoke and all her misery, too.

"Kill yourself, girl," the old woman had said. "Have mercy on us all."

Mercy.

Mercy.

Would it be mercy, to put an end to herself? Sarai knew those vicious words had come not from old ghost women but her own innermost self, guilt-poisoned from four thousands nights of dark dreams. She also knew that in all of the city and in the monstrous metal angel that had stolen the sky, she was the only one who knew the suffering of humans and godspawn both, and it came to her that her mercy was singular and precious. Today it had forestalled carnage, at least for a time. The future was blind, but she couldn't feel, truly, that it would be better without her in it. She gathered herself from her wild scatter. She gave up the sky with its signal-fire stars, and flew instead down to Weep to find out what her mercy had set in motion.

🌿 41 🌿

WITCHLIGHT

The goddess was real, and she was alive.

Lazlo had dreamed her before he knew the Mesarthim were blue, and that had seemed uncanny enough. How much more now that he'd seen her *alive*, her lovely face an exact match to the one in his dreams. It was no coincidence.

It could only be magic.

When wagons arrived to retrieve the downed silk sleigh and its passengers, the four of them stuck to a simple story of mechanical failure, which was questioned by no one. They downplayed the event to such a degree that the day carried on as usual, though Lazlo felt as though he'd left "usual" behind forever. He processed everything as well as could be expected— considering that "everything" entailed near death at the hands of savage ghosts—and he found within himself, rising through all the consternation and fright, a strange bubble of gladness. The girl from his dreams wasn't a figment, and she wasn't the goddess of despair, and she wasn't *dead*. All day long he kept tipping back his head to look up at the citadel with new eyes, knowing she was inside it. How was it possible?

How was any of it possible? Who was she, and how had she come into his dreams? He was fretful as he laid himself down to sleep that night, hoping that she would return. Unlike the previous night, when he'd sprawled facedown on the bed, shirtless and unselfconscious, without even tying the drawstring of his breeches, tonight he was prey to a peculiar formality. He put on a shirt, tied his drawstring, tied back his hair. He even glanced at himself in the mirror—and felt foolish to be concerned for his appearance, as though she would somehow see him. He had no idea how it worked, this magic. She was up there and he was down here, but he couldn't shake the feeling that he was expecting a visitor—which would have been a new experience for him in any setting, but was particularly, uh, provocative in this one. To be lying in bed, waiting for a goddess to pay him a call...

He blushed. Of course it wasn't like that. He stared at the ceiling, a tension in his limbs, and felt as though he were acting the part of a sleeper in a play. It wouldn't do. He had to actually fall asleep in order

453

to dream, and it wasn't coming easily, with his mind racing from the mania of the day. There was a kind of euphoria, he had discovered, in nearly dying and then not. Add to that his anxiousness as to whether she would come. He was all nerves and fascination and bashfulness and a deep, stirring hope.

He remembered, marveling, how he had taken her hand last night and held it in his own, sensing the realness of it, and of her, and the connection that had blazed between them when he had. In reality he would never have dared to do such a bold thing. But he couldn't quite convince himself that it *wasn't* reality, in its way. It hadn't occurred in the physical realm, that much was true. His hand had not touched her hand. But…his *mind* had touched *her* mind, and that seemed to him a deeper reality and even greater intimacy. She had gasped when he touched her, and her eyes had flown wide. It had been real to her, too, he thought. Her lashes, he recalled, were golden red, her eyes pellucid blue. And he remembered how she had looked at him as though transfixed, the first time, nights ago, and again last night. No one had ever looked at him like that before. It made him want to check the mirror again to see what she had seen—if perhaps his face had improved without his knowing it—and the impulse was so vain and unlike him that he flung an arm over his eyes and laughed at himself.

His laughter subsided. He remembered, too, the

welling blood and her warning—"Everyone will die"—and the furious way she had grappled in the doorway of the citadel, fighting to warn him yet again.

He would be dead if it weren't for her.

"*Go!*" she had screamed as hands caught at her, reeling her back inside. How fierce and desperate she had looked. Was she all right? Had she been hurt? In what conditions did she exist? *What was her life?* There was so much he wanted to know. Everything. He wanted to know everything, and he wanted to help. Back in Zosma, when Eril-Fane had stood before the scholars and spoken with shadowed countenance of Weep's "problem," Lazlo had been overcome by this same deep desire: to help, as though someone like him had any chance of solving a problem like this.

It struck him as he lay here with his arm slung across his eyes, that the girl was tied up in Weep's problem in ways he could not yet understand. One thing was clear to him, though. She wasn't safe, and she wasn't free, and Weep's problem had just grown much more complicated.

Whom had she defied with that scream, he wondered, and what price might she have paid for it? Worrying about her redoubled his anxiety and pushed sleep even further away, so that he feared it would never come. He was anxious that he might miss her visit, as though his dreams were a door she might even now be knocking on, and finding no one at home.

Wait, he thought. *Please wait for me.* And finally he calmed himself with what he thought of, self-mockingly, as "housekeeping concerns." He'd never had a guest before, and he didn't know how to go about it. *How* to receive her if she came, and *where*. If there were etiquette guidelines for hosting goddesses in one's dreams, he had never found that book at the Great Library.

It wasn't simply a question of parlors and tea trays—though there was that, too. If she were coming in reality he would be limited *by reality*. But dreams were a different matter. He *was* Strange the dreamer. This was his realm, and there were no limits here.

* * *

Sarai watched the dreamer fling his arm across his eyes. She heard him laugh. She took note of his unnatural stillness, recognizing it as restrained restlessness, and waited impatiently for it to soften into sleep. Her moth was perched in a shadowed corner of the window casement, and she waited there a long time after he fell still, trying to determine when he had truly crossed over. His arm was still crooked over his face, and without being able to see his eyes, she couldn't tell if he might be faking. Ambush was on her mind, for obvious reasons, and she couldn't reconcile the violence of the morning with the quiet of this night.

She had found none of the panic or preparation that she had expected. The damaged silk sleigh had been hauled back to its pavilion, and there it lay forlorn, one pontoon deflated. The mechanist-pilot was asleep in her bed, her head on her husband's shoulder, and though the earlier chaos flared through her dreams—and his, in smaller measure—the rest of the outsiders were untroubled. Sarai's determination, from her moths' gleanings of the night's first crop of dreams, was that Soulzeren had told her husband but no one else of the . . . encounter . . . at the citadel.

The Zeyyadin were all likewise in the dark. No panic. No awareness, that Sarai could tell, of the threat that lurked over their heads.

Had Eril-Fane kept it secret? Why would he?

If only she could ask him.

In fact, at the same time that her moth was perched in the window casement watching sleep claim Lazlo Strange, Sarai was watching it *not* claim the God-slayer.

She had found him. She hadn't even been looking, just assuming he'd be missing as he had been all these nights Sarai had nightly called on Azareen and found her all alone.

Really, she still was alone. She was in her bed, curled in a ball with her hands over her face, not asleep, as Eril-Fane was likewise not asleep in the small sitting room just outside the door, chairs pushed aside and a bedroll laid out on the floor. He wasn't lying on it, though. His back was to the wall, and his face was in his hands. Two rooms, door closed between them. Two warriors with their faces in their hands. Sarai, watching them, could see that everything would be better if the faces and hands were to simply...switch places. That is, if Azareen were to hold Eril-Fane while he held her.

How anguished they both were, and how still and quiet and determined to suffer alone. From Sarai's vantage point, she beheld two private pools of suffering so close together they were nearly adjacent—like the connecting rooms with the shut door between them. Why not open the door, and open their arms, and close them again around each other? Did they not understand how, in the strange chemistry of human emotion, his suffering and hers, mingled together, could...countervail each other?

At least for a time.

Sarai wanted to feel scorn for them for being such fools, but she knew too much to ever scorn them. For years she'd seen Azareen's love for Eril-Fane blasted in the bud like Sparrow's orchids by one of Feral's blizzards. And why? Because the great Godslayer was incapable of love.

Because of what Isagol had done to him.

And, as Sarai had slowly come to understand— or rather, for years *refused* to understand until finally there was no denying it—because of what he himself had done. What he had forced himself to do to ensure the future freedom of his people: killing children, and, with them, his own soul.

That was what had finally broken through her blindness. Her father had saved his people and destroyed himself. As strong as he looked, inside he was a ruin, or perhaps a funeral pyre, like the Cusp—only instead of the melted bones of ijji, he was made up of the skeletons of babies and children, including, as he had always believed, his own child: *her*. This was his remorse. It choked him like weeds and rot and colonies of vermin, clogging and staining him, stagnant and fetid, so that nothing so noble as love, or—gods above—*forgiveness*, could ever claim space in him.

He was even denied the relief of tears. Here was something else that Sarai knew better than anyone: The Godslayer was incapable of crying. The city's name was a taunt. In all these years, he had been unable to weep. When Sarai was young and cruel, she had tried to make him, ever without success.

Poor Azareen. To see her curled up like that and skinned of all her armor was like seeing a heart flayed from a body, laid raw on a slab, and labeled *Grief.*

And Eril-Fane, savior of Weep, three years' plaything of the goddess of despair? What label for him, but *Shame.*

And so Grief and Shame abided in adjoining rooms

459

with the door shut between them, holding their pain in their arms instead of each other. Sarai watched them, waiting for her father to fall asleep so that she might send her sentinel to him—if she dared—and know what he was hiding in his hearts as he hid his face in his great hands. She couldn't forget his look of horror when he had seen her in the doorway, but nor could she understand why he'd kept her secret.

Now that he knew she was alive, what did he plan to do about it?

* * *

And so here were the four who had flown to the citadel and lived to tell the tale—though they apparently *hadn't* told it. Sarai watched them all, the sleeping and the sleepless. She was many other places, too, but most of her focus was split between her father and the dreamer.

When she was certain that Lazlo had at last subsided into dreams—and he had finally moved his arm so that she could see his face—she detached her moth from the casement and went to him. She couldn't quite bring herself to touch him, though, and hovered in the air above him. It would be different now. That much she knew. Up in the citadel, pacing, she felt as jumpy as though she were really there in the room with him, ready to spook at his slightest movement.

Through the moth's senses she smelled his sandal-wood and clean musk scent. His breathing was deep and even. She could tell that he was dreaming. His eyes moved under his lids, and his lashes, resting closed—as dense and glossy as the fur of rivercats—fluttered gently. Finally, she couldn't stay out one moment more. With a feeling of surrender, and anticipation, and apprehension, she crossed the small distance to his brow, settled on his warm skin, and entered his world.

He was waiting for her.

He was *right there*, standing straight and expectant as though he'd known she would come.

Her breath caught. *No*, she thought. Not as though he'd *known*. As though he'd *hoped*.

Her moth spooked from him and broke contact. He was too near; she wasn't prepared. But that single strobe of an instant caught the moment that his worry became relief.

Relief. At the sight of *her*.

It was only then, aflutter in the air above him, her hearts in her own far-off body drumming up a wild cadence, that Sarai realized she'd been braced for the worst, certain that today, finally, he must have learned proper disgust for her. But in that glimpse she had seen no sign of it. She took courage, and returned to his brow.

There he still was, and she beheld again the trans-formation from worry to relief. "I'm sorry," he said in his woodsmoke voice. He was farther away now. He hadn't moved, exactly, but rather shifted the conception of space in the dream so as not to crowd her at its threshold. They weren't in any version of Weep, she saw, or in the library, either. They were standing on the bank of a river, and it wasn't the tumultuous Uzumark but a gentler stream. Not Weep nor the Cusp nor the citadel were visible, but a great deal of pale-rose sky, and, beneath it, this broad path of smooth green water plied by birds with long, curved necks. Along the banks, leaning out as though to catch their own reflections, were rows of rough stone houses with their shutters painted blue.

"I frightened you," said Lazlo. "Please stay."

It was funny, the notion that *he* could frighten *her*. The Muse of Nightmares, tormentor of Weep, spooked from a dream by a sweet librarian?

"You only startled me," she said, self-conscious. "I'm not used to being greeted." She didn't explain that she wasn't used to being *seen*, that all this was new to her, or that her heartbeats were tangling together, falling in and out of rhythm like children learning how to dance.

"I didn't want to miss you, if you came," said Lazlo. "I hoped you would." There it was, the witchlight in his eyes, sparkling like sun on water. It does something to a person to be looked at like that—especially someone so accustomed to disgust. Sarai had a new, disconcerting awareness of herself, as though she'd never realized how many moving parts she had, all to be coordinated with some semblance of grace. It worked itself out so long as you didn't think about it. Start worrying, though, and it all goes wrong. How had she gone her entire life without noticing the awkwardness of arms, the way they just hang there from your shoulders like links of meat in a shop window? She crossed them—artlessly, she felt, like some arm amateur taking the easy way out.

"Why?" she asked him. "What do you want?"

"I...I don't want anything," he rushed to say. Of course, it was an unfair question. After all, it was she trespassing in his dream, not the other way around. He had more right to ask what *she* wanted here. Instead, he said, "Well, I do want to know if you're all right. What happened to you up there? Were you hurt?"

Sarai blinked. Was *she* hurt? After what he had seen and survived, he was asking if *she* was all right? "I'm fine," she said, a bit gruff due to an unaccountable ache in her throat. Up in her room she cradled her injured arm. No one in the citadel even cared that she was hurt. "You should have listened to me. I tried to warn you."

"Yes, well. I thought you were a dream. But apparently you're not." He paused, uncertain. "You're not, are you? Though of course if you were, and told me you weren't, how would I know?"

"I'm not a dream," said Sarai. There was bitterness in her voice. "I'm a nightmare."

Lazlo breathed out a small, incredulous laugh. "You're not my idea of a nightmare," he said, blushing a little. "I'm glad you're real," he added, blushing a lot. And they stood there for a moment, facing each other—though they weren't looking *at* each other, but down at the pebbled stretch of riverbank between their two pairs of feet.

Lazlo saw that hers were bare and that she was curling her toes into the pebbles and the soft mud beneath them. He had been thinking about her all day, and he had little enough to go on, but she'd clearly been a surprise to Eril-Fane and Azareen, which led him to suppose that her entire life had been lived up in the citadel. Had she ever set foot on the world? With this is mind, the sight of her bare blue toes curling into the river mud struck him with a deep poignancy.

After which the sight of her bare blue ankles and slender calves struck him with a deep allure, so that he blushed and looked away. And he thought that after all, in the midst of everything, it might be ridiculous to offer refreshment, but he didn't know what else to do, so he ventured, "Would you . . . would you care for some tea?"

Tea?

Sarai noticed, for the first time, the table at the riverside. It was actually in the shallows, its feet lost in little foaming eddies that curled against the bank. There was a linen cloth on it and some covered dishes, along with a teapot and a pair of cups. A wisp of steam escaped the pot's spout, and she found that she could smell it, spicy and floral amid the earthier scents of the river. What they called tea in the citadel was only herbs like mint and lemon balm. She had a distant memory of the taste of real tea, buried with her recollections of sugar and birthday cake. She fantasized about it sometimes—the drink itself, but this, too. The ritual of it, the setting up and sitting down that seemed to her, from outside of it, the simple heart of culture. Sharing tea and conversation (and, it was always to be hoped, cake). She looked from the incongruous setup to the landscape around it and then back to Lazlo, who'd caught a bit of his lower lip between his teeth and was watching her, anxious.

And Sarai noticed, outside the dream, that his real lip was likewise caught between his real teeth. His nervousness was palpable, and it disarmed her. She saw that he wanted to please her. "This is for *me*?" she asked with half a voice.

"I'm sorry if I've gotten anything wrong," he said, abashed. "I've never had a guest before, and I'm not sure how to do it."

"A guest," Sarai said faintly. That word. When she went into dreams, she went as a trespasser, a marauder. She had never been *invited* before. She had never been *welcome*. The feeling that came over her was all new—and extravagantly nice. "And I've never *been* a guest before," she confessed. "So I know no more about it than you do."

"That's a relief," said Lazlo. "We can make it up between us, however we like."

He pulled out a chair for her. She moved to sit. Neither had ever performed this simple maneuver, on land let alone in water, and it struck them at the same moment that there was room for error. Push the chair in too quickly or too slowly, or else sit too soon or too heavily, and misadventure ensues, perhaps even an unintended baptism of the hindquarters. But they managed it all right, and Lazlo took the chair opposite, and just like that they were two people sitting at a table regarding each other shyly through a wisp of tea steam.

Inside a dream.

Within a lost city.

In the shadow of an angel.

At the brink of calamity.

But all of that—city and angel and calamity—seemed worlds away right now. Swans swam past like elegant ships, and the village was all pastel with patches of blue shadow. The sky was the color of the blush on peaches, and insect language whirred in the sweet meadow grass.

Lazlo considered the teapot. It seemed a lot to ask of his hands to steadily pour into such dainty cups as he'd conjured, so he had the tea pour itself, which task was accomplished admirably, as though by an invisible steward. Only one drop went astray, discoloring the linen cloth, which he promptly willed clean again.

Imagine, he thought, having such power in life. And then it struck him as funny that it was the cleaning of a tablecloth that had given rise to this thought, and not the creation of an entire village and a river with birds on it, the hills in the distance, or the surprise they held in store.

He had dreamed lucidly before, but never so lucidly as this. Ever since he came to Weep, his dreams had been exceptionally vivid. He wondered: Was it *her* influence that made this clarity possible? Or had his own attention and expectancy shifted him into this state of higher awareness?

They picked up their cups. It was a relief to both of them to have something to do with their hands. Sarai tried her first sip, and couldn't tell whether the flavor—smoke and flowers—was her own memory of tea, or if Lazlo was shaping the sensory experience within his dream. Did it work like that?

"I don't know your name," he said to her.

Sarai had never, in all her life, been asked her name or told it. She had never *met* anyone before. Everyone she knew, she had always known—except for captured ghosts, who weren't exactly keen on pleasantries. "It's Sarai," she said.

"Sarai," he repeated, as though he were tasting it. *Sarai*. It tasted, he thought—but did not say—like tea—complex and fine and not too sweet. He looked at her, really looked. He wouldn't, in the world, ever look at a young woman with such directness and intensity, but it was somehow all right here, as though they had met with the tacit intent to know each other. "Will you tell me?" he asked. "About yourself?"

Sarai held her cup in both hands. She breathed the hot steam while cold water swirled around her feet. "What did Eril-Fane tell you?" she asked, wary. Through another moth's eyes, she observed that her father was no longer sitting against the wall, but had moved to the open window of Azareen's sitting room and was leaning out, staring up at the citadel. Was he imagining *her* up there? And, if so, what was he thinking? If he would sleep, she might be able to tell. She couldn't see it on his face, which was like a death mask: grim and lifeless with hollows for eyes.

"He only said that you aren't Isagol," Lazlo relayed. He paused. "Are you . . . her daughter?"

Sarai lifted her gaze to him. "Did he say that?"

Lazlo shook his head. "I guessed," he said. "Your hair." He had guessed something else, too. Hesitant, he said, "Suheyla told me that Eril-Fane was Isagol's consort."

Sarai said nothing, but truth was in her silence, and in her proud effort to show no pain.

468

"Didn't he know about you?" Lazlo asked, sitting forward. "If he'd known he had a child—"

"He knew," Sarai said shortly. A half mile away, the man in question rubbed his eyes with infinite weariness, yet still he didn't close them. "And now he knows I'm still alive. Did he say what he intends to do?"

Lazlo shook his head. "He didn't say very much. He asked that we not tell anyone what happened up there. About you or any of it."

Sarai had assumed as much. What she wanted to know was *why*, and *what next*, but Lazlo couldn't tell her that and Eril-Fane was still awake. Azareen had drifted off, finally, and Sarai landed a soft sentinel on the curve of her tearstained cheek.

She found no answers, though. Instead, she was plunged into the violence of the morning. She heard her own echoing cry of "Go!" and felt the terror bearing down, cleavers and meat hooks and the face of her own grandmother—Azareen's grandmother—twisted in unfamiliar hatred. It replayed itself over and over, relentless, and with one terrible difference: In the dream, Azareen's blades were as heavy as anchors, weighing down her arms as she strove to defend against the onslaught pouring from the angel's hand. She was too slow. It was all frantic, sluggish panic and roiling, invincible foes, and the outcome was not so lucky as it had been that morning.

In Azareen's dream, they all died, just as Sarai had told Lazlo they would.

She grew quiet at the riverside, her attention drawn away. Lazlo, observing that the cerulean hue of her face had gone a little ashen, asked, "Are you all right?"

She nodded, too quickly. *I just watched you die*, she did not say, but she had a hard time pushing the image from her mind. The warmth of his brow beneath her moth reassured her, and the sight of him across the table. Real Lazlo, dream Lazlo, alive because of her. It sank in that she was seeing a vision of the murders she had averted, and whatever shame she might have felt at Minya's tirade earlier, she didn't feel it anymore.

Deftly, she took control of Azareen's nightmare. She lightened the warrior's weapons and slowed the onslaught while the silk sleigh drifted out of range. Finally, she evanesced the ghosts, starting with Azareen's grandmother, infusing the dream with their sighs of release. The dead were free and the living were safe, and there was an end to the dream.

Sarai had finished her tea. The pot refilled her cup. She thanked it as though it were alive, and then her gaze lingered on the covered dishes. "So," she inquired, flashing a glance Lazlo's way. "What's under there?"

❧ 42 ❧

GOD OR MONSTER, MONSTER OR GOD

Lazlo had only marginally more experience with cake than Sarai did, so this was one of the things they made up between them "however they liked." It was a bit of a game. One would imagine the contents of a dish, and the other would uncover it with a small, dramatic flourish. They discovered that they could conjure splendid-*looking* confections, but were somewhat less successful when it came to flavor. Oh, the cakes weren't bad. They were sweet at least—that much was easy. But it was a bland sweetness dreamed up by orphans who'd pressed their faces to sweetshop windows (metaphorically, at least), and never had a taste.

"They're all alike," lamented Sarai, after sampling a small forkful of her latest creation. It was a marvel to behold: three tall tiers glazed in pink with sugared petals, far too tall to have fit beneath the cover it was under. "A magic trick," Lazlo had said, when it had seemed to grow with the lifting of the lid.

"Everything here is a magic trick," Sarai had replied.

But their recipes could use a bit less magic and more reality. The imagination, as Lazlo had previously noted, is tethered in some measure to the known, and they were both sadly ignorant in matters of cake. "These should be good at least," said Lazlo, trying again. "Suheyla made them for me, and I think I remember the flavor pretty well."

It *was* better: a honeyed pastry filled with pale-green nuts and rose petal jelly. It wasn't as good as the real thing, but at least it had a specificity the others lacked, and though they could easily have willed their fingers clean, that seemed a sad waste of imaginary honey, and both were inclined to lick them instead.

"I don't think we'd better attempt any dream banquets," said Lazlo, when the next attempt proved once more uninspiring.

"If we did, I could provide kimril soup," said Sarai.

"Kimril?" asked Lazlo. "What's that?"

"A virtuous vegetable," she said. "It has no flavor to tempt one to overindulgence, but it will keep you alive."

There was a little pause as Lazlo considered the practicalities of life in the citadel. He was reluctant to abandon this sweet diversion and the lightness it had brought to his guest, but he couldn't sit here with this vision of her and not wonder about the *real* her, whom he'd glimpsed so briefly and under such terrible circumstances. "Has it kept *you* alive?" he inquired.

"It has," she said. "You might say it's a staple. The citadel gardens lack variety."

"I saw fruit trees," Lazlo said.

"Yes. We have plums, thank gardener." Sarai smiled. In the citadel, when it came to food, they had been known to praise "gardener" as others might praise god. They owed an even greater debt to Wraith for that bundle of kimril tubers that had made all the difference. Such were their deities in the citadel of dead gods: an obscure human gardener and an antisocial bird. And, of course, none of it would have mattered without Sparrow's and Feral's gifts to nurture and water what little they had. How unassailable the citadel looked from below, she thought, and yet how tenuous their life was in it.

Lazlo had not missed her plural pronoun. "We?" he asked casually, as though it weren't a monumental question. *Are you alone up there? Are there others like you?*

Evasive, Sarai turned her attention to the river. Right where she looked, a fish leapt up, rainbow iridescence shimmering on its scales. It splashed back down and sank out of sight. Did it make any difference, she wondered, if Lazlo and Eril-Fane found out there were more godspawn alive in the citadel? The Rule was broken. There was "evidence of life." Did it

473

matter *how much* life? It seemed to her that it did, and anyway, it felt like betrayal to give the others away, so she said, "The ghosts."

"Ghosts eat plums?"

Having determined to lie, she did so baldly. "Voraciously."

Lazlo let it pass. He wanted to know about the ghosts, of course, and why they were armed with kitchen tools, viciously attacking their own kin, but he started with a slightly easier question, and asked simply how they came to be there.

"I suppose everyone has to be somewhere," Sarai said evasively.

Lazlo agreed, thoughtful. "Though some have more control over the *where* than others."

He didn't mean the ghosts now. He cocked his head a little and looked intently at Sarai. She felt his question forming. She didn't know what words he would use, but the gist of it boiled down to *why. Why are you up there? Why are you trapped? Why is this your life? Why everything about you?* And she wanted to tell him, but she felt her own return question burgeoning within her. It felt a little like the burgeoning of moths at darkfall, but it was something much more dangerous than moths. It was *hope*. It was: *Can you help me? Can you* save *me? Can you save* us?

When she'd gone down to Weep to "meet" the Godslayer's guests, she'd had no scope to imagine *him*. A…friend? An ally? A dreamer in whose mind the best version of the world grew like seed stock. If only it could be transplanted into reality, she thought, but it couldn't. It couldn't. Who knew better how poisonous the soil was in Weep than she who had been poisoning it for ten long years?

So instead she cut off his almost-question and asked, "Speaking of *where*, what is this place?"

Lazlo didn't press her. He had patience for mysteries. All these years, though, the mysteries of Weep had never had the urgency of this one. This was life or death. It had almost been *his* death. But he had to earn her trust. He didn't know how to do that, and so once again sought refuge in stories. "Ah, well. I'm glad you asked. This is a village called Zeltzin. Or at least this is how I imagine a village called Zeltzin might look. It's an ordinary place. Pretty, if unexceptional. But it does have one distinction."

His eyes sparkled. Sarai found herself curious. She looked around her, wondering what that distinction might be.

Earlier, while he was trying to fall asleep, Lazlo's first thought was to make an elegant sort of parlor to receive her in if she came. It seemed the proper way to go about things, if a bit dull. For some reason, then, Calixte's voice had come into his head. "Beautiful and full of monsters," she'd said. "All the best stories are." And she was right. "Any guesses?" he asked Sarai.

She shook her head. Her eyes had a bit of a sparkle, too.

"Well, I might as well tell you," said Lazlo, enjoying himself. "There's a mineshaft over there that's an entrance to the underworld."

"The underworld?" Sarai repeated, craning her neck in the direction he pointed.

"Yes. But that's not the distinction."

She narrowed her eyes. "Then what is?"

"I could also tell you that the children here are born with teeth and gnaw on bird bones in their cradles."

She winced. "That's horrible."

"But that's not the distinction, either."

"Won't you tell me?" she asked, growing impatient.

Lazlo shook his head. He was smiling. This was fun. "It's quiet, don't you think?" he asked, faintly teasing. "I wonder where everyone's gone."

It was quiet. The insects had ceased their whirring. There was only the sound of the river now. Behind the village, sweet meadows climbed toward a ridge of hills that looked, from a distance, to be covered in dark fur. Hills that seemed, Sarai thought, to be holding their breath. She sensed it, a preternatural stillness, and held hers, too. And then . . . the hills exhaled, and so did she.

"Ohhh," she breathed. "Is it—?"

"The mahalath," said Lazlo.

The fifty-year mist that made gods or monsters.

It was coming. It was fog—tongues of white vapor extruding between the knuckles of the fur-dark hills—but it moved like a living thing, with a curious, hunting intelligence. At once light and dense, there was something lithe about it, almost serpentine. Unlike fog, it didn't merely drift and settle, tumbling downward, heavier than the air. Here and there, tendrils of its curling white churn seemed to rise up and peer about before collapsing again into the tidal flow like whitecaps sucked back into the surf. It was pouring downward—pouring *itself* downward—in a glorious, relentless glissade over the meadow slopes on a straight path for the village.

"Did you ever play make-believe?" Lazlo asked Sarai.

She gave a laugh. "Not like this." She was frightened and exhilarated.

"Shall we flee?" he asked. "Or stay and take our chances?"

The tea table had vanished, and the chairs and dishes, too. Without noticing the transition, the pair of them were standing, knee-deep in the river, watching the mahalath swallow the farthest houses of the village. Sarai had to remind herself that none of it was real. It was a game within a dream. But what were the rules? "Will it change us?" she asked. "Or do we change ourselves?"

"I don't know," said Lazlo, to whom this was also

new. "I think we could choose what we want to become, or we could choose to let the dream choose, if that makes sense."

It did. They could exert control, or relinquish it to their own unconscious minds. Either way, it wasn't a mist remaking them, but themselves. God or monster, monster or god. Sarai had an ugly thought. "What if you're already a monster?" she asked in a whisper.

Lazlo looked over at her, and the witchlight in his eyes said that she was nothing of the sort. "Anything can happen," he said. "That's the whole point."

The mist poured forth. It swallowed the drifting swans one by one. "Stay or go?" Lazlo asked.

Sarai faced the mahalath. She let it come. And as its first tendrils wrapped around her like arms, she reached for Lazlo's hand, and held it tight.

43

A Singularly Unhorrible Demon

Inside a mist, inside a dream, a young man and woman were remade. But first they were *un*made, their edges fading like the evanescent white bird, Wraith, as it phased through the skin of the sky. All sense of physical reality slipped away—except for one. Their hands, joined together, remained as real as bone and sinew. There was no world anymore, no riverbank or water, nothing beneath their feet—and anyway, no feet. There was only that one point of contact, and even as they let go of themselves, Lazlo and Sarai held on to each other.

And when the mist passed on its way, and the remade swans lorded their magnificence over the humble green river, they turned to each other, fingers interlaced, and looked, and looked, and looked.

Eyes wide and shining, eyes unchanged. His were

still gray, hers were still blue. And her lashes were still honey red, and his as glossy black as the pelts of rivercats. His hair was still dark, and hers was still cinnamon, and his nose was the victim of velvet-bound fairy tales, and her mouth was damson-lush.

They were both in every way unchanged, save one.

Sarai's skin was brown, and Lazlo's was blue.

They looked, and looked, and looked at each other, and they looked at their joined hands, the brown-and-blue pattern of their fingers reversed, and they looked at the surface of the water, which hadn't been a mirror before but was now because they willed it so. And they gazed at themselves in it, side by side and hand in hand, and they beheld neither gods nor monsters. They were so nearly unchanged, and yet that one thing—the color of their skin—would, in the real world, change everything.

Sarai looked at the rich earthen color of her arms, and she knew, though it was hidden, that she bore an elilith on her belly like a human girl. She wondered what the pattern was, and wished that she could take a peek. The other hand, the one joined with Lazlo's, she gently withdrew. There seemed no further pretext for holding it, though it had been rather nice while it lasted.

She looked at him. *Blue.* "Did you choose this?" she asked.

Lazlo shook his head. "I left it to the mahalath," he said.

"And it did this." She wondered why. Her own change was easier to understand. Here was her humanity externalized, and all her longing—for freedom, from disgust, from the confines of her metal cage. But why should *he* come to *this*? Maybe, she thought, it wasn't longing but fear, and this was his idea of a monster. "Well, I wonder what gift it has given you," she said.

"Gift? You mean magic? Do you think I have one?"

"All godspawn have gifts."

"Godspawn?"

"That's what they call us."

Us. Another collective pronoun. It glimmered between them, briefly, but Lazlo didn't call attention this time. "*Spawn*, though," he said, grimacing. "It doesn't suit. That's the offspring of fish or demons."

"The intent, I believe, is the latter."

"Well, you're a singularly unhorrible demon, if I may say so."

"Thank you," Sarai said with play sincerity, laying a modest hand across her breast. "That's the nicest thing anyone has ever said to me."

"Well, I have at least a hundred nicer things to say and am only prevented by embarrassment."

His mention of embarrassment magically conjured embarrassment. In her reflection, Sarai saw the way her brown cheeks went crimson instead of lavender, while Lazlo beheld the reverse in his own. "So, gifts," he said, recovering, though Sarai wouldn't have minded dwelling for a moment on his hundred nicer things. "And yours is . . . going into dreams?"

She nodded. She saw no need to explain the mechanics of it. Ruby's long-ago commiseration flashed through her mind. "Who would ever want to kiss a girl who eats moths?" The thought of kissing stirred a fluttering in her belly that was something like it might feel if her moths really *did* live inside of her. Wings, delicate and tickling.

"So how do I know what it is, this gift?" Lazlo asked. "How does one find out?"

"It's always different," she told him. "Sometimes it's spontaneous and obvious, and other times it has to be teased out. When the Mesarthim were alive, it was Korako, the goddess of secrets, who did the teasing out. Or so I'm told. I must have known her, but I can't remember."

The question "Told by whom?" was so palpable between them that, though Lazlo didn't ask it—except, perhaps, with his eyebrows—Sarai nevertheless answered. "By the ghosts," she said. Which happened, in this case, to be the truth.

"Korako," said Lazlo. He thought back on the mural, but he'd been so fixed on Isagol that the other goddesses were a blur. Suheyla had mentioned Letha, but not the other one. "I haven't heard anything about her."

"No. You wouldn't. She was the goddess of secrets, and her best-kept secret was herself. No one ever knew what her gift even was."

"Another mystery," said Lazlo, and they talked of gods and gifts, walking by the river. Sarai kicked at the surface and watched the flying droplets shiver ephemeral rainbows. They pointed to the swans, which had been identical before but now were strange—one fanged and made of agates and moss, another seeming dipped in gold. One had even become a svytagor. It submerged and vanished beneath the opaque green water. Sarai told Lazlo some of the better gifts she knew from Great Ellen, and slipped in among them a girl who could make things grow and a boy who could bring rain. His own gift, if the mahalath had given him one, remained a mystery.

"But what about you?" he asked her, pausing to pluck a flower that he had just willed to grow. It was an exotic bloom he'd seen in a shop window, and he would have been abashed to know it was called a passion flower. He offered it to Sarai. "If you were human, you would have to give up your gift, wouldn't you?"

He couldn't know the curse that her gift was, or what the use of it had done to her and to Weep. "I suppose so," she said, sniffing the flower, which smelled of rain.

"But then you couldn't be here with me."

483

It was true. If she were human, Sarai couldn't be in Lazlo's dream with him. But...she could be in his room with him. A heat flared through her, and it wasn't shame or even embarrassment. It was a kind of longing, but not hearts' longing. It was skin's longing. To be touched. It was limbs' longing. To entwine. It was centered in her belly where her new elilith was, and she brushed her fingers over it again and shivered. Up in the citadel, pacing, her true body shivered in kind. "It's a sacrifice I would be willing to make," she said.

Lazlo couldn't fathom it, that a goddess would be willing to give up her magic. It wasn't just the magic, either. He thought she would be beautiful in any color, but found he missed the true exquisite hue of her. "You wouldn't really want to change, though, would you?" he persisted. "If this were real, and you had the choice?"

Wouldn't she? Why else had her unconscious—her inner mahalath—chosen *this* transformation? "If it meant having a life? Yes, I would."

He was puzzled. "But you're alive already." He felt a sudden stab of fear. "You are, aren't you? You're not a ghost like the ones—"

"I'm not a ghost," said Sarai, to his great relief. "But I am godspawn, and you must see that there's a difference between being alive and having a life."

Lazlo did see that. At least, he thought he saw. He

thought that what she meant was in some way comparable to being a foundling at Zemonan Abbey: alive, but not living a life. And because he had found his way from one to the other and had even seen his dream come true, he felt a certain qualification on the subject. But he was missing a crucial piece of the puzzle. A crucial, *bloody* piece of the puzzle. Reasonably, and warmly, he sympathized. "It can't be much of a life trapped up there. But now that we know about you, we can get you out."

"Get me out? What, down to Weep?" There was a twist of incredulous amusement in Sarai's voice, and while she spoke, she reverted to her true color, her skin flushing back to blue. *So much for human*, she thought. The hard truth would brook no make-believe. As though her reversion had triggered an end to the fantasy, Lazlo reverted, too, and was himself again. Sarai was almost sorry. When he had looked like that, she could almost have believed a connection between them. Had she really wondered, wistfully, a short time earlier, if this dreamer could help her? Could *save* her? He had no clue. "You do understand, don't you," she said with undue harshness, "that they would kill me on sight."

"Who would?"

"*Anyone* would."

"No." He shook his head, unwilling to believe it. "They're good people. It will be a surprise, yes, but

485

they couldn't hate you just because of what your parents were."

Sarai stopped walking. "You think good people can't hate?" she asked. "You think good people don't *kill*?" Her breathing hitched, and she realized she'd crushed Lazlo's flower in her hand. She dropped the petals into the water. "Good people do all the things bad people do, Lazlo. It's just that when they do them, they call it justice." She paused. Her voice grew heavy. "When they slaughter thirty babies in their cradles, they call it *necessary*."

Lazlo stared at her. He shook his head in disbelief.

"That shock you saw on Eril-Fane's face?" she went on. "It wasn't because he didn't know he had a child." She took a breath. "It was because he thought he killed me fifteen years ago." Her voice broke at the end. She swallowed hard. She felt, suddenly, as though her entire head were filled with tears and if she didn't shed some of them it would explode. "When he killed *all the godspawn*, Lazlo," she added, and wept.

Not in the dream, not where Lazlo could see, but up in her room, hidden away. Tears sheeted down her cheeks the way the monsoon rains sheeted down the smooth contours of the citadel in summer, flooding in through all the open doors, a rolling deluge of rain across the slick floors and nothing to do but wait for it to stop.

Eril-Fane had known that one of the babies in the

nursery was his, but he didn't know which one. He had seen Isagol's belly swell with his child, of course, but after she was delivered of it, she had never mentioned it again. He'd asked. She'd shrugged. She'd done her duty; it was the nursery's problem now. She hadn't even known if it was a boy or a girl; it was nothing to her. And when he had walked, drenched in godsblood, into the nursery and looked about him at the squalling blue infants and toddlers, he had feared that he would see, and know: *There. That one is mine.*

If he had seen Sarai, cinnamon-haired like her mother, he would have known her in an instant, but he hadn't, because she wasn't there. But he hadn't known that; for all he knew her hair was dark like his own, like all the rest of the babies. They made a blur of blue and blood and screams.

All innocent. All anathema.

All dead.

Lazlo's eyes were dry but wide and unblinking. *Babies.* His mind rejected it, even as, under the surface, puzzle pieces were snapping together. All the dread, and the shame he'd seen in Eril-Fane. Everything about the meeting with the Zeyyadin, and . . . and the way Maldagha had laid her hands on her stomach. Suheyla, too. It was a maternal gesture. How stupid he'd been not to see it, but then how could he, when he'd spent his life among old men? All the things that hadn't quite made sense now shifted just enough, and it was like tilting the angle of the sun so that instead of glancing off a window-pane and blinding you, it passed through it to illuminate all that was within.

He knew Sarai was telling the truth.

A great man, and also a good one. Is that what he had thought? But the man who had slain gods had also slain their babies, and Lazlo understood now what it was he'd feared to find in the citadel. "Some of us know better than others the...state...it was left in," he had said. Not the skeletons of gods, but infants. Lazlo hunched over, feeling ill. He pressed a palm hard to his forehead. The village and the monster swans vanished. The river was no more. It all blinked out, and Lazlo and Sarai found themselves in his little room—the Godslayer's little room. Lazlo's sleeping body wasn't stretched out on the bed. This was one more dream setting. In reality he was sleeping in the room, and in the dream he was standing in it. In reality a moth perched on his brow. In the dream the Muse of Nightmares stood beside him.

The Muse of Nightmares, Sarai thought. As much as ever. She had, after all, brought nightmare to this dreamer to whom she had come seeking refuge. In his sleep, he murmured, "No." His eyes and fists were squeezed tight shut. His breathing was quick, and so was his pulse. All the hallmarks of nightmare. How well Sarai knew them. All she'd done was tell the truth. She hadn't even *shown* it to him. Knifeshine and spreading blood, and all the small blue bodies. Nothing would induce her to drag that festering memory into this beautiful mind. "I'm sorry," she said.

Up in the citadel, she sobbed. *She* could never be free of the fester. Her own mind would always be an open grave.

"Why are *you* sorry?" Lazlo asked her. There was sweetness in his voice, but the brightness had left it. It had gone dull somehow, like an old coin. "You're the last person who should be sorry. He's supposed to be a hero," he said. "He let me believe it. But what kind of hero could do . . . *that*?"

In Windfall, the "hero" in question was lying stretched out on the floor. He was as still as a sleeper but his eyes were open in the dark, and Sarai thought again how he was as much a ruin as he was a man. He was, she thought, like a cursed temple, still beautiful to look at—the shell of something sacred—but benighted within, and none but ghosts could ever cross the threshold.

"What kind of hero?" Lazlo had asked. What kind, indeed. Sarai had never let herself rise to his defense. It was unthinkable, as though the bodies themselves were a barrier between her and forgiveness. Nevertheless, and not quite knowing what she was going to say, she told Lazlo, speaking softly, "For three years, Isagol . . . made him love her. That is . . . she didn't *inspire* love. She didn't strive to be worthy of it.

She just reached into his mind...or his hearts or his soul...and played the note that would make him love her against everything that was in him. She was a very dark thing." She shuddered to think how she herself had come from the body of this very dark thing. "She didn't take away his conflicting emotions, although she could have. She didn't make him *not hate* her. She left his hate there, right beside the love. She thought it was funny. And it wasn't...it wasn't *dislike* beside *lust*, or some trivial pale versions of hate and love. You see, it was *hate*." She put everything she knew of *hate* into her voice—and not her own hate, but Eril-Fane's and the rest of the victims of the Mesarthim. "It was the hate of the used and tormented, who are the children of the used and tormented, and whose own children will be used and tormented. And it was *love*," she went on, and she put that into her voice, too, as well as she was able. Love that sets forth the soul like springtime and ripens it like summer. Love as rarely exists in reality, as if a master alchemist has taken it and distilled out all the impurities, every petty disenchantment, every unworthy thought, into a perfect elixir, sweet and deep and all-consuming. "He loved her so much," she whispered. "It was all a lie. It was a *violation*. But it didn't matter, did it, because when Isagol made you feel something, it became real. He *hated* her. And he *loved* her. And he killed her."

She sank onto the edge of Lazlo's bed and let her

gaze roam over the familiar walls. Memories can be trapped in a room, and this one still held all the years that she'd come in this window full of righteous malice. Lazlo sank down beside her. "Hate won," she said. "Isagol left it there for her amusement, and for three years he fought a war within himself. The only way he could win was for his hate to surpass that vile, false, perfect love. And it did." Her jaw clenched. She darted a glance at Lazlo. This story wasn't hers to tell, but she thought he needed to know. "After Skathis brought Azareen up to the citadel."

Lazlo knew a little of the story already. "They got her later," Suheyla had said. Sarai knew all of it. She alone knew of the tarnished silver band that Azareen put on her finger every night and took off first thing every morning. Theirs wasn't the only love story ended by the gods, but it was the only one that ended the gods.

Eril-Fane had been gone for more than two years by the time Skathis took Azareen, and she might have been the first girl in Weep who was glad to mount the monster Rasalas and fly up to her own enslavement. She would know, at least, if her husband was still alive.

He was. And Azareen had learned how you can be glad and devastated at the same time. She heard his laugh before she saw his face—Eril-Fane's *laugh*, in that place, as alive as she had ever heard it—and she broke away from her guard to run toward it, skidding around a corner of the sleek metal corridor to the sight of him gazing at Isagol the Terrible with love.

She knew it for what it was. He had looked at her like that, too. It wasn't feigned but true, and so after more than two years of wondering what had become of him, Azareen found out. In addition to the misery of serving the gods' "purpose," it was her fate to watch her husband love the goddess of despair.

And Eril-Fane, it was his fate to see his bride led down the sinister corridor—door after door of little rooms with nothing in them but beds—and finally, Isagol's calculus failed. Love was no match for what burned in Eril-Fane when he heard Azareen's first screams.

"*Hate* was his triumph," Sarai told Lazlo. "It was who he became to save his wife, and all his people. So much blood on his hands, so much hate in his hearts. The gods had created their own undoing." She sat there for a moment, mute, and felt an emptiness within her where for years her own sustaining hate had been. There was only a terrible sadness now. "And after they were slain and all their slaves were freed," she said heavily, "there was still the nursery, and a future full of terrible, unguessable magic."

The tears that had, until now, flowed only down Sarai's real cheeks, slipped down her dream ones, too. Lazlo reached for her hands and held them in both of his own.

"It's a violence that can never be forgiven," she said, her voice husky with emotion. "Some things are too terrible to forgive. But I think...I think I can understand what they felt that day, and what they faced. What were they to do with children who would grow into a new generation of tormentors?"

Lazlo reeled with the horror of it all, and with the incredible feeling that after all his own youth had been merciful. "But...if they'd been embraced instead, and raised with love," he said, "they wouldn't have become tormentors."

It sounded so simple, so clean. But what had the humans known of Mesarthim power besides how it could be used to punish and oppress, terrify and control? How could they even have imagined a Sparrow or a Feral when all they knew was the likes of Skathis and Isagol? Could one reach back in time and expect them to be as merciful as it was possible to be fifteen years later with a mind and body unviolated by gods?

Sarai's own empathy made her queasy. She'd said she could never forgive, but it would seem she already had, and she flushed with confused dismay. It was one thing not to hate, and another to forgive. She told Lazlo, "I feel a little like him sometimes, the love and hate side by side. It's not easy having a paradox at the core of one's own being."

"What do you mean? What paradox? Being human and godsp—" Lazlo couldn't bring himself to call her *spawn*, even if she called herself that. "Human and Mesarthim?"

"There's that, too, but no. I mean the curse of knowledge. It was easy when we were the only victims." *We.* She'd been looking down at their hands, still joined, hers curled inside his, but she glanced up now and didn't retreat from the pronoun. "There are five of us," she admitted. "And for the others there is only one truth: the Carnage.

"But because of my gift—or curse—I've learned what it's been like for the humans, before and since. I know the insides of their minds, why they did it, and how it changed them. And so when I see a memory of those babies being..." Her words choked off in a sob. "And I know that was my fate, too, I feel the same simple rage I always have, but now there's...there's outrage, too, on behalf of those young men and women who were plucked from their homes to serve the gods' purpose, and desolation for what it did to them, and guilt...for what *I've* done to them."

She wept, and Lazlo drew her into an embrace as though it were the most natural thing in the world that he should draw a mournful goddess against his shoulder, enfold her in his arms, breathe the scent of the flowers in her hair, and even lightly stroke her temple with the edge of his thumb. And though there was a layer of his mind that knew this was a dream, it was momentarily shuffled under by other, more compelling layers, and he experienced the moment as though it were absolutely real. All the emotion, all the sensation. The texture of her skin, the scent of her hair, the heat of her breath through his linen shirt, and even the moisture of tears seeping through it. But far more intense was the utter, ineffable tenderness he felt, and the solemnity. As though he had been entrusted with something infinitely precious. As though he had taken an oath, and his very life stood surety to it. He would recognize this later as the moment his center of gravity shifted: from being one of one—a pillar alone, apart—to being half of something that would fall if either side were cut away.

Three fears had gnawed at Lazlo, back in his old life. The first: that he would never see proof of magic. The second: that he would never find out what had happened in Weep. Those fears were gone; proof and answers were unfolding minute by minute. And the third? That he would always be alone?

He didn't grasp it yet—at least not consciously—but he no longer was, and he had a whole new set of fears to discover: the ones that come with cherishing someone you're very likely to lose.

"Sarai." *Sarai.* Her name was calligraphy and honey. "What do you mean?" he asked her gently. "What is it you've done to them?"

And Sarai, remaining just as she was—tucked into his shoulder, her forehead resting against his jaw—told him. She told him what she was and what she did and even…though her voice went thin as paper… *how* she did it, moths and all. And when she was finished telling and was tense in the circle of his arms, she waited to see what he would say. Unlike him, she couldn't forget that this was a dream. She was outside it and inside it at once. And though she didn't dare look at him while she told him her truth, her moth watched his sleeping face for any flicker of expression that might betray disgust.

There were none.

Lazlo wasn't thinking about the moths—though he did recollect, now, the one that had fallen dead from his brow on his first morning waking up in Weep. What really seized him was the implication of nightmares. It explained so much. It had seemed to him as though fear were a living thing here, because *it was*. Sarai kept it alive. She tended it like a fire and made sure it never went out.

If there were such a goddess in a book of olden tales, she would be the villain, tormenting the innocent from her high castle. The people of Weep *were* innocent—most of them—and she *did* torment them, but…what choice did she have? She had inherited a story that was strewn with corpses and clotted with enmity, and was only trying to stay alive in it. Lazlo felt many things for her in that moment, feeling her tension as he held her, and none of them were disgust.

He was under her spell and on her side. When it came to Sarai, even nightmares seemed like magic. "The Muse of Nightmares," he said. "It sounds like a poem."

A poem? Sarai detected nothing mocking in his voice, but she had to see his face to confirm it, which meant sitting up and breaking the embrace. Regretfully, she did. She saw no mockery, but only... witchlight, still witchlight, and she wanted to live in it forever.

She asked in a hesitant whisper, "Do you still think I'm a...a singularly unhorrible demon?"

"No," he said, smiling. "I think you're a fairy tale. I think you're magical, and brave, and exquisite. And..." His voice grew bashful. Only in a dream could he be so bold and speak such words. "I hope you'll let me be in your story."

44

AN EXTRAORDINARY SUGGESTION

A poem? A fairy tale? Was that really how he saw her? Flustered, Sarai rose and went to the window. It wasn't just her belly now that felt a flutter like wild soft wings, but her chest where her hearts were, and even her head. *Yes,* she wanted to say with shy delight. *Please be in my story.*

But she didn't. She looked out into the night, up at the citadel in the sky, and asked, "Will there *be* a story? How can there be?"

Lazlo joined her at the window. "We'll find a way. I'll talk to Eril-Fane tomorrow. Whatever he did then, he must want to atone for it. I can't believe he means to hurt you. After all, he didn't tell anyone what happened. You didn't see how he was after, how he was..."

"Broken?" supplied Sarai. "I did see him after. I'm

looking at him right now. He's on the floor of Azareen's sitting room."

"Oh," said Lazlo. It was something to wrap his head around, how she could have so many eyes in the world at once. And Eril-Fane on Azareen's floor, that took some getting used to, too. Did they live together? Suheyla had said that it wasn't a marriage anymore, whatever it was between them. As far as he knew, Eril-Fane still lived *here*.

"He should come home," he said. "*I* can sleep on the floor. This is his room, after all."

"It isn't a good place for him," she said, staring unseeing out the window. Her jaw clenched. Lazlo saw the muscle work. "He's had a lot of nightmares in this room. Many of them were his own, but . . . I had a hand in plenty."

Lazlo shook his head in wonder. "You know, I thought it was foolish, that he was hiding from his nightmares. But he was right."

"He was hiding from *me*, even if he didn't know it." A great wave of weariness broke over Sarai. With a sigh, she closed her eyes and leaned against the window frame. She was as light-headed as she was heavy-limbed. What would she do once the sun rose and she couldn't stay here, in the safety of this dream?

She opened her eyes and studied Lazlo.

In the real room, her moth took stock of real Lazlo,

499

the relaxation of his face, and his long, easy limbs, loose in slumber. What she wouldn't give for restful sleep like that, not to mention the degree of control he had within his dreams. She wondered at it. "How did you do that earlier?" she asked him. "The mahalath, the tea, all of it. How do you shape your dreams with such purpose?"

"I don't know," he said. "It's new to me. I mean, I had some lucidity in dreams before, but not predictably, and never like this. Only since you came."

"Really?" Sarai was surprised. "I wonder why."

"Isn't it like this with other dreamers?"

She let out a soft laugh. "Lazlo," she said. "It isn't anything like this with other dreamers. To start with, they can't even see me."

"What do you mean, they can't see you?"

"Just that. It's why I came right up and looked at you that first time, so shamelessly." She wrinkled her nose, embarrassed. "Because I never imagined you'd be able to see me. With other dreamers I can scream right in their face and they'd never know it. Believe me, I've tried. I can do anything at all in a dream except *exist*."

"But...why would that be? What a bizarre sort of condition to your gift."

"A bizarre condition to a bizarre gift, then. Great Ellen—she's our nurse, she's a ghost—she never saw a gift like mine in all her years in the nursery."

The crease between Lazlo's brows—the new one the Elmuthaleth sun had made for him—deepened.

500

When Sarai spoke of the nursery, and the babies, and the gifts—*years* of them—questions lined up in his mind. More mysteries of Weep; how endless was the supply of them? But there was a more personal mystery confronting him now. "But why should I be able to see you if no one else can?"

Sarai shrugged, as baffled as he was. "You said they call you Strange the dreamer. Clearly you're better at dreams than other people."

"Oh, clearly," he agreed, self-mocking and more than a little pleased. *Much* more than a little, as the idea sank in. All this while, from the moment Sarai appeared at the riverbank and squished her toes into the mud, the entire night had been so extraordinary he'd felt... effervescent. But how much *more* extraordinary was it, now that he knew it was extraordinary for her, too?

She wasn't quite looking effervescent, though, if he had to be honest with himself. She looked... tired.

"You're awake now?" he asked, still trying to grasp how it worked. "Up in the citadel, I mean."

She nodded. Her body was in her alcove. Even in that confined space, it was pacing—like a menagerie ravid, she thought—with just a whisper of her awareness left behind to guide it. She felt a stab of sympathy for it, abandoned not only by her kin, but by herself, left empty and alone while she was here, weeping her tears onto a stranger's chest.

No, not a stranger. The only one who saw her.

"So, when I wake up," he went on, "and the city wakes up, you'll just be going to sleep?"

Sarai experienced a thrum of fear at the thought of falling asleep. "That's the usual practice," she said. "But 'usual' is dead and gone." She took a deep breath and let it out. She told him about lull, and how it didn't work anymore, and how, as soon as her consciousness relaxed, it was as though the doors of all her captive terrors' cages slid wide open.

And, while most people might have a few terrors rattling their cages, she had . . . all of them.

"I did it to myself," she said. "I was so young when I began, and no one ever told me to consider the consequences. Of course, it seems so obvious now."

"But you can't just banish them?" he asked her. "Or transform them?"

She shook her head. "In other people's dreams I have control, but when I'm asleep," she said, "I'm powerless, just like any other dreamer." She regarded him evenly. "Except you. You're like no other dreamer."

"Sarai," said Lazlo. He saw how she sagged against the window frame, and put out his arm to support her. "How long has it been since you've slept?"

She hardly knew. "Four days? I'm not sure." At his look of alarm, she forced a smile. "I sleep a little," she said, "in between nightmares."

"But that's mad. You know you can actually die of sleep deprivation."

Her answering laugh was grim. "I didn't know that, no. You don't happen to know how long it takes, do you? So I can plan my day?" She meant it as a joke, but there was an edge of desperation to the question.

"No," said Lazlo, feeling spectacularly helpless. What an impossible situation. She was up there alone, he was down here alone, and yet somehow they were together. She was inside his dream, sharing it with him. If he had her gift, he wondered, could *he* go into *her* dreams and help her to endure them? What would that mean? What terrors did she face? Fighting off ravids, witnessing the Carnage again and again? Whatever it was, the notion of her facing them alone gutted him.

A thought came to him. It seemed to land as lightly as a moth. "Sarai," he asked, speculative. "What would happen if you were to fall asleep right now?"

Her eyes widened a little. "What, you mean *here*?" She glanced toward the bed.

"No," he said quickly, his face going hot. In his head it was clear: He wanted to give her a haven from her nightmares—to *be* a haven from them. "I mean, if you keep the moth where it is, on me, but fall asleep up there, could you...do you think that maybe you could stay here? With me?"

When Sarai was silent, he was afraid the suggestion went too far. Was he not, in a way, inviting her to... spend the night with him? "I only mean," he rushed to explain, "if you're afraid of your own dreams, you're welcome here in mine."

A light frisson of shivers went down Sarai's arms. She wasn't silent because she was offended or dismayed. Quite the opposite. She was overwhelmed. She was welcome. She was *wanted*. Lazlo didn't know about the nights she'd trespassed without his invitation, tucking a little piece of her mind into a corner of his, so that the wonder and delight of it could help her to endure...everything else. She needed rest, badly, and though she joked with him about dying of sleep deprivation, she was, in fact, afraid.

The idea that she could stay *here*, be safe *here*—with *him*...it was like a window swinging open, light and air rushing in. But fear, too. Fear of *hope*, because the instant she understood what he was proposing, Sarai wanted so badly for it to work, and when did she ever get what she wanted? "I've never tried it before," she said, striving to keep her voice neutral. She was afraid of betraying her longing, in case it all should come to nothing. "Falling asleep might sever the tether," she said, "and cut the moth loose."

"Do you want to try?" asked Lazlo, hopeful, and trying to disguise it.

"There can't be much time before sunrise."

"Not much," he agreed. "But a little."

She had another thought. She was poking the idea

for weaknesses, and so frightened of finding them. "What if it works, but my terrors come, too?"

Lazlo shrugged. "We'll chase them away, or else turn them into fireflies and catch them in jars." He wasn't afraid. Well. He was only afraid it wouldn't work. Anything else they could handle, together. "What do you say?"

For a moment Sarai didn't trust her voice. As casual as they strove to seem, they both felt something momentous take shape between them, and—though she didn't for a minute question his intentions—something intimate, too. To sleep inside his dream, when she wasn't even certain she'd be aware it *was* a dream. Where she might not have control...

"If it does work," she whispered, "but I'm powerless..."

She faltered, but he understood. "Do you trust me?" he asked.

It wasn't even a question. She felt safer here than she ever had anywhere. And anyway, she asked herself, what real risk was there? *It's just a dream*, she answered, though of course it was so much more.

She looked at Lazlo, bit her lip and let it go, and said, "All right."

45

STRANGE AZOTH

In the makeshift alchemical laboratory in the windowless attic of the crematorium, a small blue flame touched the curved glass base of a suspended flask. The liquid there heated and changed state, rising as vapor through the fractionating column to catch in the condenser and trickle in droplets into the collection flask.

The golden godson retrieved it and held it up to a glave to examine it.

Clear fluid. It might have been water to look at it, but it wasn't. It was azoth, a substance even more precious than the gold it could yield, because, unlike gold, it had multiple, wondrous applications and but a single source in all the world: himself—at least as long as its key component remained secret.

A vial lay empty on the worktable. It was labeled SPIRIT OF LIBRARIAN, and Thyon felt a twinge of...

distaste? Here was vital essence of the no-name peasant foundling who had the unforgivable habit of *helping him for no good reason*, all while looking guileless, as though it were a normal thing to do.

Maybe it was distaste. Thyon pushed the empty vial aside to clear space for his next procedure. Or maybe it was discomfort. The whole world saw him the way he wanted to be seen: as an unassailable force, complete unto himself and in full command of the mysteries of the universe.

Except for Strange, that is, who knew what he really was. His jaw clenched. If only, he thought, Lazlo would have the courtesy to...cease to exist...then perhaps he could be grateful to him. But not while he was there, always *there*, a benign presence laughing with warriors or doing, gladly, whatever needed to be done. He'd even formed the habit of helping the caravan's cook scrub the big soup pot out with sand. What was he trying to prove?

Thyon shook his head. He knew the answer, he just couldn't understand it. Lazlo wasn't trying to prove anything. Nothing was strategy with him. Nothing was deception. Strange was just Strange, and he'd offered up his spirit with no strings attached. Thyon *was* grateful, even if he was resentful in equal—or greater—measure. He had drawn too much of his own spirit, and that was a dangerous game. Lazlo's jibe that it would make him ugly had not missed its mark, but that wasn't his only concern. He had seen the spirit-dead. Most didn't last long, either taking their own lives or wasting away from a lack of will even to eat. The will to live, it would seem, existed in this mysterious clear fluid that Strange had given of without a second thought.

And Thyon was much restored, thanks to the reprieve. He was taking another stab at alkahest, using the Strange azoth this time. Usually he felt a stir of eagerness at this part of a chemical procedure—a thrill to create something no one else could, and alter the very structure of nature. Alkahest was a universal solvent, true to its name, and had never failed him before. He'd tested it tirelessly back at the Chrysopoesium, and it had dissolved every substance he'd touched it to, even diamond.

But not mesarthium. The damnable metal frightened him in its unnaturalness, and he felt already the ignominy of defeat. But scientific method was Thyon's religion, and it dictated the repeat of experiments—even of failures. So he cooked a new batch of chemicals, and took the alkahest over to the north anchor to test it again. It wasn't in its final preparation, of course, or else it would eat through its container. He would make the final mixture at the last moment to activate it.

And then, when nothing happened—as nothing *would*—he would apply the neutralizing compound to *de*activate it so it didn't just drip down the impervious metal and eat its way into the ground.

He was going to take a nap after. That was what he was thinking about—*beauty sleep, you Strange bastard*—as he walked through the moonless city of Weep with a satchel of flasks slung over his shoulder. He was going to repeat his experiment and record its failure, and then he was going to bed.

There wasn't even a moment, not even a second, in which Thyon Nero considered that the experiment might not fail.

46

JUST A DREAM

Sarai called the rest of her moths home early, leaving just the one on Lazlo's brow. She hesitated only to recall the one watching over her father.

Watching him, she corrected herself. *Not watching* over *him*. That wasn't what she was doing.

Here she'd finally found him, and she couldn't even look into his mind.

It was a relief, she admitted to herself, finally giving up and drawing the moth off the wall and out the window, back up into the air. She was afraid to know what she would find in his dreams now that he knew she was alive. Could it be that after everything there was still some capacity for hope in her—that he might be *glad* she wasn't dead?

She shook it off. Of course he wouldn't be glad, but

tonight she didn't have to know it. She left him to his thoughts, whatever they might be.

The journey from rooftops to terrace was long for such small fluttering scraps as moths, and she had never been so impatient as in those minutes while they rose through the heights of the air. When they finally arrived and fluttered back through the terrace door, she saw the ghosts standing guard and remembered with a start that she was a prisoner. She'd all but forgotten, and didn't dwell on it now. Most of her awareness was with Lazlo. She was still in his room with him when, up in her own, she parted her lips to receive her moths home.

She turned away from him in the dream, even though she knew he couldn't see her real mouth, or the moths vanishing into it. Their wings brushed over her lips, soft as the ghost of a kiss, and all she could think was how the sight would disgust him.

Who would ever want to kiss a girl who eats moths?

I don't "eat" them, she argued with herself.

Your lips still taste of salt and soot.

Stop thinking of kissing.

And then: the unusual experience of lying down on her bed in full dark—her real body in her real bed—in the stillness of knowing both citadel and city were sleeping, and with a thread of her consciousness still stretched down into Weep. It had been years since she'd gone to bed before sunrise. As Lazlo had earlier lain stiffly, his very eagerness for sleep keeping sleep at bay, so did Sarai, a heightened awareness of her limbs giving rise to brief doubts as to how she arranged them when she wasn't thinking about it. She achieved something like her natural sleep position—curled on her side, her hands tucked under one cheek. Her weary body and wearier mind, which had seemed, in her exhaustion, to be drifting away from each other like untethered boats, made some peace with the tides. Her hearts were beating too fast for sleep, though. Not with dread, but agitation lest it shouldn't work, and...excitement—as wild and soft as a chaos of moth wings—lest it should.

In the room down in the city, she stood by the window awhile and talked with Lazlo in a newly shy way, and that sense of the momentous did not die down. Sarai thought of Ruby's envious laments about how she "got to *live*." It had never felt true before, but now it did.

Was it living, if it was a dream?

Just a dream, she was reminded, but the words had little meaning when the knots of the hand-tied rug under her imaginary feet were more vivid than the smooth silk pillow beneath her actual cheek. When the company of this dreamer made her feel *awake* for the first time, even as she tried to sleep. She was unsettled, standing there with him. Her mind was unquiet. "I wonder if it might be easier to fall asleep," she ventured finally, "if I'm not talking."

"Of course," he said. "Do you want to lie down?" He blushed at his own suggestion. She did, too. "Please, be comfortable," he said. "Can I get you anything?"

"No, thank you," said Sarai. And with a funny feeling of repeating herself, she lay down on the bed, here much as she had up above. She stayed close to the edge. It wasn't a large bed. She didn't think he would lie down, too, but she left room enough in case he did.

He stayed by the window, and she saw him make as though to put his hands in his pockets, only to discover that his breeches didn't have pockets. He looked awkward for a moment before remembering this was a dream. Then pockets appeared, and his hands went in.

Sarai folded hers once more under her cheek. This bed was more comfortable than her own. The whole room was. She liked the stone walls and wood beams that had been shaped by human hands and tools instead of by the mind of Skathis. It was snug, but that was nice, too. It was cozy. Nothing in the citadel was cozy, not even her alcove behind the dressing room, though that came closest. It struck her with fresh force that this was her father's bed, as the bed in the alcove had been his before it was hers. How many times had she imagined him lying awake there, plotting murder and revolt? Now, as she lay here, she thought of him as a boy, dreading being stolen and spirited up to the citadel. Had he dreamed of being a hero, she wondered, and if he had, what had he imagined it would be like? Nothing like it was, she was sure. Nothing like a ruined temple that only ghosts could enter.

And then, well...it wasn't sudden, exactly. Rather, Sarai became aware that something was softly different, and she understood what it was: She was no longer in multiple places, but just one. She had misplaced her awareness of her true body reposed in her true bed, and of the moth on Lazlo's brow. She was only here, and it felt all the more real for it.

Oh. She sat up, the full realization hitting her. She was *here*. It had worked. The moth's tether had not snapped. She was asleep—oh blessed rest—and instead of her own unconscious fraught with prowling terrors, she was safe in Lazlo's. She laughed—a little incredulous, a little nervous, a little pleased. Okay, a lot pleased. Well, a lot nervous, too. A lot *everything*. She was asleep in Lazlo's dream.

He watched her, expectant. The sight of her there—her blue legs, bare to the knees, entangled in his rumpled blankets, and her hair mussed from his pillow—made for an aching-sweet vision. He was highly conscious of his hands, and it wasn't from the awkwardness of not knowing what to do with them,

514

but from knowing, rather, what he *wished* to do with them. It tingled along his palms: the aching urge to touch her. His hands felt wide awake. "Well?" he asked, anxious. "Did it work?"

She nodded, breaking into a wide, wondering smile that he could hardly help but mirror back at her. What a long, extraordinary night it had been. How many hours had passed since he had closed his eyes, hoping she would come. And now...in some way he couldn't entirely wrap his mind around, she was...well...that was it, wasn't it? He had entirely wrapped his mind around *her*.

He held a goddess in his mind as one might cup a butterfly in one's hands. Keeping it safe just long enough to set it free.

Free. Could it be possible? Could she ever be free? Yes.

Yes. Somehow.

"Well then," he said, feeling a scope of possibility as immense as oceans. "Now that you're here, what shall we do?"

It was a good question. With the infinite possibilities of dreaming, it wasn't easy to narrow it down. "We could go anywhere," said Lazlo. "The sea? We could sail a leviathan, and set it free. The amphion fields of Thanagost? Warlords and leashed wolves and drifting ulola blossoms like fleets of living bubbles. Or the Cloudspire. We might climb it and steal emeralds from the eyes of the sarcophagi, like Calixte. Do you fancy becoming a jewel thief, my lady?"

Sarai's eyes sparkled. "It does sound fun," she said. It all sounded marvelous. "But you've only mentioned real places and things so far. Do you know what I'd like?"

She was sitting on her knees on the bed, her shoulders straight and hands clasped in her lap. Her smile was a brilliant specimen and she wore the moon on her wrist. Lazlo was plain dazzled by the sight of her. "What?" he asked. *Anything*, he thought.

"I'd like for the wingsmiths to come to town."

"The wingsmiths," he repeated, and somewhere within him, as though with a whirr of gears and a ping of sprung locks, a previously unsuspected vault of delight spilled open.

"Like you mentioned the other day," said Sarai, girlish in her demure posture and childlike excitement. "I'd like to buy some wings and test them out, and after that perhaps we might try riding dragons and see which is more fun."

Lazlo had to laugh. The delight filled him up. He thought he'd never laughed like this before, from this new place in him where so much delight had been waiting in reserve. "You've just described my perfect day," he said, and he held out his hand, and she took it.

She rose to her knees and slid off the side of the bed, but at the moment that her feet touched the floor, a great concussion *thoom*ed in the street. A tremor shook the room. Plaster rained from the ceiling, and all the excitement was stricken from Sarai's face. "Oh gods," she said, in a rasp of a whisper. "It's happening."

"What is? What's happening?"

"The terrors, my nightmares. They're here."

47

THE TERRORS

"Show me," said Lazlo, who still wasn't afraid. As he'd said before, if her terror spilled over, they'd take care of it.

But Sarai shook her head, wild. "No. Not this. Close the shutters. Hurry!"

"But what is it?" he asked. He moved toward the window, not to close the shutters but to look out. But before he could, they slammed before him with a crack and rattle, and the latch fell securely into place. Eyebrows raised, he turned to Sarai. "Well, it seems you're not powerless here after all."

When she just looked at him blankly, he pointed to the shutters and said, "You did that, not me."

"I did?" she asked. He nodded. She stood up a little straighter, but she had no time to gather her courage, because outside the *thoom* came again, lower now and with subtler tremors, and then again and again in rhythmic repetition.

Thoom. Thoom. Thoom.

Sarai backed away from the window. "He's coming," she said, shaking.

Lazlo followed her. He reached for her shoulders and held them gently. "It's all right," he said. "Remember, Sarai, it's just a dream."

She couldn't feel the truth of his words. All she felt was the approach, the closing-in, the dread, the dread that was as pure a distillation of fear as any emotion Isagol had ever made. Sarai's hearts were wild with it, and with anguish, too. How could she have deployed *this*, again and again, into the dreams of the helpless sleepers of Weep? What kind of monster was she?

It had been her most powerful weapon, because it was their most potent fear. And now it was stalking her.

Thoom. Thoom. Thoom.

Great, relentless footsteps, closer, louder.

"Who is it?" Lazlo asked, still holding Sarai's shoulders. Her panic, he found, was catching. It seemed to pass from her skin to his, moving up from his hands, up his arms in coursing vibrations of fear. "Who's coming?"

"Shhh," she said, her eyes so wide they showed a full ring of white, and when she whispered it was breath shaped into words, and made no sound at all. "He'll hear you."

Thoom.

Sarai froze. It didn't seem possible for her eyes to widen any further, but they did, and in that brief moment of silence when the footsteps ceased—that terrible pause that every household in Weep had dreaded for two hundred years—Sarai's panic overpowered Lazlo's reason, so that they were both *in it*, living it, when the shutters, without warning, were ripped from their hinges in a havoc of splintering wood and shattered glass. And there, just outside, was the creature whose footsteps shook the bones of Weep. It was no living thing, but moved as though it were, as sinuous as a ravid, and shining like poured mercury. It was all mesarthium, smooth bunched muscle shaped for crouching and leaping. The flanks of a great cat, the neck and heavy hump of a bull, wings as sharp and vicious as the wings of the great seraph, though on a smaller scale. And a head...a head that was made for nightmares.

Its head was *carrion.*

It was metal, of course, but like the relief on the walls of Sarai's rooms—the songbirds and lilies so real they mocked the master carvers of Weep—it was utterly true to life. Or rather, true to *death.* It was a dead thing, a rotten thing, a skull with the flesh peeling off, revealing teeth to the roots in a grimace of fangs, and in the great black eye sockets were no eyes but only a terrible, all-seeing light. It had horns thick as arms, tapering to wicked points, and it pawed at the ground and tossed its head, a roar rumbling up its metal throat.

It was Rasalas, the beast of the north anchor, and it wasn't the true monster. The true monster was astride it:

Skathis, god of beasts, master of metal, thief of sons and daughters, tormentor of Weep.

Lazlo had only the crudely drawn mural to go on, but he beheld now the god who had stolen so much—not just sons and daughters, though that was the dark heart of it. Skathis had stolen the sky from the city, and the city from the world. What tremendous, insidious power that took, and here was the god himself.

One might expect a presence to rival the Godslayer's—a dark counterpart to his light, as two quell kings faced off across a game board.

But no. He was nothing next to the Godslayer. Here was no dark majesty, no fell magnificence. He was of ordinary stature and his face was just a face. He was no demon-god from myth. But for his color—that extraordinary blue—there was nothing extraordinary about him besides the cruelty in his face. He was neither handsome nor ugly, distinguished only by the malice that burned in his gray eyes, and that serpent smile of cunning and venom.

But he rode upon Rasalas, and that more than made up for any shortfall of godly grandeur, the beast an extension of his own psyche, every prowling, pawing step and toss of the head his own. Each growl that echoed up that metal throat was his as surely as if issued from his own flesh throat. His hair was of sullen brown, and he wore on it a crown of mesarthium shaped as a wreath of serpents swallowing each other by the tails. They moved about his brow in sinuous waves of devouring, round and round, relentless. He was clothed in a coat of velvet and diamond dust with long, fluttering tails in the shape of knife blades, and his boots were white spectral leather buckled with lys.

It was an accursed thing to flay a spectral and wear its skin. Those boots might almost have been of human leather, so deeply wrong were they.

But none of the terrible details could account for the purity of dread that surged through the room—through *the dream*, though both Lazlo and Sarai had lost their grip on that fact, and were prey to the torrents of the unconscious. That pure dread, as Lazlo had witnessed again and again since arriving in Weep, was a collective horror that had been building for two full centuries. How many young men and women had been taken up in all that time, and returned with no memories after this moment—this moment at their door or window when the leering god came calling. Lazlo thought of Suheyla and Azareen and Eril-Fane, and so many others, taken just like this, no matter what their families did to keep them safe.

Again the question beat at his mind. *Why?* All the stolen girls and boys, their memories taken and much more than that.

The nursery, the babies. *Why?*

On the one hand it was obvious, and certainly nothing new. If there has ever been a conqueror who did not exact this most devastating tithe from his subjects, he is unknown to history. The youth are the spoils of war. Chattel, labor. No one is safe. Tyrants have always taken who they wanted, and tyrants always will. The king of Syriza had a harem even now.

But this stood apart. There was something *systematic* in the taking, something shrouded. That was what nudged at Lazlo's mind—but briefly, only to be churned under by the overwhelming dread. Just a few minutes earlier he had thought, nonchalant, that he could catch Sarai's terrors like fireflies in a jar. Now the enormity of them reached out to catch *him*.

"Strange the dreamer," said Skathis, extending one imperious hand. "Come with me."

"No!" cried Sarai. She grabbed at Lazlo's arm and clutched it to herself.

Skathis grinned. "Come now. You know there is no safety and no salvation. There is only surrender."

Only surrender. Only surrender.

What flooded Sarai was the emotion of everyone ever left behind, every family member or fiancé, childhood sweetheart or best friend who could do nothing but surrender as their loved one was taken up. Rasalas reared up on its hind legs, its huge, clawed paws coming down hard on the window ledge, crumbling it away. Sarai and Lazlo stumbled backward. They clung together. "You can't have him!" choked Sarai.

"Don't worry, child," said Skathis, fixing her with his cold eyes. "I'm taking him for *you*."

She shook her head, hard, at the idea that this thing should be done in her name—as Isagol had taken Eril-Fane for her own, so would Skathis take Lazlo for her. But then . . . that very idea—the paradox of it, of Skathis taking Lazlo *from* her to bring him *to* her—split Sarai back into two people, the one in the citadel and the one in this room, and uncovered the border between dream and reality that had become lost in the fear. This was just a dream, and as long as she knew that, she wouldn't be powerless in it.

All the fear washed away like dust in a rainstorm. *You are the Muse of Nightmares*, Sarai told herself. *You are their mistress, not their thrall.*

And she threw up one hand, not forming in her mind a precise attack, but—as with the mahalath—letting some deeper voice within herself decide.

It decided, apparently, that Skathis was already dead.

Before Sarai's and Lazlo's eyes, the god jerked, eyes widening in shock as a hreshtek suddenly burst out through his chest. His blood was red—as red as the paint in the mural, in which, it occurred to Lazlo, Skathis was depicted just like this: stabbed from behind, the sword slitting out right between his hearts. A red bubble appeared at his lips, and very quickly he was dead. *Very* quickly. This was no natural depiction of his death, but a clear reminder of it. *You're dead, stay dead, leave us alone.* Rasalas the beast froze in place—all mesarthium dying with its master—while on its back the lord of the Mesarthim collapsed in on himself, withering, *deflating*, until nothing remained but a bloodless, spiritless husk of blue flesh to be carried off, with a terrific screech, in a flash of melting white, by the great bird, Wraith, appearing from nowhere and vanishing the same way.

The room was quiet, but for quick breathing. The nightmare was over, and Lazlo and Sarai clung together, staring into the face of Rasalas, frozen in a snarl. Its great feet were still up on the window ledge, claws sunk into the stone. Lazlo reached out a shaking arm and yanked the curtain closed. The other arm he left in Sarai's possession. She was still clinging to it, both of her own arms wrapped around it as though she meant to dig in her heels and wrestle Skathis for him. She'd done better than that. She had vanquished the god of beasts. Lazlo was sure he had done none of it.

"Thank you," he said, turning to her. They were so very near already, her body pressed against his arm.

His turning brought them nearer, face-to-face, his tilted down, hers up, so that the space between them was hardly more than the wisp of tea steam that, earlier in the night, had drifted up between them at the riverbank tea table.

It was new to both of them—this nearness that mingles breath and warmth—and they shared the sensation that they were absorbing each other, melting together in an exquisite crucible. It was an intimacy both had imagined, but never—they now knew—successfully. The truth was so much better than the fantasy. The wild, soft wings were in a frenzy. Sarai couldn't think. She wanted only to keep on melting.

But there was something in the way. She was still blinking away the afterimage of Rasalas's gleaming teeth, and the knowledge that it was all her fault. "Don't *thank* me," she said, letting go of Lazlo's arm and looking down, breaking the gaze. "I brought that here. You should throw me out. You don't want me in your mind, Lazlo. I'll just ruin it."

"You ruin nothing," he said, and his woodsmoke voice had never been sweeter. "I might be asleep, but this has still been the best night of my life." Marveling, he gazed at her eyes, her cinnamon brows, the perfect curve of her blue cheek, and that luscious lip with the crease in the center, sweet as a slice of ripe fruit. He dragged his eyes up from it, back to hers. "Sarai," he said, and if ravids purred it might sound something like the way he said her name. "You must see. *I want you in my mind.*"

And he wanted her in his arms. He wanted her in his life. He wanted her *not* trapped in the sky, *not* hunted by humans, *not* hopeless, and *not* besieged by nightmares whenever she closed her eyes. He wanted to bring her to a real riverbank and let her sink her toes into the mud. He wanted to curl up with her in a real library, and smell the books and open them and read them to each other. He wanted to buy them both wings from the wingsmiths so that they could fly away, with a stash of blood candy in a little treasure chest, so that they could live forever. He'd learned, the moment he glimpsed what lay beyond the Cusp, that the realm of the unknowable was so much bigger than he'd guessed. He wanted to discover *how much* bigger. With her.

But first…first he just really, really, *really* wanted to kiss her.

He searched her eyes for acquiescence and found it. Freely she gave it. It was like a thread of light passing from one to the other, and it was more than acquiescence. It was complicity, and desire. Her breathing shallowed. She stepped in, closing that little space. There was a limit to their melting, and they found it, and defied it. His chest was hard against hers. Hers was soft against his. His hands closed on her waist. Her arms came round his neck. The walls gave forth

527

a shimmer like sunrise on fierce water. Countless tiny stars spent themselves in radiance, and neither Sarai nor Lazlo knew which of them was making it. Perhaps they both were, and there was such brilliance in the endless careless diamonds of light, but there was awareness, too, and urgency. Under the skin of dreaming, they both knew that dawn was near, and that their embrace could not survive it.

So Sarai rose to her toes, erasing the last little gap between their flushed faces. Their lashes fluttered shut, honey red and rivercat, and their mouths, soft and hungry, found each other and had just time to touch, and press, and sweetly, sweetly open before the first wan morning light seeped in at the window, touched the dusky wing of the moth on Lazlo's brow, and—in a puff of indigo smoke—annihilated it.

🌿 48 🌿

No Place in the World

Sarai vanished from Lazlo's arms, and Lazlo vanished from Sarai's. The shared dream ripped right down the middle and spilled them both out. Sarai woke in her bed in the citadel with the warmth of his lips still on hers, and Lazlo woke in the city, a moth-shaped puff of smoke diffusing on his brow. They sat up at the same moment, and for both, the sudden absence was the powerful inverse of the presence they'd felt just an instant before. Not mere physical presence—the heat of a body against one's own (though that, too)—but something more profound.

This was not the frustration one feels at waking from a sweet dream. It was the desolation of having found the place that *fits*, the one true place, and experiencing the first heady sigh of *rightness* before being torn away and cast back into random, lonely scatter.

The place was each other, and the irony was sharp, since they couldn't *be* in the same place, and had come no closer to each other in physical reality than her screaming at him across her terrace while ghosts clawed and tore at her.

But even knowing that was true—that they hadn't been in the same place all this long night through, but practically on different planes of existence, him on the ground, her in the sky—Sarai could not accept that they hadn't been *together*. She collapsed back on her bed, and her fingers reached wonderingly to trace her own lips, where a moment before his had been.

Not really, perhaps, but truly. That is to say, they might not have *really* kissed, but they had *truly* kissed. Everything about this night was true in a way that transcended their bodies.

But that didn't mean their bodies *wanted* to be transcended.

The ache.

Lazlo fell back on his pillows, too, raised fists to his eyes and pressed. Breath hissed out between his clenched teeth. To have been granted so tiny a taste of the nectar of her mouth, and so brief a brush with the velvet of her lips was unspeakable cruelty. He felt set on fire. He had to convince himself that liberating a silk sleigh and flying forthwith to the citadel was not a viable option. That would be like the prince charging up to the maiden's tower, so mad with desire that he forgets his sword and is slain by the dragon before even getting near her.

Except that the dragon in this case was a battalion of ghosts whom no sword could harm, and he didn't have a sword anyway. At best he had a padded pole, a true hero's weapon.

This problem—by which he meant not the interrupted kiss, but this whole ungodly impasse of city and citadel—would not be solved by slaying. There had been too much of that already. How it *would* be solved, he didn't know, but he knew this: The stakes were higher than anyone else realized. And the stakes, for him now, were personal.

From the day the Godslayer rode through the gates in Zosma and issued his extraordinary invitation, throughout the recruitment of experts and all their endless speculation, to finally laying eyes on Weep, Lazlo had felt a certain freedom from expectation. Oh, he wanted to help. Badly. He'd daydreamed about it, but in all of that, no one was looking to *him* for solutions, and he hadn't been looking to himself for them, either. He'd merely been wistful. "What could *I* do?" went the refrain. He was no alchemist, no builder, no expert on metals or magnets.

But now the nature of the problem had changed. It wasn't just metals and magnets anymore, but ghosts and gods and magic and vengeance, and while he wouldn't call himself an expert in any of those things, he had more to recommend him than the others did, starting with an open mind.

And open hearts.

Sarai was up there. Her life was at stake. So Lazlo didn't ask himself *What could* I *do?* that morning as the second Sabbat of Twelfthmoon dawned in the city of Weep, but "What *will* I do?"

It was a noble question, and if destiny had seen fit to reveal its staggering answer to him then, he would never have believed it.

✳ ✳ ✳

Eril-Fane and Azareen came for breakfast, and Lazlo saw them through the lens of everything he'd learned in the night, and his hearts ached for them. Suheyla set out steamed buns and boiled eggs and tea. They sat down, all four of them, on the cushions around the low stone table in the courtyard. Suheyla knew nothing yet but what she sensed: that something had happened, that something had changed. "So," she asked. "What did you find up there, really? I take it that the story about the pontoon was a lie."

"Not exactly a lie," said Lazlo. "The pontoon did spring a leak." He took a sip of tea. "With some help from a meat hook."

Suheyla's cup clattered onto her saucer. "A meat

hook?" she repeated, eyes wide, then narrow. "How did the pontoon happen to encounter a meat hook?"

The question was directed at Lazlo, since he seemed more inclined to speak than the other two. He turned to Eril-Fane and Azareen. It seemed their business to do it, not his.

They began with the ghosts. In fact, they named a great many of them, beginning with Azareen's grandmother. There were more than Lazlo realized. Uncles, neighbors, acquaintances. Suheyla wept in silence. Even a cousin who'd died a few days ago, a young man named Ari-Eil, had been seen. They were all pale and sick with the implications. The citizens of Weep, it would seem, were captive even in death.

"Either we've all been damned and the citadel is our hell," said Suheyla, shaking, "or there's another explanation." She fixed her son with a steady gaze. She wasn't one to give credence to hell, and was braced for the truth.

He cleared his throat and said, with enormous difficulty, "There is a . . . survivor . . . up there."

Suheyla paled. "A *survivor*?" She swallowed hard. "Godspawn?"

"A girl," said Eril-Fane. He had to clear his throat again. Every syllable seemed to fight him. "With red hair." Five simple words—*a girl with red hair*—and what a torrent of emotion they unleashed. If silence

533

could crash, it did. If it could break like a wave and flood a room with all the force of the ocean, it did. Azareen seemed carved of stone. Suheyla gripped the edge of the table. Lazlo reached out a hand to steady her.

"Alive?" she gasped, and her gaze was pinned to her son. Lazlo could see the ricochet of feeling in her, the tentative surge of hope flinching back toward the firmer ground of dread. Her grandchild was alive. Her grandchild was godspawn. *Her grandchild was alive.* "Tell me," she said, desperate to hear more.

"I have nothing more to tell," said Eril-Fane. "I only saw her for an instant."

"Did she attack you?" asked Suheyla.

He shook his head, seeming puzzled. It was Azareen who answered. "She warned us," she said. Her brow was furrowed, her eyes haunted. "I don't know why. But we would all be dead if it weren't for her."

A brittle silence settled. They all traded looks across the table, so stunned and full of questions that Lazlo finally spoke.

"Her name is Sarai," he said, and their three heads swung to face him. He had been silent, set apart from the violence of their emotion. Those five words—"a girl with red hair"—created such an opposite effect in him. Tenderness, delight, desire. His voice carried all of it when he said her name, in an echo of the ravid's purr in which he'd said it to her.

"How could you know that?" asked Azareen, the first to recover from her surprise. Her tone was blunt and skeptical.

"She told me," Lazlo said. "She can go into dreams. It's her gift. She came into mine."

They all considered this. "How do you know it was real?" Eril-Fane asked.

"They're not like any dreams I've had before," Lazlo said. How could he put it into words, what it was like being with Sarai? "I know how it sounds. But I dreamed her before I ever saw her. Before I even saw the mural and knew the Mesarthim were blue. That was why I asked you that day. I thought she must be Isagol, because I didn't know about the—" He hesitated. This was their secret shame, and it had been kept from him. The godspawn. The word was as terrible as the name Weep. "The children," he said instead. "But I know now. I . . . I know all of it."

Eril-Fane stared at him, but it was the blind, unblinking stare of someone seeing into the past. "Then you know what I did."

Lazlo nodded. When he looked at Eril-Fane now, what did he see? A hero? A butcher? Did they cancel each other out, or would butcher always trump hero? Could they exist side by side, two such opposites, like the love and hate he'd borne for three long years?

"I had to," said the Godslayer. "We couldn't suffer them to live, not with magic that would set them above us, to conquer us all over again when they grew up. The risk was too great." It all had the ring of something oft repeated, and his look appealed to Lazlo to understand. Lazlo didn't. When Sarai told him what Eril-Fane had done, he'd believed the Godslayer must repent of it now. But here he was, defending the slaughter.

"They were innocent," he said.

The Godslayer seemed to shrink in on himself. "I know. Do you think I wanted to do it? There was no other way. There was no place for them in this world."

"And now?" Lazlo asked. He felt cold. This wasn't the conversation he had expected to be having. They should have been figuring out a plan. Instead, his question was met with silence, the only possible interpretation of which was: There was *still* no place for them in this world. "She's your daughter," he said. "She's not some monster. She's afraid. She's *kind*."

Eril-Fane shrank further. The two women closed ranks around him. Azareen flashed Lazlo a warning look, and Suheyla reached for her son's hand. "And what of our dead, trapped up there?" she asked. "Is that kind?"

"That isn't her doing," Lazlo said, not to dismiss the threat, but at least to exonerate Sarai. "It must be one of the others."

Eril-Fane flinched. "Others?"

How deep and tangled the roots of hatred were,

thought Lazlo, seeing how even now, with remorse and self-loathing like a fifteen years' canker eating him from within, the Godslayer could hardly tell whether he *wished* the godspawn unslain or *feared* them so.

As for Lazlo, he was uneasy with the information. He felt sick in the pit of his stomach to fear that he couldn't trust Eril-Fane. "There are other survivors," was all he said.

Survivors. There was so much in that word: strength, resilience, luck, along with the shadow of whatever crime or cruelty had been survived. In this case, *Eril-Fane* was that crime, that cruelty. They had survived *him*, and the shadow fell very dark on him.

"Sarai saved us," Lazlo said quietly. "Now we have to save her, and the others, too. You're Eril-Fane. It's up to you. The people will follow your lead."

"It isn't that simple, Lazlo," said Suheyla. "There's no way you could understand the hate. It's like a disease."

He was beginning to understand. How had Sarai put it? "The hate of the used and tormented, who are the children of the used and tormented, and whose own children will be used and tormented."

"So what are you saying? What do you mean to do?" He braced himself, and asked, "Kill them?"

"No," said Eril-Fane. "No." It was an answer to the question, but it came out as though he were warding off a nightmare or a blow, as though even the idea was an assault, and he couldn't bear it. He put his face in his hand, head bowed. Azareen sat apart, watching him, her eyes dark and liquid and so full of pain that she might have been made of it. Suheyla, eyes brimming with tears, laid her one good hand on her son's shoulder.

"I'll take the second silk sleigh," he had said, lifting his head, and while the women's eyes were wet, his were dry. "I'll go up and meet with them."

Azareen and Suheyla immediately objected. "And offer yourself as sacrifice?" demanded Azareen. "What would that accomplish?"

"It seems to me you barely escaped with your lives," Suheyla pointed out more gently.

He looked to Lazlo, and there was a helplessness in him, as though he wanted Lazlo to tell him what to do. "I'll talk to Sarai tonight," he volunteered. "I'll ask if she can persuade the others to call a truce."

"How do you know she'll come again?"

Lazlo blushed, and worried they could see it all written on his face. "She said she would," he lied. They'd run out of time to make plans, but she didn't need to say it. Night couldn't come soon enough, and he was sure she felt the same. And next time he wouldn't wait until the precise strike of dawn before drawing her close. He cleared his throat. "If she says it's safe, we can go up tomorrow."

"We?" said Eril-Fane. "No. Not you. I'll risk no one but myself."

Azareen looked sharply away at that, and in the bleakness of her eyes, Lazlo saw a shade of the anguish of loving someone who doesn't love himself.

"Oh, I'm going with you," Lazlo said, not with force but simple resolve. He was imagining disembarking from the sleigh onto the seraph's palm, and Sarai standing before him, as real as his own flesh and blood. He had to be there. Whatever look these musings produced upon his face, Eril-Fane didn't try to argue him out of it. As for Azareen, neither would she be left behind. But first, the five up in the citadel had to agree to it, and that couldn't happen until tomorrow.

Meanwhile, there was today to deal with. Lazlo was to go to the Merchants' Guildhall this morning and ask Soulzeren and Ozwin, privately, to conjure some likely excuse for delaying the launch of the second silk sleigh. Everyone would be expecting them to follow up yesterday's failed ascension with a success, which of course they couldn't do, at least not yet.

As for the secret, it would be kept from the citizens. Eril-Fane considered keeping it from the Tizerkane, too, for fear that it would cause them too much turmoil and prove too difficult to hide. But Azareen was staunch on their behalf, and argued that they needed to be ready for anything that happened. "They can bear it," she said, adding softly, "They don't need to know all of it yet."

She meant Sarai, Lazlo understood, and whose child she was.

"There's something I don't understand," he said as he prepared to take his leave. It seemed to him it was the mystery at the center of everything to do with the godspawn. "Sarai said there were thirty of them in the nursery that day."

Eril-Fane looked sharply down at his hands. The muscles in his jaw clenched. Lazlo was uncomfortable pressing onward in this bloody line of inquiry—and he was far from certain he really wanted an answer— but it felt too important not to delve deeper. "And though that's... no small number, it's got to be just a fraction." He was imagining the nursery as a row of identical cribs. Because he hadn't been in the citadel and seen how everything was mesarthium, he substituted rough wooden cribs—little more than open crates—like the ones the monks kept infant orphans in at the abbey.

Here was the thing that nagged at Lazlo like a missing tooth. He himself had been an infant in a row of identical cribs, and he shared a name with countless other foundlings to show for it. There had been a lot of them—a lot of Stranges—and... there were *still* a lot of them. "What about all the others?" he asked, looking from Eril-Fane to Azareen, and lastly to Suheyla, who, he suspected, had been delivered of one herself. "The ones who weren't babies anymore? If the Mesarthim were doing this all along…" *This?* He shuddered at his own craven circumlocution, using so meaningless a word to obscure so hideous a truth. *Breeding.* That was what they'd been doing. Hadn't they?

Why?

"Over two centuries," he pressed, "there had to have been *thousands* of children."

Their three faces all wore the same bleak look. He saw that they understood him. They might have stepped in and saved him coming out with it, but they didn't, so he put it bluntly. "What happened to all the rest?"

Suheyla answered. Her voice was lifeless. "We don't know," she said. "We don't know what the gods did with them."

49

VEIL OF REVERIE

There was no beauty sleep for Thyon Nero. Quite the opposite.

"It might not kill you," Strange had said. "But it will make you ugly." Thyon recalled the jest—the easy teasing tone of it—as he drew another long, ill-advised syringeful of spirit from his own overtaxed veins. It couldn't be helped. He had to make more azoth at once. A control batch, as it were, after the...inexplicable...results of last night's test.

He had washed all his glassware and instruments carefully. He might have requested an assistant to do such menial chores, but he was too jealous of his secret to let anyone into his laboratory. Anyway, even if he'd had an assistant, he would have washed these flasks himself. It was the only way to be certain that there were no impurities in the equation, and no unknown factor that might affect the results.

He had always eschewed the mystical side of alchemy and focused on pure science. Such was the basis of his success. Empirical reality. Results—repeatable, verifiable. The solidity of truth you could hold in your hands. Even as he read the stories in *Miracles for Breakfast*, he was mining it for clues. It was science he was after—traces of science, anyway, like dust shaken from a tapestry of wonder.

And when he *re*read the stories, still it was research.

When he read them to fall asleep—a habit that was as deep a secret as the recipe for azoth—it was possible that he might drift into a kind of reverie that felt more mystical than material, but they were fairy tales, after all, and it was only in those moments when his mind shut off its rigor. Whatever it was, it was gone by morning.

But morning had come. He might have no windows to attest to it, but he had a watch, ticking steadily. The sun had risen, and Thyon Nero wasn't reading fairy tales now. He was distilling azoth, as he had done hundreds of times before. So why had that shimmering veil of reverie been drawn over him now?

He shook it off. Whatever accounted for the results of his experiments, it wasn't mystical, and neither was mesarthium itself, and neither was spirit. There was a scientific explanation for everything.

Even "gods."

🌿 50 🌿

THE WHOLE DAY TO GET THROUGH

In the citadel and in the city, Sarai and Lazlo each felt the tug of the other, like a string fixed between their hearts. Another between their lips, where their kiss had barely begun. And a third from the pit of her belly to his, where new enticements stirred. Soft, insistent, delirious, the tug. If only they could gather up the strings and wind themselves nearer, nearer, until finally meeting in the middle.

But there was the whole day to get through before it was time, again, for dreams.

Waking from her first kiss, still flush with the magic of the extraordinary night, Sarai had been buoyant, and alive with new hope. The world seemed more beautiful, less brutal—and so did the future—because Lazlo was in it. She lay warm in her bed, her fingers playing over her own smile as though encountering it for the first time. She felt new to herself—not an obscene thing that made ghosts recoil, but a poem. *A fairy tale.*

In the wake of the dream, anything seemed possible. Even freedom.

Even love.

But it was hard to hold on to that feeling as reality reasserted itself.

She was still a prisoner, for starters, with Minya's army preventing her from leaving her room. When she tried to shoulder through them to the door, they gripped her arms—right over the bruises they'd made the day before—and hauled her back. Less Ellen never came with her morning tray, nor did Feyzi or Awyss with the fresh pitcher of water they always brought first thing. Sarai had used the last of her water yesterday to clean the wound on her arm, and woke dehydrated—no doubt her weeping in the night hadn't helped—with nothing to drink.

She was thirsty. She was hungry. Did Minya mean to starve her?

She had nothing at all until Great Ellen came in sometime in early afternoon with her apron full of plums.

"Oh, thank goodness," said Sarai. But when she looked at Great Ellen, she was disturbed by what she saw. It was the ghost's beloved face, matronly and broad, with her round red "happiness cheeks," but there was nothing happy to be found in her affect, as flat as all the ghosts in Minya's army. And when she spoke, the rhythm of her voice was not her own, but recognizably Minya's. "Even traitors must be fed," she said, and then she dropped the hem of her apron and dumped the plums onto the floor.

"What...?" asked Sarai, jumping back as they went rolling every way. As the ghost turned away, Sarai saw how her eyeballs strained to stay fixed for as long as possible on her, and she read pain in them, and apology.

Her hands shook as she picked up the plums. The first few she ate still crouched there. Her mouth and throat were so dry. The juice was heavenly, but it was tainted by the manner of its delivery, and by the horror of Minya using Great Ellen in such a way. Sarai ate five plums, then crawled around on the floor until she had gathered up all the rest of them and shoved them into the pockets of her robe. She could have eaten more, but she didn't know how long they'd have to last her.

Yesterday, trapped alone in her room, she'd felt despair. Today, she didn't reprise it. Instead, she got mad. At Minya, of course, but the others, too. The ghosts had no free will, but what about Feral and Ruby and Sparrow? Where were they? If it were one of *them* being punished, she wouldn't just accept it and go about her day. She would fight for them, even against Minya.

Did they really believe she had betrayed them? She

hadn't chosen humans over godspawn, but life over death—for all their sakes. Couldn't they see that?

Under the influence of lull, Sarai's days had been nothing but dreamless gray moments between one night and the next. This day was the opposite. It would not end.

She watched the squares of sunlight that her windows threw on the floor. They ought to have moved with the angle of the sun, but she was sure they were frozen in place. Of course today would be the day the sun got stuck in the sky. The gears of the heavens had gotten gummed up, and now it would be daytime forever.

Why not *nighttime* forever?

Lazlo and nighttime forever. Sarai's belly fluttered, and she yearned for the escape that nightfall would bring—if indeed it ever came.

Sleep would help pass the time, if she dared.

She certainly needed it. The little rest she'd gotten, asleep in Lazlo's dream, hadn't even begun to allay her fatigue. These past days, hunted by nightmares, she'd felt their presence even while she was awake. She felt them now, too, and she was still afraid. She just wasn't *terrified* anymore, and that was rather wonderful.

She considered her options. She could pace, bitter and frantic and feeling every second of her deprivation and frustration as the sun dawdled its way across the sky.

Or she could go to the door, stand in front of her

547

ghost guards, and scream down the corridor until Minya came.

And then what?

Or she could fall asleep, and maybe fight nightmares—and maybe *win*—and hurry the day on its way.

It wasn't a choice, really. Sarai was tired and she wasn't terrified, so she lay down in her bed, tucked her hands under her cheek, and slept.

* * *

Lazlo looked up at the citadel and wondered, for the hundredth time that day, what Sarai was doing. Was she sleeping? If she was, was she fending off nightmares on her own? He stared at the metal angel and focused his mind, as though by doing so he could give her strength.

Also for the hundredth time that day, he remembered the kiss.

It might have been brief, but so much of a kiss—a first kiss, especially—is the moment before your lips touch, and before your eyes close, when you're filled with the sight of each other, and with the compulsion, the pull, and it's like . . . it's like . . . finding a book inside another book. A small treasure of a book hidden inside a big common one—like . . . spells printed on dragonfly wings, discovered tucked inside a cookery book, right between the recipes for cabbages and corn. That's what a kiss is like, he thought, no matter how brief: It's a tiny, magical story, and a miraculous interruption of the mundane.

Lazlo was more than ready for the mundane to be interrupted again. "What time is it?" he asked Ruza, glaring at the sky. Where it showed around the citadel's edges, it was damnably bright and blue. He'd never felt anger at the sky before. Even the interminable days of the Elmuthaleth crossing had passed more quickly than this one.

"Do I look like a clock?" inquired the warrior. "Is my face round? Are there numbers on it?"

"If your face were a clock," Lazlo reasoned slowly, "I wouldn't ask you what time it was. I'd just look at you."

"Fair point," admitted Ruza.

It was an ordinary day, if at least ten times longer than it ought to have been. Soulzeren and Ozwin did as asked and produced a credible reason to delay a second launch. No one questioned it. The citizens were relieved, while the faranji were simply occupied.

Thyon Nero wasn't the only one exhausting himself—though he was the only one siphoning off his own vital essence to do it. They were all deeply engaged, hard at work, and competitive. Well, they were all deeply engaged and competitive, and all with the exception of Drave were also hard at work—though, to be fair, this wasn't his fault. He'd have liked nothing better than to blow something up, but it was clear to everyone, himself included, that he and his powder were on hand as a last resort.

When all else fails: *explosions.*

This did not sit well with him. "How am I supposed to win the reward if I'm not allowed to *do* anything?" he demanded of Lazlo that afternoon, waylaying him outside the Tizerkane guard station where he'd stopped to talk with Ruza and Tzara and some of the other warriors.

Lazlo was unsympathetic. Drave was being compensated for his time, just like everyone else. And as for the reward, Drave's personal fortune wasn't high on his list of priorities. "I don't know," he answered. "You might come up with a solution to the problem that doesn't involve destruction."

Drave scoffed. "Doesn't involve destruction? That's like me asking you not to be a mealy-mouthed poltroon."

Lazlo's eyebrows shot up. *"Poltroon?"*

"Look it up," snapped Drave.

Lazlo turned to Ruza. "Do *you* think I'm a poltroon?" he asked, the way a young girl might ask whether her dress was unflattering.

"I don't know what that is."

"I think it's a kind of mushroom," said Lazlo, who

knew very well what *poltroon* meant. Really, he was surprised that Drave did.

"You are absolutely a mushroom," said Ruza.

"It means 'coward,'" said Drave.

"Oh." Lazlo turned to Ruza. "Do you think I'm a coward?"

Ruza considered the matter. "More of a mushroom," he decided. To Drave: "I think you were closer the first time."

"I never said he was a mushroom."

"Then I'm confused."

"I take it as a compliment," Lazlo went on, purely for the infuriation of Drave. It was petty, but fun. "Mushrooms are fascinating. Did you know they aren't even plants?"

Ruza played along, all fascinated disbelief. "I did *not* know that. Please tell me more."

"It's true. Fungi are as distinct from plants as animals are."

"I never said anything about mushrooms," Drave said through gritted teeth.

"Oh, I'm sorry. Drave, you wanted something."

But the explosionist had had enough of them. He flung out a hand in disgust and stalked off.

"He's bored, poor man," said Tzara, with a flat lack of pity. "Nothing to destroy."

"We could at least give him a small neighborhood

to demolish," suggested Ruza. "What kind of hosts *are* we?"

And Lazlo felt a . . . fizz of uneasiness. A bored explosionist was one thing. A bored, disgruntled explosionist was another. But then the conversation took a turn that drove all thoughts of Drave from his head.

"I can think of a way to keep him busy," said Shimzen, one of the other warriors. "Send him up in a silk sleigh to blow the godspawn into blue stew."

Lazlo heard the words, but they were spoken so evenly, so casually, that it took him a moment to process them, and then he could only blink.

Blue stew.

"As long as I don't have to clean it up," said Ruza, just as casually.

They had been briefed, earlier, on the . . . situation . . . in the citadel. Their blasé demeanor was certainly a cover for their deep disquiet, but that didn't mean they weren't absolutely in earnest. Tzara shook her head, and Lazlo thought she was going to chide the men for their callousness, but she said, "Where's the fun in that? You wouldn't even get to watch them die."

His breath erupted from him in a gust, as though he'd been punched in the gut. They all turned to him, quizzical. "What's the matter with *you*?" asked Ruza, seeing his expression. "You look like someone served you blue stew for dinner." He laughed, pleased with his joke, while Shimzen slapped him on the shoulder.

Lazlo's face went tight and hot. All he could see was Sarai, trapped and afraid. "How can you speak like that," he asked, "when you've never even met them?"

"*Met* them?" Ruza's eyebrows went up. "You don't *meet* monsters. You slay them."

Tzara must have seen Lazlo's anger, his... stupefaction. "Trust me, Strange," she told him. "If you knew anything about them, you'd be happy to drop the explosives yourself."

"If you knew anything about *me*," he replied, "you wouldn't think I'd be happy to kill anyone."

They all squinted at him, puzzled—and annoyed, too, that he was spoiling their amusement. Ruza said, "You're thinking of them as people. That's your problem. Imagine they're threaves—"

"We didn't kill the threave."

"Well, that's true." Ruza screwed up his face. "Bad example. But would you have looked at me like that if I had?"

"I don't know. But they're not threaves."

"No," Ruza agreed. "They're much more dangerous."

And that was true, but it missed the point. They were *people*, and you didn't laugh about turning *people* into stew.

Especially not Sarai.

"You think good people can't hate?" she'd asked Lazlo last night. "You think good people don't kill?"

How naïve he'd been, to imagine it was all a matter of understanding. If only they knew her, he'd told himself, they couldn't want to hurt her. But it was so clear to him now: They could *never* know her. They'd never let themselves. Suheyla had tried to tell him: The hate was like a disease. He saw what she meant. But could there ever be a cure?

Could the people of Weep ever accept the survivors in the citadel—or, like the threave in the desert, at least suffer them to live?

51

POLTROONS

"There is a magnetic field between the anchors and the citadel," Mouzaive, the natural philosopher, was telling Kether, artist of siege engines, in the guildhall dining room. "But it's like nothing I've seen before."

Drave, who was irrationally furious to find mushrooms on his plate, sat at the next table. The sullen look on his face gave no hint that he was listening.

Mouzaive had invented an instrument he called a cryptochromometer that used a protein extracted from birds' eyes to detect the presence of magnetic fields. It sounded like a lot of flummery to Drave, but what did he know?

"Magnetic anchors," mused Kether, wondering how he might appropriate the technology for his own engine designs. "So if you could shut them off, the citadel would just...float away?"

"That's my best guess."

"How's it floating, anyway, something that big?"

"A technology we can't begin to fathom," said Mouzaive. "Not ulola gas, that's for certain."

Kether, who was keen on appropriating *that* technology, too, said sagely, "If anything's certain, it's that nothing's certain."

Drave rolled his eyes. "What's making it?" he asked, gruff. "The magnetic field. Is there machinery inside the anchors or something?"

Mouzaive shrugged. "Who knows. It could be a magical moon pearl for all I can tell. If we could get inside the damned things, we might find out."

They discussed the metallurgists' progress, and Thyon Nero's, speculating who would breach the metal hulls first. Drave didn't say another word. He chewed. He even ate the mushrooms while phrases like "breach the hulls" rang in his mind like bells. He was supposed to sit back while the Fellerings and Nero vied for the reward? As though Nero even needed it, when he could just make gold any day of the week.

He'd be damned if this bunch of poltroons were going to keep him from throwing his hat in the ring.

Or more like blowing the damned ring up.

52

AMAZING, BUT SCORCHED

Sparrow *had*, in fact, tried to visit Sarai, but ghosts blocked the corridor and wouldn't let her through. The little girl ghost, Bahar, dripping with river water and dolor, told her solemnly, "Sarai can't play right now," which sent a chill up her spine. She went to the Ellens in the kitchen to see if they knew how she was, but she found them grim and silent, which sent another chill. They were never like this. It had to be Minya's doing, but Minya had never oppressed the nurses as she did the other ghosts. Why now?

Minya was nowhere to be found, and neither were Ruby or Feral.

Sometimes they all just needed a little time to themselves. That was what Sparrow told herself that afternoon in the citadel. But she needed the opposite.

She needed her family. She hated not being able to go to Sarai, and she was furious that she couldn't even find Minya to appeal to her. She went to the heart of the citadel and called out through the narrow opening that had once been a door. She was sure Minya must be inside, but she never answered.

Even the garden couldn't soothe her today. Her magic felt feeble, as though some river within herself were dry. She imagined herself weeping, and Feral holding her to comfort her. He would smooth her hair with his hands and murmur soothing things, and she would look up, and he would look down, and . . . and it wouldn't be anything like when Ruby had kissed him, all sucking noise and storm clouds. It would be sweet, so sweet.

It could happen, she thought. *Now, with everything so fraught.* Why not? The tears were easy enough to produce; she'd been holding them back all day. As for Feral, he could only be in his room. Sparrow wandered up the corridor, past her own room and Ruby's, all silent behind their curtains.

She would feel very stupid later for imagining that Ruby wanted time to herself. She never did. To Ruby, thoughts were pointless if there was no one to tell them to the instant you had them.

She came to Feral's door, and all was *not* silent behind *his* curtain.

"How do I know you won't burn me?" Feral had asked Ruby days earlier.

"Oh, that could only happen if I completely lost track of myself," she'd said. "You'd have to be *really* good. I'm not worried."

It had been something of a slap, and Feral had not forgotten it. It created a conundrum, however. How could he make her eat those words, without getting burned up for his trouble?

These were dark days, and it was good to have a challenge to take his mind off ghosts and doom: make Ruby completely lose track of herself, while not ending up a pile of char. Feral applied himself. The learning curve was delicious. He was keenly attuned to Ruby's pleasure, in part because *it could kill him*, and in part because…he liked it. He liked her pleasure; he'd never liked her better than when she was soft against him, breathing in surprised little gasps or looking up at him from under her lashes, her eyelids heavy with hedonic contentment.

It was all very, very satisfying, and never so much as when, finally, she made a sound like the sighing of doves and violins, and…set fire to his bed.

The scent of smoke. A flash of heat. Her lips were parted and her eyes glowed like embers. Feral pushed himself away, already summoning a cloud; he had rehearsed emergency plans in his head. The air filled with vapor. The silk sheets, clenched in Ruby's fists, burst into flame, and an instant later the cloud burst forth rain, severing the dove-and-violin sigh and dousing her before the rest of her bonfire could kindle.

She gave a little shriek and came upright in an instant. Rain lashed down at her whilst Feral stood back safe and smug. To his credit, he kept the cloud no longer than strictly necessary, on top of which, it wasn't even cold. It was a tropical cloud. He thought this quite a nice gesture, but the romance was lost on Ruby.

"How...how...*rude*!" she exclaimed, shaking water from her arms. Her blue breasts glistened. Her hair sluiced rivers down her back and shoulders.

"*Rude?*" Feral repeated. "So the polite thing would be to uncomplainingly burn up?"

She glared at him. *"Yes."*

He surveyed the scene. "Look," he pointed out. "You've scorched my sheets."

She had. There were sodden, black-edged holes where she'd clenched them in her fists. "Do you expect me to *apologize*?" Ruby asked.

But Feral shook his head, grinning. He didn't mean to rebuke her. On the contrary, he was gloating. "You lost track of yourself," he said. "You know what that means, don't you? It means I'm *really* good."

Her eyes narrowed. Still entangled in Feral's sheets, she went full Bonfire, lighting up like a torch and taking the whole bed with her.

Feral groaned, but could only watch as his sheets, pillows, mattress—everything that was not mesarthium—flamed and were eaten up, leaving nothing behind but hot metal and a smoking naked girl with her eyebrows raised as though to say, *How's that for scorched sheets?* She didn't really look mad, though. A grin tugged at one corner of her mouth. "I suppose you *have* improved," she allowed.

It felt like winning at quell, only much better. Feral laughed. He'd known Ruby all his life and been annoyed by her for half of it, but now he was simply amazed by the turn things could take between two people, and the feelings that could grow while you distracted yourself from the end of the world. He walked back over to her. "You've destroyed my bed," he said, congenial. "I'll have to sleep with you from now on."

"Oh really. Aren't you afraid I'll incinerate you?"

He shrugged. "I'll just have to be less amazing. To be on the safe side."

"Do that and I'll kick you out."

"What a dilemma." He sat on the edge of the bare bed frame. "Be less amazing, and stay alive. Or be amazing, and get scorched." Mesarthium didn't hold heat; it was already back to normal, but Ruby's skin was not. It was hot—like a summer day or a really good kiss. Feral leaned toward her, intent upon the latter, and froze.

At the same moment, they became aware of a movement in their peripheral vision. The curtain. It had been pushed aside, and Sparrow was standing there, stricken.

53

TARNISHED HEARTS

Sarai's dreams that day were not without their terrors, but, for a change, she was not without defenses. "We'll chase them away," Lazlo had said, "or else turn them into fireflies and catch them in jars."

She tried it, and *it worked*, and at some point in the evening, she found herself striding through a dark wood in a Tizerkane breastplate, carrying a jar full of fireflies that had recently been ravids and Rasalas and even her mother. She held up the jar to light her way, and it lit her smile, too, fierce with triumph.

She didn't meet Lazlo in the dream, not exactly. Perhaps her unconscious preferred to wait for the real thing. But she did relive the kiss, exactly as it had been—melting sweet and all too brief—and she woke exactly when she had before. She didn't bolt upright in bed this time, but lay where she was, lazy and liquid with sleep and well-being. At dawn, solitude had greeted her, but not this time. Opening her eyes, she gave a start.

Minya was standing at the foot of her bed.

Now she did bolt upright. "Minya! Whatever happened to respecting the curtains?"

"Oh, the curtains," said Minya, dismissive. "Why worry about curtains, Sarai, unless you've something to hide?" She looked sly. "Ruby and Feral do, you know. But curtains, well, they don't block out sounds very well." She made exaggerated smooching noises and it reminded Sarai of how they would giggle and gasp when she told them about the things that humans did in their beds. It was a long time since she'd done that.

Ruby and Feral, though? It didn't really surprise her. While she'd been wrapped up in her own misery, life in the citadel had gone on. *Poor Sparrow*, she thought. "Well, I'm not hiding anything," she lied.

Minya didn't believe her for a second. "No? Then why do you look like that?"

"Like what?"

Minya studied her, her flat gaze roving up and down so that Sarai felt stripped. *Seen*, but not in a good way. Minya pronounced, as though diagnosing a disease, "*Happy*."

Happy. What a notion. "Is *that* what this feeling is?" she said, not even trying to hide it. "I'd forgotten all about it."

564

"What do *you* have to be happy about?"

"I was just having a good dream," said Sarai. "That's all."

Minya's nostrils flared. Sarai wasn't supposed to have good dreams. "How is that possible?"

Sarai shrugged. "I closed my eyes, lay still, and—"

Minya was furious. Her whole body was rigid. Her voice took on the spittle-flying hiss normally reserved for the word *vengeance*. "*Have you no shame?* Lying there all silky and wanton, having good dreams while our lives fall apart?"

Sarai had plenty of shame. Minya might as well have demanded *Have you no blood?* or *Have you no spirit?* because shame as good as ran in her veins. But... not right now. *"I think you're a fairy tale."* Funny how light she felt without it. *"I think you're magical, and brave, and exquisite."*

"I'm through with shame, Minya," she said. "And I'm through with lull, and I'm through with nightmares, and I'm through with vengeance. Weep has suffered enough and so have we. We have to find another way."

"Don't be stupid. There *is* no other way."

"A lot of things could happen," Sarai had told Ruby, not believing it herself. That had been days ago. She believed it now. Things *had* happened. Unbelievable things. But where the citadel was concerned, nothing could happen unless Minya let it.

Sarai had to persuade her *to let it*.

For years she'd stifled her own empathy and kept it in for fear of Minya's wrath. But now so much depended on it—not just her love, but all their lives. She took a deep breath. "Minya," she said, "you have to listen to me. Please. I know you're angry with me, but please try to open your mind."

"Why? So you can put things in it? I'm not forgiving your humans, if that's what you think."

Your humans. And they *were* her humans, Sarai thought. Not just Eril-Fane and Lazlo, but all of them. Because her gift had forced her—and *allowed* her—to know them. "Please, Min," she said. Her voice fluttered as though it were trying to fly away, as she herself wished she could do. "Eril-Fane didn't tell anyone what happened yesterday. He didn't tell them about me, or the ghosts."

"So you *have* seen him," Minya said with vindication. "You used to be a terrible liar, you know. I could always tell. But you seem to be improving."

"I wasn't lying," said Sarai. "I hadn't seen him, and now I have."

"And is he well, our great hero?"

"No, Minya. He's never been well. Not since Isagol."

"Oh stop," protested Minya, pressing a hand to her chest. "You're breaking my hearts."

"What hearts?" asked Sarai. "The hearts you tarnish with miserable ghosts so that you can hold on to your hate?"

"The hearts I tarnish with miserable ghosts? That's good, Sarai. That's really poetic."

Sarai squeezed her eyes shut. Talking to Minya was like getting slapped in the face. "The point is, he didn't tell anyone. What if he's sick about what he did, and wants to make amends?"

"If he can bring them all back to life, then I'll certainly consider it."

"You know he can't! But just because the past is blood doesn't mean the future must be, too. Couldn't we try talking to him? If we promise him safe conduct—"

"Safe conduct! You're worrying about *his* safety? Will Weep promise *us* safe conduct? Or don't you need us anymore? Maybe we aren't a good enough family for you now. You have to yearn for the man *who killed our kind.*"

Sarai swallowed. Of course she needed them. Of course they were her real family and always would be. As for the rest, she wanted to deny it out of hand. When Minya put it like that, it appalled even her. "That's ridiculous," she said. "This isn't even about him. It's about us, and our future."

"Do you really think he could ever love you?" the little girl asked. "Do you really think a human could ever stand the sight of you?"

Until a week ago, Sarai would have said no. Or she wouldn't have said anything, but only *felt* the *no* as shame, wilting and withering her like an unwatered flower. But the answer had changed, and it had changed *her*. "Yes," she said, soft but resolute. "I *know* a human could stand the sight of me, Minya, because there is one who can see me."

The words were out. She couldn't take them back. A flush spread up her chest and neck. "And he stands the sight of me quite well."

Minya stared. Sarai had never seen her gobsmacked before. For an instant, even her anger was wiped clean away.

It came back. "Who?" she asked in a deadly seethe of a voice.

Sarai felt a tremor of misgiving for having opened the door to her secret. But she didn't see that Lazlo could be kept secret much longer, not if there was to be any chance of the future that she hoped for. "He's one of the faranji," she said, trying to sound strong for his sake. Lazlo deserved to be spoken of with pride. "You've never seen such dreams, Min. The beauty he sees in the world, and in me. It can change things. I can feel it."

Did she think she could sway her? Did she imagine Minya would ever listen?

"So that's it," said the girl. "A man makes eyes at you, and just like that you're ready to turn your back on us and go play house in Weep. Are you so hungry for love? I might expect as much of Ruby, but not of you."

Oh, that bright little treacherous voice. "I'm not turning my back on anyone," said Sarai. "The point is that humans don't have to despise us. If we could just *talk* to them, then we would see if there might be a chance—a chance for us to *live*, and not merely exist. Minya, I can bring a message for Eril-Fane. He could come up tomorrow, and then we'd know—"

"By all means," said Minya. "Bring him, and your lover, too. Bring all the faranji, why don't you. How convenient if we could take them all out at once. That would be a big help, actually. Thank you, Sarai."

"Take them all out," she repeated, dull.

"Was I not clear? Any human who sets foot in the citadel will die."

Tears of futility burned Sarai's eyes. Minya's mind, like her body, was immutable. Whatever accounted for the unnatural stasis that had kept her a child for fifteen years, it was beyond the reach of reason or persuasion. She would have her carnage and her vengeance and drag everyone into it with her.

"You could give Minya a nice warm hug," Sparrow had said to Ruby in the garden. She hadn't meant it, and the poisonous thought—the shocking, inconceivable, unthinkable notion of the five of them doing harm to one another—had made Sarai ill. She felt ill now, too, looking into the burning eyes of the little girl who'd given her a life, and asking herself how... how she could just stand by and let her start a war.

She wanted to scream.

She wanted to scream *her moths*. "You were quite clear," she spat. Her moths were burgeoning. They wanted out. *She* wanted out. The sun had set. The sky was not full dark, but it was dark enough. She faced the small tyrant, heir to Skathis in cruelty at least, if not in gift. Her fists clenched. Her teeth clenched. The scream built in her, as violent as the first one, years ago, that she'd held in for weeks, so certain it was bad.

"Bad would be good," Minya had said then. "We *need* bad."

And thus had the Muse of Nightmares been born, and Sarai's fate decided in those few words.

"Go on, then," said Minya now. Her fists, too, were clenched, and her face was wild, half mad with rage and resentment. "I can see you want to. Go down to your humans if that's all you care about! Your lover must be waiting. Go to him, Sarai." She bared her small white teeth. "Tell him *I can't wait to meet him*!"

Sarai was trembling. Her arms were stiff at her sides. Leaning toward Minya, she opened her mouth, and screamed. No sound came out. Only moths. All at Minya, right at Minya. A torrent of darkness, frantic wings, and fury. They spewed at her. They *poured* at her. They flew in her face and she gave a cry, trying to duck out of their path. They dipped when she did. She couldn't escape them. They beat their wings at her face and hair, the stream of them parting around her like a river around a rock. Past her, out of the alcove, over the heads of the ghosts standing guard, and out into the twilight.

Sarai stood where she was, still screaming, and though no sound came out—her voice having gone— her lips shaped the words *Get out! Get out! Get out!* until Minya picked herself up from her cower, and, with a terrible look, turned and fled.

Sarai collapsed onto her bed, heaving with silent sobs, and her moths winged down and down. They didn't divide, because her mind would not divide. She thought only of Lazlo, so that was where they flew, straight to the house and the window she knew so well, into the room where she hoped to find him sleeping.

But it was early yet. His bed was empty and his boots gone, so the moths, fluttering with agitation, had no choice but to settle down and wait.

🌿 54 🌿

Too Lovely Not to Devour

Lazlo didn't want to talk to anyone except Sarai. He just didn't think he could keep his composure through any more talk of the "godspawn," be it well meant or ill. He half considered climbing in his window to avoid Suheyla, but he couldn't do that, so he went in by the green door and found her in the courtyard. Supper was waiting. "Don't worry," she told him straightaway. "Just a light meal. I know you're probably eager for sleep."

He was, and he could have done well enough without supper, but he made himself pause. Sarai was her grandchild, after all, her only one. He'd been angry that morning that she and Eril-Fane hadn't met the news of her existence gladly, but in light of what the Tizerkane reaction had been, he saw that theirs had been generous, if honest. He tried to appreciate what this all meant for her.

She set out bowls of soup and hung a fresh disc of bread from the big hook. It had seeds and petals baked into it in a pattern of overlapping circles—a light meal, maybe, but she must have spent hours on it. Usually she was effortlessly chatty, but not tonight. He saw a shy but shamefaced curiosity in her, and several times she'd seemed about to speak, and then think better of it.

"The other day," he said, "you told me just to ask. Now it's my turn. It's all right. You can ask."

Her voice was timorous. "Does...does she hate us very much?"

"No," he said, "she doesn't hate you at all," and he felt confident that it was true. She'd talked of the paradox at the core of her being, and the curse of knowing one's enemies too well to be able to hate them. "Maybe she used to, but not anymore." He wanted to tell her that Sarai understood, but that absolution could come only from Sarai.

He ate fast, and Suheyla made him tea. He declined it at first, eager to go, but she said it would help him fall asleep faster.

"Oh. Then that would be wonderful."

He drained it in a gulp, thanked her, paused to press her hand, and went at last to his room. He opened the door and...halted on the threshold.

573

Moths.

Moths were perched on the wooden headboard and the pillows and the wall behind the bed, and when the door opened, they lifted into the air like leaves stirred by a wind.

Sarai, he thought. He didn't know what to make of their numbers. They overwhelmed him, not with fear—or, gods forbid, disgust—but with *awe*, and a prickle of dread.

Maybe he brought all the dread with him from the guard station and the brutal, bloody words of his friends, and maybe the moths brought some of it on their furred twilight wings. He understood one thing in the swirl of creatures: Sarai was waiting for him.

He closed the door. He would have washed and shaved his face, cleaned his teeth, brushed his hair, changed. He blushed at the thought of taking off his shirt, though he knew she'd seen him sleeping that way before. He settled for brushing his teeth and taking off his boots, and then he lay down. Overhead, moths clustered on the ceiling beam like a branch in dark bloom.

He realized, once he was settled, that he'd left enough room on the bed for Sarai—on the side she'd chosen in the dream—though all that was needed was his brow for her moths to perch on. Some other time it might have made him laugh at himself, but not tonight. Tonight he only felt her absence from a world that didn't want her.

He didn't move over, but closed his eyes, feeling the moths all around him—*Sarai* all around him. He was breathless for sleep to come so that he could be with her, and tonight there was no euphoria keeping him awake. There was only a slow sinking, and soon enough—

* * *

The moth, the brow.

The threshold of the dream.

Sarai found herself in the amphitheater market. She craved the color and sweetness of Dreamer's Weep, as she thought of it, but here were neither. The place was empty. A wind scoured through, blowing scraps of refuse past her ankles, and a terrible pit of fear opened in her. Where was all the color? There should have been silks fluttering, music in the air, and laughter drifting down from the children on their high wires. There were no children on the high wires, and all the market stalls were bare. Some even looked *burned*, and there wasn't a sound to be heard.

The city had stopped breathing.

Sarai stopped breathing, too. Had *she* made this place, to reflect her despair, or was it Lazlo's creation?

That seemed impossible. Her soul needed Dreamer's Weep, and she needed him.

There he was, right there, his long hair wild in the wind. His face was somber, the easy joy gone from it, but there was still—Sarai breathed again—such witchlight in his eyes. She had witchlight in her own. She felt it go out from her like something that could touch him. She stepped forward, following in its path. He stepped forward, too.

They came to stand face-to-face—arm's reach without reaching. The three strings that joined them wound them ever nearer. Hearts, lips, navels. Closer, still not touching. The air between them was a dead place, as though both of them were carrying their hopelessness before them, hoping for the other to dash it away. They held everything they had to say, every desperate thing, and they didn't want to say any of it. They just wanted it to vanish—*here*, at least, in this place that was theirs.

"Well," remarked Sarai. "*That* was a long day."

This earned a surprised laugh from Lazlo. "The longest," he agreed. "Were you able to sleep at all?"

"I was," she reported, finding a small smile. "I turned my nightmares into fireflies and caught them in a jar."

"That's good," Lazlo breathed. "I was worried." He blushed. "I may have thought about you a few times today."

"Only a few?" she teased, blushing, too.

"Maybe more," he admitted. He reached for her hand. It was hot, and so was his. The edges of their hopelessness dissolved, just a little.

"I thought about you, too," said Sarai, lacing their fingers together. Brown and blue, blue and brown. She was transfixed by the sight of them. She murmured, "And it's only fair to tell you that I dreamed of you."

"Oh? I hope I was well behaved."

"Not *too* well behaved." Coyly, she added, "No better than this morning, when the sun so rudely rose."

She meant the kiss; he understood. "*The sun.* I still haven't forgiven it." The space between them could only shrink, not grow. Lazlo's voice was music—the most beautiful smoky music—when he caught Sarai up in his arms, and said, "I want to catch it in a jar and put it away with the fireflies."

"The moon on a bracelet and the sun in a jar," said Sarai. "We really wreak havoc on the heavens, don't we?"

Lazlo's voice sank deeper in his throat. Smokier. Hungrier. "I expect the heavens will survive," he said, and then he kissed her.

How had they survived a whole day on the merest touch that was last night's kiss? If they'd known then what a kiss *was*, they couldn't have. It would have been unbearable to come so close—to *barely feel* and *almost taste* and be snatched apart before...well, before *this*. But they hadn't known.

And now they did.

Now, right now, they learned. Sarai leaned into Lazlo, her eyes closing in anticipation. His were slower. He wanted to see her. He didn't want to miss even a second of her face. Her smooth cerulean loveliness held him spellbound. There was a dusting of nearly invisible freckles on the bridge of her nose. The glide of their faces was as slow as poured honey, and *her lips*. Ever so slightly, they parted. The bottom one, voluptuous as dew-bright fruit, parted from its fellow—*for him*—and it was the most enticing thing he'd ever seen. A blaze of desire surged through him and he leaned into the honey-slowness, pushing the hopelessness out of his way to take that sweet, soft lip between his own.

The searing softness, the melt.

When Lazlo had wished to discover, with Sarai, the realm of the unknowable, he had thought of great, huge mysteries like the origin and nature of gods. But right now, he'd have given it all up for this small mystery, this tiny, newest, and best mystery of Weep. This kiss.

This exact kiss.

Lips. The wonder of lips that could brush or press, part and close, and—parting, closing—catch the other's lip in the sweetest of bites. Not a true bite. Not teeth. Ah, teeth were still a secret. But the tip of the tongue, well. Hopelessness had little chance against the discovery of the tip of the tongue. And the thing that was almost blinding, unfathomable, was this: Heady as it was—so heady he felt dizzy from it, tipsy—still he sensed that even *this* was only the threshold to another realm of the unknowable. A door pushed just ajar, and the thinnest sliver of light hinting at radiance beyond.

He felt light and heavy at the same time. Burning, floating. He'd never suspected. He'd been aware of girls, of course, and had all the sorts of thoughts that young men have (the better ones, anyway; better young men *and* better thoughts) and of course he wasn't ignorant of the…biology of things. But he'd never had any inkling of what he now sensed lay beyond that tantalizing door. It was a radiance that felt rich and deep and huge and *close* and secret and delirious and…sacred.

It was his future with the girl he held in his arms, and whatever he had felt and feared on his walk home from the guard station, now he was certain: There *would be* a future.

Hope was easy, after all. Here in this place, anyway.

He drew her closer, his arms full around her waist, and lost himself in the marvel of her, of this. He breathed the scent and taste of her, and shivered when her fingers traced up his arms to the nape of his neck. She wove them through his hair and awakened more sensation, a fire of pleasure that radiated down his shoulders and up his scalp, nudging at that tantalizing door with all its luminous secrets. When he broke the kiss, finally, it was to press his face to hers. The ridge of his brow to hers, his cheekbone, rough, against hers, smooth.

"Sarai," he breathed against her cheek. He felt like a glass filled with splendor and luck. His lips curved into a smile. He whispered, "You have ruined my tongue for all other tastes," and understood finally what that phrase meant.

Sarai pulled back, just enough that they could look at each other. Her amazement mirrored his own, her gaze the equivalent of a whispered *Oh*, husky and astonished and awakened.

The laughter reached them first—children's laughter—and then the color. They broke their gaze to look around, and saw the city no longer holding its breath. There were swallowtail flags snapping on the domes, and the sky was a mosaic of kites. And the market stalls were no longer empty, but coming to life as though opening for the morning, with vendors in long aprons setting out their wares. Flocks of brilliant butterflies moved through like schools of fish, and the upper levels of the amphitheater were espaliered with jeweled fruit trees.

"That's better," sighed Sarai. Up in the citadel, her tears dried on her cheeks. The clench of her fists and stomach relaxed.

"Much better," Lazlo agreed. "Do you think *we* just did that?"

"I'm certain of it."

"Well done, us," he said, then added, with exaggerated nonchalance, "I wonder what would happen if we kept kissing."

In a similar display of feigned indifference, Sarai shrugged and said, "Well, I guess we *could* find out."

They knew they had to talk about the day, and the future, and all the hate and despair and helplessness, but...not just yet. That place in their minds that had worked their mahalath transformations was coloring Dreamer's Weep with their snatched and grabbed happiness. Everything else could wait. "Lazlo," Sarai whispered, and she asked him a question to which he already knew the answer. "Do you still want me in your mind?"

"Sarai," he replied. "I want you..." His arms were already around her. He drew her even closer. "In my mind."

"Good." She bit her lip, and the sight of her fine white teeth bearing down on that decadent, delicate lip planted at least an unconscious thought in his mind regarding the potential of teeth in kissing. "I'm going to go to sleep," she told him. "I'm already lying in my bed." She didn't mean to sound seductive, but in her sudden shyness, her voice sank to a whisper, and Lazlo heard it like a purr.

He swallowed hard. "Do you need to lie down here?" In the dream, he meant, because she had last time.

"I don't think so. Now that we know it works, I think it'll be easy." She touched the tip of her nose to the tip of his. *Shaped by fairy tales*, she thought, which made it better than every straight nose in the world. "But there is one thing you can do for me."

"What is it?" asked Lazlo. "Anything."

"You can kiss me some more," she said.

And he did.

* * *

Up in the citadel, Sarai's body fell asleep, and as soon as it did, she stopped being the girl lying on the bed, and she stopped being the moth perched on Lazlo's brow, and became only—and gloriously—the girl in his arms.

Kissing, it turned out, was one of those things that only got better the more of it one did, and became more...interesting...as one gained confidence. Oh, the ways that lips could know each other, and tongues, how they could tease and tingle. Tongues, how they could *lick*.

Some things, thought Sarai, were too lovely to devour, while others were too lovely *not* to.

And together they learned that kissing wasn't just for mouths. That was a revelation. Well, one mouth was needed, of course. But that mouth might decide to take a small sojourn down to the soft place under the jaw, or the tender, exquisite spot just below the ear. Or the earlobe. Who knew? Or the neck. *The entire neck!* And here was a cunning quirk of physiology. Sarai found that she could kiss Lazlo's neck while he kissed hers. Wasn't that lucky? And it was immensely rewarding to feel his tremors when her lips found a place that felt particularly good. Almost as rewarding as when *his* found such a place on *her*. And if not his lips, oh.

His teeth.

Even up in the citadel, the teeth caused her to shiver.

"I never knew about necks," Sarai whispered between fast, hot kisses.

"Neither did I," said Lazlo, breathless.

"Or *ears*."

"*I know*. Who could have guessed about *ears*?"

They were still, all this while, in the marketplace of Dreamer's Weep. Sometime early in the kiss—if one could, with generosity, call it *a* kiss—a convenient tree grew up from a crack in the cobbles, tall and smooth and canted at just the right angle for *leaning* when the dizziness became too much. This was never going any farther than leaning. There was, even in their delectation of necks, an innocence born of perfect inexperience combined with...politeness. Their hands were hot, but they were hot in safe places, and their bodies were close but chaste.

Well.

What does the body know of chastity? Only what the mind insists upon, and if Lazlo's and Sarai's minds insisted, it was not because their bodies failed to present a compelling argument. It was just that it was all so new and so sublime. It might take weeks, after all, just to master necks. Sarai's fingertips did, at some point in the heedless flow of dream time, find themselves slipping under the hem of Lazlo's shirt to play ever so lightly over the bare skin of his waist. She felt him shiver and she sensed—and he did, too—how very much remained to be discovered. She tickled him on purpose and the kiss became a laugh. He tickled back, his hands emboldened, and their laughter filled the air.

They were lost inside the dream, no awareness of the real—of rooms or beds or moths or brows. And so it was that in the giddy, sultry world of their embrace, the real Lazlo—fast asleep in the city of Weep—turned over on his pillow, crushed the moth, and broke the dream.

55

DISFAITH

In the real city, Thyon Nero walked to the anchor, his satchel slung over his shoulder. Last night, he had made the same walk with the same satchel. He had been weary then, and thinking about napping. He ought to have been wearier now, but he was not.

His pulse was reedy. His spirit, depleted by his own depredations, pulsed too fast through his veins, twinning with a whirr and discordant jangle of...of disbelief crashing against evidence, producing a sensation of *disfaith*.

He had stumbled onto something that refused to be believed. His mind was at war with itself. Alchemy and magic. The mystical and the material. Demons and angels, gods and men. What was the world? What was the *cosmos*? Up in the black, were there roads through the stars, traveled by impossible beings? What had he entered into, by coming across the world?

He reached the anchor. There was the whole broad face of it, visible to any passerby—not that there were likely to be passersby at this late hour of night—and there was the alley with its mural depicting the wretched, bloody gods. The alley was where he'd been doing his testing, where no one would see him if they happened by. If he could have had a fragment of mesarthium to experiment on in his laboratory, he would have been spared these late-night outings, this risk of discovery. But no fragments existed, for the simplest of reasons: Mesarthium could not be cut. There were no *scraps* to be had. There was only this massive slab of it—and the other three identical ones at the southern, eastern, and western edges of the city.

He returned to his site in the alley, and shifted the debris he had leaned there to screen it from view. And there, at the base of the impregnable anchor, where smooth mesarthium met the stones it had crushed two hundred years ago underneath its awful weight, was the solution to Weep's problem.

Thyon Nero had done it.

So why hadn't he sent at once for Eril-Fane, and earned himself the envy of all the other delegates and the gratitude of Weep? Well, he had to confirm the results first. Rigor, always. It might have been a fluke.

It wasn't. He knew that much. He didn't understand it, and he didn't believe it, but he knew.

"Stories will be told about me." That was what he had said to Strange back in Zosma—his reason for coming on this journey. It wasn't his main reason, but never mind. That had been *escape*—from the queen and his father and the Chrysopoesium and the stifling box that was his life. Whatever his reason, he was here now and a story was unfurling before him. A legend was taking shape.

He set down his satchel and opened it. More vials and flasks than last night, and a hand glave to see by. He had several tests to perform this time. The old alkahest and the new. The notes he took were habit and comfort, as though his tidy writing could transform mystery into sense.

There was a gaping rent in the metal. It was knee-high, a foot wide at the bottom, and deep enough to reach your arm into. It looked like an ax chop, except that the edges weren't sharp, but smooth, as though they had been melted.

The new tests proved what Thyon already knew—not what he understood or believed, but what he *knew*, in the way that a man who falls on his face knows the ground.

Mesarthium was conquered.

There was a legend taking shape. But it wasn't his.

He packed up his satchel and leaned the debris back up against the anchor, to screen the rent from sight. He stood at the mouth of the alley, all reedy pulse and ravaged spirit, wondering what it all meant. Weep gave no answer. The night was silent. He slowly walked away.

* * *

Across the street, Drave watched, and when the alchemist was gone, he disengaged from the shadows, crept to the mouth of the alley, and went in.

56

THE DREAMSMITHS

"No no no no no," said Lazlo, bolting upright in his bed. The moth lay on his pillow like a scrap of sooty velvet. He prodded it with his finger and it didn't move at all. It was dead. It was Sarai's and he had killed it. The bizarre, tenuous nature of their connection struck him with new force—that a *moth* should be their only link. That they could be sharing such a moment and lose it in an instant because *he rolled over on his pillow and crushed a moth.* He cupped the poor thing on his palm, then set it gently on the night table. It would vanish at dawn, he knew, and be reborn at next nightfall. He'd killed nothing... besides his own ardor.

It was funny, really. Absurd. Infuriating. And *funny.*

He flopped back onto his pillows and looked up at the moths on his ceiling beam. They were stirring, and he knew that Sarai could see him through their eyes. With a mournful smile, we waved.

Up in her room, Sarai laughed, voicelessly. The look on his face was priceless, and his body was limp with helpless vexation. *Go back to sleep*, she willed him. *Now.*

He did. Well, it took ten hours—or perhaps ten minutes—and then Sarai was standing before him with her hands on her hips.

"Moth killer," she admonished him.

"I'm sorry," he said. "I really loved that moth, too. That one was my favorite."

"Better keep your voice down. This one will get its feelings hurt and fly away."

"I mean *this one's* my favorite," he revised. "I promise not to smoosh it."

"Be sure that you don't."

They were both smiling like fools. They were so full of happiness, and Dreamer's Weep was colored by it. If only real Weep could be so easily set right. "It was probably for the best, though," Lazlo ventured.

"Oh?"

"Mm. I wouldn't have been able to stop kissing you otherwise. I'm sure I'd be kissing you still."

"That would be terrible," she said, and took a prowling step closer, reaching up to trace a line down the center of his chest.

"Wretched," he agreed. She was lifting her face

to his, ready to pick up where they'd left off, and he wanted to melt right back into her, breathe the nectar and rosemary of her, tease her neck with his teeth, and make her mouth curve into its feline curl.

It thrilled him that he could make her smile, but he had the gallant notion that he should make best efforts, now, to do so in other ways. "I have a surprise for you," he said before she could kiss him and undermine his good intentions.

"A surprise?" she asked, skeptical. In Sarai's experience, surprises were bad.

"You'll like it. I promise."

He took her hand and curled it through his arm, and they walked through the marketplace of Dreamer's Weep, where mixed among the commonplace items were wonderful ones like witch's honey, supposed to give you a fine singing voice. They sampled it, and it did, but only for a few seconds. And there were beetles that could chew gemstones better than any jeweler could cut them, and silence trumpets that, when blown, blasted a blanket of quiet loud enough to smother thunder. There were mirrors that reflected the viewer's aura, and they came with little cards to tell what the colors meant. Sarai's and Lazlo's auras were a matching shade of fuchsia that fell smack between pink for "lust" and red for "love," and when they read it, Lazlo blushed almost the same hue, whereas Sarai went more to violet.

They glimpsed the centaur and his lady; she held a parasol and he a string market bag, and they were just another couple out for a stroll, buying vegetables for their supper.

And they saw the moon's reflection displayed in a pail of water—never mind that it was daytime—and it wasn't for sale but "free" for whoever was able to catch it. There were sugared flowers and ijji bones, trinkets of gold and carvings of lys. There was even a sly old woman with a barrel full of threave eggs. "To bury in your enemy's garden," she told them with a cackle.

Lazlo shuddered. He told Sarai how he'd seen one in the desert. They stopped for sorbet, served in stemmed glasses, and she told him about Feral's storms, and how they would eat the snow with spoonfuls of jam.

They talked, walking along. She told him about Orchid Witch and Bonfire, who were like her younger sisters, and he told her of the abbey, and the orchard, where once he'd played Tizerkane warriors. He paused before a market stall that did not strike her as especially wonderful, but the way he beamed at it made her take a second look. "Fish?" she inquired. "That's not my surprise, is it?"

"No," he said. "I just love fish. Do you know why?"

"Because they're delicious?" she hazarded. "*If* they are. I've never tasted fish."

"Sky fish being hard to come by."

"Yes," said Sarai.

"They can be tasty," he said, "but it's actually *spoiled* fish to which I am indebted."

"Spoiled fish. You mean … *rotten*?"

"Not quite rotten. Just gone off, so you wouldn't yet notice, but eat it and get sick."

Sarai was bemused. "I see."

"You probably don't," said Lazlo, grinning.

"Not in the slightest," Sarai agreed.

"If it weren't for spoiled fish," he said, like the telling of a secret, "I would be a monk." Even though he'd been leading up to this disclosure in the spirit of silliness, when he got to it, it didn't feel silly. It felt like the narrowest of escapes, being sent to the library that day so long ago. It felt like the moment the silk sleigh crossed some invisible barrier and the ghosts began to dissolve. "I would be a monk," he said with deepening horror. He took Sarai by the shoulders and said, with resonant conviction, "I'm glad I'm not a monk."

She still didn't know what he was talking about, but she sensed the shape of it. "I'm glad, too," she said, hardly knowing whether to laugh, and if ever there was a status—*non-monk*—worth celebrating with a kiss, this was it.

It was a good kiss, but not so fully committal as to require reconjuring the leaning tree. Sarai opened her eyes again, feeling dreamy and obscure, like a sentence half translated into a beautiful new language.

The fish stall was gone, she saw. Something else was in its place. A black tent with gold lettering.

WHY NOT FLY? she read. Why not fly? No reason *she* could think of.

Why not fly?

She turned to Lazlo, thrilled. Here was his surprise. "The wingsmiths!" she cried, kissing him again. Arm in arm, they entered the tent. In the way of dreams, they walked into a black tent but entered a large bright courtyard, open to the sky. There were balconies on all four sides, and everywhere were mannequins clad in outlandish garbs—feather suits, and dresses made of smoke and fog and glass. All were complete with goggles—like Soulzeren's, but weirder, with luminous yellow lenses and mysterious clockwork gears. One even had a butterfly proboscis, curled up like a fiddlehead.

And each mannequin, of course, was crowned by a glorious pair of wings.

There were butterfly wings, to go with the proboscis. One pair was sunset orange, swallow-tailed, and scalloped in black. Another, an iridescent marvel of viridian and indigo with tawny spots like cats' eyes. There were even moth wings, but they were pale as the moon, not dusk-dark like Sarai's moths. Bird wings, bat wings, even flying fish wings. Sarai paused before a pair that was covered in soft orange *fur*. "What kind are these?" she asked, stroking them.

"Fox wings," Lazlo told her, as though she might have known.

"Fox wings. Of course." She lifted her chin and said with decision, "I'll take the fox wings, please, good sir."

"An excellent choice, my lady," said Lazlo. "Here, let's try them on and see if they fit."

The harness was just like the ones in the silk sleigh. Lazlo buckled it for her, and picked out his own pair. "Dragon wings," he said, and slipped into them like sleeves.

WHY NOT FLY? the gold letters asked. No reason in the world. Or if there were ample reasons in *the world*—physics and anatomy and so on—there was at least no reason *here*.

And so they flew.

Sarai knew flying dreams, and this was better. It had been her wish when she was little, before her gift manifested and stole her last hope of it. Flying was freedom.

But it was also *fun*—ridiculous, marvelous *fun*. And if there had been sunlight just moments ago, it suited them now to have stars, so they did. They were low enough to pick like berries from a branch, and string onto the bracelet with her moon.

Everything was extraordinary.

Lazlo caught Sarai's hand in flight. Remembered the first time he'd caught it and felt the same unmistakable shock of the real. "Come down over here," he said. "Onto the anchor."

"Not the anchor," she demurred. It loomed suddenly below them, jutting up from the city. "Rasalas is there."

"I know," said Lazlo. "I think we should go and visit him."

"What? *Why?*"

"Because he's turned over a new leaf," he said. "He was tired of being a half-rotted monster, you know. He practically begged me for lips and eyeballs."

Sarai gave a laugh. "He did, did he?"

"I solemnly swear," said Lazlo, and they hooked their fingers together and descended to the anchor. Sarai alighted before the beast and stared. Lips and eyeballs indeed. It was still recognizably Skathis's beast, but only just. It was Skathis's beast as remade in Lazlo's mind, and so what had been ugly was made beautiful. Gone was the carrion head with its knife-fang grin. The flesh that had been falling from the bones—mesarthium flesh, mesarthium bones—covered the skull now, and not just with flesh but fur, and the face had the delicate grace of a spectral mingled with the power of a ravid. Its horns were a more refined version of what they'd been, fluting out to tight spirals, and the eyes that filled the empty sockets were large and shining. The hump of its great shoulders had shrunk. All its proportions were made finer. Skathis might have been an artist, but he'd been a vile one. Strange the dreamer was an artist, too, and he was the antidote to vile.

"What do you think?" Lazlo asked her.

"He's actually lovely," she marveled. "He would be out of place in a nightmare now."

"I'm glad you like him."

"You do good work, dreamsmith."

"Dreamsmith. I like the sound of that. And you're one, too, of course. We should set up a tent in the marketplace."

"*Why not dream?*" Sarai said, painting a logo onto the air. The letters glimmered gold, then faded, and she imagined a fairy-tale life in which she and Lazlo worked magic out of a striped market tent and kissed when there were no customers. She turned to him, shrugged the broad flare of her fox wings back from her shoulders, and wrapped her arms around his waist. "Have I told you that the moment I first stepped into your dreams I knew there was something special about you?"

"I don't believe you have, no," said Lazlo, finding a place for his arms about her shoulders, wild windswept hair and wings and all. "Please go on."

"Even before you looked at me. *Saw* me, I mean, the first person who ever did. After that, of course I knew there was something, but even before, just seeing Weep in your mind's eyes. It was so magical. I wanted it to be real, and I wanted to come down and bring Sparrow and Ruby and Feral and Minya and live in it, just the way you dreamed it."

"It was all the cake, wasn't it? Goddess bait."

"It didn't hurt," she admitted, laughing.

Lazlo sobered. "I wish I could make it all real for you."

Sarai's laugh trailed away. "I know," she said.

The hopelessness didn't come back to either of them, but the reasons for it did. "It was a bad day," said Lazlo.

"For me, too."

They told each other all of it, though Lazlo didn't think it necessary to repeat the warriors' actual words. "It made me think it was impossible," he said. He traced her cheek with his finger. "But I've thought things were impossible before, and so far, none of them actually were. Besides, I know Eril-Fane doesn't want any more killing. He wants to come up to the citadel," he told her. "To meet you."

"He does?" The fragile hope in her voice broke Lazlo's hearts.

He nodded. "How could he not?" Tears came to her eyes. "I told him you could ask the others to call a truce. I can come, too. I'd rather like to meet you."

There had been a soft longing in Sarai's eyes, but now Lazlo saw it harden. "I've already asked," she said.

"And they said *no*?"

"Only one of them did, and only her vote matters."

It was time to tell him about Minya. Sarai had described Ruby and Sparrow and Feral to him already, and even the Ellens, because they all fit in the loveliness here, and the sweetness of this night. Minya didn't. Even the thought of her infected it.

She told him first how Minya had saved the rest of them from the Carnage, which she had witnessed, and she told him the strange fact of her agelessness. Last, she told him of her gift. "The ghost army. It's hers. When someone dies, their souls are pulled upward, up toward...I don't know. The sky. They have no form, no ability to move. They can't be seen or heard, except by her. She catches them and binds them to her. Gives them form. And makes them her slaves."

Lazlo shuddered at the thought. It was power over death, and it was every bit as grim a gift as the ones the Mesarthim had had. It cast a dark pall over his optimism.

"She'll kill anyone who comes," Sarai said. "You mustn't let Eril-Fane come. *You* mustn't come. Please don't doubt what she can and will and *wants* to do."

"Then what are we to do?" he asked, at a loss.

There was, of course, no answer, not tonight at least. Sarai looked up at the citadel. By the light of the low-hanging stars, it looked like an enormous cage. "I don't want to go back yet," she said.

Lazlo drew her closer. "It's not morning yet," he

said. He waved his hand and the citadel vanished, as easily as that. He waved it again and the anchor vanished, too, right out from under their feet. They were in the sky again, flying. The city shone far below, glavelight and golden domes. The sky glimmered all around, starlight and infinity, and altogether too many seconds had passed since their last kiss. Lazlo thought, *All of this is ours, even the infinity*, and then he *turned* it. He turned *gravity*, because he could.

Sarai wasn't expecting it. Her wings were keeping her *up*, but then *up* became *down* and she tumbled, exactly as Lazlo had planned it, right into his arms. She gave a little gasp and then fell silent as he caught her full against him. He wrapped his wings around them and together they fell, not toward the ground but away, into the depths of the sky.

They fell into the stars in a rush of air and ether. They breathed each other's breath. They had never been this close. It was all velocity and dream physics— no more need to stand or lean or fly, but only fall. They were both already fallen. They would never finish falling. The universe was endless, and love had its own logic. Their bodies curved together, pressed, and found their perfect fit. Hearts, lips, navels, all their strings wound tight. Lazlo's palm spread open on the small of Sarai's back. He held her close against him. Her fingers twined through his long dark hair. Their mouths were soft and slow.

Their kisses on the ground had been giddy. This one was different. It was reverent. It was a promise, and they trailed fire like a comet as they made it.

He knew it wasn't his will that brought them to their landing. Sarai was a dreamsmith, too, and this choice was all her own. Lazlo had given her the moon on her wrist, the stars that bedecked it, the sun in its jar on the shelf with the fireflies. He had even given her wings. But what she wanted most in that moment wasn't the sky. It was the world and broken things, and hand-carved beams and tangled bedcovers, and a lovely tattoo round her navel, like a girl with the hope of a future. She wanted to know all the things that bodies are for, and all the things that hearts can feel. She wanted to sleep in Lazlo's arms—and she wanted to *not* sleep in them.

She wanted. She wanted.

She wanted to wake up holding hands.

Sarai wished and the dream obeyed. Lazlo's room replaced the universe. Instead of stars: glaves. Instead of the cushion of endless air, there was, beneath her, the soft give of feathers. Her weight settled onto it, and Lazlo's, onto her, and all with the ease—the rightness—of choreography meeting its music.

Sarai's robe was gone. Her slip was pink as petals, the straps gossamer-fine against the azure of her skin. Lazlo rose up on his elbow and gazed down at her in wonder. He traced the line of her neck, dizzy with this new topography. Here were her collarbones, as he had seen them that first night. He leaned down and kissed the warm dip between them. His fingertips traced up the length of her arm, and paused to roll the fine silk strap between them.

Holding her gaze, he eased it aside. Her body rose against his, her head falling back to expose her throat. He covered it with his mouth, then kissed a path down to her bare shoulder. Her skin was hot—

And his mouth was hot—

And it was still all only a beginning.

✳ ✳ ✳

That was not what Thyon Nero saw when he came to peer in Lazlo's window. Not lovers, and no beautiful blue maiden. Just Lazlo alone, dreaming, and somehow *radiant*. He was giving off...bliss, Thyon thought, the way a glave gives light.

And...was that a *moth* perched on his brow? And...

Thyon's lip curled in disgust. On the wall above the bed, and on the ceiling beams: wings softly stirring. *Moths.* The room was infested with them. He knelt and picked up some pebbles, and weighed them on his palm. He took careful aim, drew back his hand, and threw.

602

57

THE SECRET LANGUAGE

Lazlo shot upright, blinking. The moth spooked from his brow and all the others from the wall, to flutter up to the ceiling and beat around the beams. But he wasn't thinking about the moths. He wasn't thinking. The dream had pulled him down so deep that he was underneath thought, submerged in a place of pure feeling—and *what* feeling. *Every* feeling, and with the sense that they'd been stripped down to their essence, revealed for the first time in all their unspeakable beauty, their unbearable fragility. There was no part of him that knew he was dreaming—or, more to the point, that he was suddenly *not* dreaming.

He only knew that he was holding Sarai, the flesh of her shoulder hot and smooth against his mouth, and then he wasn't.

Twice before, the dream had broken and stolen

her away, but those other times he'd understood what was happening. Not now. Now he experienced it as though Sarai herself—flesh and breath and hearts and hope—melted to nothing in his arms. He tried to hold on to her, but it was like trying to hold on to smoke or shadow, or—like Sathaz from the folktale— the reflection of the moon. Lazlo felt all of Sathaz's helplessness. Even as he sat up in his bed in this room where Sarai had never been, the air seemed to cling to the curves of her, warm with traces of her scent and heat—but empty, forsaken. Devoid.

Those other times he'd felt frustration. This was *loss*, and it tore something open inside him. "No," he gasped, surfacing fast to be spilled back into reality like someone beached by the crash of a wave. The dream receded and left him there, in his bed, alone— stranded in the merciless intransigence of reality, and it was as bleak a truth to his soul as the nothingness of the Elmuthaleth.

He exhaled with a shudder, his arms giving up on the sweet, lost phantom of Sarai. Even her fragrance was gone. He was awake, and he was alone. Well. He was awake.

He heard a sound—a faint, incredulous chuff— and spun toward it. The shutters were open and the window ought to have been a square of dim cut from the dark, plain and empty against the night. Instead, a silhouette was blocked in it: a head and shoulders, glossed pale gold.

"Now *that*," drawled Thyon Nero, "looked like a really good dream."

Lazlo stared. Thyon Nero was standing at his window. He had been watching Lazlo sleep, watching him *dream*. Watching him dream *that dream*.

Outrage coursed through him, and it was disproportionate to the moment—as though Thyon had been peering not just into the room but into the dream itself, witness to those perfect moments with Sarai.

"Sorry to interrupt, whatever it was," Thyon continued. "Though really you should thank me." He tossed a spare pebble over his shoulder to skitter across the paving stones. "There are *moths everywhere*." They were all still there, settling on the ceiling beams. "There was even one on your face."

And Lazlo realized that the golden godson hadn't just spied on him. He had actually awakened him. It wasn't sunrise or a crushed moth that had broken this dream, but Thyon Nero pitching pebbles. Lazlo's outrage transformed in an instant to *rage*—simpler, hotter—and he shot out of bed as fast as he had shot out of sleep.

"What are you doing here?" he growled, looming in the space of the open window so that Thyon, surprised, stumbled back. He regarded Lazlo with narrow-eyed wariness. He'd never seen him angry before, let alone wrathful, and it made him seem *bigger* somehow, an altogether different and more dangerous species of Strange than the one he had known all these years.

Which shouldn't surprise him, considering why he'd come.

"That's a good question," he said, and turned it back on Lazlo. "What *am* I doing here, Strange? Are you going to enlighten me?" His voice was hollow, and so were his eyes, his sunken cheeks. He was gaunt with spirit loss, his color sickly. He looked even worse than he had the day before.

As for Lazlo, he was surprised at his own rage, which even now was ebbing away. It wasn't an emotion he had much experience with—it didn't fit him—and he knew it wasn't really Thyon who had provoked it, but his own powerlessness to save Sarai. For an instant, just an instant, he had felt the searing anguish of losing her—but it wasn't real. She wasn't lost. Her moths were still here, up on the ceiling beams, and the night wasn't over. As soon as he fell back to sleep she'd return to him.

Of course, he had to get rid of the alchemist first. "Enlighten you?" he asked, confused. "What are you talking about, Nero?"

Thyon shook his head, scornful. "You've always been good at that," he said. "That hapless look. Those innocent eyes." He spoke bitterly. "Yesterday, you almost had me convinced that you helped me *because I needed it*." This he said as though it were the most absurd of propositions. "As though any man ever walked up to another and offered the spirit from his veins. But I couldn't imagine what motive you could have, so I almost *believed* it."

Lazlo squinted at him. "You should believe it. What other motive could there be?"

"That's what I want to know. You pulled me into this years ago, all the way back at the Chrysopoesium. Why, Strange? What's your game?" He looked wild as well as ill, a sheen of sweat on his brow. "Who are you really?"

The question took Lazlo aback. Thyon had known him since he was thirteen years old. He knew who he was, insofar as it was knowable. He was a Strange, with all that that implied. "What's this about, Nero?"

"Don't even think about playing me for a fool, Strange—"

Lazlo lost patience and cut him off, repeating, in a louder voice, "*What's this about, Nero?*"

The two young men stood on opposite sides of the open window, facing each other across the sill much as they had once faced each other across the Enquiries desk, except that now Lazlo was uncowed. Sarai watched them through her sentinels. She had awakened when Lazlo did, then collapsed back on her pillows, squeezing her eyes tight shut to block out the sight of the mesarthium walls and ceiling that hemmed her in. Hadn't she said she didn't want to come back here yet? She could have cried in her frustration. Her blood and spirit were coursing fast and her shoulder was hot as though from Lazlo's real breath. The pink silk strap had even slipped down, just like in the dream. She traced it with her fingers, eyes closed, recalling the feeling of Lazlo's lips and hands, the exquisite paths of sensation that came alive wherever he touched her. What did the faranji mean, coming here in the middle of the night?

The two spoke in their own language, as meaningless to her as drums or birdsong. She didn't know what they were saying, but she saw the wariness in their posture, the mistrust in their eyes, and it set her on edge. Lazlo pushed his hair back impatiently with one hand. A beat passed in silence. Then the other man reached into his pocket. The movement was quicksilver-sudden. Sarai glimpsed a glint of metal.

Lazlo saw it, too. A knife. Flashing toward him.

He jerked back. The bed was right behind him. He bumped against it and ended up sitting. In his mind's eye, Ruza shook his head, despairing of ever making a warrior of him.

Thyon gave him a scathing look. "I'm not going to kill you, Strange," he said, and Lazlo saw that it was not a knife that lay across his open palm, but a long sliver of metal.

His heartbeats stuttered. Not just metal. *Mesarthium.*

Understanding flooded him and he surged back to his feet. For the moment, he forgot all his anger and Thyon's cryptic insinuations and was simply overcome by the significance of the achievement. "You did it," he said, breaking into a smile. "The alkahest worked. Nero, you did it!"

Thyon's scathing look was wiped away, replaced with uncertainty. He'd convinced himself this was part of some ploy, some trickery or treachery with Strange at its center, but suddenly he wasn't sure. In Lazlo's reaction was pure wonder, and even he could see it wasn't feigned. He shook his head, not in denial, but more like he was shaking something off. It was the same feeling of disfaith he'd experienced at the anchor—of disbelief crashing against evidence. Lazlo wasn't hiding anything. Whatever the meaning of this enigma, it was a mystery to him as well.

"May I?" Lazlo asked, not waiting for an answer. The metal seemed to call out to him. He took it from Thyon's hand and weighed it on his own. The ripple of glavelight on its satin-blue sheen was mesmerizing, its surface cool against his dream-fevered skin. "Have you told Eril-Fane?" he asked, and when Thyon didn't answer, he pulled his gaze up from the metal. The scorn and suspicion were gone from the alchemist's face, leaving him blank. Lazlo didn't know exactly what this breakthrough would mean for Weep's problem, which was far more complicated than Thyon knew, but there was no doubt that it was a major accomplishment. "Why aren't you gloating, Nero?" he asked. There was no grudge in his voice when he said, "It's a good episode for your legend, to be sure."

"Shut up, Strange," said Thyon, though there was less rancor in the words than in all the ones that came before them. "Listen to me. It's important." His jaw clenched and unclenched. His gaze was sharp as claws. "Our world has a remarkable cohesion—a set of elements that make up everything in it. *Everything in it.* Leaf and beetle, tongue and teeth, iron and water, honey and gold. Azoth is..." He groped for a way to explain. "It's the secret language they all understand. Do you see? It's the skeleton key that unlocks every door." He paused to let this sink in.

"And you're unlocking the doors," said Lazlo, trying to guess where he was going with this.

"Yes, I am. Not all of them, not yet. It's the work of a lifetime—the Great Work. *My* great work, Strange. I'm not some gold maker to spend my days filling a queen's coin purse. I am unlocking the mysteries of the world, one by one, and I haven't come across a lock yet, so to speak, that my key will not fit. The world is my house. I am its master. Azoth is my key."

He paused again, with significance, and Lazlo,

seeking to fill the silence, ventured a wary, "You're welcome?"

But whatever Thyon's point was, it was apparently *not* gratitude for the part Lazlo had played in giving him his "key." Aside from a narrowing of his eyes, he continued as though he hadn't heard. "Mesarthium, now"—he paused before laying down his next words with great weight—"is *not* of this world."

He said it as though it were a great revelation, but Lazlo just raised his eyebrows. He knew that much already. Well, he might not know it the way that Thyon knew it, through experiments and empirical evidence. Still, he'd been sure of it since he first set eyes on the citadel. "Nero," he said, "I should have thought that was obvious."

"And that being the case, it should be no surprise that it does not understand the secret language. The skeleton key does not fit." In a voice that brooked no doubt, he said, "Azoth of this world does not affect mesarthium."

Lazlo's brow furrowed. "But it did," he said, holding up the shard of metal.

"Not quite." Thyon looked at him very hard. "Azoth distilled from *my* spirit had no effect on it at all. So I ask you again, Lazlo Strange... *who are you?*"

58

ONE-PLUM WRATH

Sparrow leaned against the garden balustrade. The city lay below, cut by the avenue of light—moonlight now—that slipped between the great seraph's wings. It looked like a path. At night especially, the cityscape was muted enough to lose its sense of scale. If you let your eyes go just out of focus, the avenue became a lane of light you might walk straight across, all the way to the Cusp and beyond. Why not?

A breeze stirred the plum boughs, shivering leaves and Sparrow's hair. She plucked a plum. It fit perfectly in her hand. She held it there a moment, looking out, looking down. Ruby had thrown one. Reckless Ruby. What would it feel like, Sparrow wondered, to be wild like her sister, and take what—and who—you wanted and do as you liked? She laughed inwardly. *She* would never know.

Drifting down the corridor toward Feral's room, she'd been daydreaming of a kiss—a single sweet kiss—only to discover...

Well.

She felt like a child. On top of everything else—her chest aching as though her hearts had been stomped on, and the shock that had her still gasping—she was *embarrassed*. She'd been thinking of a kiss, while they were doing... *that*. It was so far beyond anything she knew. Sarai used to tell them about the things humans did together, and it had been so scandalous, so remote. She'd never even imagined doing it herself, and for all of her sister's fixation on kissing, she'd never imagined her doing it, either. Especially not with Feral. She squeezed her eyes closed and held her face in her hands. She felt so stupid, and betrayed, and... left behind.

She weighed the plum in her hand, and for just a moment it seemed to represent everything she wasn't—or perhaps every sweet, insipid thing she *was*.

Ruby was fire—fire and wishes, like torch ginger—and she was... fruit? No, worse: She was *kimril*, sweet and nourishing and *bland*. She drew back her arm and hurled the plum as far out as she could. Instantly she regretted it. "Maybe I'll hit one of them," Ruby had said, but Sparrow didn't want to hit anyone.

Well, maybe Ruby and Feral.

As though conjured by her thoughts, Ruby stepped

out into the garden. Seeing her, Sparrow plucked another plum. She didn't throw it at her, but held it, just in case. "What are you doing awake?" she asked.

"I'm hungry," said Ruby. For hungry children growing up in the citadel of the Mesarthim, there had never been a pantry worth raiding. There were only the plum trees Sparrow kept in perpetual fruit.

"It's no wonder," she said. She weighed the plum in her palm. "You've been...active lately."

Ruby shrugged, unrepentant. She walked the herb path and scents rose up around her. She was wild-haired as ever—or even more so, from her recent exertions—and had put on a slip with a robe, unbelted, its ties flittering behind her like silky kitten tails.

Ruby lolled against the balustrade. She picked a plum and ate it. Juice dripped down her fingers. She licked them clean and gazed out at the Cusp. "Are you in love with him?" she asked.

"What?" Sparrow scowled. *"No."*

She might have made no answer at all, Ruby ignored it so completely. "I didn't know, you know. You could have told me."

"What, and ruin your fun?"

"Martyr," said Ruby, mild. "It was just something to do, and he was someone to do it with. The only boy alive."

"How romantic."

"Well, if it's romance you want, don't expect too much from our Feral."

"I don't expect anything from him," said Sparrow, annoyed. "I don't want him *now*."

"Why not? Because I've had my way with him? Don't tell me it's like when we used to lick the spoons to claim our place at table."

Sparrow tossed up the plum and caught it. "It is a little like that, yes."

"Well then. The spoons were always fair game again after a wash. The same ought to go for boys."

"Ruby, really."

"What?" Ruby demanded, and Sparrow couldn't tell if she was joking, or truly saw no difference between licked spoons and licked boys.

"It's not about the *licking*. It's obvious who Feral wants."

"No, it's not. It's just because I was there," she said. "If you'd gone to him, then it would be you."

Sparrow scowled. "If that's true, then I really don't want him. I only want someone who wants only me."

Ruby thought it *was* true, and to her surprise, it bothered her. When Sparrow put it like that, she rather thought that she, too, would like someone who wanted only her. She experienced an utterly irrational flare of pique toward Feral. And then she remembered what he'd said right before they both looked up and saw Sparrow in the door. "I'll have to sleep with you from now on."

Her cheeks warmed as she considered this. At first blush, it was anything but romantic. "I'll *have* to" made it sound as though there was no other choice, but of course there was. There was spare bedding; he only had to ask the chambermaids for it. If he preferred to come to her, well. Until now, *she* had always gone to *him*. And he'd said "from now on." It sounded like...a promise. Had he meant it? Did she want it?

She reached out and took a windblown curl of Sparrow's hair into her plum-sticky hand. She gave it a gentle tug. A wistful air came over her, the closest she could come to remorse. "I just wanted to know what it was like," she said, "in case it was my last chance. I never wanted to take him away from you."

"You didn't. It's not like you tied him down and forced him." Sparrow paused, considering. "You didn't, did you?"

"Practically. But he didn't scream for help, so..."

Sparrow launched the plum. It was close range, and hit Ruby on her collarbone. She said, "Ow!" though it hadn't really hurt. Rubbing at the place of impact, she glared at Sparrow. "Is that it, then? Have you spent your wrath?"

"Yes," said Sparrow, dusting off her palms. "It was one-plum wrath."

"How sad for Feral. He was only worth one plum. Won't he mope when we tell him."

"We needn't tell him," said Sparrow.

"Of course we need," said Ruby. "Right now he probably thinks we're both in love with him. We can't let *that* stand." She paused at the railing. "Look, there's Sarai."

Sparrow looked. From the garden, they could see Sarai's terrace and Sarai on it. It was far; they could really only make out the shape of her, pacing. They waved, but she didn't wave back.

"She doesn't see us," said Sparrow, dropping her hand. "Anyway, she's not really there."

Ruby knew what she meant. "I know. She's down in the city." She sighed, wistful, and rested her chin in her hand, gazing down to where people lived and danced and loved and gossiped and didn't ever eat kimril if they didn't want to. "What I wouldn't give to see it just once."

59

GRAY AS RAIN

Sarai hadn't been out on her terrace since the attack on the silk sleigh. She'd kept to her alcove since then, trying to preserve some privacy while under heavy guard, but she couldn't take it anymore. She needed air, and she needed to move. She was always restless when her moths were out, and now her confusion was compounding it.

What was this about?

She paced. Ghosts were all around her, but she was barely aware of them. She could still make no sense of Lazlo's exchange with the faranji, though it clearly had something to do with mesarthium. Lazlo was tense, that much she understood. He handed back the piece of metal. The other man left—finally—and she expected Lazlo to go back to sleep. To come back *to her*.

Instead, he put on his boots. Dismay sparked through her. She wasn't thinking now of exquisite paths of sensation or the heat of his lips on her shoulder. That had all been driven out by a thrum of unease. Where was he going at this time of night? He was distracted, a million miles away. She watched him pull on a vest over his loose linen nightshirt. The impulse to reach for him was so strong, but she couldn't, and her mouth was alive with questions that she had no way to ask. A moth fluttered around his head, its path a scribble.

He saw it and blinked back into focus. "I'm sorry," he said, uncertain whether she could hear him, and put out his hand.

Sarai hesitated before perching on it. It had been a long time since she'd tried contact with a waking person, but she knew what to expect. She did *not* expect to slip into a dreamspace where she could see and talk to him, and indeed she didn't.

The unconscious mind is open terrain—no walls or barriers, for better or worse. Thoughts and feelings are free to wander, like characters leaving their books to taste life in other stories. Terrors roam, and so do yearnings. Secrets are turned out like pockets, and old memories meet new. They dance and leave their scents on each other, like perfume transferred between lovers. Thus is meaning made. The mind builds itself like a sirrah's nest with whatever is at hand: silk threads and stolen hair and the feathers of dead kin. The only rule is that there are no rules. In that space, Sarai went where she wanted and did as she pleased. Nothing was closed to her.

The conscious mind was a different story. There was no mingling, no roaming. Secrets melted into the dark, and all the doors slammed shut. Into this guarded world, she could not enter. As long as Lazlo was awake, she was locked out on the doorstep of his mind. She knew this already, but he didn't. When the moth made contact, he expected her to manifest in his mind, but she didn't. He spoke her name—first aloud in the room and then louder in his mind. "Sarai?"

Sarai?

No response, only a vague sense that she was near—locked on the far side of a door he didn't know how to open. He gathered that he'd have to fall asleep if he wanted to talk to her, but that was impossible right now. His mind was buzzing with Thyon's question.

Who are you?

He imagined that other people had a place in the center of themselves—right in the center of themselves—where the answer to that question resided. Himself, he had only an empty space. "You know I don't know," he had told Thyon, uncomfortable. "What are you suggesting?"

"I am suggesting," the golden godson had replied, "that you are no orphan peasant from Zosma."

Then who?

Then *what*?

Azoth *of this world*. That was what Thyon had said. Azoth of this world did not affect mesarthium. Azoth distilled from the alchemist's own spirit had no effect on it at all. And yet he had cut a shard off the anchor, and that was proof enough: *Something* had affected mesarthium, and that something, according to Thyon, was Lazlo.

He told himself Nero was mocking him, that it was all a prank. Maybe Drave was hiding just out of sight, chuckling like a schoolboy.

But what sort of prank? An elaborate ruse to make him think there was something special about him? He couldn't believe that Nero would go to the trouble, particularly not now, when he was so obsessed with the challenge at hand. Thyon Nero was many things, but frivolous just wasn't one of them.

But then, maybe Lazlo just wanted it to be true. For there to be something special about him.

He didn't know what to think. Mesarthium was at the center of this mystery, so that was where he was going—to the anchor, as though Mouzaive's invisible magnetic fields were pulling him there. He left the house, Sarai's moth still perched on his hand. He didn't know what to tell her, if she could even hear him. His mind was awhirl with thoughts and memories, and, at the center of everything: the mystery of himself.

"So you could be anyone," Sarai had said when he told her about the cartload of orphans and not knowing his name.

He thought of the abbey, the monks, the rows of cribs, the wailing babies, and himself, silent in their midst.

"Unnatural," Brother Argos had called him. The word echoed through Lazlo's thoughts. *Unnatural.* He'd only meant Lazlo's silence, hadn't he? "Thought sure you'd die," the monk had said, too. "Gray as rain, you were."

A fizz of shivers radiated out over Lazlo's scalp and down his neck and spine.

Gray as rain, you were, but your color came normal in time.

In the silent street of the sleeping city, Lazlo's feet slowed to a stop. He lifted the hand that had, moments ago, been holding the piece of mesarthium. The moth's wings rose and fell, but he wasn't looking at the moth. The discoloration was back—a grime-gray streak across his palm where he'd clutched the slender shard. He knew that it would fade, so long as he wasn't touching mesarthium, and return as soon as he did. And all those years ago, his skin had been gray and had faded to normal.

The sound of his heartbeats seemed to fill his head.

What if he hadn't been ill at all? What if he was . . . something much stranger than the name Strange was ever intended to signify?

622

Another wave of shivers swept over him. He'd thought it was some property of the metal that it was reactive with skin, but he was the only one who had reacted to it.

And now, according to Thyon, *it* had reacted to *him*.

What did it mean? What did any of it mean? He started walking again, faster now, wishing Sarai were by his side. He wanted her hand clasped in his, not her moth perched on it. After the wonder and ease of flying in so real-seeming a dream, he felt heavy and trudging and trapped down here on the surface of the world. That was the curse of dreaming: One woke to pallid reality, with neither wings on one's shoulders nor goddess in one's arms.

Well, he might never have wings in his waking life, but he *would* hold Sarai—not her phantom and not her moth, but *her*, flesh and blood and spirit. Somehow or other, he vowed, that much of his dream would come true.

✷ ✷ ✷

As Lazlo quickened his pace, so did Sarai. Her bare feet moved swiftly over the cool metal of the angel's palm, as though she were trying to keep up. It was unconscious. As Ruby and Sparrow had said, she wasn't really here, but had left just enough awareness in her body so that she knew when to turn in her pacing and not walk up the slope that edged the seraph's hand and right over the edge.

Most of her awareness was with Lazlo: perched on his wrist, and pressed against the closed door of his consciousness. She felt his quickened pulse, and the wave of shivers that prickled his flesh, and she experienced, simultaneously, a surge of emotion radiating out from him—and it was the kind of trembling, astonished awe one might feel in the presence of the sublime. Clear and strong as it was, though, she couldn't grasp its cause. His feelings reached her in waves, like music heard through walls, but his thoughts stayed hidden inside.

Her other ninety-nine moths had flown off and were spinning through the city in clusters, searching for some hint of activity. But she could find nothing amiss. Weep was quiet. Tizerkane guards were silent silhouettes in their watchtowers, and the golden faranji returned directly to his laboratory and locked himself inside. Eril-Fane and Azareen were sleeping—she in her bed, he on the floor, the door closed between them—and the silk sleighs were just as they'd been left.

Sarai told herself that there was nothing to worry about, and then, hearing the words in her mind, gave a hard—if voiceless—laugh. *Nothing to worry about?*

Nothing at all. What could there possibly be to worry about?

Just discovery, carnage, and death.

Those were the worries she'd grown up with, and they were dulled by familiarity. But there were new worries, because there was new hope, and desire, and...and *love*, and those were neither familiar nor dull. Until a few days ago, Sarai could hardly have said what there was to live for, but now her hearts were full of reasons. They were full and heavy and burdened with a fearsome urgency *to live*—because of Lazlo, and the world they built when their minds touched, and the belief, in spite of everything, that *they could make it real*. If only the others would let them.

But they wouldn't.

Tonight she and Lazlo had sought solace in each other and found it, and they had *hidden* in it, blocking out reality and the hate they were powerless against. They had no solution and no hope, and so they'd reveled in what they did have—each other, at least in dreams—and tried to forget all the rest.

But there was no forgetting.

Sarai caught sight of Rasalas, perched on the anchor. She usually avoided the monster, but now she sent a cluster of her moths winging nearer. It had been beautiful in the dream. It might have served as a symbol of hope—if it could be remade, then anything could—but here it was as it had ever been: a symbol of nothing but brutality.

She couldn't bear the sight. Her moths broke apart and spun away, and that was when a sound caught her ear. From down below, in the shadow of the anchor, she heard footsteps, and something else. A sullen creak, low and repetitive. Flowing more of her attention into these dozen-some moths, she sent them down to investigate. They honed in on the sound and followed it into the alley that ran along the base of the anchor.

Sarai knew the place, but not well. This district was abandoned. No one had lived here in all the time she'd been coming down to Weep, so there was no reason to send moths here. She'd all but forgotten the mural, and the sight arrested her: six dead gods, crudely blue and dripping red, and her father in the middle: hero, liberator, butcher.

The creaking was louder now, and Sarai could make out the silhouette of a man. She couldn't see his face, but she could smell him: the yellow stink of sulfur and stain.

What's he *doing here?* she wondered with distaste. Sight confirmed what her other senses told her. It was the peeling-faced one whose dreams had so disturbed her. Between his ugly mind and rancid hygiene, she hadn't made contact with him since that second night, but only passed him by with wincing revulsion. She'd spent less time in his mind than in any of his fellows', and so she had only a passing notion of his expertise, and even less of his thoughts and plans.

Perhaps that had been a mistake.

He was walking slowly, holding a sort of wheel in his hands—a spool from which he was unwinding a long string behind him. That was the rhythmic creaking: the wheel, rusty, groaning as it turned. She watched, perplexed. At the mouth of the alley, he peered out and looked around. Everything about him was furtive. When he was certain no one was near, he reached into his pocket, fumbled in the dark, and struck a match. The flame flared high and blue, then shrank to a little orange tongue no bigger than a fingertip.

Bending down, he touched it to the string, which of course wasn't a string, but a fuse.

And then he ran.

❦ 60 ❦

SOMETHING ODD

Thyon dropped the shard of mesarthium onto his worktable and dropped himself, heavily, onto his stool. With a sigh—frustration on top of deep weariness— he rested his brow on his hand and stared at the long sliver of alien metal. He'd gone looking for answers, and gotten none, and the mystery wouldn't let him go.

"What are you?" he asked the mesarthium, as though it might tell him what Strange had not. "Where did you come from?" His voice was low, accusatory.

"Why aren't you gloating?" Strange had asked him. "You did it."

But what, exactly, had he done? Or, more to the point, why had it worked? The vial labeled SPIRIT OF LIBRARIAN was lying just a few inches from the metal. Thyon sat like that, staring hard at the two things—the vial with its few remaining drops of vital essence, and the bit of metal the essence had enabled him to cut.

And maybe it was because he was dazed with spirit loss, or maybe he was just tired and halfway to dreaming already, but though he looked with all the rigor of a scientist, his gaze was filtered by the shimmering veil of reverie—the same sense of wonder that attended him when he read his secret book of miracles. And so, when he noticed something odd, he considered all possibilities, including the ones that oughtn't to have been possible at all.

He reached for the metal and examined it more closely. The edges were uneven where the alkahest had eaten away at it, but one facet was as perfectly smooth as the surface of the anchor. Or it had been. He was certain.

It wasn't anymore. Now, without a doubt, it bore the subtle indentations of…well, of *fingers*, where Lazlo Strange had clutched it in his hand.

⚜ 61 ⚜

HOT AND ROTTEN AND WRONG

As Sarai had felt waves of Lazlo's feelings even through the barriers of his consciousness, so did he feel the sudden blaze of hers.

A fry of panic—no thoughts, no images, just a slap of *feeling* and he jerked to a halt, two blocks from the anchor, and then, flooding his senses: the tang of sulfur, hot and rotten and wrong.

It was the stink of Drave, and it felt like a premonition, because just then Drave came into view at the top of the street, rounding the corner at a dead run. His eyes widened when he caught sight of Lazlo, but he didn't slow. He just came pelting onward as though pursued by ravids. All in an instant: the panic, the tang, and the explosionist. Lazlo blinked.

And then the world went white.

A bloom of light. Night became day—brighter than day, no darkness left alive. Stars shone pale against bleached-bone heavens, and all the shadows died. The moment wavered in tremulous silence, blinding, null, and numb.

And then the blast.

It hurled him. He didn't know it. He only knew the flash. The world went white, and then it went black, and that was all there was to it.

Not for Sarai. She was safe from the blast wave—at least her body was, up in the citadel. The moths near the anchor were incinerated in an instant. In the first second before her awareness could flow into her other sentinels, it was as though fire scorched away her sight in pieces, leaving ragged holes rimmed in cinders.

Those moths were lost. She had some eighty others still on wing in the city, but the blast ripped outward so fast and far it seized them all in its undertow and swept them away. Her senses churned with their tumbling, end over end, no up, no down. She dropped to her knees on the terrace, head spinning as more moths died, more holes melting from her vision, and the rest kept on reeling, out of her control. It was seconds before she could pull her senses home to her body—most of them, at least. Enough to stop the spinning as her helpless smithereens scattered. Her mind and belly heaved, sick and dizzy and frantic. The worst was that she'd lost Lazlo. The moth on his hand had been peeled away and snuffed out of existence, and for all she knew, he had been, too.

No.

An explosion. She understood that much. The roar of the blast was curiously muted. She crawled toward the edge of the terrace and lay over it, her chest against the metal, and peered over the edge. She didn't know what to expect to see down in Weep. Chaos—chaos to match the churn of her wind-scattered senses? But all she saw was a delicate blossom of fire from the district of the anchor, and fronds of smoke billowing in slow motion. It looked like a bonfire from up here.

Ruby and Sparrow, peering over the balustrade in the garden, thought the same.

It was...pretty.

Maybe it wasn't bad, Sarai thought—she prayed—as she reached back out for her remaining sentinels. Many were crushed or crippled, but several dozen could still fly, and she hurled them at the air, back toward the anchor, to where she'd lost Lazlo.

Vision at street level was nothing like the calm view from overhead. It was almost unrecognizable as the landscape of a moment ago. A haze of dust and smoke hung over everything, lit lurid by the fire blazing at the blast sight. It didn't look like a bonfire from down here, but a conflagration. Sarai searched with her dozens of eyes, and nothing quite made sense. She was almost sure this was where she'd lost Lazlo, but the topography had changed. Chunks of stone stood in the street where before no stones had been. They'd been hurled there by the blast.

And under one was pinned a body.

No, said Sarai's soul. Sometimes that's all there is: an infinite echo of the smallest of words. *No no no no no* forever.

The stone was a chunk of wall, and not just any chunk. It was a fragment of the mural, hurled all this way. Isagol's painted face gazed up from it, and the gash of her slit throat gaped like a smile.

Sarai's mind had emptied of everything but *no*. She heard a groan and her moths flurried to the body—

—and as quickly away from it again.

It wasn't Lazlo, but Drave. He was facedown, caught while running from the chaos he had caused. His legs and pelvis were crushed under the stone. His arms scrabbled at the street as though to pull himself free, but his eyes were glazed, unseeing, and blood bubbled from his nostrils. Sarai didn't stay to watch him die. Her mind, which had shrunk to the single word *no*, unfurled once more with hope. Her moths wheeled apart, cutting through the blowing smoke until they found another figure sprawled out flat and still.

This was Lazlo. He was on his back, eyes closed, mouth slack, his face white with dust except where blood ran from his nose and ears. A sob welled up in

Sarai's throat and her moths slashed the air in their haste to reach him—to touch him and know if his spirit still flowed, if his skin was warm. One fluttered to his lips, others to his brow. As soon as they touched him, she fell into his mind, out of the dust and smoke of the fire-painted night and into...a place she'd never been.

It was an orchard. The trees were bare and black. "Lazlo?" she called, and her breath made a cloud. It streamed from her and vanished. Everything was still. She took a step, and frost crackled beneath her bare feet. It was very cold. She called for him again. Another breath cloud formed and faded, and there was no answer. She seemed to be alone here. Fear coiled in her gut. She was in his mind, which meant he was alive—and her moth that was perched on his lips could feel the faint stir of breath—but where was he? Where was *she*? What was this place? She wandered among the trees, parting the whip boughs with her hands, walking faster and faster, growing more and more anxious. What did it mean if he wasn't here?

"Lazlo!" she called. "Lazlo!"

And then she came into a clearing and he was there—on his knees, digging in the dirt with his hands. "Lazlo!"

He looked up. His eyes were dazed, but they brightened at the sight of her. "Sarai? What are you doing here?"

"Looking for you," she said, and rushed forward to

throw her arms around him. She kissed his face. She breathed him in. "But what are *you* doing?" She took his hands in hers. They were caked with black dirt, his nails cracked and broken from scraping at the frozen earth.

"I'm looking for something."

"For what?"

"My name," he said, with uncertainty. "The truth."

Gently, she touched his brow, swallowing the fear that wanted to choke her. Being thrown like that, he had to have hit his head. What if he was injured? What if he was...damaged? She took his head in her hands, wishing savagely that she were down in Weep, to hold his real head in her lap and stroke his face and be there when he woke, because of course he would wake. Of course he was fine. Of course. "And...you think it's here?" she asked, not knowing what else to say.

"There's something here. I know there is," he said, and...something was.

It was caked in dirt, but when he pulled it out, the soil fell away and it glimmered white as pearl. It was...a feather? Not just any feather. Its edges met the air in that melting way, as though it might dissolve. "Wraith," said Sarai, surprised.

"The white bird," said Lazlo. He stared at the feather, turning it over in his hand. Fragmented images flittered at the edge of memory. Glimpses of white feathers, of wings etched against stars. His brow furrowed. Trying to catch the memories was like trying to catch a reflection. As soon as he reached for them, they warped and vanished.

For her part, Sarai wondered what a feather from Wraith was doing here, buried in the earth of Lazlo's unconscious mind. But it was a dream—from a blow to the head, no less—and likely meant nothing at all.

"Lazlo," she said, licking her lips, fear hot and tight in her throat and her chest. "Do you know what's happened? Do you know where you are?"

He looked around. "This is the abbey orchard. I used to play here as a boy."

"No," she said. "This is a dream. Do you know where *you* are?"

His brow furrowed. "I...I was walking," he said. "To the north anchor."

Sarai nodded. She stroked his face, marveling at what it had come to mean to her in so short a span of time— this crooked nose, these rough-cut cheeks, these river-cat lashes and dreamer's eyes. She wanted to stay with him, that was all she wanted—even here, in this austere place. Give them half a minute and they could turn it into paradise—frost flowers blooming on the bare black trees, and a little house with a potbellied stove, a fleece rug in front of it just right for making love.

The last thing she wanted to do—the very last thing—was push him out a door where she couldn't follow. But she kissed his lips, and kissed his eyelids, and whispered the words that would do just that. She said, "Lazlo. You have to wake up now, my love."

And he did.

* * *

From the quiet of the orchard and Sarai's caress, Lazlo woke to...quiet that wasn't silence, but sound pulled inside out. His head was stuffed with it, bursting, and he couldn't hear a thing. He was deaf, and he was choking. The air was thick and he couldn't breathe. Dust. Smoke. Why...? *Why was he lying down?*

He tried to sit up. Failed.

He lay there, blinking, and shapes began to resolve from the dim. Overhead, he saw a shred of sky. No, not sky. Weep's sky: the citadel. He could see the outline of its wings.

The outline of wings. *Yes.* For an instant, he captured the memory—white wings against stars—just a glimpse, accompanied by a sensation of weightlessness that was the antithesis of what he was feeling now, sprawled out on the street, staring up at the citadel. Sarai was up there. *Sarai.* Her words were still in his mind, her hands still on his face. She had just been with him....

No, that was a dream. She'd said so. He'd been walking to the anchor, that was it. He remembered... Drave running, and white light. Understanding slowly seeped into his mind. Explosionist. Explosion. Drave had done this.

Done *what*?

A ringing supplanted the silence in his head. It was low but growing. He shook it, trying to clear it, and the moths on his brow and cheeks took flight and fluttered around his head in a corona. The ringing grew louder. Terrible. He was able to roll onto his side, though, and from there get his knees and elbows under him and push up. He squinted, his eyes stinging from the hot, filthy air, and looked around. Smoke swirled like the mahalath, and fire was shooting up behind an edge of shattered rooftops. They looked like broken teeth. He could feel the heat of the flames on his face, but he still couldn't hear its roar or anything but the ringing.

He got to his feet. The world swung arcs around him. He fell and got up again, slower now.

The dust and smoke moved like a river among islands of debris—pieces of wall and roof, even an iron stove standing upright, as though it had been delivered by wagon. He shuddered at his luck, that nothing had hit him. That was when he saw Drave, who hadn't been so lucky.

Stumbling, Lazlo knelt beside him. He saw Isagol's eyes first, staring up from the mural. The explosionist's eyes were staring, too, but filmed with dust, unseeing.

Dead.

Lazlo rose and continued on, though surely only

a fool goes toward fire and not away from it. He had to see what Drave had done, but that wasn't the only reason. He'd been going to the anchor when the blast hit. He couldn't quite remember the reason, but whatever it was, it hadn't let him go. The same compulsion pulled him now.

"My name," he'd told Sarai when she asked what he was looking for. "The truth."

What truth? Everything was blurred, inside his head and out. But if only a fool goes toward a fire, then he was in good company. He didn't hear their approach from behind him, but in a moment he was swept up with them: Tizerkane from the barracks, fiercer than he'd ever seen them. They raced past. Someone stopped. It was Ruza, and it was so good to see his face. His lips were moving, but Lazlo couldn't hear. He shook his head, touched his ears to make Ruza understand, and his fingers came away wet. He looked at them and they were red.

That couldn't be good.

Ruza saw, and gripped his arm. Lazlo had never seen his friend look so serious. He wanted to make a joke, but nothing came to mind. He knocked Ruza's hand away and gestured ahead. "Come on," he said, though he couldn't hear his own words any better than Ruza's.

Together they rounded the corner to see what the explosion had wrought.

62

A CALM APOCALYPSE

Heavy gray smoke churned skyward. There was an acrid stink of saltpeter, and the air was dense and grainy. The ruins around the anchor's east flank were no more. There was a wasteland of fiery debris now. The scene was apocalyptic, but...it was a calm apocalypse. No one was running or screaming. No one lived here, and that was a mercy. There was no one to evacuate, no one and nothing to save.

In the midst of it all, the anchor loomed indomitable. For all the savage power of the blast, it was unscathed. Lazlo could make out Rasalas on high, hazy in the scrim of dust-diffused firelight. The beast seemed so untouchable up there, as though it would always and forever lord its death leer over the city.

"Are you all right?" Ruza demanded, and Lazlo

started to nod before he realized he'd heard him. The words had an underwater warble and there was still a tinny ringing in his ears, but he could hear. "I'm fine," he said, too on edge to be relieved. The panic was leaving him, though, and the disorientation, too. He saw Eril-Fane giving orders. A fire wagon rolled up. Already the flames were dying down as the ancient timbers were consumed. Everything was under control. It seemed no one had even been hurt—except for Drave, and no one would mourn for him.

"It could have been so much worse," he said, with a sense of narrow escape.

And then, as if in answer, the earth gave a deep, splintering *crack* and threw him to his knees.

* * *

Drave had wedged his charge into the breach Thyon's alkahest had made in the anchor. He'd treated it like stone, because stone was what he knew: mountainsides, mines. The anchor was like a small mountain to him, and he'd thought to blow a hole in it and expose its inner workings—to do quickly what Nero was doing slowly, and so win the credit for it.

But mesarthium was not stone, and the anchor not a mountain. It had remained impervious, and so the bulk of the charge, meeting perfect resistance from above, had had nowhere to blow but . . . *down.*

✳ ✳ ✳

A new sound cut through the ringing in Lazlo's ears—or was it a feeling? A rumbling, a roar, he could hear it with his bones.

"Earthquake!" he hollered.

The ground beneath their feet might have been the city's floor, but it was also a roof, the roof of something vast and deep: an unmapped world of shimmering tunnels where the Uzumark flowed dark and mythic monsters swam in sealed caverns. How deep it went no one knew, but now, all unseen, the intricate subterranean strata were collapsing. The bedrock had fractured under the power of the blast, and could no longer support the anchor's weight. Fault lines were spidering out from it like cracks in plaster. *Huge* cracks in plaster.

Lazlo could barely keep his feet. He'd never been in an earthquake before. It was like standing on the skin of a drum whilst some great hands beat it without rhythm. Each concussion threw him, staggering, and he watched in sick astonishment as the cracks grew to gaping rifts wide enough to swallow a man. Lapis paving stones buckled. The ones at the edges toppled inward and vanished, and the rifts became chasms.

"Strange!" Ruza hollered, dragging him back. Lazlo let himself be dragged, but he didn't look away.

It struck him like a hammer blow what must happen next. His astonishment turned to horror. He watched the anchor. He saw it shudder. He heard the cataclysmic rending of stone and metal as the ground gave way. The great monolith tilted and began to sink, grinding down through ancient layers of rock, ripping through them as though they were paper. The sound was soul-splitting, and this apocalypse was calm no longer.

The anchor capsized like a ship.

And overhead, with a sickening lurch, the citadel of the Mesarthim came loose from the sky.

63

WEIGHTLESS

Feral was asleep in Ruby's bed.

Ruby and Sparrow were leaning over the garden balustrade, watching the fire in the city below.

Minya was in the heart of the citadel, her feet dangling over the edge of the walkway.

Sarai was kneeling on her terrace, peering over the edge.

In all their lives, the citadel had never so much as swayed in the wind. And now, without warning, it pitched. The horizon swung out of true, like a picture going crooked on a wall. Their stomachs lurched. The floor fell away. They lost purchase. It was like floating. For one or two very long seconds they hung there, suspended in the air.

Then gravity seized them. It flung them.

Feral woke as he was thrown out of bed. His first

thought was of Ruby—first, disoriented, to wonder if she'd shoved him; second, as he tumbled...*down-hill?*...if she was all right. He hit the wall, smacking his head, and scrambled to stand. "Ruby!" he called. No answer. He was alone in her room, and her room was—

—sideways?

Minya was thrown off the walkway but caught the edge with her fingers and hung there, dangling in the huge sphere of a room, some fifty feet up from the bottom. Ari-Eil stood nearby, as unaffected by the tilt as he was by gravity or the need to breathe. His actions weren't his own, but his thoughts were, and as he moved to grab Minya by the wrists, he was surprised to find himself conflicted.

He hated her, and wished her dead. The conflict was not to do with her—except insofar as it was she who kept him from dissolving into nothing. If she died, he would cease to exist.

Ari-Eil realized, as he plucked Minya back onto the walkway, that he did not wish to cease to exist.

In the garden. On the terrace. Three girls with lips stained damson and flowers in their hair. Ruby, Sparrow, and Sarai went weightless, and there were no walls or ghosts to catch them.

Or, there were ghosts, but Minya's binding was too strict to allow them the choice they might or might not have made: to catch godspawn girls and keep them from falling into the sky. Bahar would have helped, but couldn't. She could only watch.

Hands clutched at metal, at plum boughs.

At air.

And one of the girls—graceful in all things, even in this—slipped right off the edge.

And fell.

It was a long way down to Weep. Only the first seconds were terrible.

Well. And the last.

🌿 64 🌿

What Version of the World

Lazlo saw. He was looking up, aghast, at the unimaginable sight of the citadel tilting off its axis, when, through the blowing smoke and grit he saw something plummet from it. A tiny far-off thing. A mote, a bird.

Sarai, he thought, and shunned the possibility. Everything was unreal, tinged with the impossible. Something had fallen, but it couldn't be her, and the great seraph couldn't be keeling over.

But it was. It seemed to lean as though to take a better look at the city below. The delegates had debated the anchors' purpose, assuming they kept the citadel from drifting away. But now the truth was revealed. They held it up. Or they *had*. It tipped slowly, still buoyed on the magnetic field of the east, west, and south anchors, but it had lost its balance, like a table with one leg cut away. It could only tip so far before it would fall.

The citadel was going to fall on the city. The impact would be incredible. Nothing could survive it. Lazlo saw how it would be. Weep would be ended, along with everyone in it. *He* would be ended, and so would Sarai, and dreams, and hope.

And love.

This couldn't be happening. It couldn't end this way. He had never felt so powerless.

The catastrophe in the sky was distant, slow, even serene. But the one on the ground was not. The street was disintegrating. The sinking anchor sheared its way through layers of crust and sediment, and the spidering cracks met and joined and became pits, calving slabs of earth and stone into the darkness below, where the first froth of the Uzumark was breaking free of its tunnels. The roar, the thunder. It was all Lazlo could hear, all he could feel. It seemed to inhabit him. And through it all, he couldn't take his eyes off the anchor.

Impulse had drawn him this far. Something stronger took over now. Instinct or mania, he didn't know. He didn't wonder. There was no space in his head for thinking. It was throbbing full of horror and roar, and there was only one thing that was louder—the need to reach the anchor.

The sheen of its blue surface pulled at him. Unthinking, he took a few steps forward. His hearts were in his throat. What had been a broad avenue was fast becoming a ragged sinkhole with black water boiling up to fill it. Ruza caught his arm. He was screaming. Lazlo couldn't hear him over the din of destruction, but it was easy to read the words his mouth formed.

"Get back!" and "Do you want to die?"

Lazlo did not want to die. The desire to *not die* had never been so piercing. It was like hearing a song so beautiful that you understood not only the meaning of art, but life. It gutted him, and buoyed him, ripped out his hearts and gave them back bigger. He was desperate to *not die*, and even more than that, to *live*.

Everyone else was falling back, even Eril-Fane—as though "back" were safe. Nowhere was safe, not with the citadel poised to topple. Lazlo couldn't just retreat and watch it happen. He had to *do* something. Everything in him screamed out for action, and instinct or mania were telling him *what* action:

Go to the anchor.

He pulled free of Ruza and turned to face it, but still he hesitated. "My boy," he heard in his mind—old Master Hyrrokkin's words, kindly meant. "How could *you* help?" And Master Ellemire's, *not* kindly meant. "I hardly think he's recruiting librarians, boy." And always, there was Thyon Nero's voice. "Enlighten me, Strange. In what version of the world could *you* possibly help?"

What version of the world?

The dream version, in which he could do anything, even fly. Even reshape mesarthium. Even hold Sarai in his arms.

He took a deep breath. He'd sooner die trying to hold the world on his shoulders than running away. Better, always, to run *toward*. And so he did. Everyone else followed sense and command, and made for whatever fleeting safety they could find before the final cataclysm came. But not Lazlo Strange.

He pretended it was a dream. It was easier that way. He lowered his head, and ran.

Over the suicide landscape of the collapsing street, around the turbulent froth of the escaping Uzumark, over churned-up paving stones and smoking ruins, to the sheen of the blue metal that seemed to call to him.

Eril-Fane saw him and bellowed, "Strange!" He looked from the anchor to the citadel, and his horror deepened, a new layer added to the grief of this doom: the daughter who had survived all these years, only to die now. He halted his retreat, and so did his warriors, to watch Lazlo run to the anchor. It was madness, of course, but there was beauty in it. They realized, all of them—in that moment if they hadn't already—how fond of the young outsider they'd grown. And even if they knew death was coming for them, none of them wanted to see him die first. They

650

watched him climb over shifting rubble, losing his footing and slipping, rising again to scrabble forward until he reached it: the wall of metal that had seemed insurmountable, shrinking now as the earth sucked it under.

Even though it was sinking, still he looked so small before it. It was *absurd* what he did next. He put up his hands and braced it, as though, with the strength of his body, he could hold it up.

There were carvings of gods in just this pose. In the Temple of Thakra, seraphim upheld the heavens. It might have been absurd to see Lazlo attempt it, but nobody laughed, and nobody looked away.

And so they saw, all together, what happened next. It had the feel of a shared hallucination. Only Thyon Nero understood what he was seeing. He arrived on the scene out of breath. He'd run from his laboratory with his shard of mesarthium clutched in his hand, desperate to find Strange and tell him... tell him what?

That there were fingerprints in the metal, *and it might mean something*?

Well, he didn't need to tell him. Lazlo's body knew what to do.

He gave himself over, as he had to the mahalath. Some deep place in his mind had taken control. His palms were pressed full against the mesarthium, and they throbbed with the rhythm of his heartbeats. The metal was cool under his hands, and . . .

. . . *alive.*

Even with all the tumult around him, the noise and quaking and the ground shifting under his feet, he sensed the change. It felt like a hum—that is, the way your lips feel when you hum, but all over. He was unusually aware of the surface of himself, of the lines of his body and the planes of his face, as though his skin were alive with some subtle vibrations. It was strongest where his hands met the metal. Whatever was awakening within him, it was waking in the metal, too. He felt as though he were absorbing it, or it was absorbing him. It was becoming him, and he it. It was a new sense, more than touch. He felt it most in his hands, but it was spreading: a pulse of blood and spirit and . . . *power.*

Thyon Nero had been right. It would seem that Lazlo Strange was no orphan peasant from Zosma.

Elation swept through him, and with it his new sense unfurled, growing and reaching out, seeking and finding and *knowing.* He discovered a scheme of energies—the same unfathomable force that kept the citadel in the sky—and he could feel it all. The four anchors and the great weight they upheld. With the one tipping out of alignment, the whole elegant scheme had torn, frayed. The balance was upset, and Lazlo felt, as clearly as though the seraph were his own body slowly falling to earth, how to put it right.

It was the wings. They had only to fold. *Only!* Wings whose vast sweep shadowed a whole city, and he had only to fold them like a lady's fan.

In fact, it was that easy. Here was a whole new language, spoken through the skin, and to Lazlo's amazement he already knew it. He willed, and the mesarthium obeyed.

In the sky above Weep, the angel folded its wings, and the moonlight and starlight that for fifteen years had been held at bay came flooding in, seeming sun-bright after such long absence. It spiked in shafts through the apocalypse of smoke and dust as the citadel's new center of gravity readjusted to the three remaining supports.

Lazlo felt it all. The hum had sunk into the center of him and broken open, flooding him with this new perception—a whole new sense attuned to mes-arthium, and he was master of it. Balancing the cit-adel was as simple as finding his footing on uneven ground. Effortlessly, the great seraph came right, like a man straightening up from a bow.

For the minutes it took Lazlo to perform this feat, he was focused on it wholly. He had no awareness of his surroundings. The deep part of him that could feel the energies followed them where they led, and it wasn't only the angel that was altered. The anchor was, too. All those who were standing back and watching saw its unassailable surface seem to turn molten and flow down and outward: underground, to seal the cracks in the broken bedrock—and over the streets, to distribute its weight more evenly over its compromised foundation.

And then there was Rasalas.

Lazlo was unaware that he was doing it. It was his soul's mahalath, remaking the monster as he had in his dream. Its proportions flowed from bunched and menacing to lithe and graceful. Its horns thinned, stretching longer to coil spiral at the ends, as sinuously as ink poured into water. And as the anchor redistributed its weight, seeming to melt and pour itself out, the beast rode it down, ever nearer the surface of the city, so that by the time it stopped, by the time it all stopped—the earth shaking, the grit blowing, the angel taking its new pose in the sky—this was what witnesses beheld:

Lazlo Strange in a lunge, head bowed as he leaned into the anchor, arms extended, hands sunk to the wrists in fluid mesarthium, with the remade beast of the anchor perched above him. It was Skathis's monster, shaped now not of nightmare, but grace. The scene...the scene was a marvel. It carried with it the hearts-in-throat abandon of Lazlo's rush to the anchor, all the certainty of death, and hope like a small mad flame flaring in a dark, dark place as he had lifted his arms to hold up the world. If there was any justice, the scene would be carved into a monument of demonglass and placed here to commemorate the salvation of Weep.

The *second* salvation of Weep, and its new hero.

Few will ever witness an act destined to become legend. How does it happen, that the events of a day, or a night—or *a life*—are translated into story? There is a gap in between, where awe has carved a space that words have yet to fill. This was such a gap: the silence of aftermath, in the dark of the night on the second Sabbat of Twelfthmoon, at the melted north anchor of Weep.

Lazlo had finished. The elegance of energies was restored. City and citadel were safe, and all was *right*. He was suffused with well-being. This was who he was. *This was who he was.* He might not know his true name, but the place at his center wasn't empty anymore. Blood on his face, hair pale with the dust of collapsing ruins, he lifted his head. Perhaps because he hadn't watched it all happen but felt it, or perhaps because...it had been *easy*, he didn't grasp the magnitude, quite, of the moment. He didn't know that here was a gap slowly filling with legend, much less that it was *his* legend. He didn't feel like a hero, and, well... he didn't feel like a monster, either.

Nevertheless, in the space where his legend was gathering up words, *monster* was surely among them.

He opened his eyes, coming slowly back to awareness of the world outside his mind, and found it echoing with silence. From behind him came footsteps, many and cautious. It seemed to him they gathered up the silence like a mantle and carried it along with them, step by step. There were no cheers, no sighs of relief. There was barely breath. Seeing his hands still sunk into the metal, he drew them out like pulling them out of water. And . . . he stared at them.

Perhaps he ought not have been surprised by what he saw, but he was. It made him feel inside a dream, because it was only in a dream that his hands had looked like this. They were no longer the brown of desert-tanned skin, and neither were they the gray of grime and sickly babies.

They were vivid azure blue.

Blue as cornflowers, or dragonfly wings, or a spring—not summer—sky.

Blue as tyranny, and thrall, and murder waiting to happen.

Never had a color meant so much, so deeply. He turned to face the gathering crowd. Eril-Fane, Azareen, Ruza, Tzara, the other Tizerkane, even Calixte and Thyon Nero. They stared at him, at his face that was as blue as his hands, and they struggled—all save Thyon—with an overwhelming upsurge of cognitive dissonance. This young man whom they had found at a library in a distant land, whom they had taken into their hearts and into their homes, and whom they valued above any outsider they had ever known, was also, impossibly, godspawn.

65

WINDFALL

They were all so still, so speechless and frozen, their expressions blank with shock. And so this was the mirror in which Lazlo knew himself: hero, monster. Godspawn.

He saw, in their shock, a struggle to reconcile what they thought they knew of him with what they saw before them, not to mention what they had just seen him *do*, and what it meant as their gratitude vied with mistrust and betrayal.

Under the circumstances—that is, their being *alive*—one might expect their acceptance, if not quite elation to match Lazlo's own. But the roots of their hate and fear were too deep, and Lazlo saw hints of revulsion as their confusion smeared one feeling into the next. And he could offer them no explanation. He had no clarity, only a muddy swirl of his own, with streaks of every color and emotion.

He fixed on Eril-Fane, who in particular looked dazed. "I didn't know," he told him. "I promise you."

"*How?*" gasped Eril-Fane. "How is it possible that *you* are . . . *this*?"

What could Lazlo tell him? He wanted to know that himself. How had a child of the Mesarthim ended up on an orphan cart in Zosma? His only answer was a buried white feather, a distant memory of wings against the sky, and a feeling of weightlessness. "I don't know."

Maybe the answer was up in the citadel. He tilted back his head and gazed at it, new elation blooming in him. He couldn't wait to tell Sarai. To *show* her. He didn't even have to wait for nightfall. He could *fly*. Right now. She was up there, real and warm, flesh and breath and laughter and teeth and bare feet and smooth blue calves and soft cinnamon hair, and he couldn't wait to show her: The mahalath had been right, even if it hadn't guessed his gift.

His gift. He laughed out loud. Some of the Tizerkane flinched at the sound.

"Don't you see what this means?" he asked. His voice was rich and full of wonder, and all of them knew it so well. It was their storyteller's voice, both rough and pure, their *friend's* voice that repeated every fool phrase they threw at him in their language lessons. They *knew* him, blue or not. He wanted to push past this ugliness of age-old hates and soul-warping fears and start a new era. For the first time, it truly seemed possible. "I can move the citadel," he said. He could free the city from its shadow now, and Sarai from her prison. What *couldn't* he do in this version of the world in which he was hero and monster in one? He laughed again. "Don't you see?" he demanded, losing patience with their suspicion and scrutiny and the unacceptable absence of celebration. "The problem," he said, "is solved."

No cheers broke out. He didn't expect any, but they might at least have looked glad not to be dead. Instead they were just overwhelmed, glancing at Eril-Fane to see what he would do.

He came forward, his steps heavy. He might have been called the Godslayer for good reason, but Lazlo didn't fear him. He looked him right in the eyes and saw a man who was great and good and human, who had done extraordinary things and terrible things and been broken and reassembled as a shell, only then to do the bravest thing of all: He had kept on living, though there are easier paths to take.

Eril-Fane stared back at Lazlo, coming to terms with the new complexion of his familiar face. Time passed in heartbeats, and at last he held out his great hand. "You have saved our city and all our lives, Lazlo Strange. We are greatly in your debt."

Lazlo took his hand. "There is no debt," he said. "It's all I wanted—"

But he broke off, because it was then, in the silence after the earth settled and the crackle of the fire died down, that the screams reached them, and, a moment later, carried by a terror-stricken rider, the news.

A girl had fallen from the sky. She was blue.

And she was dead.

* * *

Sound and air were stolen, and joy and thought and purpose. Lazlo's wonder became its own dark inverse: not even despair, but nothingness. For despair there would have to be acceptance, and that was impossible. There was only *nothing*, so much *nothing* that he couldn't breathe.

"Where?" he choked out.

Windfall. Windfall, where ripe plums rain down from the gods' trees and there is always the sweet smell of rot.

The plummet, he recalled, sick with sudden memory. Had he seen her fall? No. *No.* He'd told himself then it couldn't be her, and he had to believe it now. He would know if Sarai had…

He couldn't even form the word in his mind. He *would* feel her fear—the way he had just before the blast, when that urgency of feeling had hit him, along with Drave's sulfur stink, like a premonition. That could only have come from her, by way of her moth.

Her moth.

Something pierced the nothingness, and the something was dread. Where were Sarai's moths? Why weren't they here? They had been, when he lay on the ground, unconscious. "You have to wake up now, my love."

My love.

My love.

And they'd been with him when he staggered down the street toward the fire. When had they gone? And where?

And *why*?

He asked the question, but slammed the door on any answers. A girl was dead, and the girl was blue, but it couldn't be Sarai. There were four girls in the citadel, after all. It felt filthy to hope it was one of the others, but he hoped it nonetheless. He was near enough to the melted remains of the anchor to reach back and touch it, and he did, instantly drawing on its power. And Rasalas—Rasalas remade—lifted its great horned head.

It was like a creature awakening from sleep, and when it moved—sinuous, liquid—and shook open its massive wings, a bone-deep terror stirred in all the warriors. They drew their swords, though their swords were useless, and when Rasalas leapt down from its perch, they scattered, all but Eril-Fane, who was stricken by a terror closer to Lazlo's own. A girl, fallen. A girl, dead. He was shaking his head. His hands balled into fists. Lazlo didn't see him. He didn't see anyone but Sarai, bright in his mind, laughing, beautiful, and alive—as though picturing her that way proved that she was.

With a leap, he mounted Rasalas. His will flowed into the metal. Muscles bunched. The creature leapt, and they were airborne. Lazlo was flying, but there was no joy in it, only the detached recognition that *this* was the version of the world he had wished for just moments ago. It was staggering. He could reshape mesarthium and he could fly. That much had come to pass, but there was a piece missing, the most important piece: to hold Sarai in his arms. It was a part of the wish, and the rest had come true, so it had to, too. A stubborn, desperate voice inside of Lazlo bargained with whatever might be listening. If there was some providence or cosmic will, some scheme of energies or even some god or angel answering his prayers tonight, then they had to grant this part, too.

And ... it could be argued that they did.

Rasalas descended on Windfall. It was a quiet neighborhood usually, but not now. Now it was chaos:

wild-eyed citizens caught in a nightmare carnival in which there was but one attraction. All was hysteria. The horror of the averted cataclysm had all poured into it, mixing with old hate and helplessness, and as the beast descended from the sky, the fervor rose to a new pitch.

Lazlo was barely aware of it. At the center of it all, in a pocket of stillness within the roiling nest of screams, was the girl. She was arched over a garden gate, head tilted back, arms loose around her face. She was graceful. *Vivid.* Her skin was blue and her slip was ... it was *pink*, and her hair, spilling loose, was the orange-red of copper and persimmons, cinnamon and wildflower honey.

And blood.

Lazlo *did* hold Sarai in his arms that night, and she was real and flesh, blood and spirit, but not laughter. Not breath. Those had left her body forever.

The Muse of Nightmares was dead.

❧ 66 ❧

GOD AND GHOST

Of course it was a dream. All of it, another nightmare. The citadel's sickening lurch, the helpless silk-on-mesarthium glide down the seraph's slick palm, flailing wildly for something to hold on to and finding nothing, and then...falling. Sarai had dreamed of falling before. She had dreamed of dying any number of ways since her lull stopped working. Of course...those other times, she'd always awakened at the moment of death. The knife in the heart, the fangs in her throat, the instant of impact, and she'd bolt upright in her bed, gasping. But here she was: not awake, not asleep.

Not alive.

Disbelief came first, then surprise. In a dream, there were a hundred thousand ways that it might go, and many of them were beautiful. Fox wings, a flying carpet, falling forever into the stars.

In reality, though, there was only the one way, and it wasn't beautiful at all. It was sudden. Almost too sudden to hurt.

Almost.

White-hot, like tearing in half, and then nothing.

Surrounded by ghosts as she had always been, Sarai had wondered what it was like at the last, and how much power a soul had, to leave the body or stay. She had imagined, as others had before her and would after, that it was somehow a matter of will. If you just clung tightly enough and refused to let go, you might... well, you might get to *live*.

She wanted so badly to live.

And yet when her time came, there was no clinging, and no choice. Here was what she hadn't counted on: There was her body to hold on *to*, but nothing to hold on *with*. She slipped out of herself with the sensation of being shed—like a bird's molted feather, or a plum dropped from a tree.

The shock of it. She had no weight, no substance. She was in the air, and the dreamlike unreality of floating warred with the gruesome truth beneath her. Her body. She... *it*... had landed on a gate, and was curved over it backward, hair streaming long, ginger blossoms raining down from it like little flames. The column of her throat was smooth cerulean, her eyes glassy and staring.

Her pink slip looked lewd to her here, hiked up her bare thighs—all the more so when a crowd began to gather.

And scream.

An iron finial had pierced through her breastbone, right in the center of her chest. Sarai focused on that small point of red-slick iron and...hovered there, over the husk of her body, while the men, women, and children of Weep pointed and clutched their throats and choked out their raw and reeling screams. Such vicious noise, such contorted faces, they were barely human in their horror. She wanted to scream back at them, but they wouldn't hear her. They couldn't see her, not *her*— a trembling ghost perched on the chest of her own fresh corpse. All they saw was calamity, obscenity. Godspawn.

Her moths found her, those that remained. She'd always thought they would die when she did, but some vestige of life was in them yet—the last tatters of her own, till sunrise could turn them to smoke. Frantic, they fluttered at her dead face and plucked wildly at her bloody hair—as though they could lift her up and carry her back home.

They could not. A dirty wind purled them away and there was only the screaming, the hateful twisted faces, and...the truth.

It was all *real*.

Sarai was dead. And though she had gone beyond breathing, the realization choked her, like when she woke from a nightmare and couldn't get air. The sight of her poor body...like *this*, exposed to *them*. She wanted to gather herself into her own arms. And her body...it was only the beginning of loss. Her soul would go, too. The world would resorb it. Energy was never lost, but *she* would be lost, and her memories with her, and all her longing, and all her love. Her love.

Lazlo.

Everything came rushing back. The blast, and what came after. Dying had distracted her. With a gasp she looked up, braced for the sight of the citadel plunging from the sky. Instead she saw...*the sky*—moonlight shafting through smoke, and even the glimmer of stars. She blinked. The citadel wasn't falling. The seraph's wings were folded.

Truth skittered away again. *What was real?*

The frenzy around her, already unbearable, grew wilder. She wouldn't have believed the screams could get any louder, but they did, and when she saw why, her hearts—or the memory of them—gave a lurch of savage hope.

Rasalas was in the sky, and Lazlo was astride him. *Oh glory*, the sight! The creature was remade, and... Lazlo was, too. He was Lazlo of the mahalath, as blue as skies and opals, and he took Sarai's breath away. His long dark hair streamed in the gusts of wingbeats as Rasalas came down to land, and Sarai was overcome with the wild joy of reprieve. If Rasalas was flying, if Lazlo was *blue*, then it was, after all, just a dream.

Oh gods.

Lazlo slid from Rasalas's back and stood before her, and if her despair was grim before that surge of joy, how wretched it was after. Her hope could not survive the grief she saw in him. He swayed on his feet. He couldn't get his breath. His beautiful dreamer's eyes were like burnt-out holes, and the worst thing was: He wasn't looking at *her*. He was staring at the body arched over the gate, dripping blood from the ends of its cinnamon hair, and that was what he reached for. Not *her*, but *it*.

Sarai saw his hand tremble. She watched him trace the slim pink strap hanging limp from her dead shoulder, and remembered the feel of his hand there, easing the same strap aside, the heat of his mouth on her skin and the exquisite paths of sensation, in every way as though it had really happened—as though their bodies had come together, and not just their minds. The cruelty of it was a knife to her soul. Lazlo had never touched her, and now he was, and she couldn't feel a thing.

He eased the strap back into place. Tears streaked down his cheeks. The gate was tall. Sarai's dead face, upside down, was higher than his upturned one. He gathered her hair to him as though it were something worth holding. Blood wicked into his shirt and smeared over his neck and jaw. He cupped the back of her neck. How gently he held the dead thing that had been her. Sarai reached down to touch his face, but her hands passed right through him.

The first time she ever went into his dream, she had stood right in front of him, secure in her invisibility, and wistful, wishing this strange dreamer might fix his sweet gray eyes on *her*.

And then he had. Only him. He had *seen* her, and his seeing had given her being, as though the witchlight of his wonder were the magic that made her real. She had lived more in the past nights than in all the dreams that came before, much less her real days and nights, and all because he saw her.

But not anymore. There was no more witchlight and no more wonder—only despair worthy of Isagol at her worst. "Lazlo!" she cried. At least, she shaped the name, but she had no breath or tongue or teeth to give it sound. She had nothing. The mahalath had come and remade them both. He was a god, and she was a ghost. A page had turned. A new story was beginning. You had only to look at Lazlo to know it would be brilliant.

And Sarai could not be in it.

* * *

Lazlo didn't feel the page turn. He felt the book slam shut. He felt it fall, like the one long ago that had shattered his nose, only this one shattered his life.

He climbed the stone base of the gate and reached up for Sarai's body. He placed one hand under the

670

small of her back. The other still cradled her neck. As carefully as he could, he lifted her. Strangled sobs broke from him as he disengaged her slender frame from the finial that pinned it in place. When she came free, he stepped back down, folding her to his chest, at once gutted and filled with unspeakable tenderness. Here at last were her real arms, and they would never hold him. Her real lips, and they would never kiss him. He curled over her as though he could protect her, but it was far too late for that.

How could it be that in his triumph he had saved *everyone but her*?

In the furnace of his grief, rage kindled. When he turned around, holding the body of the girl he loved—so light, so brutally unalive—the blanket of shock that had muted the screaming was thrown off, and the sound came roaring at him, as deafening as any explosion, louder than the rending of the earth. He wanted to roar back. Those who hadn't fled were pressing close. There was menace in their hate and fear, and when Lazlo saw it, the feeling inside him was like the blast of fire rising up a dragon's throat. If he screamed, it would burn the city black. That was how it felt. That was the fury that was in him.

"You do understand, don't you," Sarai had said, "that they would kill me on sight?"

He understood now. He knew they *hadn't* killed her, and he knew they would have, given the chance.

671

And he knew that Weep, the city of his dreams, which he had just saved from devastation, was open to him no longer. He might have filled the place at the center of himself with the answer to who he was, but he had lost so much more. Weep *and* Sarai. The chance of home and the chance of love. Gone.

He didn't scream. Rasalas did. Lazlo wasn't even touching him. He didn't need to now; nearness was enough. Like a living thing, the beast of the anchor spun on the closing crowd, and the sound that rippled up and blasted from its metal throat wasn't fury but *anguish.*

The sound of it crashed against the screaming and overwhelmed it. It was like color drowning color. The hate was black and the fear was red, and the anguish, it was blue. Not the blue of cornflowers or dragonfly wings or skies, and not of tyranny, either, or murder waiting to happen. It was the color of bruised flesh and storm-dark seas, the bleak and hopeless blue of a dead girl's eyes. It was *suffering*, and at the bottom of everything, like dregs in a cup, there was no deeper truth in the soul of Weep than that.

The Godslayer and Azareen reached Windfall just as Rasalas screamed. They pushed through the crowd. The sound of pain carved them open even before they saw . . .

They saw Lazlo and what he held in his arms—the slender, slack limbs, the wicking flowers of blood, the cinnamon spill of hair, and the truth that it betrayed. Eril-Fane staggered. His gasp was the rupture of the small, brave hope growing inside his shame, and when Lazlo mounted Rasalas with Sarai clutched to his chest, he dropped to his knees like a warrior felled in battle.

Rasalas took flight. Its wingbeats stirred a storm of grit, and the crowd had to close its eyes. In the darkness behind their shut lids they all saw the same thing: no color at all, only *loss* like a hole torn in the world.

Azareen knelt behind her husband. Trembling, she wrapped her arms around his shoulders. She curved herself against his back, laid her face to the side of his neck, and wept the tears that he could not. Eril-Fane shuddered as her tears seared his skin, and something inside him gave way. He pulled her arms tight against his chest and crushed his face into her hands. And then, and there, for everything lost and everything stolen, both from him and by him in all these long years, the Godslayer started to sob.

Sarai saw everything, and could do nothing. When Lazlo lifted her body down, she couldn't even follow. Some final invisible mooring line snapped, and she was cast adrift. At once, there was a sensation of... unraveling. She felt herself beginning to come apart. Here was her evanescence, and it was like dying all over again. She remembered the dream of the mahal-ath, when the mist unmade her and all sense of physical being vanished, but for one thing, one solid thing: Lazlo's hand gripping hers.

Not now. He took her body and left her soul. She cried out after him, but her screams were silent even to herself, and with a flash of metal and a swirl of smoke, he was gone.

Sarai was alone in her final fading, her soul diffusing in the brimstone air.

Like a cloud of breath in an orchard when there's nothing left to say.

❦ 67 ❦

PEACE WITH THE IMPOSSIBLE

The city saw the new god rise into the sky, and the citadel watched him come.

The smooth gleam of Rasalas poured itself upward, wingbeat by wingbeat, out of the smoke that still churned, restless, around the rooftops of Weep. The moon was finally setting; soon the sun would rise.

Ruby, Sparrow, and Feral were at the garden's edge. Their faces were stricken, ashen, and so were their hearts. Their grief was inarticulate, still entangled in their shock. They were just beginning to grasp the task that lay ahead: the task of *believing* that it had really happened, that the citadel had really tilted.

And Sarai had really fallen.

Only Sparrow had seen her, and only out of the corner of her eye. "Like a falling star," she had said, choking on sobs, when she and Ruby had finally unclenched their hands from the balustrade and the plum boughs that had saved them from sharing her fate. Ruby had shaken her head, denying it, *rejecting* it, and she was shaking it still, slowly and mechanically, as though she couldn't stop. Feral held her against him. Their rasping, sob-raw breathing had settled into rhythm. He was watching Sarai's terrace, and he kept expecting her to emerge. He kept *willing* her to. His plea of "Come on, come on," was an unspoken chant, timed to the shaking of Ruby's head. But deep down he knew that if there were any chance that she was there—that Sarai was still *here*— he would be marching down the corridor to prove it with his own eyes.

But he wasn't. He couldn't. Because his gut already knew what his head refused to accept, and he didn't want it proven.

Only Minya didn't dither with disbelief. Nor did she appear to be afflicted by grief, or any other feeling. She stood back by the arcade, just a few steps into the garden, her small body framed in an open archway. There was no expression on her face beyond a kind of remote...alertness.

As though she was listening for something.

Whatever it was, it wasn't wingbeats. Those, when they came, drubbing at the air and peppered by the amazed cries of the others, brought her blinking out of her transfixion, and when she saw what revealed itself, rising up in the air in front of the garden, her shock was like a blow.

For a moment, every ghost in the citadel felt their tethers fall slack. Immediately the feeling passed. Minya's will was reasserted, the tethers once more drawn taut, but they all felt, to a one, a gasp of freedom too fleeing to exploit. What torment—like a cage door no sooner swinging open than it slammed shut again. It had never happened before. The Ellens could attest that in fifteen years, Minya's will had never faltered, not even in her sleep.

Such was her astonishment at the sight of man and creature surging over the heads of Ruby, Feral, and Sparrow to land, amid gusting wingbeats, in the patch of anadne blossoms in the center of the garden. White flowers whirled like snow and her draggled hair streamed back from her face as she squinted against the draft.

Mesarthim. Mesarthium. Man and beast, strangers both, blue and blue. And before she knew *who*, and before she knew *how*, Minya grasped the full ramifications of Lazlo's existence, and understood that *this changed everything*.

What she felt, first and foremost, faced with the solution to her problem and Weep's, wasn't *relief*, but—slow and steady and devastating, like a leak that would steal all the air from her world—the certain loss of control.

She held herself as still as a queen on a quell board, her eyes cut as narrow as the heat pits on a viper, and watched them come.

Lazlo dismounted. He'd seen the others first—their three stricken faces at the garden railing—and he was highly aware of the ghosts, but it was Minya he scanned for and fixed on, and her to whom he went with Sarai clasped to his chest.

They all saw what he held, the unbearable broken form of her, the pink and red and cinnamon so brutally beautiful against the blue of her skin and his. It was Ruby who drew in a low, racking sob. Red glimmered in her hollow eyes. Her fingertips kindled into ten blue tapers and she didn't even feel it. Sparrow's sorrow was manifest in the withering of flowers around her feet. Her gift, which they had never even known worked in reverse, was leeching the life out of all the plants she touched. And nor did Feral consciously summon the sheaves of cloud that coalesced around them, blocking out the sky, the horizon, the Cusp, shrinking the world to *here*—this garden and this garden alone.

Only Minya was purposeful. As Lazlo drew nearer, so did her ghosts.

There were a dozen positioned around the garden and many more inside the gallery, ever ready to repel invasion. And though Lazlo's gaze didn't waver from Minya, he felt them behind him. He *saw* them behind her, through the arcade, and as Weep's dead answered Minya's call, moving toward the arches that had for fifteen years stood open between garden and gallery, Lazlo closed them.

Her will summoned the ghosts, and his barred their way. It was the opening exchange of a dialogue in power—no words spoken, only magic. The metal of the arches turned fluid and flowed closed, as they had not done since Skathis's time, cutting Minya off from the bulk of her army. Her back was to the gallery, and the flow of the mesarthium made no sound, but she felt it in the muting of the souls on the ends of her tethers. Her jaw clenched. The ghosts in the garden glided into position, flanking Lazlo from behind. He didn't turn to face them, but Rasalas did, a growl of warning rumbling up its metal throat.

Ruby, Sparrow, and Feral watched it all with held breath.

Lazlo and Minya faced each other, and they might have been strangers, but there was more between them than the corpse of Sarai. Minya understood it, even if Lazlo didn't. This faranji could control mesarthium, which meant that he was Skathis's son.

And hence, her brother.

Which revelation stirred no feeling of kinship, but only a burn of bitterness—that he should inherit the gift that should have been hers, but with none of the hardship that had made her so desperate for it.

Where had he come from?

He had to be the one Sarai had spoken of, and who had made her so defiant. "I know a human could stand the sight of me," she had said, blazing with a boldness Minya had never seen. "Because there is one who can see me, and he stands the sight of me quite well."

Well, she'd been misinformed or lying. This was no human.

Beast faced ghosts, as man faced girl. The seconds between them were fraught with challenge. Power bristled, barely held in check. In Minya, Lazlo saw the merciless child who had tried to kill him, and whose devotion to bloodshed had filled Sarai with despair. He saw an enemy, and so his fury found a focus.

But. She was an enemy who caught ghosts like butterflies in a net, and he was a man with his dead love in his arms.

He fell to his knees before her. Hunched over his burden, he sank down on his heels so that he was just her height. He looked her in the eyes and saw no empathy there, no glint of humanity, and braced himself for a struggle. "Her soul," he said, and his voice had never been rougher—so raw it was practically bloody. He didn't know how it worked or what it would mean. He only knew that some part of Sarai might yet be saved, and *must be*. "You have to catch it."

680

Someone else—almost anyone else—might have seen his heartbreak and forgiven his tone of command.

But not Minya.

She'd had every intention of catching Sarai's soul. That was what she'd been listening for. From the moment she learned Sarai had fallen, she had stretched her senses to their limits, waiting, hardly breathing, alert to the telltale skim of passing ghosts. That was what it was like: straining to hear, but with her whole being. And like with listening, the subtle skim of a soul could be drowned out by a nearer, louder presence.

Like an arrogant, trespassing man astride a winged metal beast.

This stranger dared to come here and break her focus in order to command her to do what she was doing already?

As though, if not for him, she would let Sarai drift away?

"Who do you think you are?" she seethed through clenched teeth.

Who *did* Lazlo think he was? Orphan, godspawn, librarian, hero? Maybe he was all of those things, but the only answer that came to him, and the only relevant context, was Sarai—what she was to him, and he to her. "I am...I'm Sarai's..." he began but couldn't finish. There wasn't a word for what they were. Neither married nor promised—what time had there been for promises? Not yet lovers, but so much more than friends. So he faltered in his answer, leaving it unfinished, and it was, in its way, simply and perfectly true. He was Sarai's.

"Sarai's *what*?" demanded Minya, her fury mounting. "Her protector? Against *me*?" It enraged her, the way he held her body—as though Sarai belonged to him, as if she could be more precious to him than to her own family. "Leave her and go," she snarled, "if you want to live."

Live? Lazlo felt a laugh rise up his throat. His new power surged in him. It felt like a storm ready to burst through his skin. "I'm not going anywhere," he said, his fury matching hers, and to Minya, it was a challenge to her family and her home—everything she'd spent herself on and poured herself into, every moment of every day, since gods' blood spurted and she saved who she could carry.

But saving them had only been the beginning. She'd had to *keep* them alive—four *babies* in her care, inside a crime scene of corpses and ghosts, and herself just a traumatized child. Her mind was formed in the desperate, keep-alive pattern of those early weeks and months as she spent herself out and burned herself up. She didn't know any other way. There was nothing left over, *nothing*, not even enough to grow. Through sheer, savage will, Minya poured even her life force into the colossal expenditure of magic necessary to hold on to her ghosts and keep her charges safe—and not just safe but *loved*. In Great Ellen, she had given them a mother, as best she could. And in the effort of it all, she had stunted herself, blighted herself, whittled herself to a bone of a thing. She wasn't a child. She was barely a person. She was *a purpose*, and she hadn't done it all and *given everything* just to lose control now.

Power flared from her. Ruby, Feral, and Sparrow cried out as the dozen ghosts who remained in the garden—Great Ellen among them—unfurled and flew at Lazlo with their knives and meat hooks, and Great Ellen with her bare hands shaping themselves into claws as her teeth grew into fangs to shame even Skathis's Rasalas.

Lazlo didn't even think. From the towering wall of metal that was backdrop to the garden—and made up the seraph's shoulders and the column of its neck—a great wave of liquid metal peeled itself away and came pouring down, flashing with the first rays of the rising sun, to freeze into a barrier between himself and the chief onslaught. At the same moment, Rasalas leapt. The creature didn't bother itself with ghosts but knocked Minya to the ground like a toy to a kitten, and pinned her there, one metal hoof pressing on her chest.

It was so swift—a blur of metal and she was down. The breath was knocked out of her, and...the fury was knocked out of Lazlo. Whatever she was, this cruel little girl—his own would-be murderer, not least—the sight of her sprawled out like that at Rasalas's mercy shamed him. Her legs were so impossibly thin, her clothes as tattered as the beggars in the Grin. She didn't give up. Still her ghosts came at him, but the metal moved with them, flowing to block them, catching their weapons and freezing around them. They couldn't get near.

He went and knelt by Minya. She struggled, and Rasalas increased the pressure of its elegant hoof against her chest. Just enough to hold her, not enough to hurt. Her eyes burned black. She hated the pity she saw in Lazlo's. It was a thousand times worse than the fury had been. She gritted her teeth, ceased her ghosts' attack, and spat out, "Do you want me to save her or not?"

He did. Rasalas lifted its hoof and Minya slid out from beneath it, rubbing the place on her chest where it had pinned her. How she hated Lazlo then. In compelling her by force to do what she'd been planning anyway, it felt as though he'd *won* something, and she'd lost.

Lost *what*?

Control.

The queen was vulnerable on the quell board with no pawns to protect her. This new adversary possessed the gift she'd always craved, and up against it, she was nothing. His power swept hers aside like a hand brushing crumbs from a table. His control of mesarthium gave them their freedom in every way they'd ever daydreamed—but Minya didn't even know if *she* would be counted among *them*, or would be swept aside just like her power and her ghosts. They could leave her behind if they wanted, if they decided they didn't trust her—or simply didn't *like* her—and what could she do? And what of the humans, and the God-slayer, and revenge?

It seemed to her the citadel swayed beneath her, but it was steady. It was her world that swayed, and only she could feel it.

She rose to her feet. Her pulse beat in her temples. She closed her eyes. Lazlo watched her. He felt an ache of tenderness for her, though he couldn't have said why. Maybe it was simply because with her eyes closed she really looked like a six-year-old child, and it brought home that once upon a time she had been: just a six-year-old child with a crushing burden.

When she settled into a stillness of deep concentration, he let himself hope what he had so far only wondered: that it might be possible Sarai was not lost to him.

That she was, even now, adrift—like an ulola flower borne by the wind. *Where was she?* The very air felt alive with possibility, charged with souls and magic.

There was a man who loved the moon, but whenever he tried to embrace her, she broke into a thousand pieces and left him drenched, with empty arms.

Sathaz had finally learned that if he climbed into the pool and kept very still, the moon would come to him and let him be near her. Only near, never touching. He couldn't touch her without shattering her, and so—as Lazlo had told Sarai—he had made peace with the impossible. He took what he could get.

Lazlo had loved Sarai as a dream, and he would love her as a ghost as well.

He finally acknowledged that what he carried in his arms was not Sarai but only a husk, empty now of the mind and soul that had touched his in their dreaming. Carefully he laid her down in the flowers of the garden. They cushioned her like a bower. Her lifeless eyes were open. He wished to close them, but his hands were sticky with her blood, and her face, it was unmarred, even serene, so he leaned in close and used his lips: the lightest touch, catching her honey-red lashes with his lower lip and brushing down, finishing with a kiss to each smooth lid, and then to each cheek, and finally her lips. Light as the brush of a moth wing across the sweet ripe fruit with its crease in the middle, as soft as apricot down. Finally, the corners, sharp as crescents, where her smile had lived.

The others watched, with breaking hearts or hardened ones, and when he stood and stepped back and turned to Minya, he felt like Sathaz in the pool, waiting for the moon.

He didn't know how it worked. He didn't know what to look for. Really, it wasn't so different from waiting for her in a dream when she might appear anywhere and his whole being clenched into a knot of eagerness. He watched Minya's face, alert to any change in her expression, but there was none. Her little grubby visage was mask-still until the moment her eyes sprang open.

There was a light in them. *Triumph*, Lazlo thought, and his hearts gave a leap of joy because he thought it meant that she'd found Sarai, and bound her.

And she had.

Like an etching in the air that slowly filled with beauty, Sarai was gathered out of nothingness and bound back into being. She was wearing her pink slip, and it bore no blooms of blood. The smooth blue of her chest was unpierced by the iron finial, and her hair was still studded with flowers.

For Sarai, the sensation of *re-raveling* was like being saved from drowning, and her first breaths drawn with phantom lungs—which were, like everything about her new state, illusion, but illusion given form—were the sweetest she had ever known.

She was not alive and she knew it, but...whatever

her new state might lack, it was infinitely preferable to the unmaking that had almost devoured her. She laughed. The sound met the air like a real voice, and her body had mass like a real body—though she knew it followed a looser set of rules. And all the pity and outrage she'd felt on behalf of Minya's bound ghosts deserted her. How could she ever have thought evanescence was kinder? Minya had *saved* her, and Sarai's soul flowed toward her like music.

That was what it felt like to move. Like music come to life. She threw her arms around Minya. "Thank you," she whispered, fierce, and let her go.

Minya's arms had not responded, and neither had her voice. Sarai might have seen the cool flicker of her gaze if she weren't so swept up in the moment. None of her old fears could compare with the wrenching loss she had just escaped.

And there was Lazlo.

She stilled. Her ghost hearts beat like real ones, and her cheeks flushed—all the habits of her living body taking root in her phantom one. Lazlo. There was blood on his chest and witchlight in his eyes. He was blue and ablaze with power, and with *love*, and Sarai flew to him.

Tears streamed down his cheeks. She kissed them away.

I'm dead, she thought, but she couldn't feel that

it was true any more than she'd felt the dreams she shared with Lazlo were false. For him it was the same. She felt, in his arms, the way she had in his mind: exquisite, and all he knew was gladness and second chances and the magic of possibility. He knew the touch of her dream lips, and he had even kissed her dead face in soft farewell. He bent now and kissed her ghost, and found her mouth full and sweet and smiling.

He felt her smile. He tasted it. And he saw her joy. Her cheeks were flushed and her eyes were shining. He bent his head to kiss her shoulder, moving the pink strap aside a fraction with his lips, and he was breathing in her scent—rosemary and nectar—when she whispered in his ear. The brush of her lips sent shivers coursing through him, and the words, they sent chills.

He froze.

The lips were hers, but the words were not. "We're going to play a game," she said, and her voice was all wrong. It was bell-bright and as sweet as icing sugar. "I'm good at games. You'll see. Here's how this one goes." He looked up from Sarai's shoulder. He locked eyes with Minya and the light of triumph in hers had all-new meaning. She smiled, and Sarai's lips whispered her words in Lazlo's ear.

"There's only one rule. You do everything I say, or I'll let her soul go. How does that sound?"

Lazlo drew back sharply and looked at Sarai. The smile he had tasted was gone from her lips, and the joy from her eyes. There was only horror now as their new truth came clear to them both. Sarai had sworn to herself that she would never again serve Minya's twisted will, and now . . . now she was powerless against it. She was dead and she was saved and she was caught and she was powerless.

No.

She wanted to scream it—*No!*—but her lips formed Minya's words and not her own. "Nod if you understand," she whispered to Lazlo, and she hated every syllable, and hated herself for not resisting, but there *was* no resisting. When her soul had shaken loose from her body she'd had nothing to hold on to it with; no arms to reach with or hands to grip with. Now she had no will to resist with.

Lazlo understood. The little girl held the thread of Sarai's soul, and so she as good as held the thread to his—and to his power, too.

What would she do with it? What would she make *him* do? It was a game, she'd said. "Nod if you understand."

He understood. He held Sarai in his arms. Her ghost, her fate, and Weep's fate, too. He stood on the citadel of the Mesarthim, and it was not of this world, and he was not who he had been. "So you could be anyone," Sarai had said once. "A prince, even."

But Lazlo was not a prince. He was a god. And this was not a game to him.

He nodded to Minya, and the space where his legend was gathering up words grew larger.

Because this story was not over yet.

TO BE CONTINUED

ACKNOWLEDGMENTS

It's thank-you time!

First: Jane. To my amazing agent, Jane Putch, for getting me through this year: *Thank you*. Remember that night in Pittsburgh when I had a second cocktail and told you the whole plot of the book? Your enthusiasm was like fuel, then and on so many occasions before and since. You are truly an incredible partner.

To the teams at Little, Brown Books for Young Readers and Hodder & Stoughton, who didn't bat an eye when this supposed stand-alone mutated into a duology, and changed main character *and* title. Um, yeah. Thanks for being cool with all that! And thank you for doing what you do so brilliantly, from beginning to end.

To Tone Almhjell and Torbjørn Amundsen for several rounds of crucial feedback—including the all-important thumbs-up at the end, when I'd lost all context. Thank you so much. Tone, we're going to figure out an easier way to do this book-writing thing, right? Any day now?

To Alexandra Saperstein for unwavering excitement and support. Tag! Your turn to finish a book next! (Also: adventure. Remember: A woman should have squint lines from looking at France, not just from writing in dim light....)

A couple of folks let me steal their cool names. Thank you, Shveta Thakrar, for the use of *thakrar* for my fictional term, and an even bigger thanks to Moonrascal Drave, whose name I put to a less noble use. Even on my final proof pass I was wondering if I should change my explosionist's name because I felt terrible using *Drave* for such a creepy character! Please know that the real Drave is a cool guy and great friend to SFF. (Bonus points if you know the other recent SFF book in which his name appears.)

Thank you to my parents, always and forever.

And most of all, to Jim and Clementine, my people. For fun and adventure and normalcy and silliness and sanity and coziness and constancy and book time and superheroes and creativity and inspiration and lazy days and crazy days and castles and cake and cats and dreams and toys and plays and home and *so much love*. You are everything to me.

4-4-18
6-5-19
8